THE OUTLAW HEARTS FAMILY SAGA

OUTLAW HEARTS (Sourcebooks)

DO NOT FORSAKE ME (Sourcebooks)

LOVE'S SWEET REVENGE (Sourcebooks)

THE LAST OUTLAW (Sourcebooks)

A CHICKADEE CHRISTMAS (Short story in an anthology
titled CHRISTMAS IN A COWBOY'S ARMS (Sourceboks)

BLAZE OF GLORY (Amazon)

SHADOW TRAIL (Amazon)

SHADOW TRAIL
By Rosanne Bittner

This book is a work of fiction. All characters and their names, and all incidents in this story are a product of the author's imagination and meant only for entertainment reading that includes adult content and 1800's "Old West" culture.

Cover design by Mandy Koehler Designs.

Editing by Michelle Crean, Editor/Web Site Designer

Dedicated to my husband, Larry, who quietly finds things to do while I spend daily hours in my office at the computer. As of May 2023 I have been published for 40 years with 75 books in print, much of it possible because of a husband who has always believed in me and my writing. We will be married 58 years in October 2023, through which we have faced many, many "life" challenges. And here we are, still together, because we believe marriage is forever, as do the characters in my books, which is why my stories always turn out to be memorable family sagas and testaments to enduring love. Our life together has been no different.

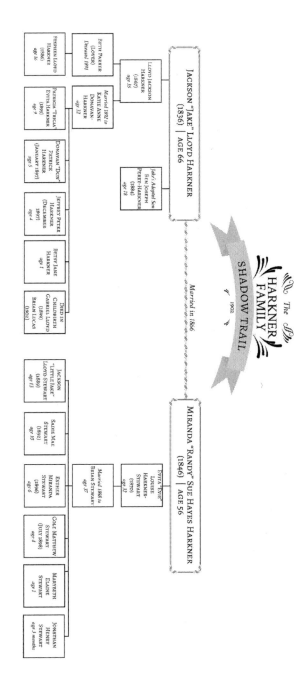

The HARKNER FAMILY

SHADOW TRAIL

1902

JACKSON "JAKE" LLOYD HARKNER
(1836) | AGE 66

Married in 1866

MIRANDA "RANDY" SUE HAYES HARKNER
(1846) | AGE 56

Jackson "Jake" Lloyd Harkner's line

LLOYD JACKSON HARKNER
(1867)
age 35

Married 1892 to

KATIE ANNE DONAVAN-HARKNER
age 32

- **BETH PARKER (LOVER)**
  Deceased 1891

  - **STEPHEN LLOYD HARKNER**
    (1886)
    age 16

- **PATRICIA "TRICIA" EVITA HARKNER**
  (1893)
  age 9

- **DONAVAN "DON" PATRICK HARKNER**
  (JANUARY 1897)
  age 5

- **JEFFREY PETER HARKNER**
  (DECEMBER 1897)
  age 4

- **BETSY JANE HARKNER**
  age 1

- **DIED IN CHILDBIRTH**
  GABRIEL LLOYD (1899)
  BRIAN LUCAS (1902)

Jake's Adopted Son
BEN JOSEPH PERRY-HARKNER
(1884)
age 18

Miranda "Randy" Sue Hayes Harkner's line

EVITA "EVIE" LOUISE HARKNER-STEWART
(1870)
age 32

Married 1888 to
BRIAN STEWART
age 37

- **JACKSON "LITTLE JAKE" LLOYD STEWART**
  (1889)
  age 13

- **SADIE MAE STEWART**
  (1892)
  age 10

- **ESTHER MIRANDA STEWART**
  (1896)
  age 6

- **COLE MATTHEW STEWART**
  (JULY 1898)
  age 4

- **MARYBETH ELAINE STEWART**
  age 1

- **JONATHAN HENRY STEWART**
  age 3 months

PART 1

There it was. Something Miranda had not seen in years. The look in his eyes was pure outlaw Jake, that one side of him she had never been able to control.

CHAPTER ONE

Denver: June 1902

Dallas blinked at the bright sunlight when she walked out of Denver's Union Station. She thought how the sun should be the same everywhere, but she swore it was much brighter out west. Maybe it was because most of this country was high and treeless.

She glanced behind her, waiting for the porter to bring her bags. She smiled wryly at the fact that she had convinced the man to help her, even though he was very busy helping someone else at the time. As a woman who had been consorting with men from all walks of life for years, she knew every way there was to talk a man into whatever she wanted.

Except for Jake Harkner. Jake was one of a kind, and he was her reason for making this long, arduous trip to Denver. She realized that after the way she had betrayed him all those years ago, it was not likely she could talk him into what she needed from him now, but she had to try. It would not help when he learned what she had been hiding from him for all these years.

Denver was bigger than she had expected, especially after living in the little town of Shelter, Wyoming for so long. People milled about everywhere, and vendors on the street in front of the train station sold everything from cookies to balloons. A man bumped into her, then excused himself and kept going, nearly running into two children who were chasing each other.

Horses and carriages clattered up and down the street, mixed with automobiles and their chugging engines and air horns. Sometimes one of the new-fangled modes of transportation would backfire, causing shouts from startled people and sending horses into a panic.

The lonesome sound of train whistles added to the bedlam that was topped off with bells that clanged from Denver's tramway system. The sights and sounds of progress, mixed with memories of Jake, took Dallas's thoughts to the past ... to Missouri ... so long ago ... when life was still slow, beautiful, and peaceful.

The war changed all that ... changed some people forever. It bred outlaws, ruthless men who had no real place to call home, men who took what they needed from others, lonely men from brutal childhoods ... like an outlaw from Texas named Jake Harkner. Jake was in his late twenties when she'd known him in every way a woman could know a man. And handsome, so handsome that her memory of him caused her to put her hand to her heart. By the time wanted posters started showing up with Jake's face on them, he had earned the nickname of *The Handsome Outlaw*.

But Jake was too torn inside to care about looks. He'd been so incredibly lonely and desperate, so angry at life itself. When she knew him, he'd been running from the law for ten or twelve years, running from dreadful childhood memories, from himself and the fact that he had killed his own father. Over the last few years, she had followed the stories written about him by an award-winning Chicago reporter named Jeff Truebridge. She had also read Truebridge's book about Jake, *Jake Harkner, The Legend and the Myth*.

But Jake was no myth. She still could hardly believe he had married and settled and now helped run a big ranch south of Denver. She figured his wife must be quite something to put up with a man like Jake. According to the book, Miranda Harkner was ten years younger than Jake.

That wife could have been me. She wondered if memories from their good times together might stir the "old" Jake she had known. Then again, if Jake still was as angry with her as when he left her, he might toss her right off his ranch. That was the more likely outcome of her visit. Her only winning card was the real reason she was here.

"Sorry for the wait, Ma'am." The porter's words interrupted Dallas's thoughts. He unloaded two carpetbags and a hatbox from a cart he'd used to bring her bags out. "Real busy today. I had trouble finding this cart." He straightened and faced Dallas with a big grin on his chubby face. "I don't usually do this so much anymore, you know. I am being promoted to assistant conductor and will soon be taking tickets and such. But I certainly don't mind helping a pretty woman."

Dallas took the hint. He expected a tip, as well he should. She reached into her drawstring handbag and pulled out a silver dollar, then smiled as fetchingly as an ageing woman could. The porter was no young man himself, so he was easier to sweet-talk than a younger man might be. She grasped his hand and put the coin into his palm. "You have been very kind, uh —" She glanced at his badge. "Henry?"

"Yes, ma'am!" Henry looked at the coin. "Ma'am, this is an extravagant tip. Thank you! Is there anything else I can do for you?"

Dallas decided to take advantage of the moment. She needed to know a little more about Jake before her surprise visit. "Yes," she answered. "You can tell me the best way to get to the J&L ranch and how long it might take to get there. Do you know of it? And do you know a man named Jake Harkner?"

The porter lit up like firecracker. His cheeks even turned redder. "Do I *know* him? *Everybody* in these parts knows about the J&L and its owner. Jake Harkner is famous in these parts."

"In more places than just here," Dallas told him. She placed another silver dollar in the porter's palm, hoping the generous tip would keep him talking.

"Thank you, Ma'am!" Henry's ruddy complexion grew redder as he shoved the coins into his pants pocket. "I should tell you that if you are headed for the J&L, you have quite a trip ahead of you through rugged country."

"I have already been on a rugged trip just getting this far, Henry. I am tougher than I look."

Henry adjusted his cap. "I hope so. I have never seen the ranch's homestead myself. They say that getting that far is not easy. And it is difficult for a strange man to be allowed close to the homestead because Harkner and his son guard that place like a fortress on account of Jake's reputation. He knows how to make enemies without even trying. And getting there is a two or three-day trip, most of it on J&L land." He looked Dallas over curiously, his eyes lingering on her very full bosom.

Dallas laughed inwardly at how much men liked breasts. She'd worn a dress that was cut to show just enough cleavage to entice a man of any age, another tool to get whatever she wanted. She brushed at her pale blue day dress as Henry kept talking, then adjusted the brim of her peach basket leghorn hat, trimmed with the same material as her dress. One of the girls who worked for her at Dallas's Pleasure Emporium had made her clothes. They might all be a bunch of whores, but some were good cooks and seamstresses.

"And why would you be wanting to find Jake, if I may ask?" The affable Henry gave her his best smile.

"No, you may *not* ask. For now, let's just say I am an old friend, so tell me the best type of transportation I need to get to Jake's ranch."

Henry folded his arms and raised his chin a little, obviously trying to impress her with his knowledge and authority. "Well, ma'am, first off, you'd better take a horse-drawn carriage. The road into the J&L is rough, dusty, and long. Some of these new-fangled motor cars cannot make the whole trip. Either way, it will cost you plenty to go that far. It would be better if you could find one of the J&L men here in town. Sometimes they come to Denver to pick up supplies, things they don't have enough of in the smaller towns. Jake himself, he does not leave the ranch much anymore, not after that last big gunfight that was in the news about three years ago."

Just as Dallas suspected, Henry was a talker, and he seemed to be proud to give her the impression that he knew Jake. She gladly let him ramble on, drinking in every word because she needed to learn all she could about Jake's current situation ... and about the woman he had married.

"They say no man ever came closer to death than Jake

did after that gunfight," the porter told her. "He went up against ten or twelve men who all wanted the reputation of shooting him down. A few days earlier, those men had shot and wounded one of Jake's grandsons, sniper style, just to rile Jake. The kid was only about twelve. And they shot Jake's adopted son, too, a big kid named Ben, 15 or so at the time. They shot that poor kid's arm off. If you don't think that would put hell fire in Jake Harkner, think again."

"I know Jake well, and I don't doubt his reaction one bit."

"They say those outlaws gave Jake a letter when he got back from a big trip to Chicago ... took his wife there to visit an old friend and enjoy the honeymoon they never got to have in all their years together. I heard that in that letter those men threatened two of Jake's little granddaughters. After learning what happened to his son and grandson, Jake went after them men with the vengeance of Satan. Some say the scene he left behind was a real bloodbath. Word now is that Mrs. Harkner has a good hold on the man because of how bad wounded he was. She insists he stays close to home."

"And Jake does what she wants?"

"Oh, yes, ma'am. If you saw those two together, you would understand."

Dallas chuckled. "That sure doesn't sound like the Jake I knew. Did the gunfight leave him wounded enough to slow him down?"

Henry shook his head. "Ma'am, if you think Jake staying home more now means he has softened, do not think that for a minute. You would still be hard pressed to find a man anywhere around who would be willing to go up against him. I was a waiter at a cattlemen's ball back a few years ago here in Denver when Jake shot a man smack in the forehead, close range. I saw the whole thing. The man had just shot Jake's grown son. Everybody figured he was dead, including Jake. I watched Jake walk right up to that shooter and blow the man's head half off. *Boom!* That big .44 of Jake's about shook the whole room. It was an awful sight. Some tried to call it murder, but Jake managed to go free on account of what the shooter had done to his son. They called it a crime of passion, but Jake is still on the watch list of a judge here in Denver. He reminded Jake that he cannot be judge and jury, but Jake does not seem to worry about wasting bullets when it comes to revenge."

Good. That is just the kind of man I need. Someone who will kill for somebody he cares about. "I am well aware of Jake's quick temper," Dallas said aloud. "And I know the story. At least Jake's son lived. Tell me a little more about the J&L."

Henry smiled eagerly. "Oh, the J&L is one of the biggest ranches around. The brand stands for Jake and Lloyd, father and son. I hear tell the homestead is like its own village. Jake's wife and daughter run a little school there, along with Jake's son's wife. And they have a small supply store for local farmers and ranchers. Jake runs a gunsmith shop there, too. And his daughter's husband is a full-fledged doctor. Brian Stewart, his name is. And the daughter, she's real religious, even runs a chapel on the ranch."

Dallas smiled fetchingly, eager to keep the man talking. "I find it hard to believe Jake has a Bible-thumping daughter."

"Funny, isn't it?" Henry chuckled. He looked her over, again taking a good look at her bosom. Dallas knew the hard lines of her face and the fact that she had known Jake Harkner made Henry wonder. Everyone knew the kind of women Jake ran with before he married. She might be in her fifties now, but she did all she could to stay in shape. Indeed, she had a lot fewer customers nowadays, but the girls at Dallas's Pleasure Emporium brought her a nice income up in Wyoming's outlaw country. Still, she hated the fact that a hard life and too many years on this earth had added a few pounds to her still-curvy body and too many wrinkles to her once milky-smooth complexion.

Shadows from the past sometimes kept her awake at night. She vividly remembered the wild times she'd had with Jake, but eventually she'd betrayed him in an underhanded way that he probably had never forgiven her for. Once he left, she continued doing what she did best. She told herself it was to survive, but damned if she did not enjoy the pleasure of a man in her bed. "How might I find a Harkner cowboy here in Denver?" she asked Henry, ignoring the obvious curiosity in his gaze.

"Can't be sure any are here at all, but you should try taking a cab to Johnson's Supply Station. Any cab driver will know where that is. The men who work there might be able to tell you if anybody from the ranch is expected any time soon. I am sure a J&L man would be willing to take you back to the homestead for free. Cowboys don't mind traveling with a pretty woman."

"Thank you for the compliment, Henry." Dallas folded her arms. "And before I go, tell me what you know about Jake's wife. You must have seen her at that cattlemen's ball."

The man's eyes brightened again. "Oh, yes, ma'am. I have seen her more than once. Miranda Harkner is a damn good-looking woman. *Damn* good looking. I saw her again three years ago when she and Jake came back from that trip to Chicago. Oh, by the way, did you read about how Jake stopped a train robbery on that trip? Woo-hoo!" The porter laughed and slapped his thigh. "They sure did pick the wrong train to rob! I wish I had been there to see it -- them men being greeted by Jake Harkner himself! He took them all down."

Dallas put a hand on his arm. "Stick to the subject. I asked about Jake's wife. Do they really get along as well as rumors have it?"

The porter frowned. "Why would you want to know about that?"

"Again, it's none of your business."

Henry grinned. "Yes, ma'am." He adjusted his cap again. "Well, Miranda Harkner is educated and real sophisticated, not the type to marry an outlaw. Know what I mean? But she is by-God damn tough, I expect, putting up with a man like Jake. As far as them getting along, Jake looks at that woman like she just came down from heaven itself. I doubt there is a couple stuck together any tighter than those two. Happy does not even come close to what you see when they are together. And Jake is real protective of her. Same with his daughter and daughter-in-law. You will almost never see a Harkner woman walking around alone."

Dallas sighed. It obviously was not going to be easy to get Jake away from the J&L ... or his wife. "Hail a cab for me, will you? I want to go to that supply store and see if I can find a ride to the Harkner ranch."

"Yes, ma'am." Henry chuckled and shook his head, then walked across the street to talk to a man sitting in the driver's seat of a mule-drawn cab. An automobile ahead of the cab backfired, causing the mule to rear up and bray wildly. It took a moment for the driver to calm the animal down. After a moment of discussion, the carriage driver snapped the reins against the mule's rear and turned the carriage, dodging a much bigger carriage to come over to where Dallas waited. She thanked Henry and gave him another coin, smiling inside at how rich she'd become by running a whorehouse that welcomed men like Henry with open arms. Henry piled her baggage into the back of the carriage and ordered the driver to take Dallas to Johnson's Supply Station.

"Thanks for your help and for all the information," Dallas called to Henry as the cab driver yelled, "Git up there!" Dallas settled against the leather seat, her heart pounding at the thought of seeing Jake again. She hung on to her hat against a sudden mountain breeze and hoped she would be lucky enough to find someone to take her to the J&L.

Would Jake even recognize her? Whether he did or not, she had no doubt she would recognize him. A man like Jake Harkner usually never changed much. Seeing him again could be a wonderful, heartfelt reunion ... or a heart-breaking disaster.

CHAPTER TWO

"SHE IS, UH, *FISSATO*, YES?" Frank swallowed nervously as he watched Jake Harkner finish polishing the old Colt Dragoon pistol that Frank's boss, Henry Till, had asked him to pick up for him.

"Frank, you need to use English with people out here," Jake told him, "especially if you want to become a citizen."

"*Si*, I know!" The young Italian nodded his head vigorously. "But you speak Spanish, no?"

"I speak Spanish, yes. My mother was Mexican. And I grew up in Texas. Three quarters of the people in Texas know Spanish, probably because most of those three quarters are from Mexico in the first place. Either way, I grew up speaking English. My father ..."

Frank noticed a darkness move into Jake's eyes. *The father you killed,* he thought.

"My father was an American from the east," Jake finished.

Frank swallowed, a little worried about the darkness to Jake's demeanor. He decided it might be important to change the subject. "I meant to say, uh." He thought for a moment. "Fixed! Yes, Mister Till said he thought you would have the gun fixed by now, so he sent me here because I wanted very much to meet the famous Jake Harkner."

Jake frowned. "Do not call me famous, Frank. And yes, that old gun is fixed, but I would recommend that Henry put it in his case of vintage guns. I would hate to find out someone on the Twisted Tree ended up getting shot by accident. Tell Henry this gun is mostly for show. He can shoot it for fun, but it would be best if no one is in close range. I cannot guarantee its precision. Do you want me to wrap it?"

"Oh, *si*! I mean, yes!" Frank eyed Jake closely as the older man wrapped the gun in brown paper and tied string around it. "Mister Till told me he will pay you at the Fourth of July picnic," Frank said as he watched. "I am *eccitato* for celebrate your country's *indipendenza*."

Jake chuckled. "I take it that means you look forward to our Independence Day celebrations." He handed Frank the gun. "Tell Henry and Bessie hello from Jake and Randy. And the cost is five dollars because I had to make a couple of the parts myself, with the help of our blacksmith."

"You are *talentuoso* with guns. Yes? I mean, talented."

"Some talents are a blessing, Frank, and some are a curse." Jake took a cigarette from a box of Duke's Best on the countertop and struck a match to light it. "*My* talent happens to be a curse, because men usually die from it. If I had always used it just as a gunsmith for a living, I would have avoided a hell of a lot of trouble in my life, not just for me, but for my whole family. Then again, running from the law led me to my wife, so one good thing came of it. Still, you'd be best to stay out of that kind of trouble, Frank, and enjoy the freedom of being a man who gets along with the law."

"*Si,* I know. But back in Italy they talk about how

exciting life is in America's wild west. It is why I left my family in New York and came here, to learn about the cowboy life, and learn about the outlaws and the Indians."

Jake snickered and took another drag on the cigarette. "Frank, it sounds like you have read too many of those penny dreadfuls. I guess the better term now is dime novels. I find it sad to say that there are hardly any Indians left, except for those sent to remote reservations. And the only truth you will find about me is in the book my reporter friend in Chicago wrote. Jeff Truebridge is a good friend, and he writes reality without glamorizing or exaggerating. I figured if people would pay to read about my sorry life, I could make a little extra money and contribute to the financial stability of my kids and grandkids."

Frank frowned with concern. "But it is not just your past that is exciting. It was not so long ago you were in that big shootout with those men who said they would hurt your granddaughters."

"I don't care to talk about that."

"I understand. Oh, and I read you are Catholic, like me. So remember that a priest can *intercedere* with God Himself to forgive everything from the past, Mr. Harkner. People say you are a good man in spite of -" The young man's smile faded when he noticed Jake's friendly attitude begin to change. The tall, hard man straightened, as though ready to protect himself from something he did not want to discuss. "I am sorry, Mr. Harkner. I get *eccitato* when I meet someone so famous, and then I talk too much." He stepped back a little at the look in Jake's dark eyes.

"Frank, the Pope himself couldn't guarantee heaven for me, and you would be wise to remember that out here you're better off *listening* instead of talking. If you talk this way to Henry's ranch hands, you will end up with a broken nose and a lot of bruises."

Frank swallowed. "*Si,* I will remember. I am just, how you say, nervous? You are such an image of the American West that I have heard about."

"I am an image of the worst elements out here, so don't go making me more than I am, Frank. You're young, and you're new here. I'll give you that. Just don't try prying into things better left alone."

Frank started to turn when he heard a young girl screaming. "Grampa! Grampa! Grampa!" The door to the shop flew open, and a girl of perhaps eight or ten years old ran inside, tears streaming down her face. She ran around the end of the counter and shook with sobs. "Outlaw is dead! He's dead!"

Jake reached down and pulled the girl into his arms as he straightened. "Sadie Mae, maybe that mean old rooster is just sick."

"No! He's dead! He's all stiff and everything. He died all alone!" The girl wrapped her arms around her grandfather's neck and her legs around his waist.

Jake hugged her close. "Let's go to the hen house and I'll look at him myself," Jake told her. "That ornery old son-of-a-gun hates me worse than any man who's ever tried to kill me. If he's still alive, seeing me will wake him up real fast."

The little girl rested her head on Jake's shoulder. "Grampa, if he's dead, can we bury him in the family plot like a person? I don't want somebody to just throw him out for the wolves. Tell me we can bury him."

"Yes, we can bury him."

"Can I wrap him in my old blanket?"

"You can do whatever you want."

"Why'd he die, Grampa?"

"Everything gets old and dies, baby girl."

"You will, too, won't you Grampa? I don't want you to die. I was so scared that last time everybody thought you were killed. I thought you died all alone."

"Dying is just a fact of life, Sadie Mae. And it is lonely even if a lot of people are around. But once I am gone, you will have a whole, great big family here who will always take care of you – your mother and father, Uncle Lloyd and Aunt Katie, grandma, all your brothers and cousins, and all the ranch hands who love you like their own."

"But I just want you. Nobody can hurt any of us when you are around."

Jake patted her back. "Honey, I'm the *reason* for a lot of hurt in this family. Come on, now. Let's go see what's wrong with Outlaw."

Grandpa and granddaughter walked out, Sadie Mae still clinging to Jake. Frank picked up his boss's gun and followed them. He noticed a beautiful older woman with blond hair hurrying to join them. Several other family members also walked in their direction.

"Jake, what's wrong?" the woman asked. "I heard Sadie Mae screaming all the way back at the house." She put her hand on his arm and looked at him lovingly.

"Outlaw. She says he's dead."

"Oh, no! I shouldn't have sent her out this morning to find some extra eggs."

"Wouldn't matter," Jake answered. "She would have found that feathered scoundrel sooner or later. Actually, I wondered why he wasn't crowing his head off like usual this morning."

The woman and others followed Jake and his grand-daughter toward the hen house. Frank watched, enthralled at meeting the infamous Jake Harkner. *That woman must be his wife. She is so pretty for an older woman. And look at Jake, so good to his granddaughter. He does not look like a man who has killed so many.* He was surprised at how Jake Harkner's countenance had changed in seconds to gentle and fatherly when his granddaughter came running to him.

Frank's attention was interrupted when a broad-shouldered cowboy who looked perhaps in his mid-thirties rode his horse close to the shop. The man's hat was off, and his long, dark hair was tied into a tail at the back of his neck. "You're Henry Till's new man, aren't you?" the man asked Frank as he dismounted. "Henry pointed you out to me last time I was at the Twisted Tree to buy a horse."

Frank swallowed and nodded. "*Sí.* I am Frank Ricci."

The man walked closer, his stature intimidating. He was tall and dark and looked very much like Jake. Frank figured he must be Jake's son, whose reputation was not a lot better than Jake's. Men at the Twisted Tree often talked about Jake and Lloyd Harkner both, mostly with the attitude that they would not want to tangle with either man.

"I came here to pick up a gun Mister Harkner repaired for my boss," Frank explained.

The man reached out to shake Frank's hand. "I'm Lloyd Harkner." He looked past Frank, observing Jake and the others all walking together. Sadie Mae was still crying. "Do you know what the hell is going on?" Lloyd asked. "Where is everybody going?"

"To the hen house, I think," Frank answered. He let go of Lloyd's hand, rubbing his own hand on his pants leg because it hurt a little from Lloyd's very firm handshake. "That little girl came running to your father to say a rooster named Outlaw has died," he explained.

Lloyd frowned. "Shit," he commented. He handed the

reins to Frank. "Tie my horse for me, will you?" He walked off to follow the others.

Surprised by the family closeness he'd just witnessed, Frank stood there holding Henry's gun in one hand and the reins to a handsome Palomino gelding in the other. Jake Harkner's reputation seemed a stark contrast to the man walking to the hen house now, his granddaughter still crying in his arms, and several family members walking beside and behind him.

Why on earth was everyone so upset over a dead rooster?

CHAPTER THREE

Dallas clung to the side railing of the wagon seat, stiffening a little at each bounce and sway. The big, boxy supply wagon carrying her definitely was not built for comfortable passenger travel, but it was a free ride to the J&L. Three more supply wagons lumbered behind hers, all loaded to capacity and pulled by teams of huge plow horses. After finding J&L men who were headed to the ranch with supplies, she'd spent the night at the newly-built Oxford Hotel in Denver and met up with them early this morning for the long journey south ... and to Jake.

The lead driver, Vance Kelly, had introduced the wagon drivers as Lou Younger, Billy Dooley, and Charlie McGee – *from Tennesse*, the man had added when introduced. Apparently, "from Tennessee" had become a sort of nickname always added when Charlie was introduced. Two outriders, Calvin Malloy and Bailey Keller, accompanied them for protection. Dallas guessed all of them to be between thirty and fifty years old, except for Vance, who looked closer to Jake's age, which by now was mid-sixties.

Another rut caused Dallas to let out a startled gasp.

"You ok, ma'am?" Vance asked. "I warned you this would be a rough ride." His blue eyes spoke of a mischievious man who had seen and done just about everything one could accomplish in life, and probably loved every minute of it.

"I'll manage," Dallas answered. "I've led a hard life and suffered a lot worse than getting my brains jangled by ruts and rocks."

"Well, that there dress is real pretty," Vance told her. "It's too bad you will have had to wear it these next two days and sleep in it on top of a pile of flour sacks tonight, but that's how it is. I reckon you will want to look nice when you get to the Harkner place, so you should know that tomorrow we're takin' a few supplies to the Twisted Tree ranch east of here. They have a little rooming house there, so you'll be able to clean up and change. We should make Jake's place by noon the next day." He studied the trail ahead as though always alert for trouble. "Meantime, enjoy the views. The J&L is 150,000 acres of grassland, streams, the big ol' Rocky Mountains, you name it. It's not the biggest ranch in Colorado, but close to it. 'Course there are a lot of new laws comin' through, disputes over ranchers and farmers and open grazing. Jake's son, Lloyd, keeps up with the business end of things and us cowboys do most of the dirty work. But Jake and Lloyd do their share."

"How many cattle do you and the men have to look after?"

"We ain't even sure. Thirty, forty thousand maybe. The count changes every spring, dependin' on how hard a winter we have. Used to be nobody kept an exact count, but now buyers and the government want more accurate records. Believe me, it's not easy keeping it all straight."

"How did Lloyd and Jake end up with such a big ranch in the first place?"

Vance shrugged. "The way I understand it, Lloyd always wanted to do this. Soon as him and Jake was done with bein' lawmen in Indian country, they came here and started buyin' up what they could with money Lloyd inherited from his first wife. They had a son named Stephen. The wife died about ten or eleven years ago and Lloyd married his current wife when the family still lived in Guthrie. Funny, ain't it? Jake being a marshal back then?"

"Yes," Dallas agreed. "He was far from a lawman when I knew him."

Vance chuckled. "It was actually a punishment. Jake went to prison years ago but got an early release on account of some woman testified he didn't do some of the things he went up for. But the judge decided Jake still had lessons to learn, so he told Jake that since he knows so much about outlaws and the raw side of life, he'd make a good marshal. He sent him to the worst place any man would want to serve as a lawman. No Man's Land in Oklahoma. Told Jake he had to serve there for three years. I guess he figured it would teach Jake a lesson, but Jake is not a very good student."

"I am betting Jake did just fine," Dallas told him. "He was a wild, angry, vengeful man when I knew him. I'll bet he still has that side to him, which he would need in a place packed with outlaws and low-lifes." *I just hope he doesn't still feel vengeful against me.*

"Yes, ma'am. He's still a short-tempered man who can be real mean when he figures it's necessary."

"How about you, Vance?" Dallas teased. "Are you wild and vengeful?"

Vance looked her over with a grin. "No, ma'am. I am for peace and harmony."

"And you are a poor liar," Dallas told him. "I know men, and I know Jake. He wouldn't hire a man if he wasn't good with a gun and willing to use it to defend the J&L and Jake's family. That means hard-nosed men who don't hesitate to pull a weapon when necessary."

Vance shrugged. "Believe what you want."

Dallas liked Vance, who was extremely sociable, and quite good looking for his age. His sparkling blue eyes spelled mischief, and she loved that in a man. "I'm glad to know I can clean up before we reach the homestead. Thank you for that, Vance."

"Well, ma'am, if there is one thing I understand real good, it's women. I know they like to take baths and smell good. And you have me wondering how you look with that red hair hangin' down all long and pretty."

Dallas shoved at his arm. "Probably not as good looking as you think. I'm no young woman, Vance."

"Age doesn't matter to me." Vance laughed and slapped the horses' rears with a web of reins. "Giddap there!," he ordered. "Don't go getting lazy on me."

Dallas was not surprised it took three days of travel over J&L land to get to the homestead. *Three or four days with these heavy wagons, two by horseback if everything goes right,* Vance had told her. *Weather's good, so I expect we will make it the third morning.* She had expected a hard trip because she had lived in big country like this for eight years now, most of it up in Wyoming ... in places occupied by mostly men ... men who needed a woman's attention and who were willing to pay good money for it. "I sure appreciate this," she said aloud.

Vance shrugged. "I don't mind making the trip beside a

pretty woman," he answered. "You said you're a friend of Jake's from a long time ago. I don't mean any insult, ma'am, but everybody knows, well, the kind of women Jake always hung with. He has a soft spot for saloon women, on account of being raised by that kind. They sometimes risked a beating to hide him from his pa. Jake had a real cruel childhood, an alcoholic father who killed his ma and little brother when Jake was still too little to do anything about it. I expect you know he finally killed his pa. Shot him to death."

"I know the story." *And I've seen his scars.* "Vance, the answer to what you are wondering is yes, I was that kind of woman when I knew Jake. In fact, I still am. You might as well know it. I run a house of prostitution up in Shelter, Wyoming. And I have to say, of all the men I've been with, Jake was the best-looking hunk of male who ever walked. He was good with those guns of his, and good with women."

"Well, ma'am, I have known Jake only these last few years. He's still a lady-killer, and maybe he used to run with the wild ones, but he don't have eyes for anybody but his wife now." He glanced at Dallas, taking inventory with his gaze. "How many years since you've seen Jake?"

"Close to 40 years. I was only 19 when last I saw him, but Jake never lit in one place for long. That was in Missouri, during the War between the States." She shook her head sadly. "I saw a lot of death and destruction because of that war. So did Jake, except he was the *cause* of some of it. He hung with a bad element back then, robbed banks and trains, did some gun running. My brother was in the same gang. He and Jake and the others had their own way of taking part in the war, and it had nothing to do with favoring north or south." Her grip on the seat railing tightened again with another jolt from ruts in the road. "Anyway, a lot of wild adventures over the years led me from Missouri to outlaw country in Wyoming. That's where I run my business now." Dallas shook her head. "You know, Vance, some of the things I'm hearing just don't fit my Jake. He sure never was a one-woman man."

"*Your* Jake? You'd better not let his *wife* hear you call him that."

Dallas chuckled. "That's just how I think of him, but I'm not sure that, once he sees me, he won't tell you to turn around and take me right back to Denver. We didn't exactly part on good terms, but that was forty years ago, and I'm hoping he's softened a little."

Vance watched ahead. "If you want to change your mind, I can leave you at the Twisted Tree and go on ahead and check with Jake before I take you all the way to the homestead," he offered.

"I'll take my chances." *Jake loved me once. Maybe he will help me.* "One thing I know for sure is Jake would never hurt a woman, not physically anyway. I gave him a good reason to lay into me once, but he didn't. I'm betting he treats his wife real good."

"Real good?" Vance snickered. "Hell, he described it in that book when he said she's the air he breathes. All us men, we keep a good eye on Miranda. She's a fine woman - straightened Jake out the best she could. Hell, when she first set eyes on Jake back in Kansas, she saw him shoot a bounty hunter, right in front of her in a supply store. Scared her to death. She pulled out a little gun from her handbag and shot Jake. Jake gets teased about that something awful, now that folks know about it."

Dallas shook her head. "I read about that. I thought maybe that was just made up in order to make the book even more entertaining."

"No, ma'am, it's not made up. Later on Miranda found Jake and felt so bad about it that she took out the bullet, and that's how it all started. Her father had been a doctor, so she knew what to do. I reckon that's when they fell in love. Miranda was a young widow, you know. Jake, he took off, thinking he was no good for her, but he knew she was heading west and he got worried about her traveling alone, so he went after her. Found her dying of snakebite, and the next thing you know, they were married. Ever since, he watches her and the Harkner women like a hawk, always afraid his past will come calling and cause trouble. It has happened too often."

The past has come calling again, Dallas wanted to answer, *and I brought it with me.* She took a deep breath against nervousness, excited about seeing Jake again, yet dreading it. *Jake, I have no choice. I don't know where else to turn.*

"What is Jake's home like?" she asked, hoping to change the subject.

"Oh, Jake and his son and daughter each have real big, fancy log homes. Jake's is the biggest. The great room stretches from a parlor end to the kitchen end with nothing in between but big ol' pine beams that support a high ceiling, so's you can see the front door from either end. Jake wanted it that way so he can see who's coming to the door from wherever he sits. There's big stone fireplaces on both ends of the great room, and the whole family gathers there every Sunday."

Vance suddenly yanked on the reins, trying to avoid a rock, but too late. He and Dallas bounced straight up, and Dallas had to grab Vance's arm to keep from sliding off the seat. Charlie McGee from Tennessee let out a howl and rode up on Dallas's side of the wagon.

"Hey, Vance, I thought you knew how to handle those horses," he teased.

"You just go on about your business," Vance answered. "The day Jake gets a dollar's worth of work out of you is the day I'll get drunker than a skunk and celebrate."

Charlie just laughed and rode ahead of them.

"Jake has ten grandkids now," Vance blabbed on. He thought a moment. "No, it's eleven. Lloyd's wife lost a baby three or four months ago, or it would be twelve. She lost another baby just a couple years ago, so she took this one real hard. So did Lloyd."

"That's too bad." Dallas repinned her hat, knocked loose in the last bounce that nearly threw her out of her seat. "Jake was far from the sort of man who would settle and have a family when I knew him." She eyed Vance. "Something tells me you are not a family man either."

Vance laughed and snapped the reins again. "No, ma'am, but I do love married women. They are the only kind I consort with."

Dallas couldn't help a loud guffaw. "Vance Kelly, you'll get yourself killed!"

"Everybody tells me that. But it's not a bad way to go, don't you think?"

Dallas laughed again. "I think you thrive on danger and on challenges," she answered. "And I might remind you that I'm *not* married, Vance Kelly, so there's no sense in being interested in me."

He winked. "Ah, but you sure are a pretty woman. Older women are the best. They know how to give a man pleasure."

Dallas laughed more. "You do know your women." She wrapped her left arm around his shoulders. "Are you consorting with any married women at the moment?"

"Well, one was too scared of losing her husband's money to let it go on, and the last one had to move away when her husband got a better job somewhere in California. So, I'm free for the taking."

Dallas chuckled. "Are some of the ranch hands married?"

"Sure. There's Jakes best friend, Cole Decker. He's married to a woman a good twenty-five years younger, Gretta MacBain. Gretta used to be the most notorious prostitute in Denver, but round and about, she found a way of keeping Jake's neck out of a noose at the trial over the shooting at the cattlemen's ball. You know about that?"

"Who doesn't?"

"Well, somehow Gretta got close to Jake after that, and later her daughter – she had a daughter named Annie who was raised by a good, Christian family – anyway, the girl was kidnapped and taken to Mexico for, well, you can imagine. Jake and Cole went down there to find her. Cole came back with the girl, but he saw Jake dragged off by *banditos*, a broken leg and all. We all thought he'd been killed, but Miranda would not give up on him. He finally made it home, and Randy, she saw him on the rise and she ran to him on bare feet through snow. It was something to see, her learning Jake was alive. It brought tears to everybody's eyes, even all the men. Ain't nobody like Randy, and Jake knows it. The man would die for her, and he sure would never do anything that could mean losing her."

Dallas shook her head. "I never thought he'd end up with a somebody like that. Jake always hung out with the painted women in honky-tonks."

Vance chuckled. "He might know a lot of women from the wrong side of the tracks on account of how he grew up, but there ain't no way now that he would ever do wrong by

Randy. 'Course, today you'd never know what Jake used to be like if you judged him by his kids and grandkids. They all think he walks on water. That daughter of his, Evie, she sees nothing but the good in her father. Still calls him Daddy." He snickered. "That last shootout Jake was in, though, that just about killed Miranda. Lloyd, too." He shook his head. "I've never seen so much blood in my life. There is no logical reason Jake should still be alive. Most think it's only because of his daughter's prayers. There seems to be a lot of power in that woman's connection to God Himself."

They rode on in silence for several long seconds. "To answer your earlier question, ma'am, there's several other married men on the J&L," Vance told her. "They all have their own cabins. The place is starting to look like a small town."

One of the horses balked and jerked the wrong way. Vance pulled on the reins and shouted "Whoa!" as he slowly pushed on the wagon brake. "Let's give these varmints a breather!" he shouted to the other men. "And I expect the woman here could use one, too. Somebody bring her some water."

Dallas patted Vance's knee. "I will be fine, Vance. Don't let me interfere with how soon you get these supplies to the J&L."

"We all need a rest," Vance told her. "It's no problem."

Vance climbed down and reached for Dallas to help her down also. "Stretch your legs, Ma'am." He wrapped the reins around a post nailed to the wagon bed. "By the way, I like to talk and I maybe told you more than I should have."

Dallas put a hand to his chest. "Vance, I think you can tell I have no plans to bring harm to Jake or his family.

Besides, you did not tell me one thing others don't already know. So don't worry about it."

Vance shook his head. "You don't know what Jake can be like when he is upset with somebody."

"Oh I *do* know what he is like, believe me."

Vance nodded to her and walked away. Dallas watched after him. *Such a gentleman.* She had no doubt all the men on the J&L were ordered to be gentlemen around the women. The thing she remembered most about Jake was his attitude toward the female sex. He should have beat her solidly after what she did to him all those years ago, but not Jake. Mean as he could be, he wouldn't touch a woman wrongly. Most people who knew him figured his penchant to fiercely protect women came from seeing his father beat his mother to death when Jake was too little to help her.

Jake was a man of many moods, but in spite of how she had betrayed him once, she felt confident he would never lay a hand on her. Still, the way the man could look at someone he hated, and the way he could use words as a weapon to express his wrath could bring a person to their knees. She found it amusing that his wife seemed to have so much control over the man. *That woman must have you roped and tied real good, Jake. I can't wait to meet her.*

CHAPTER FOUR

Miranda sat in front of the bedroom dressing table performing her nightly ritual of vigorously brushing her hair. She glanced at her husband in the mirror and put down the brush. "Can you believe Sadie Mae asked us to sing a hymn over Outlaw's grave?"

Jake chuckled. "I'm sure the men who were there struggled not to laugh, but they didn't want to hurt her feelings. I'll never understand why Sadie Mae loved that demon rooster so much." He rested against the head of their bed, which was extra long and wide, hand-built for a big man. "Do you know how many times I wanted to shoot that beast? At least now I won't be the butt of all the jokes about that rooster being the only thing that could win a fight with me. He knew I was a sonofabitch, but so was he."

"Well I'm glad no one there said anything bad about Outlaw, including you." Randy returned to brushing her hair. "Sadie Mae and Tricia are probably crying themselves to sleep tonight. Tricia stayed over at Evie's so she and Sadie Mae can cry together. Those girls usually turn to you when they are afraid or upset, but this time they probably decided that since you hated Outlaw so much, you might not understand their tears."

Jake snickered. "If they knew everything about me, they would *run* from me, not give me those hugs."

"You love those hugs, you big sap. What they *should* know is that a threat to them is the reason you nearly died three years ago. Then again, they would probably feel bad and cry over that, too."

Jake sighed and shook his head. "Speaking of grandkids, which ones are sleeping downstairs? Those bedrooms are almost never empty. They all love to sleep at Grandma's house."

"They love being close to Grandpa just as much as Grandma." Randy's heart swelled with love. All her grandchildren helped make up for the fact that she couldn't have any more children of her own after Evie was born. She and Jake had a son and a daughter, but those two children had produced many, many grandchildren they could dote on. "Esther is down there," she answered Jake, "and Donavan and Jeffrey and even little Betsy Jane, so all of Katie's little ones are here. Stephen and Young Jake are at the bunkhouse, which I totally disagree with. God knows what they see and here out there. Evie has the girls plus Cole, Marybeth and Johnny." She finished brushing and faced Jake. "I'm worried about Katie, Jake. She's never been quite the same after losing Gabriel, and now this latest stillborn. It's been four months since she lost him, and she is still suffering depression. I know Lloyd is worried about her, too. I can see it in his eyes."

"Me, too, and Lloyd doesn't need that right now. He has a lot on his shoulders with the size of this ranch and all the responsibilities that come with it. I worry about his penchant for whiskey when things go bad. Thanks to my beloved, whiskey soaked father, that desire for drink got passed down to my son."

Randy laid the brush aside and pushed some hair behind her ears. "Jake, I know Lloyd has had a problem a couple of times, but you have always given him good advice. He respects that. And he loves you too much to let it happen again. You taught him well."

"I still worry about it. If he'd actually seen with his own eyes what my father was like –"

"Jake, don't go there."

"I've stayed away from alcohol all these years for Lloyd's sake, and yours, and because of how it turned my father into Lucifer himself. God knows I've had plenty of reason over the years to get drunk and blow my own brains out. The only thing that stopped me was you and the kids." Jake shifted, grimacing a little at pain from old wounds. "And the only things I've taught our son are how to shoot straight and stay away from whiskey."

"You know better. Lloyd could not ask for a better father. If you had been conscious enough to see what he was like when he brought you home on the brink of death three years ago, you would know what you mean to him. He's grown even stronger since what happened to you. He has his father's broad shoulders and can handle whatever the J&L or family life throws at him."

Jake smiled sadly and shook his head. "You refuse to see the bad in me, don't you?"

He started coughing, the deep, heavy cough that frightened Randy. He'd had pneumonia too many times, starting during the years he'd spent in a cold, damp prison. She feared a damaged lung he suffered from the bullet wound that had collapsed that lung and left him nearly lifeless three years ago. Another bout with pneumonia would surely kill him. She hurried to his side and rubbed his shoulders until he stopped coughing, then poured him a glass of water.

"Sorry," Jake told her as he took the glass.

He drank down the water while Randy ran a hand through his dark, wavy hair, still thick for a man his age but showing streaks of gray. "Don't say you're sorry. You can't help it. But that cough does scare me."

"I'm fine."

Randy walked back to the dressing table and removed her housecoat, putting some of her face cream on her arms. "You are not fine at all. Just remember that the whole *family* loves and needs you. Me most of all. I'm just glad at how peaceful and absolutely wonderful these last three years have been as a whole for you and me." She set down the jar of cream and faced Jake again. He wore only knee-length long johns and no shirt, and she admired his still strong, firm build. "You are a tough, ornery man with a big, big heart, Jake Harkner."

Jake reached for a cigarette. "Believe what you want."

"I've seen the proof. And put that cigarette down. I sat with you for too many months just hoping you would keep breathing to see you inhale all that smoke now." Randy removed her slippers. "You have smoked too much for too long. I know you do some sneak smoking when you leave the house. I just don't want to watch. And I swear, you have breathed in more gun smoke than cigarette smoke over the years. Between that and how loud those guns of yours are, I'm surprised you can hear *or* breathe."

Jake sighed, putting back the cigarette. "I will remind

you that I've been a good boy for these last three years. Those .44's hanging over the front door are probably starting to rust. I think I'll take them to my shop and clean and oil them." He watched Randy climb into bed. "I might not be running around getting into gunfights anymore, but the sad part is that a few *other* things have slowed a little. Every bone and muscle in my body protests every time I climb on a horse or pitch hay or help drag a dead deer or elk out of the trees when we go hunting."

Randy crawled under the covers and scooted beside her husband. "That other thing you mentioned hasn't slowed all that much, Mr. Harkner, especially for a 67-year-old man. And don't forget that everything I do makes me a lot more tired now than it did ten years ago, so I am perfectly happy going to bed just to sleep. I'm slowing down, too, you know."

"Yeah?" Jake pulled her closer and leaned over to kiss her. "You are ten years younger than me, and a beautiful, desirable woman. I'm worried about keeping up."

Randy kissed him back, then ran a hand over his hard-muscled arms. "You can be such a charming liar. And speaking of ageing, you are one of those men who will never have a big belly and probably never lose this lean muscle. It's just how you are built, and I don't see all that much change from when we first met."

"I was meatier, like Lloyd is now."

"*Meatier?*" Randy laughed. "I'm not sure that's even a word." She squeezed his upper arms. "And I'd say this is pretty hard meat." She kissed his chest and ran her hands over the places where chest hair didn't grow anymore because of the scars ... scars from wounds no man should have survived, one of them shaped like a cross right over his heart where his own mother's crucifix had saved his life when a bullet slammed into it. She met his dark eyes.

There were demons in his soul. She knew that. His father had put them there. But they never showed themselves when he was beside her. Ugly things from the past vanished when they lay together like this, and she still loved the safety of being in his arms ... this place where no harm could come to her. "Some men seem to get better with age, and you are one of them," she told him lovingly. "Here you are, covered with scars from beatings as a boy and gunshot wounds from so many battles you didn't deserve, and you are still in surprisingly great shape, except for that cough."

Jake grinned. "Spoken from the viewpoint of a woman still in love with a man who doesn't deserve one damn ounce of that love."

"And you still see me as the twenty-year-old you met back in Kansas. I see the wrinkles you claim aren't there, and the touches of gray in my hair, so it really doesn't matter if we don't make love quite so often. When we do, it's as beautiful as it ever was, but all I really need is you here beside me." She kissed his chest again. "Every time I see these scars, it reminds me how close I came to truly losing you. It was bad enough when you disappeared for so long in Mexico." She moved her arms around his neck. "Believe me, all I need is for you to hold me. Nothing else is important."

"Is that so?" Jake moved fully on top of her. "Well, it *is* important for a man to know he can still please his wife."

Randy smiled and ran a finger over his full lips. He still had that great smile that she loved. For as long as she'd known him, he's scrubbed his teeth daily with baking soda. For all the wild, lawless things he'd done in life, he had a penchant for cleanliness. She believed it was his way of scrubbing away everything he hated about himself, all the bad things he believed he'd done, maybe even a way of scrubbing away bad memories. "You know darn well that your just *being* here pleases me," she told him.

"I'd like to please you a little more than that, Mrs. Harkner." He reached over her to a table on her side of the bed and picked up a peppermint stick. He bit off a piece. "This stuff helps my cough," he told her. He ran the remaining piece of peppermint over her lips.

Randy grinned. "You are so bad."

"I've heard those words before, but they were usually spoken by some man aiming a gun at me, and seldom spoken lovingly."

"Well, I know what that peppermint really means." Randy took the remaining candy into her mouth and bit it into pieces in a ritual they had used many times over the years before making love. The candy led to a better mood and sweet kisses.

Jake nuzzled her neck, kissed her behind her ear. "This is all your fault, you know," he told her. He gently stroked some her hair away from her face. "I love watching you brush out this beautiful hair, but I think you do it on purpose just to make me want you." He ran a hand over her breasts. "And these are just as full and lovely as always. Don't be talking about a thicker waist either. You have always been a tiny woman and you still are." Jake pushed up her gown and ran a hand under the waistline of her panties. "Let's get these off."

"I didn't plan on this."

"You know me. You should *always* plan on it. And you'd better take advantage of these moments, woman. I make no guarantees of how often I can do this as age catches up with me."

Randy bent her legs, and laughter and kisses melded as

she helped him get her panties off. "I might remind you how tired I am right now. Those kids downstairs wear me out."

"You aren't tired of *this*, I hope," Jake soothed.

"Never of this." Randy laughed more as she chewed up the pieces of peppermint.

"Well, all you have to do is lie here and I'll rock you to sleep," Jake told her. "No work on your part."

"Honestly, Jake, do you really think I could go to sleep with you inside me? If I did, you would never get over it."

Jake chuckled as he unbuttoned the front of her gown and moved it aside to kiss her breasts. "I remember back in Guthrie when you told me we shouldn't do this before going to church. I'll never figure that one out, but I told you if that was the case, we'd better stop going to church."

"And just when did you *start* going to church?" Randy asked. She closed her eyes and relished the feel of his lips at her nipple.

"I'd turn into a pillar of fire if I walked into a church." Jake unbuttoned the front of his longjohns and moved between her legs.

"Oh? I might remind you that when you finally made your one and only appearance in that church back in Guthrie, you didn't burn up," Randy reminded him.

More kisses. The talking stopped. Jake gently massaged sweet places, familiar strokes, perfect touches, movements between two people so in tune with each other's needs and thoughts that they were more like one person. Thirty-seven years of marriage did that to married couples. Randy breathed deeply and met his lips in wanton kisses as she relished a slow, deep climax from the way he had of stroking her deep inside. He moved inside her before her climax was over, making it even more erotic. Jake groaned with sweet pleasure at the feel of her insides pulling at him, deeply welcoming his hardness.

The rest came as naturally as breathing, and was the reason for a son and a daughter, six grandsons and five granddaughters, all from the blood of an outlaw. This didn't happen as often as when they were younger, but when it did, it was as good as ever.

For all these years Randy had relished being right here in her husband's arms, her safe place. Jake folded her against him now and grasped her bottom in his hands to rock her in sweet rhythm, filling her with hard love until she felt his release deep inside. Familiar touches and kisses. Familiar mating. Yet all of it was just as fulfilling and needed as it ever was.

Randy breathed in his familiar scent. This all came so easily, so naturally. They lay there wrapped around each other in the sheer joy of being alive and together. It was always that way, just glad to be alive and together. Others thought this man must be hard to live with, and too often he was, but only because of how the outside world saw him – only because old enemies insisted on coming after him – only because he could turn on a dime, from affable and patient, to ruthless and unable to control when anyone threatened someone he loved.

"Who do you belong to?" he asked softly as he nibbled her ear.

So many times he'd asked the question since the first time they did this in the back of a covered wagon ... so many years ago ... somewhere on the high plains ... young and achingly in love.

"Jake Harkner, now and forever," she always answered.

"You bet," he answered. "And we are going to keep

doing this as long as we still have breath in our bodies. *Tu eres, mi vida, mi querida esposa.*"

Randy loved it when he spoke to her lovingly in Spanish. His Mexican mother was the source of his dark, good looks. His build came from his gringo father, that viciously brutal, drunken, mysterious man none of them ever knew because at 15 years old, Jake killed him to save a young Mexican girl his father was raping. But the bullet that ripped through his father's upper back went through him and killed that young girl. Jake never got over either death, and that was the start of his outlaw life ... and the source of every decision he made from then on.

He'd never known love until they met in Kansas. His children only made that love stronger, but his childhood memories sometimes caused him to risk his freedom and his life to protect them ... to protect that precious love he always feared would be stolen away.

They lay there together until finally falling asleep. It was two hours later when Randy awoke to see her husband up and staring out the back window of their loft bedroom, the dark outline of the Rocky Mountains visible in bright moonlight. Their big, log home was quiet and dark. The end of a cigarette glowed red, and she heard Jake breathe in, then blow out.

He was smoking. She knew that when he smoked in the house now, something was bothering him. She didn't chastise him because this wasn't the right time. "What's wrong, Jake?"

He sighed deeply, still staring out the window. "I'm not sure. It's just something I feel. Something's not right, but everybody is home and safe, so I know it's not someone in the family. It's just that I heard wolves howling. That sound always makes me uneasy." He turned. "Go back to sleep.

It's probably nothing. The howling was probably because of a full moon. And we have outriders who will take care of any wolves threatening the cattle."

Randy felt the same worry they had lived with all these years. Jake's past had a way of rearing its ugly head unexpectedly. She turned over and closed her eyes. *Not now, and not ever again,* she told herself.

CHAPTER FIVE

Randy finished cleaning jelly from little Betsy Jane's mouth when the front screen door squeaked open. "Where are my puppies?" Lloyd yelled as he came inside.

"Daddy!" Six-year-old Donavan jumped up from the table and ran to Lloyd. "Lift me up!"

Lloyd, who like his father stood a good six feet three inches, grabbed the boy and raised him up, while five-year-old Jeffrey and two-year-old Betsy ran over and wrapped their arms around Lloyd's legs.

"Hold it!" Lloyd teased. "You will knock me over!" He held Donavan at his left side while he quickly removed his .45 from its holster at his right side. He handed it over to his mother when Randy walked up to greet him. "I'd better remember not to have this on me when I might be attacked by a bunch of puppies," he told her.

"Yes, you should." Randy gave Lloyd a chastising frown.

"Sorry, Mom. I usually remember to leave it off until I go out to the bunkhouse to give orders for the day. I was going to send Katie's folks over here to get the kids, but I missed these little troublemakers, so I came myself."

Randy turned and handed Lloyd's gun to Jake, who'd just reached the bottom of the steps from their loft bedroom. "Actually, the kids are finished eating and want to go outside and play," Randy told Lloyd. "I made them wash last night and they all have clean clothes on." She smiled at the sight of Lloyd walking to a chair with a child hanging onto each leg. He sat down and was attacked with hugs and kisses.

"Can we go riding today?" Donavan asked.

"Not with me, son. I have to ride out with Grandpa and some of the men to round up strays still roaming out on the plains, and we have to make sure nobody is sneaking off with any of them."

"I thought you were done with roundup," the boy pouted.

"Don, on a ranch this big, finding stray cattle is a never-ending job. And we need to corral the bull calves still out there on the plains and bring them in with the others so we can decide which ones to keep for breeding and which ones to save for market."

"What's the difference?" Jeffrey asked.

Lloyd glanced at Jake, and Randy folded her arms to give both of them a stern look. She hated when some of the young bulls had to be castrated. It was all for the sake of proper breeding and for market sales, but she still hated it. "Donavan, some of the young bulls have to be fixed so they can't mix with the cows," she told her grandson. "Otherwise they get ornery and dangerous to be around." She glanced at Jake. "Like some men I know."

Jake grinned. "You wouldn't want me to be all docile and not see you as a woman anymore, would you?"

Randy smiled wryly. "There are times." She headed for the kitchen.

"As I recall, you liked being a woman last night," Jake teased.

Both men snickered as Jake laid Lloyd's gun on top of the china cabinet.

"I can't believe you two still act like newlyweds sometimes," Lloyd joked. He stood up and shook off clinging children. "Grandma said you are all wanting to go play, so go play," he told the two boys, "but go to Evie's house first and get your sister Tricia. Sadie Mae is there, too. Don't be running around outside without the older girls to watch Betsy."

The children all headed for the screen door.

"And stay out of the horse barn and the corrals," Lloyd ordered. "It's too dangerous."

"But I want to ride my pony!" Donavan pouted.

"Then get Stephen from over at the bunkhouse. He'll saddle Peanut for you."

All three children ran outside, little Betsy toddling on fat legs to keep up with Jeffrey. Lloyd watched them head next door to his sister's house before walking to the kitchen end of the great room. He sat down across the table from Jake.

"God knows Stephen hangs out at the bunkhouse too much," he told his father. "The things he sees and hears from those men aren't fit for decent people, and Young Jake is just as bad. Evie has a terrible time keeping him from cussing." He grinned at Jake. "Like his grandpa, I might add. Those boys are only in their teens, but they think they are grown men. The other night I actually heard them joking about what whorehouses must be like and using words for naked women only those men out there would use."

"I'm sure you and Jake wouldn't know a thing about

houses of ill repute," Randy said mockingly as she poured coffee into three mugs.

Lloyd snickered as he lit a cigarette. "Well, we all know Pa grew up in places like that. Me, I was closer to eighteen and trying to be as crazy and ruthless as my notorious father when I started running with wild women. I can't believe I survived outlaw country at that age."

"You survived because Jake came and got you out of there," Randy reminded him.

"Yeah, well, those were bad times that I would rather not talk about."

"They were bad times for *all* of us," Jake said with a sigh.

Randy walked around the big kitchen table to set a mug of coffee in front of Lloyd. She leaned down to kiss his cheek as she did so. "Did you eat?"

"Yeah. You know Katie's mom. Clara Donavan never lets a human being go hungry. The best thing we ever did was have Katie's parents move here from Guthrie. They have been a big help and comfort for Katie. But we are running low on the household supplies. Vance should be back late today or early tomorrow with the supply wagons. You and Katie and Evie will soon be busy putting your own things away. That's a long list you gave to Vance." Lloyd sipped his coffee. "I just hope Vance was able to get all the feed I ordered, and some seed corn. We need to plant more corn. It's the cheapest kind of feed, and we can cut up and store the stalks to use for barn bedding in winter." He rubbed at a sore shoulder. "With the current banking situation in this country, prices are out of sight. A lot of farmers are going bankrupt. Rumors have it that we are headed for a recession, maybe a run on banks. I am thinking about taking some of our money out of the State Bank in Brighton."

"Good time to buy up more land," Jake suggested.

"Maybe. But I could have a run-in with the federal government over it," Lloyd reminded him. "Right now I am more concerned with possible cattle rustling. With a lot of farmers going broke, we have to keep an eye out. Stolen cattle mean easy money. That means hiring even more men to patrol the borders, which in turn means building more line shacks. In the meantime, I'd better not catch some sonofabitch trying to ride off with J&L cows."

"We'll take care of that problem if we run into it," Jake answered.

Randy hated talk of trouble. "Both of you be careful *how* you take care of the problem," she told them. She glanced at Jake. "Don't forget that you are still in trouble with that judge in Denver."

Jake just grinned. "Don't worry, love. I will remain your mild-mannered, ageing husband."

Lloyd nearly choked on his coffee, and Randy just shook her head. "You have never been mild-mannered in your life. As far as ageing, I see little proof." She looked over at Lloyd. "Stop laughing."

Lloyd laughed harder. "I can't help it. Using mild mannered for Pa is like calling wolves grass eaters."

Randy had to suppress her own laughter. "I would rather change the subject. We have already discussed castration, the danger of guns, and possible rustlers that could land Jake back in jail."

"Life on a ranch," Jake reminded her.

"Yes, well, mixing that and life with *you* is hard to take sometimes," Randy reminded him. She turned to Lloyd. "Son, how is Katie?"

Lloyd sobered. "That isn't the best subject either." He took another sip of his coffee. "Katie is still sleeping." He leaned back with a deep sigh and rubbed at his eyes. "I don't know what to do for her anymore. It's been four months since we lost William. I thought we had things worked out after we lost Gabriel, but she's become even more withdrawn and quiet than she was then." He leaned forward again and stared at his coffee cup. "She seemed better after we had Betsy, but now this last loss ..." He took another sip of brew, then picked up his cigarette from an ashtray and took another drag.

So much like his father, Randy thought. *His looks, his build, his voice, his laughter, his skill and bravery, even the way he smokes a cigarette. When Jake is gone, he won't really be gone at all as long as Lloyd is alive.* "Lloyd, all you can do right now for Katie is be patient and love her," she said aloud.

"I tell her all the time that I love her. I think her real problem is knowing she can't have any more babies. Brian made sure of it. He said another baby could take her life, so we're done, but Katie isn't happy about it."

"Well, Brian is a good doctor," Randy reminded him. "He knew she could die if she had another child. He did what was best for her."

"Katie is having trouble accepting that," Lloyd answered.

"Katie is a strong woman who just needs time to adjust," Jake told him. "She loves you too much to let this go on."

"I'll talk to her again, if you think it will help," Randy assured him. She rose and walked back to the counter beside the wood-burning stove and cut two thick pieces of bread from a loaf she'd warmed in the side oven. She buttered them as she spoke. "Evie talks to Katie often and prays with her. We all know how powerful your sister's prayers can be, Lloyd. And Brian will keep an eye on her."

Someone knocked on the front door. "Hey, Lloyd, you in there? The men are saddled and ready."

Jake recognized his best friend and ranch hand, Cole Decker, standing at the screen door. "Come on in and have some coffee," he yelled to Cole.

"No thanks. I've had enough this morning. Gretta makes a good cup of coffee."

"Yeah, well, I'm sure Gretta is good at a *lot* of things," Lloyd teased.

"You bet she is," Cole answered. "You jealous?"

Lloyd and Jake both laughed. Cole Decker was sometimes the brunt of bunkhouse teasing after marrying the infamous Gretta MacBain.

"I'm just glad for what a good woman she is when it comes to helping my mother," Lloyd answered. "She couldn't have managed Pa three years ago without Gretta's help."

"Hell, Gretta didn't mind. She got to give Jake those baths," Cole joked.

"I'll be glad to return the favor," Jake shot back. "Any time you say it's okay."

"Not while I'm alive, you handsome bastard," Cole answered.

"Not while I'm alive either," Randy added.

They all laughed. "You know we all love Gretta," Lloyd told Cole. "And I'm talking real love. Tell the men I'll be out there in a few."

"We'll be ready." Cole turned, then paused. "Jake, Thunder is saddled and ready, unless you're too old and crippled to ride with us."

"Old and crippled? You wish you were in near as good a shape as I am, you used-up old coot," Jake shot back.

Cole chuckled as he left. Randy loved the banter among the men, but most of all with Cole, who was Jake's most devoted friend and the man who'd gone to Mexico with him. When Jake finally returned home alive months later, Cole wept.

Lloyd took another drag on his cigarette and drank down a little more coffee, then rose and walked over to get his .45 from the top of the china cabinet. He shoved it into its holster. "Thanks for listening," he told his parents. "About Katie, I mean."

Jake smiled sadly. "Listen to your mother, not me. I can't guarantee my advice is any good at all."

"You've been the best father a man could ask for," Lloyd told him. "Don't ever think otherwise. The worst day of my life was when I thought I'd lost you. Promise me that if anything like that ever comes up again, you won't ride off alone again, Pa, no matter *what* the circumstances. Understand?"

"I understand."

Lloyd squeezed Jake's shoulder. "Thanks for the coffee, Mom. And you eat something more than just that bread, Pa. We have time. You shouldn't be riding around out there on an empty stomach." He walked out, and Jake turned to Randy.

"Our son has too much responsibility on his shoulders. He shouldn't have this estrangement going on between him and Katie."

Randy drank some of her own coffee. "You said it yourself, Jake. They are too much in love for this to last."

"I hope you're right." Jake finished his bread and coffee, then grabbed Randy's hand as he rose. He pulled her out of her chair, holding her close as he leaned down to kiss her deeply. "Meantime, I'm still worried about keeping up with my much-younger wife," he told her as he moved his lips to just above her ear.

"This much younger wife has trouble keeping up with *you*."

"Be glad you still have that problem." Jake kissed her again and gently fingered the diamond necklace he'd bought her in Chicago. It was shaped like a rose, her favorite flower. She wore it every day, as well as the diamond wedding ring he'd bought for her in Denver to replace the simple gold band he'd given her when they first married. "You know how much you mean to me, right?"

"Of course I do." Randy put a hand on his chest. "Is something wrong? I know you were upset last night when you heard those wolves."

Jake sighed and let go of her. "I don't know. Something is still eating at me, but I can't put a finger on it." He headed for the front door and grabbed his hat from a nearby wall hook. "By the way, you look extra pretty today. Don't think I didn't notice you wore a yellow dress. You know how much I like you in yellow."

"Thank you. I always wear yellow when I know you are going away."

"It's just overnight, Randy." He took his Winchester down from its bracket higher over where the .44's hung above the door.

Randy shrugged. "I know." She watched his familiar gait as he left, that slight limp from a broken leg he'd suffered at the tortuous hands of bandits in Mexico. She glanced up at his .44's and prayed nothing would happen to make him strap them on again.

She walked out onto the wide veranda built around the front and both sides of the house. What little grass they had was thick and green from recent rains, and she was pleased to see that her roses were loaded with buds. In all the places they had lived, she had always planted roses. She watched Jake mount Thunder as Lloyd and the rest of the men going with him rode off. Jake saw her watching him and trotted Thunder closer. "Woman, you have that look on your face."

"What look?"

"The one I see every time I ride out of here. Stop worrying."

Randy folded her arms, realizing how intimate they had grown. They could read each other's moods and thoughts. "I'm all right. I just didn't like hearing Lloyd talk about rustlers, but if any man can handle himself against such things, you certainly can. You just be careful out there and remember all the new laws they are starting to demand. You can't shoot first and ask questions later anymore, Jake, and you aren't wearing a marshal's badge."

"I am well aware of that."

"It's not just getting hurt you have to worry about. It's jail. That last shootout —"

"Randy." Jake spoke her name firmly. "It will be okay. I'm not going out there alone."

Randy forced back tears. "But you are worried about something."

"It has nothing to do with going out today to look for more strays. I'm sure everything is fine."

"Was that bread enough for breakfast this morning? I usually make ham and eggs to go with it."

"I wasn't that hungry. Besides, Rodriguez already headed out earlier with a chuck wagon. You know how well he feeds all of us. There isn't a better camp cook around. And Lloyd and I are only going along to see how things look and decide which men will go where. Some of the men will ride out several more miles than we will. They might be gone four to five days, but Lloyd doesn't want to leave Katie for that long. We will be back sometime tomorrow, probably before noon, so don't worry."

"I try not to, but I know you too well. Please, please be careful how you handle the situation if you spot rustlers."

Jake took his left foot out of the stirrup and reached out to her. "Come down those steps and grab my arm."

Randy smiled and did as he asked.

"Get up here," Jake told her.

She put her foot into the stirrup and let Jake lift her up in front of him. She wiggled sideways into the saddle with her right leg wrapped around the saddle horn. "This isn't very ladylike."

"Since when do I care about ladylike? I love you best when you are *not* a lady."

Randy smiled and moved her arm around him, resting the side of her head on his chest. "I'm sorry to slow you up. You know how I get sometimes."

"Yes, I do, and you don't need to worry anymore. I'm leaving my .44's behind and I have my rifle with me plus plenty of backup, so don't be worrying about rustlers." He gave her a tighter hug. "Lloyd and I will be back tomorrow, so go bake me more of that bread you know I love."

Randy turned her face to kiss him, then moved her arms around his shoulders for one more hug. "I'll never get over how safe I feel with you, and how scared I sometimes feel when you aren't with me. Ever since –"

Jake cut off the rest of her words with another kiss. "Don't talk about the ugly past, Randy. I swore men from my past would never, ever get to you again, and I meant it. Have I ever left you without one or two of the men keeping watch?" Another kiss.

"No. It just comes in sudden waves, and then it goes away again. I'm sorry."

"Don't be. You are a damn strong woman, Randy Harkner. Just living with me tells me so. You have a way of rising above the bad, and you are a fighter. You came with me to outlaw country to help me find Lloyd all those years ago. You have been through surgeries alone and birthing Evie alone. You waited four years for me to get out of prison and you were there for Evie after the awful thing that happened to her. You rose above what happened to you, and you waited faithfully for me to return from Mexico. Everybody else thought I was dead, but not you. You knew I would come. And this last thing ..." He sighed and kissed her hair. "You went through hell nursing me back to life three years ago. We are done with all that. Nothing but peace is all we should have ahead of us now."

Randy hugged him tighter, relishing the feel of his arms around her.

"Maybe you should go sleep at Evie's tonight, or maybe with Katie," Jake told her. "I don't like you being alone, even with men keeping guard. And Katie needs the company." He grasped her under the chin. "I'll be back tomorrow. Tell me you are okay with that."

"I am." Another kiss. Jake clung to her arm as she slid down from the horse. "You'd better get going," Randy told him. "The rest of the men are way ahead of you."

"I'll catch up easy enough." Jake gave her a smile. "I love you." Thunder skittered sideways, and Jake gave him a gentle kick. The animal took off at an easy lope.

Randy watched him ride away, thanking God that at least he was not still a marshal in outlaw country. How many times had she watched that high hill to the north that led to home ... waiting to see him come back from something dangerous? When he finally made it home after he was presumed dead in Mexico, she'd run to him barefoot through several inches of snow. There was no way she was going to stop to put on shoes first. Jake had come back from the dead. ... He always came back.

CHAPTER SIX

"How close are we to Jake's homestead now?" Dallas asked Vance.

"I figure about two more hours with these heavy wagons. That gets us there around noon."

Dallas scanned vast, green grassland as far as she could see to the north, the south, and the east. Some of the low hills looked carpeted, rather than grass-covered. The jagged, gray peaks of the Rockies to the west only highlighted the sloping green hills and expansive grassland at their base. She'd been living in Wyoming's outlaw country, just as uniquely beautiful, but each state seemed to have a different look to its mountains, even though it was all part of the Rockies.

This morning their little wagon train had crossed Horse Creek. Its sparkling water meandered through a valley sprawled with wildflowers, and several hundred head of cattle grazed there serenely, all part of the J&L.

The Harkners call this valley Evie's Garden, Vance had explained. *After Jake's daughter.*

"I still can't believe Jake owns all of this," Dallas told Vance aloud.

"He doesn't," Vance explained. "Not exactly. He and Lloyd share it. Jake contributes to all of it from sales of that book abut him, and with reward money he got for stopping a bank robbery once in Brighton. He got an even bigger reward from the Union Pacific and several banks when he stopped that train robbery a few years ago when him and the wife were on their way to Chicago to visit an old friend."

Dallas laughed. "When I knew Jake, *he* was the one robbing banks and trains. What a turn-around!"

"Yeah, well, Miranda completely changed that man's life. And because of his past, Jake didn't feel right keeping that reward money. He put it into Evie and Lloyd's bank funds to help support the ranch. It takes a lot of money to run something as big as the J&L. Jake is a humble man, in spite of his reputation. He feels he doesn't deserve one good thing that has ever happened to him. He gives all the credit to his wife and daughter."

"And what do *you* think?"

"I'd say he's right. Jake still can be a real sonofabitch. That last gunfight proved it. But I figure he'd have been dead a long time ago if not for Miranda. I would advise you not to go setting your eyes on Jake on account of old memories. I've seen Randy Harkner put a woman in her place. Under all that pretty hair and figure, there's a right strong woman who has that old outlaw roped in so tight it's a wonder he can breathe. All of us love to watch them together. Randy damn well knows how good looking Jake is, and she understands his demons. All men have demons, you know, but Jake's are extra strong. There is sometimes an extra darkness about the man, one of those things you can't put your finger on, but you know it's there. But Randy, she knows how to handle that man like nobody else. Don't take offense, but I reckon she is everything opposite of the kind of women Jake ran with before she came along."

Dallas felt an irrational jealousy at remembering the cabin Vance had pointed out earlier this morning. It was perched high up on what the Harkners called Echo Ridge. *Jake and Randy go there when they need to be alone. Randy wants them to be buried together up there when the time comes.*

Dallas sat a little straighter, hoping her dress was proper enough to stand up against Miranda Harkner. She'd bathed last night, and this morning she put on a mint green cotton dress with a high collar and pointed cuffs that were trimmed with lace. A wide, satin sash made her waist look smaller, and it was tied into a big bow at her side. A dark green velvet pillbox hat that complemented her red hair was perched on her head at just the right angle, and she wore just a little cheek and lip color. A glance in a mirror this morning told her she didn't look too bad for her age, which was ten years younger than Jake. That made her the same age as his wife. Maybe she could give Miranda Harkner a run for her money.

She immediately chastised herself for the thought. The fact remained Jake Harkner was not a man who forgave easily, and it sounded like his wife had a solid hold on him. She reminded herself that Jake never mentioned Miss Dallas Blackburn in that book about him. Apparently he thought she was of little consequence to his past ... or maybe he simply could not stand the thought of her existence.

"Hey, Vance!" One of the outriders named Calvin rode up beside them. "Somebody is ridin' hard this way, way out there to the right!"

Vance and Dallas watched along with rest of the wagon drivers and guards as a man headed toward them, his horse's mane and tail flying, as was the man's open jacket. A shot echoed through the crisp morning air, and the lead rider's hat flew off. He fell from the stampeding horse, his body rolling over and over several times.

Calvin charged away and caught up with the horse, managing to grab the bridle and slow it down to a stop. Vance had already braked the wagon and jumped off to run to the man who had fallen. He and Bailey Keller helped him to his feet.

Dallas watched in confusion as the man struggled to get away. Blood poured from the side of his head and down his face and neck from where the bullet had grazed him when the gunshot knocked off his hat. In the distance, a big, dark horse charged toward them.

"That's Jake Harkner!" the fleeing man almost screamed. "Don't let him hang me!"

"Hang you for what?" Vance asked. "We happen to work for the man."

Dallas noticed the captured man's gun holster was empty, as was the rifle boot on his saddle. Someone had already disarmed him, but shot at him anyway. She shook her head. That was something Jake would do.

"That's for sure Jake riding toward us," Charlie McGee shouted from the wagon behind Vance's. He let out a war whoop and laughed. "Ain't nobody but Jake would shoot towards others and not worry about hittin' anything but his target. Ain't no better shooter in all of Colorado – maybe not anywhere."

Calvin and Vance continued to struggle with the captured man while the horses of four more riders thundered toward them over the grassland, sod flying off the

horses' hooves. The rider who brought up the rear bran-
dished a rifle. That one was apparently chasing the other
three.

As the man on the dark horse came close to the wagons,
Dallas realized she would not have needed anyone to tell
her who he was.

Jake!

Her heart pounded harder. *My God, he's hardly
changed.* A little gray showed in the black, wavy hair that
sprouted from under his wide-brimmed hat, and his
complexion was darker than normal from years of riding
under the western sun. He was as tall and broad as she
remembered, but leaner now, that kind of hard leanness
familiar to older men. The rider bringing up the rear wore
his hair long like an Indian, but that didn't hide his build
and features. He was a younger version of Jake. *Must be
the son.*

"Pa, you all right?" the younger man called out, proving
her suspicion.

"I will be in a minute," Jake answered.

Dallas recognized the voice. She watched Jake
dismount and charge up to the captured man. He promptly
whacked the man across the side of the head with his rifle
butt. Dallas gasped as the man crumpled to the ground. It
was obvious that Jake Harkner had changed little in looks or
in temperament.

"You bastard!" one of the other three men who'd ridden
in ahead of Lloyd barked at Jake. "Hoot was unarmed when
you shot at him, and helpless just now when you knocked
the shit out of him!"

"He deserved it!" Jake growled, reaching down and
jerking the man to his feet. He shoved him hard toward
Vance and Bailey, who again grabbed the man's arms and

held him steady. Jake turned to the other three strangers. "I didn't shoot an unarmed man," he told the one who'd spoken up. "I *warned* him. If I meant to kill him, I *would* have! I don't usually miss my target." He walked closer. "Get down off those horses!"

"Watch yourself, Pa," Lloyd dismounted with the other three. He kept his rifle ready.

Oh, so much alike, Dallas thought. *What a pair they must have made as marshals in Indian country.* She realized Jake had not even noticed her yet. He was too absorbed in the four men he and Lloyd had corralled. And his treatment of them was pure Jake.

"What's going on, boss?" Vance asked Jake.

"*Rustling!* That's what's going on!" Jake shoved his rifle barrel into the belly of the man who'd complained about him shooting the one called Hoot. The complainer doubled over and cursed Jake. "The rest of the J&L men who rode out here with us yesterday are scattered," Jake told Vance and the others. "They are looking for more thieves like these four. Lloyd and I were headed home when we spotted these bastards camped down by Sparrow Gulch. They were branding five J&L bull calves, pretty as you please, but with their own brand!"

"Big ranchers like you won't miss five cows!" another of the men barked.

Lloyd walked up to the man who'd spouted off and landed a big fist into the man's face. His victim flew backward from the punch, then rolled to his knees and kept a hand over his face. "You broke my nose, you sonofabitch!" he cried. Blood streamed through his fingers.

"I have a great big family and a lot of cowboys to feed, you worthless thief!" Lloyd yelled. "Don't tell me I can just give away five future prize bulls!"

Dallas grinned and shook her head. *Like father, like son.*

"Your own *pa* did his share of stealin' cattle and robbin' banks back in the day," the man retorted, jerking in a sob then as he kept a hand over his nose.

"And he's killed a lot of men," the fourth man added. "That's a lot worse than stealin' a couple cows."

Jake walked up to him and shoved the end of his rifle barrel hard against the man's throat. "Then I guess killing one more man won't make much difference, *will* it?"

The man swallowed and watched Jake with wide, terror-filled eyes.

"I would have good reason to blow your head off!" Jake told him. "There are still harsh laws against rustling, mister, and out here ranchers are still given a lot of leeway when it comes to making their *own* laws!"

"Jake, watch it," Vance warned. "There's a woman with us. The men and I can handle these bastards later. Take them to the homestead and turn us loose with them in one of the barns."

Dallas's heart beat faster when Jake turned to finally notice she was there. He studied her intently.

And there it was. Jake Harkner's demeanor could change in a split second when it meant not offending or frightening a woman. "Sorry, ma'am." He looked at Vance. "Why in hell are you bringing a woman back with you?"

Vance grinned slyly. "Ask *her*. She won't tell me why, and I didn't mind comin' all this way with a pretty woman. She just said it was important and that you used to know each other."

Charlie snickered. "God knows what that means."

"Watch your mouth, Charlie," Jake warned. "Don't be insulting a lady you don't even know." He stepped closer.

"You don't know me either, do you, Jake?" Dallas found

it almost amusing that Jake paid no attention to the man
he'd nearly killed by slicing a bullet across his scalp and
then slugging him with the butt of his rifle, nor the man he'd
gouged in the gut, who was now vomiting. Their injuries
apparently meant nothing to Jake, and so far she saw not
one thing different from the Jake she'd known so many years
ago. "The years have changed me," she continued, "but they
sure haven't changed you. After 40 years, I don't blame you
for not recognizing me."

Jake pushed his hat back and squinted a little. "One
thing I never forget is a voice." He walked even closer. "I
don't forget flaming red hair either." He paused. "*Dallas?*"

"Well, I would prefer you knew me by my looks, but I
guess that's too much to expect after all this time. At least
you remembered my voice."

Their gazes held. "Jesus," Jake muttered. His eyes began
to smoulder with what Dallas was sure were bad memories.
"What the hell are you doing clear out here in Colorado,
and after all these years? Why in God's name – "

"It's a long story, Jake." *My God, you look good.*

Jake turned away and walked up to Vance. "Take her
back to Denver as soon as we unload these supplies! And
don't let her near my wife or my daughter! You got that?
And I know you and women, Vance. Stay away from that
one! She's *trouble!*"

"Pa? What's going on?"

"My fucking *past. That's* what's going on! I don't like
having this woman on my property!" Jake turned from
Vance and walked closer to his son.

"Jake, she's come a long way," Vance protested. "At least
let her rest a couple of days before she goes back."

"Rest where? In the *bunk*house?" An almost evil grin
contorted Jake's face. "That would be fitting for all the

single men on the J&L who haven't been to town in a while, and probably for half the *married* men. Women like that one aren't choosy." He stormed over to Thunder and mounted up. Before he could ride off, Lloyd grabbed Thunder's bridle.

"Pa, you've never treated a woman like this in your life. You've always welcomed women like Dixie and Gretta and others with open arms. Even Mom befriended them."

"This one is different," Jake fumed, jerking the reins and forcing Lloyd to let go.

"Jake, it's been forty years. Forty *years!*" Dallas called to him. "I didn't come all this way after all this time to make trouble. Forty years can change a person. You know that better than anybody here! Please hear me out before you send me back."

Jake whirled Thunder around and rode closer to her. "Back where?"

Dallas felt sick inside. This was not the welcome she'd hoped for. "Wyoming. The Rockies north of Cheyenne." She swallowed. "Outlaw country. A place today's laws still haven't touched. I came here ... for help."

"*Help?* You dare to come to me for help, after all these years and after what you did?"

"Yes. And I must be pretty desperate to do so, don't you think? The Jake I remember would at least have let me explain." Dallas blinked back tears and looked away.

Jake turned Thunder to face the rest of the men. "Those of you with the wagons go ahead and take them in and get them unloaded. Bailey, you take Vance's place driving the lead wagon. Vance will ride with me and Lloyd and help keep an eye on these sons of bitches we ought to hang. We'll ride ahead of the wagons and take these men to one of the barns and have someone keep an eye on them."

"What the hell is going on?" the rustler named Hoot asked, his voice broken and full of fear. "Why are you taking us back to your homestead? You gonna hang us?"

"I am sorely tempted!" Jake barked. "You should have thought twice about stealing J&L cattle!"

"Yeah? Well, *you* should hang for trying to kill an unarmed man. Don't tell me you didn't mean to blow my head off!"

"I *should* have!" Jake answered, riding closer and looking down at Hoot, whose face was swelling and turning purple. "What's your full name?"

The man's eyes teared in terror. "Harold Martin. Most call me Hoot. I had a farm south of here, but I lost it to the bank. You know how things are, Harkner. Nobody's got any money, and I have a family to feed! They say things will only get worse."

"I know the news. But what's going on today doesn't give a man the right to steal from another," Jake told him.

"You ain't one to talk!" Hoot complained.

"You could have come to us and asked for work," Lloyd told the man.

"You just remember that you will answer to the law if you kill us!" one of the other rustlers spoke up.

"That's *my* problem," Lloyd answered. "Mine and Jake's. Just like he said, out here there *is* no law but that of the cattlemen. I'd just as soon plant you under the daisies, and I could probably get away with it. *Remember* that. If I'm lucky, a *judge* will hang you! I sure as hell will do my best to ask for it."

"People are hurting for money!" Hoot shouted, putting a hand to the side of his head again. "It makes them desperate. Men like you Harkners wouldn't understand that!"

"We also don't go around stealing from the farmers,"

Lloyd blasted. "How do you think we keep the J&L running? We need money and horses and supplies, too, so don't talk to me about needing money. Now, mount up!" He turned to the others. "*All* of you!"

The rustlers grunted and groaned as they climbed into their saddles. Lloyd and Jake both handed a couple of rifles and hand guns over to Calvin and Bailey to put into the wagons. "Some of them just tossed their weapons and left them lying out there somewhere," Jake told Calvin. "Ride back where we came from and see if you can find them. If you can't, you can't." He trotted Thunder close to Bailey.

"When you get to the homestead, you drop that woman off at one of the empty cabins," he ordered. "Keep her away from my wife and daughter. I'll send someone to see what she needs for the time being until I find out what she's doing here. Understand?"

"Yes, Sir."

That woman? That's how you're going to refer to me? Dallas wanted to scream at Jake. He'd spoken as if she were a stray dog. *Damn you, Jake Harkner! You can't even say my name?* She quickly lost all hope of turning Jake's opinion of her. He didn't even want her around his wife, a woman who had actually befriended some of the other saloon women Jake called friends. But not Dallas Blackburn. Old memories would not bring back old feelings. Jake seemed almost as angry with her as he was with the rustlers.

Lloyd mounted up and trotted his horse over beside his father. "Pa, what the hell is going on? Why is that woman here?"

"I wish I knew." Jake took a cigarette from his shirt pocket and lit it. "Lloyd, you know the life I led and the women I grew up with. And you know I don't look down on them, but the woman sitting in that wagon *is* a whore of the worst sort! She won't just fuck you for money. She'll stab you in the back for it. As much as your mother and sister represent goodness and beauty, Dallas Blackburn represents evil and ugliness. Plain and simple."

"Jake, you have no right embarrassing me like this!"

Jake whirled his horse. "I have *every* right! And I don't want you talking to my men on the way to the homestead. You save your words for *me*, after we take care of these rustlers. Bailey will drop you off at a cabin where you can put up your things and rest or clean up or whatever you need to do. And stay away from the main house and my daughter and my little granddaughters. Understand?"

Dallas stiffened. "Perfectly."

"Pa, this isn't like you at all," Lloyd reminded his father.

"And of all the saloon women you've known, you haven't met one like Dallas Blackburn," Jake answered. He rode closer to the four waiting rustlers. "Get moving!" he ordered. "And if you try riding off again, I'll do more than shoot your hat off! That goes for all of you! I'm in a real bad mood right now, so I suggest you do what I say!"

The four men reluctantly headed south. Jake and Lloyd followed, rifles ready.

"When are you going to tell me more about that woman?" Lloyd asked.

"As soon as *I* know why she's here in the first place!" Jake barked. "In the meantime, make sure none of the men tries paying that woman a visit. She's trouble, in capital letters. I let Gretta live on the ranch because she's Cole's wife and she behaves like one. Dallas Blackburn won't, and I don't want trouble among the men over her. Believe me, I know a decent saloon woman from a filthy whore, and that one is a filthy whore. Her being here has brought up part of my past I never wanted to talk about, especially to your *mother!"* Jake kicked Thunder's sides and rode off, whistling at the rustlers' horses to get them moving.

Dallas watched them all ride off. *So, it's just as I feared, Jake. You still hate me passionately after all these years. And once you learn why I am here, you might hate me even worse.*

CHAPTER SEVEN

RANDY WATCHED from the veranda as Jake, Vance and Lloyd rode into the homestead with four men ahead of them. Even from a distance , she could tell the four men were injured. One of them rode slightly bent over, as though he was about to fall off his horse.

Why didn't you whistle, Jake? It was a routine they'd started back in Guthrie. When Jake was finally coming into town after hunting down outlaws, he always gave out a unique whistle to let her know he was back. Since they moved to Colorado he'd given out that whistle when he came over the rise where she always watched for him.

"Go get Brian and send him out here," Jake ordered Vance from where they all dismounted near the biggest barn.

Something wasn't right. Normally, Jake would have given that whistle, and then he would have let Lloyd take care of what needed taking care of and come straight to the house. He would always, always give her a hug and make sure things were all right before going back to whatever he needed to do. Not only had he not done that, but the way he'd barked at Vance told Randy he was angry. She watched closely as he jerked one of the men off his horse and gave him a shove toward the barn. From the way the captured men were being treated, and from Jake's mood, Randy had no doubt the men had been caught rustling cattle.

Vance headed for Evie's house to get Brian. Their son-in-law was a good doctor, and knowing Jake, the condition in which the rustlers had arrived left no surprise. They *needed* a doctor. She heard one of the wounded men scream at Jake and Lloyd. "What are you gonna do with us? You ain't no U. S. Marshal anymore, Harkner!"

"You're *lucky* all you need is a doctor's attention," Jake shouted back. "That's a lot better than being buried out there on the plains."

Most men knew Jake's reputation, so those he had just brought home were scared to death. *Don't get yourself in trouble, Jake.* Randy hurried out the door and half ran to catch up to Vance just as he stepped onto Evie's veranda. "Vance! What is going on? Jake isn't hurt, is he?"

Vance came back down the steps and removed his hat. "He ain't hurt, ma'am, but he's in a mood I ain't seen in a long time." He stepped a little closer and lowered his voice. "Maybe you should know that a woman is comin' in with the supply wagons," he told Randy. "She found J&L wagons at the supply store back in Denver and wanted us to bring her here. Says she's an old friend of Jake's, from a long time ago. I reckon you know what that means."

"I know what it means," Randy answered. "What is her name?"

Vance knit his eyebrows, looking worried. "I'd best let Jake tell you. Maybe I shouldn't even have told you as much as I did, but it's when Jake saw this woman that he got real angry, worse than his anger at those rustlers. He told us to take her right back to Denver and that he didn't want her around his family, but she's most of the way out here, so she'll be coming on in. Jake finally agreed not to make her go back right away. He told us to take her to one of the empty cabins and you and your daughter and the grandkids should stay away from her. I, uh, I already know she's no Sunday School teacher."

Randy frowned with her own worry. "Jake usually treats such women kindly."

Vance shook his head. "Not this one, honey. She's pretty hard. I don't think she's got no good in her like Gretta and some of them others. Jake seeing her set off a stick of dynamite in him, so be ready for a man in a really bad mood. I wish I could tell you more, but Jake didn't explain." He put his hat back on. "I reckon you heard Jake say to send Brian over to the barn. I'm sure you ain't surprised at Jake and Lloyd's handling of rustlers. A couple of those men need medical attention."

Brian walked through the front door with his medical bag in hand. "I heard it all," he told Vance. He hurried toward the barn.

Vance watched after him. "That son-in-law of yours is the only man on this ranch who is always calm and reasonable," he said with a smile. "Always wears them black cotton pants and white shirt with a vest. Never loses his temper. Your lovely daughter has a right fitting husband there, especially after what she's been through." He started to leave, but Evie came outside and called to him.

"I heard you talking to Mother," she said. "What do you think is wrong with Daddy? Should I go talk to him?"

Vance snickered as though the remark was almost funny. He shook his head, a warning look to his gaze. "No, Ma'am, I would *not* recommend that. Don't even be calling him Daddy. He's not behaving like the Daddy you know. And I reckon he'll be wanting to talk to your ma before anybody else. Lord knows, nobody can handle Jake like Randy can, that's sure. We'll all rest easier if she can calm him down."

Grandsons Stephen and Young Jake rode in, excited at the commotion created when Jake and the others got back.

"Hey, Vance, we just got done mending that fence in the corral where my dad keeps the breeding mares," Stephen yelled. "We saw Grandpa come back with four extra men. What happened?"

Vance warned them to stay away from the barn for a while, and especially stay away from their grandfather. "Let him explain, boys, when he's ready. You go on back to your chores."

Evie put a hand on her mother's shoulder. "Mother, I didn't hear Daddy's whistle."

"I know," Randy answered, still watching the barn. "And that worries me."

Evie reached up and tightened the combs in her long, dark hair. "It seems more like this has something to do with that woman Vance told you about. How was daddy when he left yesterday?"

Randy shrugged. "He was in a good mood. He joked around with Cole. And before he left, he pulled me up on his horse and gave me an extra hug." She turned to kiss Evie's cheek. "You go back inside and make sure all the little ones stay away from the barn. And don't let any of the kids come over to the house for now. Tell Katie. " She stepped off the veranda and headed for the main house.

"Mother, will you be okay?" Evie called to her.

Randy waved her off. "Of course I'll be okay. We are talking about Jake. I can handle that old bear." Once inside the house, Randy took the leftovers from last night's ham out of a warming oven and set the pan on the kitchen table along with a loaf of fresh-baked bread. Jake loved her bread. It was not quite one o'clock, and he probably had not eaten all morning. She walked to the front door again, peering through the screen at Jake, who was walking from the barn with a determined gait, rifle in hand. He wasn't even limping.

Randy put a hand to her chest. *So, he's so upset that he is hardly aware of that game leg.* Her heart raced a little faster. What on earth was wrong? His whole demeanor was different from anything she'd seen in him in a long time. When he came closer ... up the steps ...

"Jake!"

There it was. Something she'd not seen in years. The look in his eyes was pure outlaw Jake, so close to the Jake she'd first met back in Kansas that it startled her. "Jake?" She pushed open the screen door.

He walked right past her and into the house. Randy followed him inside and closed both the screen door and then the inner door for more privacy. Jake slammed his hat on a wall hook, after which he reached up and plunked his Winchester into the bracket over the door.

"I set out some bread and ham," Randy told him.

"I'm not hungry," he muttered. He sat down in a stuffed chair Randy kept near the door and proceded to yank off his boots.

"So, you're not talking?"

Jake paused and met her gaze, the darkness still in his eyes. "You don't want to hear what I have to say." He rose and headed for the stairs that led to their loft bedroom and wash room. "I'm going to clean up and change my shirt. I'm dusty from the trail." He looked down at her from the stairway landing. "After that, we will talk."

"Indeed we will," Randy answered. She folded her arms in a determined gesture. "But I would rather talk to the Jake who left here yesterday morning. Not the one who came back."

He turned away. "Maybe the one who came back is the *real* Jake," he answered. "The one you never should have married."

"The *real* Jake is the one I fell in love with," Randy reminded him sternly. "I *shot* that one. Remember?"

The look in Jake's eyes flickered with hints of sorrow. "Too bad you didn't hit a vital organ. You would have collected a lot of reward money and saved yourself years of heartache." He stormed up the rest of the stairs and closed the bedroom door.

Randy marched up right behind him and stood at the door. She heard drawers pulled open and slammed closed, heard water running. She frowned in wonder. Never, ever did Jake come home and half yell at her like he'd just done. Even back in Oklahoma, after hunting down some of the worst men who walked, getting into shootouts and fist fights, coming home with broken or dead men in tow, his mood changed the minute he saw her. He would be quiet and tense, but always greeted her with a kiss and a hug. In return, she never asked what he'd just been through. He always waited to tell her when he was calmer.

Something had changed, and she was not going to let him stew about it. She quietly opened the door and stepped inside the bedroom. She sat down on the edge of the bed and waited. Jake finally emerged through the curtains to the wash room wearing just knee-length longjohns, his hair damp. He stopped short when he saw her sitting there. "When did you come in?"

"A few minutes ago. You were busy washing up. I decided I would wait for you so you couldn't sneak out and ride off before we could talk. You *do* have a habit of doing that when you are upset, you know."

Jake just stood there a moment, that outlaw look still in his eyes. The room was full of him, full of anger, full of darkness. This was one of those rare moments when Randy could see his father in him, feel the terror Jake must have felt as a boy beaten with belt or rope, or with a big fist. She could imagine the dreadful revulsion of being forced to help bury his mother and little brother after they were brutally murdered before his eyes. Right now he was a mixture of that lost little boy, and the angry, intimidating outlaw spawned by that demonic boyhood. "Do you know how good you still look?" she asked.

"Don't do this, Randy. I'm not in the mood."

"Don't do what? Try to *change* that mood? I came up here for privacy while I talk to what you called the *real* Jake. Should I expect him to hit me? Or shoot me? I am not the least bit afraid of you right now, Jake Harkner, or worried what you might do, so I'm not leaving. Just tell me what I have done to deserve the attitude you came home with."

Jake closed his eyes and turned away, reaching for a blue cotton shirt hanging over the back of a pink silk cabriole chair Randy had ordered a year earlier. She thought about that lovely chair ... about Jake's words when she showed it to him in a catalogue and said she wanted to order it for their bedroom. *Go ahead,* he'd told her. *You know you don't have to ask me.*

"Jake, you have always let me have anything I want," she said aloud. "Do you think I don't know why?"

Jake pulled on the shirt and began buttoning it as he faced her again. "Why don't you tell me?"

Randy stood up and faced him squarely. "You damn well *do* know. You are a brave, able man, Jake Harkner. Other men fear you. You stood against your father as a little boy, and that made you tough. You've tried to make your heart match that toughness, but I know better. There is only one thing you are more afraid of than facing ten men all on your own, and that is losing the love of your family, most of all, *my* love, so you dote on me unnecessarily. Love scares you to death, yet you are more terrified of losing it than you are of opening your heart to it. This mood of yours has nothing to do with those rustlers out there and whatever happened with them, does it? It has something to do with the woman who is on her way here. A woman from your past. For some reason she has stirred that old fear of losing me."

His eyes betrayed his true feelings, much as he struggled against it. Randy caught a quick glance of the little boy inside the big man, begging her with unspoken words not to leave him.

"Jake, I have put up with women like that for 37 years because I understand you so well. I have even called some of them a friend. Gretta and I have actually grown close. You never once worried about telling me about *any* of the saloon women you befriended when you were a marshal back in Oklahoma, or any before that."

"This goes much farther back, *before* I met you."

"So what? I know those early years are hard for you to deal with, but surely after all this time you aren't worried about losing me. *Why?* Why is this woman different?"

"It's just ... something I've had no right keeping from you." He turned away again and took clean denim pants from the same chair. He pulled them on and began tucking in his shirt. "I should have told you about Dallas a long time ago. The where and why of it. Seeing her again just brings back ... something else you have never known about me."

"Jake, I know you lived with women like that and that you did some terrible things after you fled from Texas. I know you have always fought to put the past behind you, so I have never asked for details."

Jake finished dressing and began pulling a wide belt through the loops on his pants. "Maybe you *should* have asked for more details, because that past keeps coming back to punch me in the gut. I'm just sorry I took it out on you this time." He buckled the belt and held her gaze. Randy noticed the anger there slowly melting more and more into regrets and an almost pleading look. "I thought we were finally at peace, and that I didn't have to worry about losing you anymore. But this woman has brought that past with her, and it isn't just that I half lived with her and thought maybe I loved her. Seeing her again just threw it all in my face ... something I did, and something *she* did."

Randy stepped closer, weighing her words. She'd been through this before, and usually he ran from the moment, sometimes riding off for a day, three days, a week, needing to be alone. When he'd told her a couple of nights ago that he should have blown his own head off a long time ago, she had no doubt he had considered doing just that more than once. She'd spent thirty-seven years fighting his dark side ... that part of him that had been pounded into his soul and psyche since he was old enough to remember. The child in him believed he was bad ... worthless. Satan had power over him. A little boy as traumatized as Jake was could be unpredictable. She was determined not to let him out of this room until she was sure he was thinking straight.

"Jake, if you truly love me, then sit down on the bed beside me now and tell me about this woman. I don't care if maybe you loved her. I *did* have a husband before you came along, you know. I loved him, too, but I was young and starry-eyed, and I only had him for a couple of weeks before he died. I know now that I didn't love him the way I love you, just like I know in my heart you never loved some other woman the way you love me. You don't have to be afraid to tell me about this woman."

He shook his head. "Like I said, there is more to it than that. It's not so much the fact that I thought maybe I loved her, whatever I thought love was back then. What eats at my gut is the way she betrayed me."

Randy could feel his nervousness - something building inside. Right now he looked like a wild animal trapped in a corner. She got up and walked closer to the door. *Don't let him leave.* "What did she do?"

Jake turned away and gazed at the mountains outside the roof window. "We lived together on and off. I was just trying to maybe find a normal life, trying to figure out what love was supposed to feel like. She led me to believe she loved me in return, even though she still slept with other men for money. I never dreamed any decent woman would ever want anything to do with me, so I never even tried to see women like that. Besides, I was a wanted man." He paused and shook his head. "Anyway, I figured if Dallas ... that's her name. Dallas Blackburn. If she would agree to sleep with only me and quit the business, maybe we could get married and get out of the wild life we led."

Randy noticed his hands move into fists.

"I didn't see her for how low she really was until one night we were in the throes of ... you know. We had talked about her quitting the business. She said she would ... said she loved me and wanted to settle. We got lost in making love, if you want to call it that when it's with a whore. I had no experience with *honorable* women. Next thing I knew, a bounty hunter barged in and took a shot at me. I moved too fast for him. He winged me across the neck, but I always kept my guns hanging at the head of the bed. I'd had plenty of practice being alert to someone behind me. I managed to whip out my gun, and I shot him." He faced Randy. "Before he died he screamed at Dallas." He ran a hand through his hair and breathed heavily, seeming ready to explode. "*You bitch!* he yelled. *You said you would have him so preoccupied that I could take him easy.*"

The air hung silent and tense for a moment, until the words registered in Randy's mind. "Oh, my God," she said softly. "She set you up?"

There came the black anger again. "She wanted the reward money. I stood there stark naked, gun in hand. Mortified. Humiliated. And actually a little broken hearted that she'd done that to me. Until then we had at least been friends, but she used what feelings I had back then to stab me in the back with them."

Randy's heart ached at the thought of it – a man whose ability then to love and trust was so fragile.

"Never before or since have I wanted to shoot a woman," he told her, "or at least beat her. Memories of my father beating my mother kept me from it, but it wasn't easy holding back. She begged me not to kill her or hurt her. I could hear my mother begging that of my father, so I just grabbed my clothes and left. I never saw her again. It wasn't long after that when I met you." He breathed deeply, coughed a little. "Now you know why I fought my feelings for you. I figured I already got what I deserved for letting such feelings get away from me with Dallas, and thinking I knew a goddamn thing about love. Dallas threw it all in my face. How in hell could I let myself trust another woman ever again after that, let alone a *good* woman who was much more likely to be afraid of me and turn me in?"

Randy noticed a strange desperation in his gaze. "There is more to it than that, Jake. You said so yourself a minute ago. What are you leaving out?"

Jake stood there a moment, all brawn, all fury ... but his eyes suddenly teared. "Damn you!" He started for the door, but Randy leaned fully against it, grasping the door knob behind her back. "Don't you *dare!* You are not going to ride off without an explanation this time, Jake."

He stepped closer, towering over her. "Do you honestly think you can stop me from leaving?"

Randy raised her chin. "You tried to intimidate me once, that night in the wagon out on the plains in the middle of nowhere," she answered. "Remember? You were helping me look for my brother, and you were so damn scared of your feelings for me back then that you tried to make me hate you. You threatened to force me and use me like a whore! But you didn't scare me, Jake Harkner. I already had you all figured out, and I already loved you. What did I tell you then? Do you remember?"

His breathing came heavy and fast. "You said, *Go ahead. Act like your father, the man you <u>hate</u>.*"

"And that's who I see when you get like this," Randy said boldly. "Is that what you want? You can't make me hate you, Jake."

"Let go of that door handle," he said flatly.

"No. Not until you tell me what else is eating at you."

Jake reached behind her and gently pried her hands away. "Let go," he repeated, more gently this time. "I won't leave. I promise." He wrapped one strong hand around her wrists and held her arms behind her as he crushed her close. With his other hand he yanked the combs from her hair and let it fall, then wrapped a fist into it, clinging to her as though she were falling over a cliff and he had to hang on to save her. "I told you Dallas betrayed me, but *I* have betrayed *you*," he said, "in a whole different way."

Randy pressed her forehead against his chest. "It doesn't matter. Just tell me what is going on. I promise you won't lose me."

"*Won't* I?" Jake buried his face into her hair. "God, Randy, every time we make love, I think about it. Every time you talk about being safe in my arms, I think about it. I've kept something inside since you took that bullet out of me back in Kansas."

Randy said nothing, afraid it would end the moment and whatever he wanted to tell her. He kissed her hair as he let go of her wrists and fully embraced her.

"You have forgiven so many things," he told her. "But you might not be able to forgive this." He pulled back a little and leaned down to kiss her, a deep, almost violent kiss, as though it might be their last. He held Randy so close that she struggled to breathe. "Jake, you are hurting me."

He let go of her and pushed her gently away. "I'm sorry. I'm just ... I'm almost afraid to let go of you because this time *you* are the one who might run away."

"You are so upset you aren't making any sense, Jake. Why on earth would I leave you after all these years?"

Jake looked her over lovingly, and in a way that suggested he might never see her again. He let go of her and walked over to a chest of drawers that held his clothes and personal items ... the chest that held his mother's crumpled, bent-up crucifix that saved his life when another man's bullet slammed into his chest. "I have to show you something. Then you will understand."

Randy was stunned to see him quickly wipe at tears with his shirt sleeve. Men like Jake Harkner didn't come to tears easily. As a child toughened up in the worst ways, he'd learned that tears didn't help a thing. She watched him rummage through some of his things, then turn with something in his hand.

"I kept this in a hidden pocket in my saddle bags for years," he admitted. "Sometimes I hid it in a a cut-out in one of the barn beams. When we lived in Guthrie, I kept it in a safe in the local bank. Wherever we lived, I always found a way to hide this from you. Jess York kept it for me when I went to prison. When he knew he was dying from cancer, he put it in the local bank for me and told me where I could find it when I was let out." He walked closer, hesitated, then held out a gold chain watch.

Randy thought the watch looked familiar. Confused, she took it from him and fingered it gently, then opened it. When she studied the picture inside, she gasped, instantly overwhelmed with emotion. It was a picture of a man, a woman, a young girl and an even younger boy.

It was her family.

Confused, she turned the watch over. Engraved on the back was the name *Dr. Lawrence Baker*, her father's name. She remembered when the picture was taken, so many years ago ... just before her mother died ... before her brother ran away ... before the raid on their farm that killed her father. Wide-eyed with shock, she met Jake's gaze. "Where on earth did you get this?"

Jake stood there watching her, looking like a lost soul. "Where do you think?" His eyes brimmed with more tears, and his gaze showed literal terror that now it would all end for him ... her love, the love of his family.

Randy struggled to put it all together. *The raid on my father's farm!* She watched his eyes. "*You?*"

He faced her boldly. "Me."

CHAPTER EIGHT

THE ROOM HUNG silent and tense for several seconds as Randy wrestled with how she should feel, how she should react. This was Jake. *I belong to Jake Harkner, now and forever.* How many times had she said that in the throes of lovemaking ... such gentle, soul deep, exquisite lovemaking? He had touched and tasted every inch of her body ... had taken her to heights of passion she once never knew were possible. Now that same man had handed her a symbol of the awful raid that had left her father dead. "Tell me you didn't ... you aren't the man who killed my father, Jake ... the man who stole this watch from his dead body."

"It *could* have been me. I rode with the men who *did* kill your father. I was with them that day. The leader of ..." His voice began to break. He cleared his throat nervously. "He was Robert Blackburn. Most called him Buck. You might remember his name because he was pretty well known in Kansas and Missouri for guerilla raids during and after the war. I took part in many of those raids. Dallas was his sister. That's how I met her. I think Buck is the one who shot down your father, but I can't be sure because bullets were flying everywhere. How do I know it wasn't one of mine that maybe ricocheted off something and killed him? All I know is that I did not aim right at him during that raid."

Randy felt light-headed. She was looking at a picture of herself as a very young girl, standing there with the mother she barely remembered now, the devoted father who had lovingly raised her after her mother died, her precious little brother who ran away, never to be seen alive again. She raised her eyes to look at Jake again. Jake had come for her and saved her life when she headed west to find her brother. He'd helped her through all of it, helped her find out what happened to her brother. And he'd loved her like no other man could love.

"Seeing Dallas today brought it all back, and I knew I couldn't keep the truth about that watch from you any longer," Jake told her. "When I die, you would have found it and figured out I was part of that raid on your farm, maybe even the one who killed your father. You would have wondered why you put up with me all these years ... why you bothered mourning me after my death." He stood there, breathing heavily, almost looking like a little boy waiting for his beating. "One of the few sins I have *not* committed is lying, Randy. So please believe me when I tell you that it's most likely Buck who shot your father down," he said, his voice strained. "He took sick pleasure in killing innocent people. I didn't. But the fact remains that I rode with him, so it doesn't matter that it was someone else who shot your father. I was there that day and it *could* have been me, so I am just as guilty as the rest of them."

Randy pressed the watch to her heart and swallowed back a lump in her throat. "When did you know I was the girl in the picture?"

Jake turned and took a cigarette from a silver container on the night table. Randy didn't try to stop him. Maybe smoking would keep him from leaving. With his back to her he lit the cigarette and took a deep drag.

"It took me a few days to realize it," he answered. "The raid took place about ten days before Dallas tried to collect that bounty on me. After I killed the bounty hunter, I left, and a day or so later is when I met you in that dry goods store. That bounty hunter I shot in the supply store was a partner to the one I shot when I was with Dallas." He paused to smoke quietly, then faced Randy. "And then you shot me." He shook his head and managed a sad smile. "I fell in love with you right then and there, when you stood there looking so terrified. Those beautiful gray-green eyes of yours were wide as saucers. I had no idea who you were then. In the picture you were younger. After I ran out of that store, I was desperate to find a place to rest, maybe die. My gut was on fire."

He rubbed the back of his neck, then wiped at his eyes with his fingers. "Jesus," he muttered. "I have to get out of here."

"No!" Randy insisted. She moved to the door again. "Finish it, Jake. You owe me that."

He turned away, taking another drag on the cigarette. He stared out the window again as he spoke. "For some reason, after you shot me, I headed for the place we'd raided earlier – figured it was abandoned because we either took or destroyed everything. The crops were still trampled, every- thing broken down, most of the furniture gone. I wasn't thinking straight. I didn't realize someone might have sold everything and was making ready to leave. I had no idea it was where the beautiful woman in the supply store lived because, thank God, you weren't at the farm the day of the raid. I didn't put it all together until days later, after you took that bullet out of me and I started feeling better. You told me your father had been killed in a raid ... told me his name. That's when I knew."

Randy studied the picture again. Her family. All gone now. It was a lifetime ago. It was as though the little girl in the picture was someone else. Not her. "Did you take this watch off my father's dead body?"

Jake shook his head. "No. I swear. I got it from one of the other men later. After we settled in that night, I gambled for it." He snickered with self-loathing as he sat down on the bed. "Some winnings, huh?"

"Why didn't you sell it?" Randy continued studying the picture. "It's worth something. It has gold in it."

"I didn't keep it for its worth. I kept it because something about the family in that picture reminded me of what family is supposed to mean. I used to daydream about being part of a family like that, of being a father who loves and guides his children the way a father should. A man who loves his wife and doesn't beat her. A father who doesn't scream and terrorize his kids and drink himself into oblivion. For some reason, looking at that picture calmed me. But after I learned it was *your* family, I never looked at the picture again."

He rubbed at his eyes again, pausing and clearing his throat in a way that spoke of a man trying to stay in control. "When I realized whose watch I had, I was afraid that if I told you then, you would turn me in. So I didn't say anything. And as I healed and realized I was falling in love with you, it became more important not to tell you. I didn't have the heart for it. At the same time, I couldn't get away from you fast enough because I had no right loving you at all. When I first rode out of your life, I intended to never see you again. I sure as hell couldn't go back to Dallas, and Buck and I weren't getting along because of what his sister did to me, so I left the gang and started wandering, but I couldn't get you off my mind. I knew you were traveling west alone, so I set out to find you. I was so goddamn lonely, and so worried about you. And I felt so guilty. I just wanted to make sure you were okay."

He rested his elbows on his knees and stared at the floor. Randy waited, knowing it was best to let him continue on his own. He put the cigarette into an ashtray on the bed stand. "The rest is history. I never loved anything like I loved you, Randy, let alone realizing I could actually trust you. All those times I rode out of your life since then, I guess I was testing that trust, but I also knew you deserved so much better than being married to a wanted man and all the hell that comes with it. And the last thing I wanted was to have to tell you about that watch ... that I was with the men who raided your farm."

Randy wiped at sudden tears. "What if I had been home that day? What would have happened to me?"

Jake rose and faced her. "*Nothing!* I swear to God. Not with *me* there! I grew up watching my mother abused, and I didn't want any part of that kind of dirty work. If you had been there that day, I would have fought all of them to keep them away from you. That's the God's truth. As low and no good as I was, I never stooped that low, Randy. You must know that. I've *killed* men like Buck and his bunch for abusing a woman. I have even gone after men who rob from or beat on prostitutes. But you ... I would have known right away the beautiful, innocent woman you were. I would have taken a shower of bullets before I would have let them hurt you."

Randy's shoulders jerked in a sob. She sat down in the

chair at her dressing table and pulled a handkerchief from a pocket in her skirt.

Jake hung his head. "God, Randy, you have no idea what those tears do to me. If you want me to leave, I will leave."

Randy took a deep breath to be able to talk more. "You have no idea what bothers me about all of it, and it's not what you think." She blew her nose and wiped at her eyes. "I am crying because you said you would have died before you let those men hurt me. I just ... I needed to be sure. I always believed you would never hurt a woman. There is only one other thing I need to know." She looked at Jake pleadingly and saw the regret in his eyes when he met her gaze.

"Ask me anything," he told her.

Randy wiped tears from her cheeks again, almost afraid to ask. "When you decided to come and find me, you said it was out of guilt. But you stayed, Jake, and you married me and turned your life around and gave me two beautiful children. I need to know if you did all that out of guilt, or did you really *love* me? I know you said you fell in love with me the day I shot you, but I'm not talking about that kind of sudden desire. I am talking about the bone-deep love I have always felt for you, the kind I always thought you felt, too. But you said you felt guilty, and even now you do. Has it only been guilt all these years? If it has ..."

Before she finished, Jake had hurried over to kneel in front of her. "My God, Randy, of *course* it's all been because I love you. Coming to find you and help get you safely to Nevada *was* out of guilt." He reached out to push some hair behind her ear, then kept his hand at the side of her face. "But only at first. Deep down I knew I already loved you. I fought it, for *your* sake, because I knew life with me would be hard. But from that night I took you in that covered wagon, it was all love and nothing more. I swear it on my mother's crucifix, and you know what that means to me. Surely you feel it every time I look at you, or hold you. You must feel it when I make love to you. I have never touched another woman, not even in those two years I spent in Outlaw country after that gunfight in California. It's like I told Jeff for that book about me. You are the air I breathe. You and the kids are the only reason I fought to live three years ago, the only good and right and perfect things that ever came into my life or from my blood. And I feel so damned unworthy of all of it."

Randy glanced down at the watch again. She knew that in Jake's current mood, she had to weigh her words. She finally met his gaze, saw the fear and pleading in those dark eyes that showed violence one minute, and the gentlest of love the next. "Jake, you did not betray me," she told him. "All you did was try to keep the hurt away by not showing me this watch. But I consider it a gift. All these years I've had nothing left of my family. No pictures. None of my mother's china or jewelry. Those marauders stole or destroyed everything." She closed the watch. "Jake, that raid would have happened whether you were there or not. Those men were bent on it, and by the grace of God I wasn't home."

She folded the watch into her fist, then took hold of Jake's hand and put her own hand into his palm so that the watch was cupped between them.

"This watch landing in your hands was meant to be, Jake. *God* put it there because He was already leading you to me. What happened is not something that would make me hate you. It's something that shows me that even back then, before I ever taught you how to love, how to trust ...

you already wanted what is in this picture. *Family.* I was able to give that to you. You showing me this watch is like coming full circle for both of us. I know you think God wants nothing to do with you, but He led you back to my farm for a reason. He was bringing us together, and that is not something either of us can run from now, or deny."

Jake squeezed the watch tightly between their hands. "But I should have told you about it that night in the wagon, before I made love to you and there was no going back."

Randy shook her head. "There is your answer, Jake. There *is* no going back. Things happen the way God wants them to happen, and we've had one hell of a ride, haven't we? For a man who grew up hardly knowing the meaning of the word love, you sure know how to show it. Much as you deny it, you have truly been a good father and grandfather, and an even better husband. This watch is the best gift you have ever given me," she told him. "Better than this house or all the nice furnishings or my ring or my necklace."

Jake frowned in bewilderment. "But down inside, part of me is still the man who did some damned ugly things before we met. I've tried to make you see that, Randy, but you and Evie and the whole family keep choosing to see only that rare *good* side."

"And that is the point. You *do* have a good side. When are you going to figure out that nothing can change the fact that I love you? That *all* of us love you? I've *seen* the ugly and the ruthless. I've gone through weeks and months apart, gone through the gunfights and attacks on the family, gone through the worry and darkness of your years as a marshal in No Man's Land. I've had to jump out of bed at times when your nightmares are so bad that you are hitting at things in your sleep. But I have also seen the look on your face when Katie or Evie puts a new grandbaby in your arms, or when Sadie Mae and Tricia climb onto your lap. I couldn't be happier with the kind of husband and father you have been, so don't ever tell me again that you worry about losing me, or losing this family, or that you don't deserve all of this. *We* are the ones who worry about losing *you*. None of us ever wants to go through what we went through three years ago. Our whole world revolves around Jake Harkner, especially *my* world. Tell me you believe that."

"I want to."

"Then *do*. How much I love you will never change."

"But I don't know why Dallas is here. What if she wants something you and the family can't handle?"

"After all the things we have been through? There is *nothing* we can't handle, Jake. You must know that by now."

"Wagons comin' in!" Through the open bedroom window, they heard one of the ranch hands shout the words.

Jake immediately tensed up. "Dallas is here."

Randy clung to his hand. "Jake, have Gretta see to her needs for now. God knows Gretta can handle a woman like that. You go help Lloyd take care of those rustlers and help us unload the supply wagons. Let's bring Dallas over here later this evening to tell us why she's here. *All* of us together. I don't want you talking to her alone and then not telling us the whole story. Promise me, Jake. Don't try to handle this alone."

He leaned close and kissed her cheek. "I promise."

Randy pulled her hand away and set the watch aside. "And you don't have to tell the family about the watch, Jake," she soothed. "It's too much all at once. The important thing now is finding out what Dallas wants. All Lloyd and Evie need to know is that you knew this woman once and that she betrayed you. All right?"

Jake rose and pulled her up with him to embrace her fully. "How can you so easily forgive me?"

"Because all you have done is give me a precious gift," Randy answered. "You could have told me a long time ago, Jake, and I would have understood."

Jake crushed her close, kissing her hair. Randy could still feel his tension, his smouldering anger. "Dallas knows how I hate her. For that reason alone, it makes no sense that she has come here for some kind of help for old times' sake. That just tells me it must be serious, or she wouldn't be here at all. I don't want to put the family through hell again, Randy."

Randy breathed deeply of his familiar scent, felt the heartbeat that stopped more than once three years ago. "Jake, just stay calm and think about the grandkids. Don't show this side of you in front of them. Take one thing at a time, and trust how much we all love you."

He kept her in his arms. "I'm so damn sorry about your father. Now you know why I have always worried about losing you."

"And that is never going to happen." Randy pulled away slightly and looked up at him. "All I've ever needed to be happy is you beside me. You are my safe place."

He leaned down and kissed her teary eyes, her mouth ... tenderly ... deeply ... love and gratefulness and sorrow silently spoken. Evie called out from downstairs then.

"Mom? Is everything okay? We need you to come outside and tell us what you want brought into the house from the supply wagons." She turned her attention to Jake. "Daddy? Is everything okay?"

Jake reluctantly let go and quickly wiped at his eyes. "Is that grown woman down there ever going to stop calling me Daddy?"

"Evie is Evie." Randy managed a smile, then wiped at her own tears as Jake walked out and headed down the stairs.

"Everything is fine, Evie," he assured her.

"No, it isn't. Daddy, you look awful. What's wrong?"

Young Jake bounded through the front door before Jake could answer. "Come on, Grandpa. Uncle Lloyd needs you out at the barn, and we have supplies to unload." He walked into the kitchen area to cut himself a slice of the bread Randy had left on the table.

Evie touched her father's arm. "Daddy, what is it? You were so upset earlier, and then you and Mother came in here and closed the door and we were all worried."

"Don't be. Your mother will explain later."

"Should I take something to that woman who came in with the wagons?"

"*No!*"

Evie stepped back a little as the darkness moved back into her father's eyes.

"Leave it be, Evie," he told her. "Gretta will see to that woman."

"But I can't be rude, Daddy. You know that. Maybe she needs something. It's a long ride —"

"*Listen* to me, Evie! Stay *away* from her. I told you that Gretta will see to her."

"Jake, stay calm," Randy warned as she came down the stairs.

Jake gave Evie a quick kiss on the cheek. "I'm sorry. Your mother can explain. I'm going to talk to Lloyd." He walked out.

"Mother, what's wrong? Daddy is never short with me like that."

Randy walked closer and touched her shoulder. "It's a

long story. You know how your father gets when the worst of his past comes back to cause problems. Let's unload the supplies and then I'll explain."

"Well, I don't like this kind of unrest," Evie scowled. "And I especially don't like that look in my father's eyes. It's too much like the look he got when he shot that man in Denver. It's that look he gets when he talks about his father, or when –"

"Evie, don't worry about it. It takes time for Jake to think with reason when something from his past revisits him. You know that. And you, my precious daughter, are something that helps steer him in the right direction. Right now, just pray for God to take care of him. You know that always works."

Evie folded her arms, looking ready to cry. "If you say so."

"I *do* say so."

"But you have both been crying. I can tell."

"Such is life, Evie. God knows there isn't much your father and I can't handle together, and that is exactly what we are doing." Randy knew their daughter touched Jake in a special way. He would never forgive himself for what happened to her at Dune Hollow back in Oklahoma, at the hands of outlaws who hated U. S. Marshal Jake Harkner. In Jake's eyes, his "baby girl" was pure angel for the faith and strength she'd shown after her ordeal.

Before either woman could continue the conversation, Young Jake rushed past them and back outside. "Come on, Mom. I'll help you and Grandma unload your supplies."

Evie looked helplessly at her mother. "He is getting so tall! He looks eighteen instead of thirteen, and he's around those men in the bunkhouse too much," she complained. "I've lost my little boy."

"Evie, he is his grandfather through and through, not just in build, but in nature. The boy knows no fear, but he has a good heart. Those men out there are just helping him face real life. A young man needs to learn the good ... and the bad ... and learn to choose, just like your father did. Jake never had any guidance like Young Jake has, yet he still chose the good. It just took him longer. Now, let's help unload those wagons. We have a lot of things to put away."

They walked out together. Randy glanced in the direction from which the rest of the wagons rolled in. In the distance she saw a woman in a green dress standing on the stoop of one of the empty cabins. She couldn't see her in detail, but she noticed curly red hair and a deep green pillbox hat perched on top of the curls. She suspected the woman was still pretty. In spite of the fact that she was a prostitute Jake had known before he ever met her, Randy still couldn't help a little pang of jealousy.

I don't know why you are here, Dallas Blackburn, but if you hurt or betray my husband again, I'll show you what some proper ladies are made of, and you won't like it.

CHAPTER NINE

J‌AKE SIGNED the complaint his son-in-law wrote up for having the rustlers arrested in Brighton. "Brian, your ability to compose well-worded documents is as perfect and thorough as your doctoring," he told Evie's husband.

Brian repacked his instruments. "I do my best, Jake. Maybe some day they will be able to hook us up with a telephone and the law can come here and pick up men like these."

"Yeah! Before you break a man's nose!" The grumbled words came from the rustler Lloyd had slugged. "Your son had no right!"

Jake eyed the man darkly. "If I were you, I would be thankful that's all he did. Don't forget what the punishment has always been for stealing cattle and horses."

"*You*, for one, would gut us and drink our blood if you didn't have to remember the new laws," the man answered Jake.

"Shut up, David," Hoot Martin spoke up. "Don't tempt Satan."

"Satan is right," Jake answered. "The mood I am in

right now, don't give me ideas about what to do with all of you. I hope my son-in-law didn't waste too much laudanum on you. We might need it for the family or one of the men. He should have let all of you suffer through those stitches."

"Marshal Hal Kraemer will have something to say about how you treated us," Benny Martin spoke up. "Especially you practically blowing my brother's head off!"

"Tell him anything you want," Jake answered. "Kraemer and I have an understanding. We come from the same school of thought about outlaws."

"Takes one to know one," Hoot shot back. The bandage around his head was already blood stained.

"That's why a judge sentenced me to being a U. S. Marshal in No Man's Land," Jake answered. "He knew I could handle the worst of the worst."

"You'd be better off remembering that!" Lloyd told the rustlers. "All of you keep quiet. I can't always stop my pa from that ugly side that makes him want to hang or shoot a man." He folded the formal complaint papers. "The beams holding up this barn are damn sturdy," he reminded the rustlers, "and one thing there is plenty of on a ranch is rope."

The four rustlers glanced up, then back at Lloyd. "So, the branch doesn't fall far from the tree, does it?" Hoot answered. "You've got the same ugly in you."

"You bet," Lloyd answered. He turned to Jake. "Which of our men do you think should accompany these no-goods to Brighton?"

Jake removed his hat and ran a hand through his hair before putting it back on. "Send Tommy Tyler and Sam Hunnicut. Tommy is damn good with those guns of his, and always itching to prove it. Sam has a more steady attitude.

Maybe send Percy Bates, too. I want Terrel and Vance and Cole here. I might need them."

"For what?"Lloyd frowned. "You still haven't told me what's going on, Pa. And by the way, you look awful. You were in a piss-ass mood when we got back. I see you cleaned up already, but you were at the house for a long time, which means you've been talking to Mother. Is she okay?"

"She's fine. And I'm *still* in a piss-ass mood." Jake ordered two other ranch hands to keep an eye on the rustlers, then motioned for Lloyd and Brian to follow him outside. He and Lloyd both lit cigarettes, and Brian set his medical bag on an extra-thick fence post. "Jake, do you need aspirin or something?" he asked. "Lloyd is right. You don't look too good."

"I'm upset about Dallas Blackburn." He took a long drag on his cigarette. "In case you don't already know it, Brian, that's the woman who hitched a ride with Vance and the supply wagons. My short explanation is that I knew her before I ever met Randy, and she spells nothing but trouble. She's a whore in the worst sense – the filthy kind who *likes* that life."

"Pa, a *lot* of them like it."

"Not in the way Dallas does. She's the type who will poison your whiskey and then rob you blind while you are passed out. She's the kind who makes you think you can trust her, maybe even think she cares about you, but every kind move she makes is for something that benefits her, not because she has feelings. The last time I saw her, she'd hired a bounty hunter to shoot me while I was in bed with her so I could be caught off-guard. She wanted to collect the bounty on me. And that was *after* she told me she loved me. That's the kind of woman who is waiting over there in that cabin, and now you know why I hoped to never see her again.

She's the only woman I have ever wanted to raise a hand to. She's damn lucky I was able to control the urge."

Lloyd and Brian looked at each other in surprise.

"Jesus, Pa, that was a hell of a thing for her to do. Why haven't you ever mentioned her before?"

"Because I have tried to bury the memory. Seeing her again makes me want to wrap my hands around her throat and squeeze the life out of her. She knows damn well how I feel, and to show up after forty years only spells something bad. She can't possibly be here to stir up old memories or expect any personal help. This is something bigger."

"Then don't be trying to handle it alone," Lloyd warned. "I know you all too well, Pa. Do we have to tie you down?"

Jake took another drag on his cigarette. "Don't worry about that. I've promised Randy that the whole family can be present when Dallas tells me why she's here, so have Katie and Evie over to the house tonight after supper, seven or so. And Ben is a full-fledged legal son, so have him and Annie come, too. I suppose maybe even Stephen and Young Jake should be there. It's time they were in on these things and took over more of what's involved in running this ranch. God knows *my* days are numbered." He barely got the words out before going into another coughing fit.

Lloyd glanced at Brian with concern. Brian just shook his head. "I don't know what else to do for him, Lloyd. The man is tough as nails. I swear, being here for the rest of us is all that's holding him together."

Jake tossed his cigarette and grasped the fence rail, leaning over slightly to take a few deep breaths.

"Jake, go home and take some of that cough medicine I gave you and lie down for a while," Brian told him. "Seems like I've been treating you for pneumonia ever since I met you when you were in prison. Go rest up before we all come over this evening. Promise me you will. Do you have aspirin left at the house?"

Jake nodded. "Yeah."

"Does Mom know what that woman did to you?" Lloyd asked.

Jake took another deep breath before answering. "She does now. She knows more of the details, but I won't go into that now. It's enough to know why I'm damn sure Dallas Blackburn isn't here for a grand reunion with an old friend. I actually considered marrying that woman once ... in another life. It all happened back in Missouri. Dallas was a sister to one of the members of a gang I used to ride with. She runs a whore house up in outlaw country now, so what does that tell you?"

Lloyd closed his eyes and sighed. "It tells me a lot."

Jake took yet another deep breath and straightened. "There is more to my past than you and Evie know, Lloyd. You think I've told you all of it, but I haven't, because it's too ugly. There is more of my father in me than you realize, and I have fought it my whole life. I wanted to beat on Dallas for what she did. I've never laid a hand on a woman in my life because of what I saw my mother go through, but if any woman deserved it, Dallas did. I just grabbed my clothes and left before I could give in to that darkness. I quit the gang, and it wasn't long after that when I met your mother." He rubbed at his eyes. "I'm going to go talk to Gretta and have her deal with Dallas. I don't want my wife or someone as sweet as Evie to be around her. If anybody can stand up to Dallas Blackburn, it's Gretta MacBain. She will be damn mad about Dallas's betrayal. Gretta would never have done that to one of her customers."

Jake turned his attention to Brian. "Speaking of Evie, I

saw her for a minute just before I left the house and now she's all upset over *me* being upset. You always have a way of calming her down, Brian, so go find your wife. And thanks for patching up those men and writing up a formal complaint. We'll send those rustlers to Brighton in the morning and be rid of them. I just hope the rest of the men we left out there on the range don't find even more rustling going on. They have enough to do without having to be the law out here."

Brian grabbed his doctor's bag. "That's for sure. I'll go find Evie." He put a hand on Jake's arm. "Go rest. That's an order."

Brian walked off, and Jake turned his attention to Lloyd. "I'm sorry to bring more worry to the family, Son. You don't need this, what with running this ranch and dealing with Katie's problems."

"I'm more worried about the reason Dallas Blackburn is here. I haven't seen you this upset in a long time, Pa. Soon as you talk to Gretta, go home and rest like Brian told you to do."

Jake nodded. "I will. Besides, I'm sure your mother is anxiously waiting for me. We had some pretty serious words. She's as worried as I am."

"I'm worried, too, Pa. You've been through more than most men could ever survive. You should be sitting on the front porch in a rocking chair watching everybody else do all the work, and those guns should stay hanging over the doorway getting dusty."

Jake smiled sadly. "Men like me aren't made to sit in rocking chairs. You know that."

"And we have always had each other's backs," Lloyd reminded him. "Don't hide anything from me, Pa. I don't want to go through the hell I went through three years ago. I might be a grown man, but I still need my father."

Jake felt literal pain rush through him at the remark. "You have no idea what it means to me to hear you say that." He pressed Lloyd's arm before turning to head for Gretta's house. *I damn well know what it's like to need a father,* he thought as he walked. Lloyd's remark had struck deep. To think he'd been a good father himself meant the world to him. He made his way among the supply wagons, hating the anxiety Dallas had brought to the entire homestead. He headed past the chicken coop, where a new rooster strutted along the peak of the roof, watching him.

Why is it that roosters hate me? he wondered. The new one, which Sadie Mae had named Rocky, eyed him and crowed, then spread his black wings in a threatening pose. Jake hadn't been able to get any closer to this rooster than he had with old Outlaw.

Before he reached the door to the small frame house Cole had built for Gretta, she opened the door to greet him. "Well, well, well," she said with a smile. "Come on in, big guy. I was wondering when you would show up." She stepped aside and let him in. "Cole came home earlier to take care of a cut on his hand and he told me about that woman who came in with the supply wagons. He said you were in a bit of a rage over her being here. You seem to always end up on my doorstep when you are upset, and here you are. Randy told me once to expect that."

Jake walked into the kitchen as Gretta closed the door. "I need you to go over there and see if that woman needs anything," he told Gretta.

She walked into the kitchen to pour Jake a cup of coffee. "Why me, Jake? Greeting guests is usually something Randy or Evie would do."

"Not this time." Jake looked at her as he took the coffee, thinking how young and still pretty she was for what she had already been through in life. Gretta was blond and blue-eyed and fiesty, genuine and honest. No one pulled the wool over her eyes, and she did not shrink from her infamous past. In character and honesty, she was a far cry from Dallas Blackburn.

"Oooh, aren't we in a dark mood?" Gretta commented when she noticed the darkness in his gaze. "If I didn't know you better, I'd be afraid of you right now."

Jake sat down, putting his cup on the kitchen table and taking a cigarette from his shirt pocket. He lit it and took a deep drag. "You don't mind if I smoke, do you?"

Gretta set an ashtray on the table. "Hell, Jake, you know me better than that, but I'll bet your *wife* would mind. She worries about that cough you've had ever since you were shot."

"Randy knows when I *need* to smoke."

"And that tells me you are very upset. Cole says you told him that you didn't want any decent women around the one over there in that cabin." Gretta pulled a chair around and sat down next to him. "So, since you are sending me, I apparently don't count as decent?"

Jake closed his eyes and exhaled smoke. "Jesus, Gretta, you know that's not what I meant by asking you."

Gretta smiled and reached over to rub his shoulders. "Calm down, Jake. I'm just teasing. But it is obvious you want her greeter to be someone who understands prostitutes and that whole rotten life they lead."

Jake glanced sidelong at her. "Something like that. But believe me, this woman isn't worthy to lick the bottom of your shoes. You are a saint compared to her."

Gretta let out her familiar loud laughter at the remark. "Well, coming from you, that's one hell of a compliment."

"That's how I meant it." Jake studied her porcelain face, surrounded by a cascade of wavy blond hair. "You look nice today. And thanks for the coffee. Cole was right when he said you make the best coffee around." He took a sip.

Gretta smiled softly. "Thank you." She shook her head. "Jake, of all the men I've known in my 35 years of living, you are the only one who has come to me for advice and solace ... and nothing else. I wish other people knew what a good man you really are." She leaned back in her chair. "Of course, it's the something else that I would have enjoyed, but you are a single-vision man, and the woman in your sight is over at the main house."

"Yeah, well, as far as the 'something else,' at my age you aren't missing much. You could be my daughter, you know. Cole really robbed the cradle with you."

Dallas let loose with another howling laugh. "I might seem young in years, but I'm sure not young in experience. And as far as the 'something else,' I beg to differ with your saying I'm not missing much. I helped Randy give you those baths when you were in such bad shape you could barely breathe or get up and walk, remember? I've seen the goods, and I definitely *am* missing much."

Jake shook his head and snickered. "You do know how to make me smile when I'd rather kill somebody. Are you ever going to stop teasing me about those damn baths?"

Gretta chuckled and rubbed his shoulders again. "Hell, no. It's too much fun, and if it makes you smile, all the better. I love making you smile because you are so damn handsome when you do. And I doubt those men out there will stop teasing you about it either. Cole doesn't mind. He understands my sense of humor."

Jake set his cigarette in the ashtray and drank more coffee. "Cole is a good man."

"He's the *best*. He trusted me enough to marry me, and he built this house for me and treated me like I was a virgin when he married me. I love that man to death. We have an understanding about my past, and he never brings it up." She patted Jake's shoulder. "And I love *you,* as one hell of a good friend. For God's sake, you nearly died from rescuing my daughter from that Mexican hell-hole. So tell me why you are here. Does Randy know?"

"Of course she knows. Hell, she would probably *order* me over here if I wasn't already coming."

Gretta smiled softly. "That woman is a pretty good counselor on her own. Nobody knows you better, so if she wants you to talk to me, it must be pretty bad. It obviously has something to do with Dallas Blackburn. Is she the one you would like to kill?"

Jake sighed and leaned forward to rest his elbows on the table. "Killing her is a nice fantasy, and she would deserve it, but you know me. I would never hurt a woman." He sighed. "My past has reared its ugly head again, Gretta."

"People like us always live with that risk, don't we? All those men out there are wondering why Miss Dallas Blackburn set you off like she did. Even Lloyd doesn't know why."

"He does now. I just got done talking to him."

Gretta frowned. "Vance says you called that woman a whore, and in a very degrading tone. That's not like the Jake I know. Hell, when I was at my worst, you treated me like a lady." She took a cigarette from a tin on the table and lit her own. "So, why has the appearance of Dallas Blackburn put you in this mood?"

Jake rubbed at his eyes. "Because her being here can't

possibly be for anything good. *That's* what has put me in this mood. It's been fucking forty years since I first started living with her off and on." He smoked quietly for a few seconds. "Dallas is 57 years old now and still runs a whore-house somewhere in outlaw country in Wyoming. I have a sneaking suspicion that whatever she wants will involve gun play, but I promised Randy I was done with such things. And it doesn't make sense that Dallas would even consider thinking I would want to help her." He stood up and paced, explaining Dallas's betrayal.

"Oh, Jake, what a dirty, underhanded thing to do!" Gretta declared, shaking her head.

"The woman is rotten through and through, and appar-ently, money means more to her than love or *anything* else." Jake finally sat down again, taking another long drag on his cigarette.

Gretta touched his arm. "What do you want me to do?"

He closed his eyes and shook his head. "For now, just go see what she needs as far as personal things or bedding. See if she's hungry. You know Evie and Randy. Either one would offer that much, no matter what the woman has done." He faced her. "And don't let Dallas intimidate you. She'll know you understand her kind and she'll be a bitch to you because she'll know I sent you over there. She will see that as condescending, and she will probably be jealous of you because you are younger and we are friends."

Gretta lifted her chin in a haughty, knowing gesture. "Don't you worry about that, sweetheart. I've got her kind all figured out. I might be a hell of a lot younger, but that doesn't mean I'm not just as tough."

"That's why I'm sending you and not Randy or Evie."

Gretta chuckled. "Honey, I can understand not sending Evie. But *Randy?*" She shook her head. "You totally underestimate that wife of yours. Miss Dallas Blackburn won't intimidate her one bit. Randy has lived with you long enough to understand that dark side of life. She's had her own experiences with it. What you can do with a gun, Randy can do with a look, or the right words."

"She might be able to handle Dallas, but she shouldn't have to put up with any of this. It makes me sick what Randy has been through over the years because of my ugly past." Jake turned in his chair to face her. "I'm going to have the family over this evening. Bring Dallas over around seven. I want the family to know what's going on. I promised Lloyd and Randy both that I wouldn't try to handle things alone this time."

Gretta grabbed his hand. "Good. It hurts Randy when you *don't* share what's going on. Let her be a part of it, Jake."

"I intend to." Jake leaned forward and kissed her forehead. "You are wise beyond your age, Gretta. The reason is obvious, and I'm sorry for how life treated you."

"Hey, life treated you a lot worse. You were raised by women like me, so you understand and respect me. I love that." She stood up. "You get back over to your own house. It's been one hell of a day, and I'm sure Randy is worried."

Jake studied her very blue eyes, eyes that held wisdom beyond her age. When not painted up, and with her blond hair brushed out long and straight, she looked far different from the woman he met in Denver who strutted her stuff and was all paint and glitter, a woman with a notorious reputation because of an occupation she never chose but was forced into. "Gretta, I left out part of the story. Randy has had to forgive more than you know. Someday I'll explain it to you, but not now. First things first. The sooner I can take care of whatever it is Dallas needs, the better."

"Sure. I understand. And you know you can come and talk to me any time."

"Thanks for your help." Jake rose, and Gretta followed him out. She glanced at the distant cabin where Dallas Blackburn had been let off. The woman was watching Jake leave.

Gretta folded her arms and glared back at her. "You have met your match, Dallas Blackburn," she muttered. "And I am not talking about just me. If anybody is going to put you in your place, it will be Miranda Harkner."

JAKE WALKED inside the house to see crates of canned goods, sacks of flour and potatoes, a couple of small barrels with unknown contents, stacks of linen and towels and various other supplies sitting everywhere. Randy was in the kitchen putting away some dishes. He watched her quietly for a moment. What was she thinking? About him? About what he'd done? About a prostitute he'd half lived with before they met – a prostitute who'd tried to collect bounty on him?

He noticed the ham and bread Randy had set out for him when he first got home was still on the table. "Can I still eat?" he spoke up.

Randy turned, and there it was ... the same love in her eyes that was always there ... all the times he'd come back into Guthrie with dead and injured men in tow ... the same love that was in her eyes when he finally moved back into her life after hiding out on the Outlaw Trail for nearly two years ... the same love he saw in those gray-green eyes when he got out of prison ... when he'd rescued her from hell more than once ... the same love he saw there when he made it back from Mexico.

"Of *course* you can eat," she told him. "I was worried over the fact that you didn't eat in the first place. And you had better lie down for a while before Miss Dallas Blackburn makes her dubious appearance."

Jake grinned. "Don't tell me you see that woman as some kind of challenge, Randy."

"No. I just hate what she did to you." She walked closer, and Jake caressed the side of her face with the back of his fingers.

"There isn't a woman alive who can hold a candle to you, Randy Harkner. I just wish I could find the right words for how much I love you, and how sorry I am about that watch."

Randy smiled. "I told you *not* to be sorry. It is what it is, Jake, and there is no changing it." She moved her arms around his middle and rested her head against his chest. "Eat something. Then we will both go upstairs and sleep a while. I feel so worn out, and I know you do, too. Emotions can make a person more tired than physical work, and today we have had plenty of both. I can take my time putting away all these supplies later." She looked up at him. "I'll go outside and tell someone to let the family know we need to rest a while, so no grandchildren today."

Jake wrapped his arms around her. "Miranda Sue Harkner, what would I do without you?"

She looked up at him and they kissed lightly. "It goes both ways, Jake."

He lifted her off her feet and kissed her again. Randy glanced at his .44's that hung over the door and shivered. "Both ways," she repeated.

CHAPTER TEN

DALLAS SAT in a chair on the front stoop of the one-room cabin where she'd been left off. She'd plunked her bags inside and had finally unpinned her hat from her hair, then opened the buttons at the throat of her green dress, all the way down to her cleavage. It was hot, and apparently no one was coming to see her for a while yet.

She'd watched all the commotion of unloading the supply wagons, which now sat in front of a large shed, where she supposed long-term supplies would be stored. The Harkner homestead was a busy place, full of men riding in and out, children laughing and shouting in play, the clang of a black-smith somewhere, chickens clucking, women calling back and forth when the house supplies were being unloaded, and in the distance, cattle lowing and horses whinnying.

There were certainly plenty of men here, but she suspected that if she dared visit the bunkhouse later, Jake would have her hide. He'd already ordered Vance to stay away from her, and she shivered at Jake's attitude toward her when he first realized who she was.

Surely you will help me, Jake. What I need is right up your alley. The only thing wrong was she would have more to contend with than she'd figured on. She knew Jake supposedly had a big family, but what she'd seen here was much more than she had expected. The J&L was a Harkner empire, and she suspected Jake and his son had a firm hold on everything that went on.

She watched the young blond woman Jake had visited exit her small house not far away. The woman headed for her cabin. She wore a simple calico dress, her hair pulled back at the sides with combs, but she did not walk like most decent women. She had a strut that spoke of a woman accustomed to fetching men.

Gretta MacBain, she supposed. *Once the most outrageous prostitute in Denver.* Who had told her that? Vance? She realized he had not come around at all, probably on Jake's orders. She missed his handsome smile and blue eyes. She would love to go to bed with that man, but she'd quickly figured out that Jake was not going to allow it. Everyone seemed to be avoiding her, including Jake's wife. At least she was pretty sure that's who had come out of the main house earlier behind Jake. That woman had glanced her way, and Dallas had felt a challenge. She grinned. Did Mrs. Jake Harkner see her as someone to worry about? Did Jake tell his wife he'd once loved her?

She laughed softly to herself. She loved a challenge, and the blond woman walking her way now was definitely going to be one. How interesting that Jake himself had visited the hussy just a few minutes ago. He'd certainly been there long enough to maybe do what needed doing to get some relief for being so upset over her presence. Maybe the wife had kicked him out.

She rose as Gretta drew closer, then nodded when she reached the stoop. "I'm betting you are Gretta MacBain."

"And you'd win that bet," Gretta told her.

If looks could kill, Dallas figured she would already be dead.

Gretta came up the steps. "It's Gretta Decker now. I am married to Cole Decker, Jake's best friend. Jake gave me orders to come over here and see what you need, and to tell you to be at his house this evening around seven. The whole family will be there, so you'd better be on your best behavior."

Dallas folded her arms. "Who are *you* to give me orders?"

Gretta stepped closer. "I am a close friend of Jake and his whole family. So watch your mouth. That family has been through hell. Jake doesn't need you going over there and talking about when you and he knew each other. I don't know all the details, but I know Jake is very upset by your presence. And I know what you did."

Dallas put her hands on her hips. "And just what did I do?"

"You fucked Jake over and almost got him killed ... for money."

Dallas grinned. "I didn't just fuck him over. I just plain *fucked* him ... a *lot*. I'm sure you know he's damn good at it."

There was no time to react. Dallas felt the blow almost before she got all the words out. Gretta landed a fist into her left eye. Dallas stumbled backward and fell into the chair she'd been sitting in. Gretta leaned over her before she could get up.

"You listen to me, bitch!" Gretta warned. "Don't you *dare* say something like that in front of Jake's family! You got that? And you get it straight in your head that Jake and my husband are best friends. Not only would Jake Harkner not do something like that to a friend, but he's so sick in love with his wife that he wouldn't dream of cheating on her! I know Jake as a good friend, and nothing more! So get your filthy mind off of such thoughts and you behave like a lady over there. Understand?" She straightened. "Jake wanted me to come over here to see what you need. I can bring you some biscuits and beef stew and a coffee pot and coffee grounds. I'll have someone bring over a fresh bucket of water. There is a privy out back with some special paper. I know there are a pillow and some blankets in the cabin, so what else might you need?"

Dallas put a hand over her eye, which she could tell was already swelling and probably turning purple. "You whore! You're no better than me!"

"No? Jake said you weren't good enough to lick the bottom of my shoes. I take that as quite a compliment from a man who knows women like us pretty damn good. And you have orders to stay away from the bunkhouse tonight. If you go near there, I'll land a fist in your *other* eye!"

Dallas grabbed the arms of her chair and stood up, boiling mad. "This is one hell of a way to greet a guest!"

"The Harkner women are kind and obliging," Gretta answered. "But I am *not* a Harkner woman, and I know women like you, so I'm not worried about being kind. Normally, Jake's wife or daughter would be greeting a female guest, even if she is a prostitute, but this time I was the chosen one. I think you know why. Now, what else will you need?"

Dallas touched her aching cheekbone. "Nothing."

Gretta stepped closer again. "Why in hell are you here? If it's to make trouble for Jake, you had better have a damn good reason! Three years ago he kissed death several times in a struggle just to breathe, all from an ungodly gunfight that left him on the brink of death. *None* of us wants him and the family to go through something like that again. One more bullet wound or one more bout with pneumonia could do Jake in for good."

"He's a skilled man. He can handle what I want, and when I'm done explaining, he won't be able to say no."

"We will see about that," Gretta told her. "Either way, you mind your manners over there. No filthy talk and no hints that Jake would even *consider* being with another woman. Randy Harkner is the kindest, strongest woman I know. Don't underestimate that strength, or how far she would go to protect her family and her husband. If you smart off over there, it just might be *Randy* who blackens your other eye! I wouldn't put it past her. And Jake's daughter Evie is the closest thing to an angel who ever walked, so you dress decently and watch your dirty mouth. Got that?"

Dallas winced when she touched her eye again. "You bitch!"

"You *bet* I am. Keep pushing me and you'll find out just how far I'll go in defending Jake and Randy both." Gretta backed away. "I'll bring over the food and water. And don't leave this cabin. Understand?"

Dallas wanted to shoot her. "Perfectly. You think you're quite something, don't you? You're a pretty young thing, with that blond hair and still a skinny waist. How did someone so young end up with your reputation? It can only be because you love men and will sleep with any man with a good sized pecker between his legs."

Gretta came closer again and shoved her hard back into the chair. "How I ended up doing what I did is none of your business. I'm a married woman now, and I *behave* like one. I love my husband, and he and Jake and the other men around here treat me like a lady." She straightened. "I don't see any loving husband at *your* side," she scoffed. "And any woman who would offer Jake up for money doesn't deserve to live, so your reason for being here had *better* be worth disrupting Jake and Randy's life like you have. Got that?"

"Perfectly."

"Good! Be ready at seven to go over to Jake's place." Gretta whirled and walked away.

You cocky little twit, Dallas stewed. *I would love to put a knife into that bony little back.*

CHAPTER ELEVEN

Lloyd pulled on a clean shirt as he watched his wife use large combs to secure her hair into red curls at the crown of her head. He studied her pouty lips, her amazingly green eyes, the perfection of her face. "My God, Katie, you *do* know how beautiful you are, right?"

Katie glanced at him in her dressing table mirror as she finished tucking in more hair. "You don't need to try to compliment me, Lloyd, just to make me feel better. I know I need to lose weight. At least when I'm pregnant, I have an excuse, but we both know that isn't ever going to happen again." Her voice broke on the words.

Lloyd sighed as he tucked in his shirt. "Katie, stop it. Would you rather be dead? If Brian hadn't done what he did when we lost the last one, you would be lying out there in the family burial plot. Do you know what it would do to me if that happened? There isn't enough whiskey in Colorado to help me through something like that."

Katie broke into tears. His heart heavy for her sorrow, Lloyd walked over to kneel beside her. He touched her shoulder reassuringly. "Katie, I didn't mean to be short with you, but there are only so many ways to tell a woman how you feel about her, and I have tried them all. You are the mother of my children, the woman I have shared my bed with for ten years now. I've told you a hundred times that I don't care about a few extra pounds. You have borne six babies."

Katie grabbed a handkerchief lying on the dressing table and dabbed at her eyes. "Seven, if you count the baby I lost by my first husband. Lloyd, I've lost almost half the babies I've ever carried." More tears came.

"All the more reason to make sure you never go through that again." Lloyd rubbed her back. "Honey, tell me what to do to bring you out of this."

"I don't know. I only know you wanted lots of children, sons to help run this ranch someday. I mean, look at Evie. She's had six kids with no problems, all of them full term and born healthy. She's so strong, like you and your father. She's all Harkner. Look what she went through at Dune Hollow back in Oklahoma. My God, Lloyd, she was carrying Sadie Mae then, and she never lost that baby. You and Jake and Evie are such survivors."

Lloyd kept rubbing her back. "Katie, we all have our own strengths and weaknesses. Don't forget that my mother had to stop after two babies. She had part of her insides removed just like you did, but you have *four* healthy children, plus Stephen. Look at the big, big family Jake and my mother ended up having in spite of just two children. Think about that." Lloyd took hold of her hands. "*Look* at me, Katie."

She met his gaze, her eyes puffy and bloodshot.

"Be glad for the children we do have, Katie. And please

believe me when I tell you I don't give a damn if you've gained a few pounds, and I don't give a damn if we never have more children. I care more about your health, about growing old together." He tugged at a curl that hung down beside her neck. "And look at you. Baby, you have the kind of beauty that rises above everything else. I love wrapping my fingers into that beautiful hair when it is hanging long and loose. I have never seen eyes so green, or a complexion so fair. You remind me of fine china, and you have a mouth that begs to be kissed."

"You don't mean that."

"I damn well *do* mean it. Don't you realize that every time you walk outside, men turn their heads? I've watched them. Out of respect, they try not to show it around me, but I know what they are thinking, and believe me, they aren't thinking that you need to lose weight. They are thinking that you look damn beautiful just the way you are, and they are wishing you weren't already taken."

Katie sniffed back more tears. "You are just trying to make me feel better."

"I'm telling you the *truth*, Katie. I have never lied to you."

Katie met his dark gaze, stroked some of his long hair away from his face. "But you're so ... so strong and good looking. I've seen how neighboring ranchers' daughters look at you. I want to please you in every way, so you don't look back at them with desire."

Lloyd grinned and shook his head. "When in hell have you seen me look at other women?"

Katie shrugged. "I just know there are plenty of young women, and probably a lot of married ones, who seem to make themselves available to you for a dance or two when we go to the Fourth of July picnic at the Twisted Tree."

"And have I ever danced with any of them?"

"Well ... no."

"And there you go. And I might remind you plenty of men try getting you to dance with them at that picnic. I notice things like that, too, and I want to punch every man who approaches you."

Katie kept hold of her handkerchief and looked at her lap. "Do you mean it about not caring if we have more babies? I mean, we're still young enough. And you joke with Brian about keeping up with him and Evie. Some of our kids were born close to the same time. Tricia and Sadie Mae are like sisters, and Donavan and little Esther are almost the same age. So are Jeffrey and Cole, and –"

"Katie! Are you saying you believe I've always bedded you just to make more babies? That I wouldn't want you otherwise? What on earth have I done to make you think that?" Lloyd rose, pulling her up with him and keeping a firm hold on her arms. "This thing about our kids being close in age to Evie's is just coincidence. Neither Brian nor I ever really thought of it as some kind of race. Brian would never disrespect my sister like that." Lloyd realized he'd touched on part of the problem behind his wife's depression. He put a hand under her chin and made her look up at him. "Katie, when I make love to you it's because I *want* you. Just *you*. If I ever made you think all I wanted was a big family, I'm damn sorry. The fact is, I'm relieved we can just enjoy each other for the pure plea-sure of it now. I *need* you, Katie-girl, and in a lot more ways than in bed." He wrapped his arms around her. "Honey, I don't know what's going on with this woman from Pa's past, or what she will tell us this evening, but it might be something that means the family coming together again to support each other. I can't have you pulling away, Katie. Not now. We are so much stronger together than apart."

"I'm trying, Lloyd. I just ... I get this awful depression that I can't control. Being overweight just makes it worse. You're the kind of man who could so easily walk right into some other woman's life." Her whole body shuddered with a sob. "You're Jake Harkner's son, well-known and success-ful. There are all kinds of women out there who would gladly share your bed. And you loved Beth so deeply. I have always wondered if you love me the way you loved her, so it seemed like giving you babies would help make sure I've pleased you. And you have so many responsibilities that sometimes I feel like I'm not strong enough for all of it. And —"

"*Katie!*" Lloyd grasped her arms again and gently pushed her away to meet her gaze. "Have you *always* felt this way?"

She put a shaking hand to her cheek to wipe at another tear. "I guess maybe I have. I just want you to love me as much as you loved Beth."

"After all these years? All we've been through together? After all the babies and the losses and the way you've helped me stay away from alcohol? How in God's name can you doubt my love for you?"

Katie tried to wipe away some of the cheek color she'd stained his shirt with. "I've just been so depressed, Lloyd. Brian said he thinks it's something they call the baby blues ... that maybe I've had it since losing my first child. I've had so many babies since then that it just never totally went away. I have trouble allowing myself to be happy, trouble believing you love me just like I am."

Lloyd sighed and led her to their bed, making her sit

down beside him. "My God, Katie, why didn't you tell me this a long time ago?"

Katie shook her head. "Maybe because I think it makes me look weak, and the other Harkner women are so strong. You admire your sister and your mother so deeply, and I know you still miss Beth. And I'm scared all the time. When I saw you shot down in Denver at that cattlemen's ball and was sure you were dead, a black horror just ... swept over me. I couldn't survive without you beside me, so I do everything I can to make sure you are just mine. I want to be everything you need in a woman, Lloyd, like Evie is for Brian, and like your mother is for your father, but I'm not made of the same stuff they are."

Lloyd moved an arm around her and she leaned sideways to rest against his shoulder. "Katie Donavan Harkner, you *are* all I need in a woman. You always have been, whether you gave me one baby, or ten. I just wanted a brother or a sister for Stephen, and you gave him that. I think I love you most for the kind of mother you have been to him, and that's how he sees you ... as his real mom." He put a hand under her chin and leaned over to kiss her. "I want you for *you*, Katie. And you *are* strong, just by putting up with all the times I am too busy to come home on time, putting up with my moods and my temper, my battle with whiskey. And I'll never forget how you chased off that man who tried to kidnap Stephen back in Guthrie. He might have killed my son, but you stood there all alone and raised that rifle and scared him off."

Another kiss.

"I see you as my Katie-girl, the prettiest woman anywhere around, and you are Lloyd Harkner's *wife*. Sometimes I'm so proud of you I could bust, so you tell me what you need to get over this doubt and sadness, and I'll do it. I need you beside me, Katie, really *beside* me."

Katie kissed his cheek. "Brian said time will take care of this depression. He said now that I can't have more babies, my body needs time to adjust and rebuild ... something about a woman's hormones, he thinks. He even thinks that now I'll lose some weight. I already have lost some."

Lloyd hugged her close. "You just remember that it doesn't matter to me, okay? We will take one day ... and one night at a time. I want back in our bed, Katie. I'm tired of sleeping apart. No demands. You are still healing. I just want to be able to hold you. You trust me, don't you?"

"Of course I trust you. And I'm sorry I've made you sleep in Stephen's room since I lost the baby."

"Don't worry about it. Right now I just want you to be happy." Lloyd rose and pulled her up with him. "It's almost seven. We need to get over to the main house and find out what that woman wants out of Pa."

Katie stood up and looked him over. "I've messed up your nice, clean shirt. You will have to change it again."

"Doesn't matter." Lloyd pulled her close and leaned down to kiss her deeply, tasting her tears and wishing he knew how to stop them forever.

Katie wrapped her arms around his neck. "I love you, Lloyd."

"And you surely know how much I love you." Lloyd kissed her once more, then stepped back to unbutton his white shirt. He pulled it off, and Katie gave him a teasing smile.

"I'll bet there isn't another man around who is built like you."

Lloyd loved the hint of humor she was showing. "Play fair, Katie-girl. Don't get me wanting you right now when I can't have you. And we have no choice but to get over to my folks' house." He pulled on a clean gray and white striped shirt, praying he could take hope in thinking things would be good between them again. Whatever Dallas Blackburn wanted, he dearly hoped it wouldn't mean losing his father. After what he and Katie had been through the last couple of years, he sure as hell wasn't ready for that.

CHAPTER TWELVE

Randy forced back a smile when Dallas Blackburn walked into the house sporting a black eye. Cole had already told all of them that Gretta had socked her one for suggesting something was going on between Gretta and Jake. Stephen and Young Jake snickered when they saw Dallas's eye, and Evie reached over to touch Young Jake's arm as a gesture not to laugh.

Dallas held her chin high as she marched farther inside, Gretta right behind her. Dallas glared at Jake. "This is the kind of hospitality you show an old friend?"

Jake kept a cigarette between his lips as he spoke. "We are not friends. And you wouldn't have that black eye if you learned not to insult the wrong people."

The two younger boys could not help more stifled laughter. Dallas gave them a scolding look, then scanned the others in the room before looking at Jake again. "I feel like I am surrounded by people who want to hang me."

"Not a bad idea," Jake answered.

The boys could not help more snickers.

"Settle down, you two," Jake told Young Jake and

Stephen. He took the cigarette from his mouth and put it in an ashtray, then nodded toward one of the kitchen chairs brought into the living room area so everyone would have a place to sit. "Sit down, Dallas." He gave Gretta soft smile. "Thanks for bringing her over. You can sit down beside Cole there. He saved a chair for you."

Gretta glared at Dallas first. "You remember what I told you about watching what you say."

"Don't get your feathers in a fluff, sweetie," Dallas snapped. "I'll behave, but not because *you* told me to. You know, if you had ever come to work at Dallas's Pleasure Emporium, I would have put you in your place real fast."

"Hell, I would have ended up kicking *you* out and running the place myself," Gretta snapped.

That brought all-out laughter from the boys.

Cole grabbed Gretta's hand. "Calm down," he told her. "Don't let that woman make you be rude here in Jake's house."

"I'm sorry," Gretta apologized.

"Dallas had the remark coming," Jake told her. He turned to Dallas. "Sit down," he repeated, "and try to behave like a lady."

"A *lady*?" Dallas chuckled and took the chair Jake indicated. "I remember you as a man who wanted nothing to do with ladies, Jake. You liked your women wild."

Jake started to rise, but Randy touched his arm. "I will take care of this." She rose to face Dallas. "I will ask you to please accept our hospitality, Miss Blackburn," she said softly. "And to remember there are young people here, as well as our daughter and daughter-in-law, who are decent, Christian women. And Gretta is like part of the family also, so you will treat her as such."

Dallas looked her over. Randy wore a yellow checkered

dress that perfectly fit her waist and bosom in flattering ways, a deliberate act on her part, Dallas was sure. Randy wore her naturally-blond hair pulled back at the sides with barrettes and hanging long down her back.

"Excuse me, ma'am," Dallas said with a sly attitude, "but you have to understand how hard it is for me to realize Jake actually has such a lovely home and gracious family. And it's obvious you are the Mrs." She glanced at Jake. "Your beautiful, well-mannered, genteel wife here must have nearly passed out when you told her about us and the wild times we used to have," she said, an obvious attempt to hurt Randy.

"You misjudge," Randy answered before Jake could. She stepped directly in front of Dallas. "Believe me, after being married to Jake for 37 years, nothing you say would shock me, so stop trying. And we all know what you did to him back in those wild times, as you call them. That was a dirty, underhanded thing to do, which only shows how low you can go when the opportunity presents itself." She leaned closer. "Do not underestimate me when it comes to standing up for my husband and family, and don't think I am incapable of blackening your other eye, so be careful what you say."

Young Jake snickered again. "You tell her, Grandma!"

"Son," Brian scolded, "that is enough."

Jake tried to hide his laughter beneath a cough.

Dallas stiffened, facing Randy squarely. "Well, now, I guess you are every bit the woman Vance and Gretta both described to me. Soft and sophisticated on the outside, strong and maybe even vicious on the inside."

"Beware of the vicious side," Randy warned. She turned and waved her arm to indicate the rest of the family. "Before you explain why you are here, let me introduce you to Jake's family." She walked over to Lloyd, happy to see how tightly he was holding Katie's hand, as though they'd found their old closeness again. "This is our son, Lloyd, whom you already met on your way here, and beside him is his wife, Katie."

Dallas grinned. "No mistaking who Lloyd's father is." Her gaze shifted to the tall, dark woman sitting on Lloyd's other side. "I already know you are Jake's saint of a daughter," she said. "Like Lloyd, anyone can tell you have to be Evie, although Jake already addressed you. And that well-dressed man sitting beside you must be the doctor Vance told me about."

"Brian Stewart," Brian replied, eyeing Dallas suspiciously.

Dallas shook her head and turned to Jake again. "Leave it to you to have a passle of beautiful women around you."

Randy continued introductions. "Our grandson Jake is sitting beside Brian. He is Brian and Evie's son. He's thirteen. Beside him is sixteen-year-old Stephen, Lloyd's son by his first wife." She turned to chairs on the other side of the family circle, holding her hand out to a burly young man with white-blond hair and a missing left arm. "This is our adopted son, Ben, and his wife, Annie, who is Gretta's daughter and the young woman Jake and Cole rescued from Mexico. Ben lost his arm three years ago when enemies of Jake shot it off. That is what led to the terrible incident that left Jake on a path between life and death. I'm sure you have read about that, and it shows you what Jake will do to defend and protect his family."

"Oh, I don't doubt that," Dallas answered.

The look in Dallas's eyes made Randy secretly shiver. What was this woman up to? "Annie and Ben are married now," she told Dallas. She then indicated a man who looked perhaps in his late fifties as she introduced Cole Decker. "Cole is Gretta's husband and Jake's best friend and considered part of this family. There is a lot of love and respect sitting here in this room, Dallas, things that perhaps you never thought would surround Jake, but I suspect you would not recognize either attribute. The love spreads to several younger grandchildren who are not here." She added those last words with a bragging air and started to turn, then hesitated, facing Dallas again. "Oh, would you like something to drink? Something other than *alcohol,* I might add? I have heard that is your preferred drink, but we don't keep alcohol in this house, other than the kind that can be used to clean and treat wounds."

Dallas smiled and looked her over. "Subtle, aren't you?"

"Just saying it like it is."

"No. I don't need anything to drink," Dallas told her. "Thanks for the offer."

Randy gave her a soft smile. "The reason all of us are here together, Miss Blackburn, is that Jake, unselfish man that he is, has a tendency to try to take care of trouble all on his own, and considering your reputation and what you did to Jake, you can't possibly be here for any other reason than trouble. After what happened to Jake three years ago when he rode off alone to take care of a bad situation, I made him promise that in the future there would be no secrets. So whatever you have come here to throw at us, we are all in this together."

Dallas nodded. "Fair enough. And I promise that the reason I'm here is not a lie or a hoax of some kind. Jake is one of the few men who might be able to take care of this particular problem, and he will have a personal reason for it."

Dallas and Randy locked gazes, gauging each other.

"Jake has a big heart, and you damn well know it," Randy said. "Don't stomp on it."

"I happen to be sitting right here," Jake reminded both women. "Just get to the point, Dallas."

Dallas chuckled and shook her head. "I swear, Jake, your wife is like a she-cat protecting her kittens when it comes to you." She met Randy's gaze. "I know the man has a heart somewhere down inside that big, brawny body, but I also know how ruthless he can be. When it comes to using those guns of his and righting a wrong for someone he cares about, that big heart goes right out the window and the outlaw takes over. That's why I'm here ... for the *outlaw*."

The room hung silent for a few tense seconds. Jake reached over and pressed Randy's arm. "Sit down," he said quietly. He faced Dallas as Randy did his bidding. "I suspected gunplay. What the hell is going on, Dallas?"

Dallas sighed deeply. "I can understand none of you trusting me, especially you, Jake." She looked him over and shook her head. "I'm really sorry for what I did to you, but I was desperate. That bounty hunter had visited me earlier and waved a knife in my face while he had me pinned down. He told me if I didn't help him kill or capture you, he'd come back and mark me up for life."

"You could have told me or your brother or anybody else in his gang and we would have taken care of it," Jake reminded her.

"That bounty hunter might have got to me first. I only did what I *had* to do. At least the state I was in, that's what I believed."

"You could have warned me that he would be breaking in on us. What you did only shows you intended to keep your share of the money. Did you intend to at least pay for my burial?"

Dallas closed her eyes and then covered them with her hands. "Jake, I wasn't thinking straight. I was nineteen years old and scared. I'd stolen money from the man when he visited me that first time." She faced Jake again. "If you had seen how vicious he was about it, the dark, determined threat in his eyes, you would understand why I cooperated. After you shot him, you left so fast that I didn't get a chance to explain. And then I never saw you again. You left my brother's gang, left Missouri, and you moved around so much that you were impossible to find, so I couldn't tell you about ..." She looked around fearfully at the whole family, then at Jake. "About the baby."

Evie gasped. Randy straightened, and Jake's grip on her arm tightened. Everyone else just looked at each other.

"*What* baby?" Jake asked.

"A son I had ... by you."

CHAPTER THIRTEEN

Randy sensed the myriad of emotions in the room. She wasn't sure of her own, and she knew Jake wasn't either. He sat there just staring at Dallas. "You're lying," he finally told her.

"You were the only one I was with for a good six weeks before that," Dallas shot back. "You know that's true, because you stayed with me the whole time and we talked about me quitting my ... profession."

"I might have been staying with you, but it wasn't every single minute. I remember how you ogled every man who walked through those saloon doors below that hovel you called home, trying to determine how much money he might have on him and what he might be like in bed. People ask me how many men I've killed. Has anyone ever asked you how many men you have *slept* with?"

"Oh, dear Lord," Evie said softly.

"Jake, Annie and the boys ..."

"I know you all too well, Dallas Blackburn," Jake declared, seemingly oblivious to Randy's warning. "Enough to know that a baby you carried back then could have been fathered by any number of men."

"But I was true to only *you* those last few weeks," Dallas insisted. "That is the God's truth, Jake. And when he grew into a man, he could have been a twin to that son of yours sitting in this room right now. He was a *Harkner*, all right. Anybody could have seen that if they could have seen him and Lloyd beside each other. Big, tall, handsome, wild, and he had those dark eyes of yours. He even had your voice as a man."

Jake crushed out his cigarette. "True or not, did you tell him who you believed his father was?"

"No." Dallas closed her eyes and sighed. "I wanted to, but you left after that night I betrayed you and never came back. I couldn't find you. You moved around so much back then that it was impossible. And I know now from that book I read about you that you sometimes used different last names. As a baby, Wade wouldn't have known the difference anyway. As he grew older, I just gave up because I knew that even if I found you, you wouldn't believe me. If you did, you wouldn't have wanted him."

"Like *hell* I wouldn't! It was wrong of you not to at least give me the choice."

"It doesn't matter, Jake. By 15 years old he was an uncontrollable alcoholic. I had moved my business elsewhere by then, farther and farther west as the east and south became more and more tame. I had to go places where what I do was still legal and where men still out-numbered women. To this day, some of the old gold towns still exist, and they are still lawless. I am sure you know all about that. But it doesn't matter now. The fact remains that Wade was yours because he became the epitome of what you told me about your father. He was a mean drinker ... *real* mean."

Jake's hands moved into fists. "*Damn* you! You come here now, after all these years to tell me I have a son I never met? I could have taken him and kept him from growing up in the same world of brothels and whiskey and gambling and outlaws that *I* grew up in. And I could have saved him from *drink!*"

"Jake, after a few years you had a whole new life. There was one time I thought about telling you. It was when you went to prison and I finally knew where you were. But by then Wade was twenty years old. Was I supposed to send a mean drunk to your *wife*? At the same time I heard you were sentenced to something like ten years. I had no idea you would get out early and that a judge would send you to Oklahoma as a U. S. Marshal. Life is full of could-have-beens and mistakes and secrets, Jake. You know that better than *anyone*."

Jake rose and walked to the fireplace, bracing one arm against the mantle and looking up at the family picture that hung there. "Secrets?" he spoke up, turning to glance at Randy. "Yeah. Today has been full of secrets revealed." He turned his attention to Dallas. "In ways you don't even know about. I've been thinking how the family picture hanging over this fireplace needs updating, what with the babies who have been born since the picture was taken, and how much bigger and taller some of my grandchildren are now. Little did I know another son should be added to it. Lloyd has always been my *only* blood son, and I can't begin to –"

"I told you that it doesn't matter, Jake," Dallas interrupted. "Wade is dead."

"Oh, my," Katie said softly. She still clung tightly to Lloyd's hand.

Dallas looked at her lap. "In a sense, he finally drank

himself to death. He got raging drunk and died in a gunfight over a card game. We had been living in Shelter a few years by then, and the prostitutes there were *glad* to see him die because he beat on every woman he was ever with, even the one who gave him a child."

Jake stiffened. "A *child?*"

Randy had never seen her husband's eyes so black with fury. "Jake, stay calm and sit back down," she pleaded.

Jake ran a hand through his hair and turned away.

Randy rose and hurried over to him. She touched his arm. "Jake, please."

He looked past her, zeroing in on Dallas. "I am trying not to explode because I don't like losing my temper in front of the women in the family," he told her. He put a hand to Randy's back and walked her back to the brocade loveseat they shared. He urged her to sit back down, then sat down beside her and lit yet another cigarette and faced Dallas. "Are you saying I also have a *grandchild* I never knew?" The words came out with dark steadiness.

Dallas took a deep breath, truly looking afraid. "Yes, and she is why I am here. Her name is Dianna, but we call her Dee Dee. Wade never married the girl's mother. She ... she had worked for me, so yes, Dee Dee's mother was a prostitute. She died in childbirth. We think it was more from a head injury than birthing the baby. She went into labor after Wade slugged her in an argument. Your son was a mean, abusive drunk, just like your father. I couldn't very well burden your wife with something like that, so yes, I do have a little bit of decency in me."

Jake set the cigarette aside and rubbed at his eyes. "Jesus," he whispered.

"The girls and I were the ones who took care of Dee

Dee," Dallas continued. "But every once in a while, when Wade was actually sober, he would take her for a day or two, in the moments when he thought he might try being a real father. One thing that was different about Wade compared to your father is that he never abused Dee Dee, even when he drank. I think he truly loved her, but he didn't know how to change things and be a decent full-time father. Then ... one of those times he took her for a day or two, he got really drunk. He'd promised me he wouldn't drink at all, but I should have known better than to trust his promises. He took Dee Dee with him to a saloon and kept her on his knee while he played poker. He ran out of money, so he ... he used his own daughter in the ante, said that whoever won could take her."

"Oh, dear God," Evie moaned.

Jake let out a little groan and set his cigarette aside. Randy touched his arm, but he pulled away. "Something tells me you aren't to the worst of it yet," he told Dallas.

"My God, Jake, I'm so sorry. Maybe the younger boys shouldn't be here."

"They are old enough," Lloyd spoke up. "My son and nephew and my stepbrother over there are plenty mature enough to hear this. And they know about women like –" He paused.

"Like me?" Dallas closed her eyes and shook her head. "You can say it, Lloyd." She sighed and raised her chin to finish her story. "All right then. You have probably already figured out that Wade lost that card game. When he did, he suddenly realized what an awful thing he'd done. He shoved Dee Dee off his lap and got up, intending to shoot the man who'd won her, but he was too drunk to even get the pistol out of its holster. The man shot and killed Wade.

Then he sliced open the face of one of my girls who tried to grab Dee Dee and get her out of there. He took off with your granddaughter, Jake. She's only ten years old, about the same age as a couple of granddaughters you have living right here with your family."

"Oh, that poor girl!" Evie lamented.

Dallas kept her attention on Jake. "I've come to ask you to get Dee Dee away from the dangerous man who has her now, Jake. His name is Dennis Gates."

"Dangerous?" Jake's rage was palpable. "Dangerous *how?*"

Dallas looked around the room as though seeking an escape route. "I am hoping you will bring Dee Dee back here to live with you," she said, avoiding Jake's question. "She would be safe here, away from what goes on at my place, and free from an evil man who won't be nice to her. At the same time, you would be helping free me and my girls and the whole damn town of a very bad element in Shelter, Wyoming. The man who has Dee Dee is one of many brutes who have taken over everything in town. They shoot anybody who disagrees with them. Their leader has a lot of money and owns the Shelter gold mine. Their men come to town and raise hell and steal and take turns with my girls without paying. The girl Dennis cut up was young and pretty, and now she is scarred for life. I promised her I knew someone who might be able to get rid of the men who have caused so much turmoil and lawlessness, and their leader. His name is Ty Bolton, and Dennis Gates is his right-hand man."

"Dear Lord," Katie murmured.

"What kind of grandmother are you to let that little girl be taken?" Randy asked Dallas.

"I'm *no* kind of grandmother," Dallas shot back. "I never wanted to be one in the first place. But once you have a grandchild, even a woman like me can't help but love her. But Wade had rights as her father, and it was his day with her. I had no idea he would use his own daughter in a card game. He had never, ever done anything like that before. There was nothing I could do. By the time I learned what happened, Dee Dee was gone, to a place no one who is not a part of Ty Bolton's empire can go."

"What makes you think *I* can get in?" Jake asked.

"Because you are Jake Harkner!" Dallas nearly yelled the words. "Half the men there will run at just the mention of your name."

Jake waved her off as he rose and walked back to the fireplace.

"You know I'm right, Jake." Dallas spoke up, this time with a pleading tone. "Shelter supposedly has law and order now, but it's Ty Bolton's form of law and order. He owns the sheriff and all the deputies, and the law they keep is *their* law, which doesn't come close to *real* law and order. You know what life is like in outlaw country and in those gold towns. The rest of this land might be more civilized now, but the high plains and mountains of Wyoming are still rife with lawlessness, still a place where real lawmen won't go and the Old West still thrives. And you are one man who understands Bolton's kind of law and his kind of men. I can't find one other man willing to help. I even talked with a U. S. Marshal once, and he said Wyoming's government is too involved with its growing railroad towns and new settlers and range wars and such to start sending men to mountain towns no one else cares about. He said maybe some day, but not right now."

Jake rubbed at his forehead. "Why didn't you send me a telegram or find some other quicker way to tell me this? God only knows what has happened to that little girl by now."

"Jake, how in hell do you explain something like this in a telegram or even a letter? I knew you would probably ignore both when you saw who it was from. I had to come here in person, even though it took days longer. Before it all happened, I had decided to take Dee Dee and whatever girls wanted to go with me and move to a different town, but my son threatened to turn that gang of thieves and murderers loose on my place if I took Dee Dee away from him. That's how badly the alcohol had affected his thinking. After what you went through with your father, I don't need to explain what whiskey does to a man. He even said that if I left without telling him, he would find us and kill any of the girls who went with me, and he would take Dee Dee away with him. In his own sick way he did love her, but alcohol came first, and alcohol led him into a fight that cost him his life and his daughter."

"My God," Jake muttered. He rose and walked over close to Dallas, fists clenched. His black rage moved like a dark cloud around the room. "You should have given that girl to decent people to raise in the first place! That's what Gretta did with Annie."

Dallas rose and faced him. "It was *Wade's* choice how to raise her! A father's rights come first, and he wouldn't let me take her away."

Jake stepped closer, and Dallas backed up. "Was your *brothel* her home?"

"I always kept a good eye on her."

"What about when you were romping in bed with some *drifter*? Who watched her then?"

"Daddy, let it go," Evie spoke up. "It can't be changed now. We have to decide what to do."

Jake kept his gaze on Dallas. "You never answered my original question. You said Dennis Gates was not a nice man. Does that mean what I *think* it means?"

Dallas was visibly shaken. "Please go get her, Jake. She's only ten years old and hasn't even ..." She backed away more. "She is far from what you could call a woman. She doesn't even understand things like that. I always kept her away from it. She had her own room and we took turns watching over her so that she never ... never saw ..." She wiped at a quick tear. "Dennis has a penchant for younger women. I've never seen him ... I mean, I don't think ..."

"You know damn well why he agreed to let Wade use her for ante!" Jake yelled. "I killed my own *father* for raping a twelve-year-old girl! And I went to Mexico to get young Annie over there out of a similar situation. I broke a leg and was bullwhipped for it ... left for *dead!* My own *daughter* —" He hesitated, hating to bring up the ugliness in front of Evie. "God *damn* you, Dallas Blackburn! Do you think he would *sell* her? Make a prostitute out of her, like her *grandmother!*"

"Jake!" Randy rose. "Please calm down. Dallas didn't do this. *Wade* did it. And if he'd been sober, he would not have taken that chance. The only thing to blame for this is *whiskey!* And what's done is done. We have to decide how to handle it. Please, *please* calm down. We need to talk about this."

Jake glared at Dallas, his fists clenched. "You need to leave for now," he told her. "I can't guarantee I won't lose my temper a little too far, so just leave. I can't *look* at you right now."

He turned away and Dallas stiffened. "I'm sorry to

bring this down on you, Jake, but ... but Annie over there – she isn't related to you at all, yet you went to Mexico to rescue her. You can surely do as much for Dee Dee, because you can't take the risk that she's *not* yours. And even if she isn't, she needs someone like you to help her. You know damn well what men like Dennis Gates are capable of. You have been around men like that."

"I have *killed* men for that very reason!" Jake faced her again. "Get out! Get out *now!*" He headed toward Dallas in a rage. Dallas headed for the door, and Cole and Lloyd both jumped up and rushed over to grab Jake, pulling him back from the doorway.

"Pa, let it be!"

Dallas stopped and turned, relieved that the two men had hold of Jake. "If you decide to go after Dee Dee and you want details, the layout of the town, where Ty Bolton and his men hang out, things like that, you know where to find me," she told Jake. "As far as selling our granddaughter, that isn't likely ... yet. He will want to –" She hesitated.

"*Groom* her?" Jake roared. "*Teach* her?" He jerked away from Lloyd and Cole. "For God's sake, Dallas, you say it in such a matter-of-fact way. You should be *screaming* it in sorrow!"

Dallas closed her eyes and put a hand to her stomach. "Don't forget that I didn't get pregnant all by myself, Jake. It takes *two*, and you certainly were no more of an angel than I was, so don't blame this all on me. You left and you never came *back*!"

Jake made another move toward her.

"Pa, don't!" Lloyd grabbed his arm again.

Jake shook his head, drilling into Dallas with a gaze so dark she stepped farther back again. "Can you *blame* me for not coming back, after what you did?" Jake asked. "And you always said you had ways of *not* ending up with child, so the thought never even entered my mind."

Dallas looked away. "There isn't a woman alive who can guarantee something like that. But either way, coming here through outlaw country is a damn hard and dangerous trip, but I managed it with the help of some men I hired to get me as far as Wilcox, where I caught a train. I risked my life to get here, Jake, so I'm not *all* bad."

Jake's breathing was so labored that everyone in the room worried he might have a heart attack. "Any person who would sell out a good friend for a few bucks *is* all bad," he answered. "Why should I trust you on this? Maybe you have some other reason for wanting me to go after the girl, and Ty Bolton and all the rest. Risking it all is fine with me if this granddaughter does exist and needs my help. But if I find out you tricked me into going into country like that for some other reason, like men wanting the reputation of killing Jake Harkner, when I'm through with them, I will be coming after *you*. I will burn down your place of business and run you out along with the whole goddamn town!"

"Daddy, you wouldn't!" Evie said in a near whisper.

"I *would!*" Jake answered, still glaring at Dallas. "You think you know me, Evie, but you *don't.*"

Evie rose. "I know what you did for me at Dune Hollow! Quit making yourself out to be worse than the rumors, Daddy. You are not your *father!*"

The words seemed to startle Jake. He glanced at Evie, then turned away from Dallas. "Please leave," he told her.

Dallas raised her chin with a sniff and looked at Evie. "Your father *would* do what he threatened to do," she said. "Not one person in this family has ever seen what Jake Harkner is capable of." She stepped closer to the door, turning her attention back to Jake. "And that is the reason,

Jake, that you should realize I am not trying to trick you. Do you honestly think I would take that chance again? I am here strictly for Dee Dee's sake. I would not have come here for any other reason because I know how much Jake hates me." She turned and left.

The house quieted, and they could all hear the tap of Dallas's shoes as she walked along the veranda and off the porch.

No one spoke. Jake turned and faced his family, and the great room with its cathedral ceiling suddenly felt too small.

"I'm damn sorry all of you had to hear that. This is as far from what I expected as it can be. I thought that woman wanted personal help of some kind, and I was prepared to turn her down. This thing about a son I never knew, and a little girl who might carry my blood, changes everything. I never meant to bring new troubles to all of you."

"Pa, how could you have known?" Lloyd asked, his stance that of a man ready to stop his father if he suddenly tried to storm out. "This isn't something to try alone, that's for damn sure. I know what you are already thinking, and back in Oklahoma we always had each other's backs. I will gladly go with you to Wyoming."

Jake shook his head. "Not you. This whole place and everybody on it needs you. This could take weeks. Katie needs you right here."

Randy felt her heart sink. If there was even a remote chance that Dee Dee was really Jake's granddaughter, there would be no stopping him. Even if she wasn't his, the thought of a girl the age of his Sadie Mae or Tricia being in the hands of refuse like the man who had her now was all Jake needed to make him feel responsible to help. She stood up and faced the family.

"Everyone is dead tired," she told them. "It's been a

very, very long day for all of us. You should all leave and let me and Jake talk about this. Go home and do the same. Come back in the morning for breakfast and we will talk about what should be done."

"We can help, too, Grandpa," Young Jake told him. "Me and Stephen and Ben aren't afraid."

"Heck, I'm as good with a rifle one-handed as any man with two," Ben added.

"Daddy, you have a past that isn't pretty," Evie spoke up. "We have always known that. This is *not* the shocking news for us that you think it is."

"Do what you need to do, Jake," Cole told him. "I went along with you to Mexico. I'll be glad to go with you to Wyoming. Ain't no doubt you'll do this, but you take some help. Don't you dare go up there alone." He took hold of Grettas's arm and led her to the door.

The younger boys followed, as did Brian and Evie, who stopped beside her father and touched his arm. "I'll pray for you and mother," she told him. "And for that little girl. God will help you decide the best thing to do, Daddy."

Jake met her eyes. "I'm sorry, Evie."

"You can't hurt me or upset me," she told him. "I love you too much, and I know that no matter how much you deny that you're a good man, I know better than anybody that you are."

Jake closed his eyes and shook his head. "Believe what you want, but that God of yours has no part in this."

"Yes he does." Evie insisted. "He is working inside you right now, Daddy. He sent Dallas here, and he will guide you. And He will watch over that little girl for you until you get her out of there. You have to believe that." She wiped at tears as she left with Brian.

"This is a job for both of us, Pa, and you know it," Lloyd said.

"Son, go home for now," Jake told him. "Send those damn rustlers to Brighton in the morning and then come over and we'll talk."

Lloyd looked helplessly at his mother. "You keep an eye on him tonight."

"You can be sure I will," Randy told him.

"Even so, I'm leaving a couple of men at the house, front and back." He turned to Jake. "I don't trust you, Pa."

"Do really think there is a man on this place who can stop me if I choose to leave?" Jake scoffed.

"I will make *sure* of it, even if it takes a bullet in your ass to stop you."

The remark gave the moment a bit of humorous relief. Jake turned to his son, his face and eyes so red he looked on fire. "You would, wouldn't you?"

"You bet. And if it has to come from my own gun, then so be it. It is not just you who is affected by this, Pa. It's *all* of us, especially Mom. She needs you right now. Don't add to her worries by trying to walk off alone." Lloyd took Katie's arm but kept his gaze on Jake. "Promise me you will stay here tonight with Mom."

Jake sighed deeply as he rubbed at the back of his neck. "I'll stay."

"If I find out in the morning that you left, I'll knock the shit out of you," Lloyd warned. "And don't make Mom's night miserable over this. It's time for all of us to think straight and make some kind of plan. All right?"

Jake nodded. "All right. Thank God you have a level head."

"Yeah, well I am just as furious as you are. But it is what it is, so we have to go forward from here." Lloyd reached out and squeezed Jake's arm. "With the right men, we can get that girl out of there, Pa." He glanced at his mother. "You come and get me if you have to."

Randy folded her arms and shook her head. "How long have I lived with this, Lloyd? I won't need to come and get you."

Lloyd left reluctantly. Randy moved closer to Jake and felt heat literally radiate from his body because of his anger. She fought to hide her own terror at what she knew Jake was thinking. "I don't know what to tell you, Jake. The last thing I want is for you to ride into such danger again. But I know your heart."

Jake sighed with a groaning sound as he walked over to close and lock the front door. "Go on upstairs," he told Randy. "I'll be up soon."

Randy watched him closely. "Promise me you won't walk out that door."

"I won't." He met her gaze, love and sorrow in his eyes. "I'm sorry, Randy, sorry my past has paid us a visit again and brought danger with it. Sorry about that watch and all you've had to learn today – so much at once."

"I already told you that I consider that watch a gift. As far as danger, I have lived with it our whole married life." Randy turned to go upstairs, then stopped at the landing and watched her husband reach up and grab the gunbelt holding his .44's. He kept a cigarette between his lips as he pulled out one of the guns and set the belt aside. He whirled the chamber, checked it to be sure it was empty, cocked the gun and pulled the trigger, creating the familiar click that made Randy shudder. She well knew how loud those guns were when loaded and fired.

Jake had not touched those guns since the last awful incident from which it took him months to recover. And he wasn't getting any younger. Randy couldn't help wondering if he'd lost any of his speed and accuracy over the past three years. That could make this whole thing even more dangerous for him, let alone the fact that one more major wound or bout with pneumonia could kill him.

With a heavy heart she turned and went the rest of the way up the stairs to the bedroom.

CHAPTER FOURTEEN

Randy wished she could relax. She didn't like leaving Jake downstairs alone. God only knew what was going through his mind. Certainly sorrow was one, learning he'd had another son all these years, a son who'd fallen into the dark lifestyle of Jake's father. And now a little granddaughter was in the hands of an awful man who might abuse her, maybe even sell her.

She knew the situation was already eating at him. She had no doubt he would go to Wyoming, and as she pulled on a light blue cotton nightgown, she slowly came to the decision that she was not going to let her husband ride out of her life yet again, and into a situation that could mean he would never come back. *It's not going to be that way this time, Jake. I'm going with you.* She knew he would fight the idea, but she was not going to let him win the argument.

She wondered if the night was really warmer than normal, or if her own worry and fear made it *seem* warmer. Her stomach tightened when Jake fell into another bout of heavy coughing downstairs. She rushed out of the bedroom to see he'd come halfway up the stairs when the coughing caused him to stop and bend over.

"Jake!" Randy hurried down the stairs and past him to the kitchen to take a pitcher of water from the ice box. She poured a full glass and carried it back to Jake, who had finally managed to get the cough under control. "Drink this," she told him.

He grabbed the water and managed to drink it down, then handed back the empty glass, meeting her gaze as he did so. "I'm so goddamn sorry, Randy. You don't deserve what happened here today. Neither does the rest of the family."

Randy set the glass on a step and grasped his arm. "Come up to bed, Jake. And quit apologizing."

He stood up and grasped the railing, putting his other arm around her shoulders. They went the rest of the way up the stairs and to the bedroom.

"Get undressed and get into bed," Randy ordered. She began unbuttoning his shirt, but he grabbed her wrists.

"Don't. I'm fine now." He kept hold of her wrists. "I want to know your thoughts. I *know* you, all too well, and right now you're terrified inside. You damn well know I have to go to Wyoming, and it breaks my heart to do this to you."

"It isn't you doing this. It's a situation beyond your control, one that would never have presented itself if that woman had found a way to send Dee Dee to us in the first place." She rested her head against his chest. "She belongs to *you ... to us*. If Dallas thinks you can do something about it now, she should have contacted you much sooner, before things got this far. If the tables were turned, I would have risked death to get that girl out of there. Apparently Dallas wasn't willing to do that. But now she's willing to risk *your* life instead."

Jake finished unbuttoning his shirt. "That's Dallas for you. After the news about that last gunfight, she has probably known ever since then where I live. Maybe she has known even longer than that."

"Stop blaming her, Jake. She probably kept hoping things would get better. At least she apparently shielded Dee Dee from her lifestyle, but I do still believe she should have gotten the girl completely out of there sooner. I just think maybe she was truly afraid of this man who runs the town, and maybe afraid of her own son."

"Maybe. But I have trouble believing anything that woman says." Jake led her to the bed, where they sat down on the edge together. Jake removed his boots. "Try to relax while I get undressed."

Randy watched him, wondering if every movement and every word was something she was seeing as part of his last days on earth. "I was all set to beg you not to do this," she told him. "But I think Dallas is telling the truth. And even if that girl *isn't* your granddaughter, we can't leave a ten-year-old girl in that situation."

"I am glad you agree." Jake set his boots and socks aside and stood up to remove his denim pants. "Only a woman like you would call a child you've never met and who only *might* carry my blood, *ours*." He stepped out of his pants and tossed them aside. "I love you for that. All the grandchildren we already have love you just as much as they love their own mothers."

Randy studied his broad chest, the way his muscles worked, the way his dark skin glowed from washing up earlier. "Jake, I'm more worried about your health than about men shooting at you. God knows you *look* healthy, but your insides suffered so much damage three years ago. We are high here, but still just in the mountain foothills. Outlaw country is at a much higher elevation. You will not only be dealing with ruthless men, but the thinner air in the Wind River range and the Bighorns could kill you. It's why we haven't taken any trips higher into the Rockies ourselves when we have free time."

"I'll deal with it, just like I deal with everything else. If that God you and Evie seem to believe is in charge of my life means for me to go, He will get me through it."

His words surprised Randy. He had never even hinted that God could have anything to do with how he'd survived so much. He'd always believed God couldn't care less about a man who'd killed so many and had led such a dark life his first thirty years on this earth. She decided not to say a word to him about it. If she hinted he was actually beginning to believe that faith in God had anything to do with his life, he would deny that's what he meant.

Jake got up to set his boots near the wash room door, and as always, Randy felt the little pain in her chest at the sight of his scarred back. His father had done that to him with rough rope and the buckle end of belts and anything else he could find to hit his little boy with. Mexican bandits had added to the scars with a bull whip while he was tied to a post with an untreated broken leg that was the reason for his slight limp. *So much suffering. How is he going to get through this new problem? Especially with that cough?* "My God, Jake, this scares me. A man can only take so much."

He walked back to the bed, wearing only white ribbed cotton boxers. He propped his own pillow and crawled under a lightweight, summer blanket to lean against the headboard. He looked sidelong at her and opened his arms. "Come here."

Randy moved beside him, resting her head on his shoulder as he slipped an arm around her and rested his face against her hair. Outside, thunder rolled in the higher mountains.

"Storm coming," Randy said softly.

"In more ways than one." Jake kissed the top of her head. "I guess we both already know what needs to be done. I'll manage it somehow and come back, like always. The unfair part is that I promised you I would not ride into something dangerous again, or use those guns again after what happened three years ago. I'm so damn sorry I can't keep that promise. I don't see where I have any other choice."

Randy felt pain in her stomach at the thought. She moved an arm across his middle. "I had no doubt you would go." She leaned up and kissed his neck. "And I am going with you this time." She felt Jake instantly tense. He pulled away and straightened, facing her.

"The *hell* you are!"

Randy changed her own position to face him boldly. "Jake Harkner, I went with you years ago when Lloyd was young and angry and got in trouble on the Outlaw Trail. I ended up having to shoot two men, remember? I survived it then because I was with *you*. And I'll be with you this time, too. I am going."

"Not a chance! This is completely different and it's too damn dangerous." Jake spoke the words as a command.

"It was dangerous back then, too. And it was just you and me, Jake. This time we will be taking two or three J&L men with us."

"And we were both a whole lot younger then. This will be a hard trip, Randy, and we aren't going up against just one rancher and his men, like what we faced when we went after Lloyd. We are talking about a man who owns half the town. A crooked sheriff. A bunch of cronies lurking around every corner."

"And I will never forget the wait for months after you went to Mexico, or how it felt three years ago when I woke up to find you gone. Nor can I forget how it felt when Lloyd brought you back a bloody, dying mess, or how it felt to realize I could lose you without you even hearing me tell you once more that I love you."

"No arguing, Randy. I said no!"

"And I'm not letting you out of my sight this time. I *won't!*" Randy fought the tears that always tried to come when she was angry or desperate. "If you have to break your promise about strapping on those guns again, I want to be *with* you. I am not going to stay here through endless, sleepless nights wondering if you are dead or alive, Jake. If you don't take me with you, I'll damn well *follow* you. I'm still healthy and strong, and we are still a team. I can ride as well as any man. You know that's a fact. And you said yourself you hate breaking your promise, so if you love me, don't make me stay behind, Jake. Don't put me through that again. It's *torture.* I would rather take the risk of getting hurt."

A host of emotions moved through Jake's dark, penetrating gaze. He grasped her arms. "Baby, we've lived a pretty good life here for years, and the towns we go to have bricked streets and law and order now. But it won't be anything like that where we are going. It will be rough, filthy-talking outlaws, and dirt streets and whores and brothels, drunks and saloons and crime and still an ugly, primitive life. I know it like the back of my hand, and in dealing with it you will see me do things no woman should watch."

"But I have *seen* the ugly, Jake, at the hands of Brad Buckley. You know that. And I have seen what you can do to an enemy. Look what we survived when we first met and married, outlaws and mountain gold towns and saloons and vicious men always after you. This time you will have men with you who know how to handle guns and who also know how to handle the kind of men living up there. I am far more afraid of letting you leave again than I am of going with you. The only place I feel safe is in your arms. You are Jake Harkner. The name alone will deter a lot of them. Please don't make me stay here and sleep alone."

Obvious pain filled his eyes. "Randy," he said softly, shaking his head. "If something should happen to you, how would I live with that?"

"You would live with it because your son and grandchildren need you and you would have to go home to them. And if something should happen to you hundreds of miles away, in a place where I would never dare go alone to find your grave ... if something should happen without me being with you, able to tell you I love you ... how would I live with *that?* And what if your cough gets worse or you get pneumonia and need someone to take care of you? What if you get shot and need doctoring?"

Jake stroked some of her blond locks behind her left ear. "It's a hard ride, baby. Two or three weeks on horseback once we get off whatever train takes us as far north as possible."

"You and I go riding all the time. I'm an experienced rider. And if Dallas Blackburn could make it, so can I."

Jake closed his eyes and sighed. "You know you're crazy, don't you?"

"You *make* me crazy."

He gently pushed her down, then leaned close and

kissed the tears that trickled down her cheeks – kissed her neck, her lips. "You will be too much of a distraction."

"I'll do whatever you ask me to do." Randy ran a finger over his eyebrow, down across his full lips. "I promise. And I'll carry my own gun. Between you and the other men, I will have plenty of protection. And I went into saloons and brothels with you that first time, when we searched for Lloyd. I've heard those guns, and I've been forced to kill men in self-defense. I can do it again."

Jake moved fully on top of her and ran his hands into her hair. "And what if you end up in a situation like what happened with Buckley up at that line shack? It took you months to get over that, and I went through that hell with you. You were half out of your mind, and you still get scared when I'm not around."

"All the more reason to keep me with you this time. I'm never scared when you are beside me. We could be standing in a den of demons or a pit filled with mountain lions and I wouldn't be afraid. Not with Jake Harkner beside me."

Jake smiled sadly. "Baby, you give me way too much credit. I'm not even sure I can still shoot straight."

Randy studied the torture deep in his eyes, where those demons still lived. "You are Jake Harkner. Shooting straight is in your blood. I have a feeling it will come right back to you when you draw those guns tomorrow to practice. The last thing I want to hear is the boom of those guns, Jake, but as soon as Dallas mentioned that little girl, I knew there was no use arguing the situation."

Jake kissed her eyes softly. "How in hell did I end up with a woman like you? When we took that trip to Chicago, and I saw how perfectly you fit into that mansion of a home Peter Brown lives in, and I realized that's the kind of life you should have been living all these years –"

"Jake, stop." Randy put her fingers to his lips. "That trip was wonderful. But Colorado and this ranch have been home for so many years now that I could never live the city life. And the most successful man in the world can't compare to my Jake, in spite of all his flaws and his dark past, and in spite of how hard life has been at times. You are all man and then some, and I would never feel safe in any other man's arms. If God chooses to take you this time, I want to be right by your side. I feel strangely calm, because the thought of going with you comforts me. I'm not afraid."

"You *should* be."

"And if I was with Peter or any other man, I *would* be, because no one else loves and protects me like you do."

Jake closed his eyes and sighed as he nuzzled her neck. "Damn you, woman." He kissed her ear. "I was ready to defend you against that witch of a woman, but the way you stood up to Dallas tonight told me I didn't need to. You can be damn tough, Randy Harkner, and damn formidable for your size."

"I enjoyed putting Dallas in her place, and I was ready to blacken her other eye."

Jake snickered. "Once you get your dander up, you're a whole different woman." He kissed her. "I remember that waitress back in Guthrie, the one who unbuttoned the top buttons of her already-low dress and bent over to display her wares when she served me that coffee. You put her in her place real fast, and all with words, just like you did with Dallas."

Randy leaned up for another kiss. "I've grown used to women offering you their wares, as you call them."

Jake grinned and moved his hand over her breasts. "I'd say *your* wares are the most beautiful and fetching of any woman I've known. And you have a way of making a man want you for a lot more than that."

Randy moved her arms around his neck. "You do the same to me. You're my Jake, and you are also Daddy and Pa and Gandpa and friend, so many things to so many people who all care about you. No matter how much you fight being loved, you *are* loved, Jake, by so many, most of all, me."

"And you are responsible for all that love. Without you I would have died a long time ago, a little-known outlaw who was never loved by anyone and never loved anyone in return. And now some little girl totally innocent of my own ugly past needs me to drag her out of that world I used to live in. I'm responsible, Randy, and that means I need to go after her. I don't have any choice. You understand that, don't you?"

Randy felt the old passion rising in her heart and soul, the desperate need that always consumed them in moments like this. They had shared that need so many times when the dark world from which this man came tried to move in and take him from her.

"I am so sorry for all the hard truths you had to face today," Jake told her.

"It has been harder for you."

He kissed her eyes. "Times like this, I just want the whole world to go away and leave us alone, so it's just you and me and nobody else." He kissed her throat, moved to her mouth with kisses that grew deeper, more demanding. The energy that surged through them out of desperation brought out the passion of younger years. This kind of love-making was as natural to them as breathing ... the kind that made them both feel they could not get enough of each other ... the kind that was meant to be remembered always.

Jake moved his hand along her every curve, her taut nipples, the warmth of that place where her thighs met that sweet spot that belonged solely to Jake Harkner. Randy knew the night would end this way. It *had* to, because this was how it always ended when danger raised its evil grin. She saw it coming earlier, when Dallas Blackburn first showed up, another figure from this man's tortured past. Sharing each other, body and soul, gave them strength to face that danger. She was determined that his past would not take him from her.

Nothing more needed to be said. Jake pushed up her nightgown, and she raised her arms and let him pull it off. She knew when she first put it on that this would happen, so just like she'd done many times before, she'd not worn any underwear. After 37 years, they were totally meshed into each other's thoughts and needs.

She closed her eyes and breathed deeply of his manly scent as he trailed her body with his lips, tasting, claiming, loving every inch of her as he kissed his way downward, laying intimate claim to places she'd never allowed any other man to taste and touch. She grasped the thick waves of his hair, offering herself to him, wanting to remember every touch, remember the way his strong hands and tender kisses could command her body to react in all the ways that pleased him, while pleasing her in return. He knew every tiny part of her, as she knew every inch of him.

There was no denying they had to do this. This man knew all the right ways to arouse her to the deep climax that rippled through her body now and was quickly followed with deeper climax that made her cry out his name. Jake had a way of branding her as only his. At the same time, making love calmed him. It forced him to remember how much she needed him and that leaving her in times like this would be hurtful.

He kissed his way back to her breasts, her throat, her mouth. She tasted her own juices on his lips as he moved between her legs and filled her in order to satisfy the need he'd created deep in private places, a need only this man could satisfy with his own raging desire to please her, and to get rid of the anger in his soul.

How could any other man know her body like Jake did? And what other man could make her feel so totally safe and protected? She would ride straight into hell with him if it meant not being left behind this time. Even at his worst, she'd never been afraid of him, or of any others when she was with him. He filled her with hard thrusts, and she arched up to meet him fully in a need to prove to each other they were alive and well and were aware these moments might not last through the next challenge. They needed to literally share souls and believe they would never be apart, not even in death. She pulled at him as his life surged into her, wanting to melt right into his body and be one with him.

Jake relaxed but stayed inside her. They lay that way quietly, the bedding damp with their perspiration.

"Who do you belong to?" he asked softly.

"Jake Harkner, always and forever, and to hell and back."

She felt him swelling inside of her again. Age meant nothing in these moments. After all he'd been through, it took a hell of a lot to keep this man down, whether emotionally, physically, or sexually, especially when the danger of death parting them presented itself. That danger only created a deeper passion for life and love.

Jake rose to his knees and grasped her bottom, pulling

her to him and filling her to ecstasy again until he groaned with another release that told her she could still please him. He rolled to her side then and pulled her close. They lay there wrapped together like newlyweds.

"Do you realize how much I love you?" he whispered.

"I love you more," Randy answered softly.

"How can you," he groaned, "after the things you learned about me today?"

"Knowing you as I do, understanding your past, that makes it pretty hard to shock me, Jake. I have grown to love you far too deeply to let anything from your past change my mind." She kissed his neck.

"But I should have told you more before I allowed myself to fall in love with you."

Randy traced a finger over his lips. "You can't control love, Jake, or force it to go away. It is what it is. I already knew the worst when I met a wanted man who in turn just wanted to know what it was like to be loved. I about fell apart that first time you rode away back in Kansas. I thought I would never see you again. I wanted to beg you to stay and go west with me, but I didn't think you cared."

He kissed her softly. "Oh, I cared all right. Leaving you there was the hardest thing I've ever done in my life. I never forgot you. I had to find you again."

Randy studied the love in his eyes. "Thank God you *did* find me."

Jake closed his eyes and worked his fingers into her hair, breathing in her scent. "Randy, if you go with me, you will see the worst of Jake Harkner ... things no woman like you should see. Men are going to die, maybe brutally, and I am the one who will kill them."

"I know that. It doesn't matter. The only thing I am afraid of is letting you go without me." Randy pulled away a little and met his gaze. "Does what you just said mean you will take me with you?"

Jake pushed her damp hair away from her face. "I don't like it. Not even one little bit. But I know you. You'd hunt me down like a damn bounty hunter, and that would be a hell of a lot more dangerous for you than being with me in the first place."

"Jake, another reason I should come along is because that little girl will need a woman's love and understanding when we find her," she told him. "Just telling her you are her grandfather won't help one bit at first. All she will see is a big man with guns grabbing her away. If Grandpa is going to be there, Grandma should be, too, and not the kind of grandma Dallas is."

Jake kissed her eyes. "You're right."

Randy sat up, pulling part of the blanket over her breasts. "You had better refresh me on how to use a shotgun and let me practice using a hand gun."

Jake rolled onto his back and put a hand over his eyes. "God help me," he groaned.

Outside their roof window the sky lit up brightly, accompanied by a loud snap and an instant boom of thunder that shook the house. Its rumble rolled through the foothills and on into the higher mountains.

Indeed, a storm was coming.

CHAPTER FIFTEEN

Lloyd stood on the front porch in stockinged feet. He watched brilliant bolts of lightning turn the sky into a light show and hoped it wouldn't start a forest fire up in the mountains. Some of the bold strikes seemed to split the clouds that he could see whenever another flash occurred, making him feel split in two himself. Part of him knew full well that his place was here, with this ranch and his family. But there was always that part of him that was steadfastly loyal to his father and wanted to go with Jake to Wyoming. They were a team. Always had been. And he was still haunted by the condition Jake was in three years ago after facing alone a gang of killers. He never got over the black grief he'd felt at thinking his father would not live.

After explaining to the ranchhands why Jake would be going to Wyoming, he had made arrangements with Skeeter Keller and Percy Bates to take the rustlers to Brighton tomorrow morning. He then sent two of the men over to the main house to guard the front and back doors, just in case his father decided to try to handle things alone again. As he'd expected, every man who was left volunteered to go with Jake. There wasn't a man among them who wasn't qualified to stay and run the ranch, as well as qualified for backup firepower for Jake. They were all good cowboys as well as good with guns.

Several J&L men had backgrounds no one knew about or asked about. That's just how it was with a lot of men out here. Cowboys were private with their personal affairs, and each man respected the other for it. As long as a man was honest and loyal, worked hard, could herd and rope and brand, and could be trusted around the women, he could work on the J&L.

The plan Lloyd came up with was for the men to meet after breakfast tomorrow. But first he had to convince his father that he should go with him to Wyoming. He simply could not allow the man to go so far away and into so much danger without the backup he always gave Jake when they rode together in Oklahoma. Once that was decided, he planned to meet with the men and decide who else should go with them. With five of the men out looking for more rustlers, and two on their way to Brighton in the morning, that left nine men at home. At least three should go with Jake and the rest should stay home to work the ranch, keep guard at night, and help the boys with decisions. That would leave them a little short, but the time had come for Ben, Stephen and Young Jake to step up and start learning the ropes in helping run the J&L. It would be their full-time job someday.

Decisions. He prayed his father would agree to his plans. But he also had to get Katie to agree. He knew full well that she would not want him to leave her now, when she was still so frail and needy, but deep in his heart he hated the thought of his father facing alone the kind of men they used to face together. He took what was left of his cigarette from his lips and tossed it into the dirt beyond the porch railing just as the clouds opened up. Rain began to blow on him from a sudden gust of wind, sending him inside. He closed the front door, then sat down to remove his damp socks.

The house was quiet. Tricia and and Donavan were staying the night at Katie's parents' home. Five-year-old Jeffrey and two-year-old Betsy shared a back bedroom and were hard sleepers, and seventeen-year-old Stephen had chosen to sleep at the bunk house again. So had Young Jake, both boys probably still awake and talking with some of the men about what had gone on at the main house this evening. If not that, they would likely be joking about whore houses and naked women.

He grinned and shook his head, then rose and headed for the big leather couch in their livingroom that he'd slept on part time for several weeks now, alternating that with nights spent in one of the children's beds, his feet hanging over the end of it. Although Katie had told him earlier today she wanted him back in their bed, she had added a "not yet," and had gone off to their master bedroom without an invitation for him to join her. Using the flashes of lightning to help guide him, he walked over to the couch, hoping the blanket and pillow he'd left on it were still there.

"Lloyd."

Katie's voice startled him a little. He turned to see her standing at the bottom of the stairs.

"Katie? I didn't see you there. What's wrong?"

She remained silent for a moment. "You ... you want to go with Jake, don't you?"

What did she want him to say? He couldn't quite read her, whether she was angry or upset or just in one of her deeply depressed moods. "I can't lie, Katie. Of course I want to go, but I wouldn't leave you now. If you need me here, then here is where I will stay."

"But I understand, Lloyd. I know what it's like between you and Jake. For the last several weeks I have been making your life miserable, adding to the weight on your shoulders. Maybe it would be good for both of us if you did go with Jake, and good for you to get away from the ranch for a while and let Stephen and Ben and Young Jake start learning how to run things."

Lloyd stepped closer, hardly able to believe what she was saying. "Let's go upstairs so we don't wake the kids." He put his arm around her, noticing she'd worn a very thin nightgown. He could feel the curve of her waist, and he dearly wanted to touch more. Katie moved her own arm around his back and squeezed, a gesture he hadn't felt from her in a long time. Somewhat bewildered by her remarks and the familiar hug, Lloyd wasn't sure what to expect, and her suggestion that he go with Jake completely surprised him.

"Go ahead and finish undressing," she told him when they reached the bedroom. She sat down on the edge of the bed to wait.

The room was dimly lit by an oil lamp, its wick turned down low. Lloyd felt Katie's eyes on him as he removed his shirt and pants. "I thought you had a headache and were sleeping," he told her.

"I did have a headache, but I couldn't sleep for thinking about what happened this evening. I know how hard this has to be for your mother and Jake, and for you."

Lloyd sat down beside her in his underwear. "Life is full of hard choices, Katie. We both know that better than most."

Katie grasped his hand. "Lloyd, I saw and felt what you

went through three years ago when you thought Jake was dying. It was killing you inside." She squeezed his hand and rubbed her thumb over the back of it. "Jake is a good man. I mean, I know he can be ruthless and hard to handle sometimes, but it's usually because he has that extreme urge to protect. He has kept you from turning out like that son he never knew. When that Dallas woman told us what her son was like, I realized you might have turned out that way if not for Jake. I know your mother did her part showing you love and raising you right, but you being a man prone to drink, you needed a father like Jake, a man who understands how whiskey can destroy a man and those around him. In that respect, he's been a wonderful father. I know how close you two are." She sighed and swallowed. "I think you should go with him to Wyoming."

Lloyd moved one knee up on the bed and turned to face her. "Katie, we just had a good talk earlier. We got a few things straight between us, some misunderstandings and all. I can't leave you now. We are finally getting closer to our normal relationship."

Katie scooted farther onto the bed and took hold of his hand again. "You want to go with Jake, and I don't blame you, Lloyd. You rode together in No Man's Land, and God knows how many times you saved each other from getting shot. You have the same instincts as Jake, and you are just as good with a gun. For all we know, you're better now, because Jake is out of practice."

Lloyd grinned wryly and shook his head. "I wouldn't bet on that, believe me. And with all the hunting we've done this last couple of years, Pa is better than he ever was with a rifle."

"I'm sure you will be able to tell tomorrow with some practice." Katie continued to cling to his hand. "Either way, the two of you together are so formidable, and I look at our little Tricia and think how awful it would be if she was in the same predicament as that little girl Dee Dee. It's a sure thing Jake will go after her, just like if it was Tricia or Sadie Mae. And I trust your skills. I trust Jake completely when it comes to protecting you at all costs, and if a couple of the other hands are going along, I won't worry like I would if you were alone, just like I don't worry a whole lot when you go after rustlers." She met his gaze in the soft lamplight. "I'm telling you that if you want to go, Lloyd, you can go. We have plenty of good men to run this place while you are gone. They are all loyal to you and Jake. And your remark that it's time the boys started learning how to run things is right. Those boys would bust their buttons with pride if you put them in charge."

Lloyd watched her green eyes, those big, beautiful pools of love surrounded by long, dark lashes and set into an ivory face framed with thick, red, curly hair that spilled all over the place. "Katie, I'm not going anywhere if it will send you into worse depression."

She shook her head. "Something about our talk earlier helped me see things better. I haven't been a very good wife or a very strong one, and I've been so depressed about losing our last baby that I haven't given enough thought to what it all meant to you."

"You are all that's important, Katie. It's hard for a man to understand what losing a baby does to a woman, but I've tried."

Katie scooted closer and pressed the back of his hand to her breast. "You've been wonderful. So patient. And I've been weak and selfish in a lot of ways."

"Honey, I have never seen it that way. No one can control their emotions."

"I know. But your patience and understanding with things like that is what I love about you." She leaned closer and kissed him softly. "I want you to be happy, Lloyd, and I don't want you worried and distracted while your father is away. Deep inside you don't just want to go with him. You *need* to go with him. I want you to know I understand. I think we will both be better off and be stronger in our love if I let you go. When you get home, it will be wonderful seeing each other again. It will give both of us time to heal on the inside and appreciate each other more."

Lloyd smiled. "Now you sound more like the Katie I married." He leaned close and returned her kiss. "No lies or pretentions, Katie. Are you sure about this?"

She let go of his hand and threw her arms around his neck. "I'm sure. I can already feel a change in you at knowing you can go."

Lloyd embraced her and rolled her onto her back. "My God, woman, do you know how good it feels to hold you?" He met her mouth. She returned his kiss with heated passion, whispering when he began kissing her face, her eyes.

"It feels good to *be* held, Lloyd. I have put it off because I didn't think I was ready."

More kisses.

"But I don't want you to go without us making love," she added. "It's like we talked about earlier. We have hardly ever made love just because it feels good. I wanted babies, and you were trying to give them to me. I want to make love just to please you. Not for any other reason. And also just because you are so good at it and you take me away from worries and loss."

More hungry kisses. Her panties came off. His underwear came off.

"It took me a while to realize just how much you must love me to bring me into your life and your bed," Katie added. "I'm sorry it took so long for me to believe you love me for me and not just to make babies and bake for you and-"

"Be quiet, Katie." Lloyd stamped out her words with deeper kisses. His long hair fell around her as he moved between her legs. "It's been a long time," he said gruffly. "Just how healed are you? I don't want to hurt you."

"Brian says I am completely healed. I was just afraid to tell you, afraid I really *wasn't* ready, or that I should lose weight first. And I have belly scars, Lloyd."

"I don't give a damn. The scars only tell me what you went through to give me children." He kissed his way down to her ample bosom, down over her scars, over the warm nest he'd not touched for too long, over the insides of her thighs, back up over her soft belly, back over her nipples and to her throat. "You have always underestimated how beautiful you are, Katie-girl. I love every curve, every sweet spot, every nook and cranny."

The talking ended. He entered her with hard thrusts. Katie ran her hands over his chest and along the hard muscles of his arms. She cried out his name as she took him deep inside, and Lloyd could not remember when making love to this woman felt this good. He groaned with pounding thrusts as his life spilled into her, and for several minutes they lay wrapped together, melted into each other.

"You okay?" Lloyd asked as he kissed her behind her ear.

"Yes, but I just thought of something."

They spoke in near whispers.

"What's that?" Lloyd asked.

"Where you are going, there will be a lot of brothels."

Lloyd couldn't help a chuckle. "So what? Pa and I were around plenty of those when we rode together in Oklahoma. You know Jake. He never cheated on my mother, and I have never cheated on you."

"I know, but ..." Katie met his lips again. "Maybe we should do this a couple more times before morning. You need to get this out of your system. One look at my very handsome husband, and those women will be fighting over you."

Lloyd snickered and moved between her legs again. "Baby, whatever reason you come up with is fine with me."

In moments he was making love to her again, and for no other reason than it felt damn good.

CHAPTER SIXTEEN

"MOTHER, YOU CAN'T BE SERIOUS." Evie set her coffee aside. "You're ... well ... you're 57 years old. And the kids need their grandma here, safe and well." She glanced at her father, grateful that he had calmed down considerably since last night. How her mother managed the man when he was totally enraged always impressed her. This morning Jake sat at the table quietly drinking coffee.

"Don't look at me for answers," he told Evie. "You know your mother, once she makes up her mind."

"We all do," Lloyd said. "Give it up, sis."

Randy set a basket of homemade biscuits on the table, then straightened and put her hands on her hips. She looked sternly at both her son and her daughter. "I am not exactly falling apart, you know. I am perfectly healthy, and your father and I went alone to outlaw country eighteen years ago to find you, Lloyd, if you will remember. That's when I learned to use a shotgun, and learn I did. I shot one man with that and another with a pistol. I have every confidence that I will return home safe and well. After all, I will be with Jake. What better insurance can there be?"

Lloyd drank down some coffee. "Mom, I don't know whether to laugh or yell at you and Pa both. You talk about using a shotgun like you'd be shooting squirrels with a .22. I know that coming after me all those years ago was danger- ous, but this time you will be facing a lot more men who will be just as vicious as the ones who held me, probably *more* vicious. And if you had seen the remains of a man Pa shot with his shotgun three years ago ..."

"I know what a shotgun can do, Lloyd. I also know what Jake can do. I am certainly no novice to his abilities. And if this was just men after men, I would think twice about going, but a little girl is involved. Getting her out of there will be traumatizing enough, what with all the shooting that might take place, bloody bodies all over the place. What if that happened to Sadie Mae or Tricia, and then they had to come all the way back here with a bunch of strange men? Once we get hold of her, that girl should be with me. Her grandmother."

"But, Mom, you are hardly any bigger than a shotgun yourself," Evie reminded her.

"I don't want to hear any more about it," Randy answered. "I refuse to sit home waiting this time, not knowing what is happening to your father."

Evie looked helplessly at Jake again. He just shrugged. "I have been up against some formidable enemies in my life- time," he told Evie, "but your mother is the worst. She always wins."

"But, Daddy –"

"Evie, at least if your mother is with me, I'll know where and how she is. Besides, she threatened to run off and look for me if I *don't* take her along. I wouldn't put it past her to do just that. And she'll be the *only* woman along because I'm not taking Dallas with us. I'm leaving her off in Denver.

She can stay there or go on to Cheyenne by herself if she wants, but I don't want her coming with us to Shelter. Once we get Dee Dee, Dallas can go back to that hell hole of a business she has and stay there. We will bring Dee Dee home with us."

Lloyd shoved his plate away from him and leaned back in his chair. "I haven't said anything yet, because I wanted to hear your decision, Pa." He looked at Evie. "Sis, you can rest a little easier knowing that I am going, too. Mom will be in good hands."

"*What?*" Randy sat down to the table. "Lloyd, this is no time for you to leave Katie. And what about this ranch?"

Lloyd glanced at Jake. "Katie and I reached an understanding last night. She's the one who thinks I should go with you. She knows how restless and worried I will be having to wait around here. And we both agree it will be good for the boys to start handling more important decisions about the ranch."

Jake frowned. "You sure you didn't argue Katie into this? She needs you."

Lloyd just grinned. "I assure you, it was no argument. Quite the opposite. And it was all her idea."

Jake sighed and shook his head. "I hope you understand what it would do to Katie and your kids and to the future of this ranch if something happens to you."

"Nothing is going to happen. I'll be with you, and we'll take at least three of our best men." Lloyd lit a cigarette. "I was up half the night making plans." He grinned. "I spent the other half of the night making things right with Katie."

Jake chuckled. "Is that so?"

"It is." Lloyd sat up straighter. "Seriously, Pa, you know damn well you will get into situations where *both* of us are needed. I don't intend to see you all shot up again, and I *sure* as hell don't want to see my mother hurt … or dead. You and I together can be damn formidable, maybe even cause some of those men to back off just because they are facing *two* Harkners instead of one."

"And back here there are more rustlers to be caught," Jake reminded him. "More stray cattle to herd closer for a count, more branding to do. And we need to build up our supply of horses again, which means sending men out to look for mustangs, and then we have to break them and figure out which ones to keep and which ones to sell."

"Don't you think I know all that?" Lloyd answered. He took a deep drag on his cigarette and exhaled as he spoke. "That bunkhouse and those cabins out there are full of loyal, dependable men who know how to run this place. And Stephen and young Jake and Ben will take a lot of pride in having more responsibilities. All three of them want to go with you, but we both know they are way too young and inexperienced against men like those we are going after. We need to give them something important to do while we are gone so they won't feel bad about not going with us. This will let them show us what they are made of."

"And Katie really is all right with this?" Randy asked.

"Things are much better between us, Mom. Ask her yourself. She knows I'll be happier going with Pa, and we both feel it will be good for us to be apart for a few weeks. Don't tell me you and Pa didn't find a deeper love for each other every time he came back from hunting the scum of the earth in Oklahoma." He grasped his long hair and pulled it behind his back. "We are both okay with this decision. Katie is slowly getting stronger, and she has her parents here, which is a God-send."

Jake scooted back his chair and got up to pour himself more coffee. "I don't like your mother going with us," he told

Lloyd and Evie, "but I also know how hard it would be for her to stay here and wait again. I got up in the middle of the night and came down here to clean and oil my guns so we can get in some practice shooting this morning. I want to leave tomorrow early, so we have some planning and packing to do. We can always stop in Denver or Cheyenne and buy whatever we need or forgot." He put the coffee pot back on the stove and sat down again. "God knows I need to find out this morning if I still have what it takes as far as using those .44's." He glanced at Evie as he set his cup on the table and took his chair. She was wiping at tears. "Baby girl, you can help us with those prayers of yours. They hold more power than any shotgun or pistol. I'm counting on your connection to that God of yours to convince Him to help out. My own prayers are worthless, coming from a man who's committed every sin in the book."

Evie walked over to her father and wrapped her arms around his shoulders from behind. "Daddy, you have saved more than one child, and risked your life doing it each time. I know your past is nothing to brag about, but you have more than made up for it. God doesn't see your sins at all."

Jake patted her arm. "You just go on believing that, baby girl. I have never been able to convince you otherwise. But believe me, what might happen to some of those men won't be the work of a forgiven saint. I guess sometimes it takes a sinner to get the job done. If that's true, I'm the man for the job."

Lloyd finished his coffee and rose. "I'm going out to the barn and take care of sending those rustlers on their way. Meet me out there, Pa, and we will talk to the men and to Ben and Stephen and Young Jake about all this and what to do to take care of this place while we are gone. Then we will all get in some practice shooting." He scowled at his mother.

"I think Pa has driven you crazy and that you don't realize what you are doing, but if you actually feel better going with us, then so be it. I'll stop trying to talk some sense into you. If Pa can't change your mind, *nobody* can. I'm just glad as hell now that I *am* going." He took his wide-brimmed hat from the corner of his chair, then took hold of Evie's arm, pulling her away from Jake. "Come on, Sis. You need to go talk to Brian, and we all have a lot to do."

Evie wiped at tears and hesitated. "Daddy, I want you and Mother and the whole family at the chapel tonight so we can all pray for you and say our proper goodbyes. Tricia and Sadie Mae are going to be so distraught about this. Will you please be there? We always have a special service for things like this, and with Mother going along, it's even more important we offer our prayers for you."

Jake rubbed at his eyes, always uncomfortable with things related to God and religion. "Of course we will be there," he told Evie. "I always go to your prayer services because it's important to you." He met her gaze and gave her a grateful smile. "Evie, you just remember that God of yours has answered every prayer you ever offered, so don't you worry. I might have come back all shot up last time, but I did come back, and by some miracle only you could have created through your prayers, I lived."

Evie turned away, crying, and Lloyd put a hand to her back and led her out. Jake watched after them, then turned his attention to Randy as he finished his second cup of coffee. "You sure know how to throw a wrench into things, woman." He got up and walked around to where she sat, leaning down to kiss her.

"Jake, I think Lloyd and Katie are back together in every way, if you know what I mean. I'm happy for Lloyd. He looked so much more relaxed and happy this morning."

Jake chuckled. "Well, if you are right about them being back together in the bedroom, I can understand. I'm in a pretty good mood myself." He kissed her again.

Randy gave him a little shove. "Get out of here and let me figure out what I need to pack."

Jake snickered and headed out of the kitchen area. "After Lloyd and I talk to the men, we will get in some shooting. I'll come back for you." He pulled on his boots. "I'd better stand behind you the first time you practice with that shotgun. Evie was right. You're hardly any bigger than that gun, and it's been years. That thing will knock you right on your ass if I don't support you from behind."

"I'll get used to it." Randy rose and folded her arms. "I am guessing that part of you likes the fact that I am going with you," Randy declared. "Am I right?"

Jake shook his head. "You would be, if we were going back to Chicago or some other place. But not so much for riding into outlaw country." He gave her a sly smile. "I can't argue with the fact that it will make the nights more pleasant."

Randy smiled in return. "And mine won't be so lonely back here waiting for you. So see? There is an up-side to what sounds like a terrible idea."

Jake looked her over, sobering. "I hope you are right." He picked up his freshly-polished gun belt from where he'd hung it over a high-backed chair. He strapped it on, an all-too-familiar move, one Randy hadn't seen in almost three years. Every bullet pocket was fully loaded. She knew that once he was packed, his gear would hold both his 10-gauge shotgun and his lever-action .30-.30 Winchester. A Colt .45 would be tucked into his gunbelt at his back, and he would take two extra bandoleers loaded with more bullets.

Now he looked like the man she'd met in that supply

store so many years ago back in Kansas ... the man who'd blown away a bounty hunter right in front of her ... the man she'd shot with the tiny little gun in her purse ... and then fell in love with. For the moment, the past 37 years vanished.

CHAPTER SEVENTEEN

RANDY FELT the stark contrast between the lovely little chapel the men had built for Evie, now filled with a quiet crowd of family, cowboys, ranch hands and their wives, and the noisy practice shooting that had gone on most of the morning. Other than the littlest grandchildren, the whole family and available ranch hands watched Jake and Lloyd draw and shoot with lightning speed at targets that flew off fence posts in fractions of seconds. Jake complained about being rusty, but no one could understand why. In the first few minutes his shooting skills were back to the amazing speed and accuracy that had made him, though reluctantly, famous.

Jake had been right when he figured Randy had forgotten just how jolting the kickback from a shotgun could be. If he hadn't been standing behind her the first time she fired the gun, she would have fallen on her rump. Now her right shoulder was sore. Jake had also given her a Remington double over and under pistol that weighed only three quarters of a pound. The barrels were only three inches long, but, according to Jake, the little firearm would "do the job" in a close-up situation, and it would be easy to hide the pistol in the pocket of her riding skirt.

Jake chose Cole Decker, Charlie McGee and Terrel Adams to accompany them. The ever-loyal Cole, 64 now, was good with a gun and was the kind of friend that could be trusted in every way. He'd proved that when he went with Jake to Mexico.

He chose Charlie and Terrel because they were both not only good with a gun and loyal, but because they had no families to leave behind. Forty-five-year-old Charlie was affable and daring and had never been married. Terrel, 42, was just as capable, but Jake was already being teased about taking along "the man who loved and chased only married women." *You put him in charge of Randy, and you might never see the two of them again,* Charlie had teased.

To the surprise of everyone, Terrel had married a twice-divorced woman a year ago, but she had already left him because of his inability to be loyal to one woman. Never mind the fact that she had been unfaithful in return and had caused a bunkhouse fist fight. Terrel and Vance were often targets of bunkhouse jokes because of their reputations for chasing skirts, married or not. Either way, Terrel was a little faster with a gun than Charlie, so he would be part of their little posse that would head for Wyoming with Lloyd and Jake.

As usual, Evie had insisted on holding a prayer service for the safety of her parents, her brother, and the men going with them. Randy took a deep breath during the prayer. They would leave tomorrow, and she had to admit she was nervous. She reached over to take hold of Jake's hand as she bowed her head along with everyone else.

Evie prayed for the return of the granddaughter they'd never known, and for her father's health and safety. Jake shifted in his seat, always, always uncomfortable when Evie asked God to watch over him. Even the fact that his own mother's crucifix he'd worn in his last gun battle had stopped a bullet from crashing into his heart had not fully convinced him that God was on his side. He simply could not believe he was worthy, and as usual, he'd insisted on sitting in the last row of chairs at the back of the chappel.

Lloyd and Katie sat directly in front of them, holding hands. Before the service started, Randy noticed a new light in Katie's eyes. Thank God, things seemed to be better between her son and his wife, and Katie seemed stronger. Katie's decision to urge Lloyd to go with Jake was surprising, but it apparently had brought them closer. Perhaps this unexpected new challenge to the family would turn out to be a good thing overall.

Evie had opened the service singing *Amazing Grace*, her angelic voice accompanied by piano, played by Annie, such a beautiful young woman now. If not for Jake going after her in Mexico, Annie would likely be living in forced servitude there, or dead. Gretta, a changed woman herself, wore a simple green calico dress, her blond hair in a bun. Randy noticed Cole move an arm around her as Evie sang. Gretta, the once-notorious Denver prostitute, was now a loyal wife, and right now she was afraid for Cole.

All eleven grandchildren sat quietly together up front, except for tiny little Jonathan, born to Evie just two months ago. Brian held the sleeping baby. Brian ... the quiet, stoic Doctor Brian Stewart who was always clean shaven, his hair always neatly cut. The man never argued with Evie, or anyone else for that matter, and he treated Evie like fine china. He'd saved a few lives on this ranch, including Katie's when she lost her baby, and Jake's, more than once. Brian was always silently strong, forgiving, understanding, the perfect husband for Evie. He seldom dressed in denim pants, leather vests and cowboy boots like the other men. Instead, he wore those familiar black cotton pants, a white shirt, and a black silk vest with a watch chain hanging from its pocket.

The sight of the watch chain stabbed at Randy's heart. Her father had also been a doctor, and beside her sat a man who was there the day of the raid that killed him. She knew how deeply Jake regretted that raid, and how equally deeply he loved her and had yearned for her forgiveness. He was such a tortured, complicated man who had probably committed every sin in the book and who felt guilty sitting in his daughter's chapel, yet he was so easy to love. He let go of her hand and leaned forward, rubbing at his temples. Randy knew he was fighting those inner demons that insisted on convincing him he was not worthy to be sitting here.

Now Evie sang *Be Still My Soul,* the last words hitting home. *Be still my soul: the hour is hastening on when we shall be forever with the Lord, When disappointment, grief and fear are gone. Sorrow forgot, love's purest joys restored.*

Randy could tell it was hard for her soft-hearted daughter to get through the words ... Evie, who refused to see one bad thing about her father, who saw him not as an outlaw, but as an avenging angel. She finished the song and offered one more prayer, and then Sadie Mae and Tricia got up to sing a duet. Their hymn was *Abide With Me.*

The two little girls had sweet voices and loved to sing and show off, but Sadie Mae didn't make it through the song. She burst into tears and ran to the back of the chapel, climbing onto Jake's lap and putting her arms around his neck. She begged her grandpa to please not go away again.

Tricia ran after her as Jake stood up with Sadie Mae in his arms and carried her outside.

Everyone there reacted with a mixture of tears and pity at Sadie Mae's outburst. Evie started crying, and Brian comforted her while Randy hurried outside, followed by Lloyd and Katie. Jake was sitting on a nearby wooden bench talking to both his granddaughters. The girls were such a stark contrast, Sadie Mae a dark little beauty like her mother, Tricia with curly red hair, extremely fair skin and freckles. Jake was wiping at both girls' tears with a clean handkerchief he took from his shirt pocket, all the while trying to console the girls with promises that nothing bad would happen to him.

"But you will come back all bloody again," Sadie Mae insisted. "I don't want you to be all bloody again, Grandpa."

"Me either," Tricia added, the slender little girl shivering.

"Girls, listen to me," Jake urged. "I am not going alone this time. I will have your Uncle Lloyd with me, and Cole is going, and Charlie and Terrel. And with your Grandma along, I will be extra careful. Haven't I always come back before? Always?"

Both girls nodded through tears, taking turns wiping their faces with Jake's handkerchief. "But sometimes you get bad hurt," Sadie Mae said amid jerking sobs.

"And my Daddy might get hurt too," Tricia sobbed.

"We will have lots of help," Jake reassured them. "Lloyd and I used to go after bad men all the time when we lived in Oklahoma. We managed just fine because we know what we are doing. And we are doing this to help a cousin of yours. She's your age, and right now she's scared and hurting and in a lot of danger. If you were scared and in danger, wouldn't you want me to come after you?"

Both girls nodded.

"And when I bring this little girl home, I am going to need you two to welcome her and be her friend and play with her and love her. Can you do that?"

They both trembled with more tears as they nodded their heads. "Are you her Grandpa, too?" Sadie Mae asked.

"Yes, I am. Your mothers can explain it all to you while I am gone. The girl's name is Dianna. Her nickname is Dee Dee, and when I get her home, she will need to know we all love her and want her to live with us. This will turn out okay. Sadie Mae, your mommy is praying very hard that nobody gets hurt, and you know how strong Evie's prayers are."

Tricia sniffed and swallowed. "Did you like our song, Grandpa?"

Jake glanced at Randy, and she saw the pain in his eyes. She knew he felt guilty for all the chaos and sorrow the family had gone through too many times. He pulled both girls closer. "Your song was beautiful. Maybe you can teach your cousin to sing like that when I get her here. Just remember that I am counting on you two to welcome her and share your clothes and toys with her. Will you do that?"

They both nodded as they shared the handkerchief again.

"Good," Jake told them. "I have to talk to some of the men now, and we have a lot of packing to finish, so I want the two of you to stop crying and start picking out dresses and a couple of your doll babies Dee Dee can play with. Tricia, your Grandpa Patrick and some of the ranch hands are going to build an extra little bedroom right off of yours for Dee Dee to stay in. Sadie Mae can go stay with you as often as she wants so all three of you can be like sisters. Won't that be fun?"

Both girls nodded again, and Jake urged them to run home and start picking out clothes for Dee Dee. After one more hug the girls ran off, but Tricia stopped to reach up to Lloyd for a hug. Lloyd picked her up and walked with her. Tricia wrapped her arms around his neck. "Don't get hurt, Daddy," the girl begged.

"I'll do my best, Chicken Little." Lloyd and Katie walked both girls home while Jake remained sitting on the bench with his elbows on his knees and his head in his hand. Randy sat down beside him.

"Don't blame yourself for their tears, Jake," Randy told him.

He sighed and rubbed at his eyes. "I'm to blame for a lot more tears than theirs." He stood up. "I'm going to talk to Dallas. We've left her out of all of this, other than Gretta telling her our decision this morning. I want her to understand that we are leaving her off in Denver. She can get a room there and wait for us. I don't want her around when we reach Shelter. I don't even want to have to look at her."

"Are you sure it's wise to talk to her alone? Dallas has a way of bringing out the worst in you," Randy warned.

"I'm over that. What good does it do now to scream at her? Once we get Dee Dee, we will take her to see Dallas once more before we bring her home with us. I want it understood that Dallas will go back to Wyoming and stay there and leave Dee Dee's upbringing to us."

"Do you think Dallas will agree to that?" Randy asked. She rose to face him. "She *is* Dee Dee's grandmother."

Darkness moved into Jake's eyes. "She's *nobody's* grandmother. I don't want her around that girl ever again. She should have told me about this a long time ago. None of this would have happened if I'd known. Besides, she already said she wants us to bring Dee Dee here to raise." He turned away. "It was her idea." He smiled sadly. "How crazy is it that orphans seem to fall into my lap? Me. Jake Harkner. A man who only dreamed about being a family man 40 years ago." He faced Randy again. "And I am the most *unlikely* person for the job."

"And maybe this is exactly what the Good Lord chose for you," Randy suggested. "Beginning with the birth of Lloyd, you have spent your whole life trying to make up for your own terrible childhood. You have been the father and grandfather you wished deep inside you might have had yourself as a child."

Jake just stared at her a moment. "How do you manage to keep climbing into my head?" he asked.

"You are easier to read than you think. But keeping that dark side at bay is a never-ending job, my dear husband."

He waved her off and headed for Dallas's cabin. Randy watched after him, praying they would find Dee Dee unharmed. If she was abused or maybe even dead, she wasn't sure Jake could handle it. *You have walked on the edge of darkness your whole life, Jake.* For too many of his early years his demon of a father had beaten into him the belief that he was no good.

She had tried all their married life to convince him otherwise, but always there was that ledge he stood on, sunshine and grass at the top, rocks and darkness and death below. Sometimes that ledge would start to crumble, and always she had been able to pull him away from it. She felt it crumbling again. She would have to hang on tight to keep him from going down, especially if they found Dee Dee horribly abused, or maybe sold off to someone and they would never find her.

Evie caught up with her then. "Mother, where are the girls?"

"They went to Tricia's house to find some clothes and things for Dee Dee." Randy watched Jake pound on the door to Dallas's cabin. "Jake told them they should welcome their new cousin and share their things with her when he gets her home. He convinced them not to worry because he will have plenty of help with him." She watched the cabin door open, watched Jake go inside. It seemed almost symbolic ... as though going through that door was like walking into his past.

"What about Daddy?" Evie asked. "He's not very good at handling his granddaughters' tears."

"He sure isn't." Randy sighed and faced Evie, suddenly realizing that just in case she did not make it back, she had better let her daughter know about the pocket watch. "Evie, in the top drawer of my dressing table is a pocket watch that belonged to my father. The picture inside is of him and my mother, me and my younger brother. I want you to have it. Treasure it always. Show the watch to the children when they are old enough to understand that picture is of their great-grandparents, and the uncle you and Lloyd never knew."

Evie frowned. "Mother, why on earth haven't you ever shown that watch to me before now? Lloyd and I would have loved seeing a picture of our grandparents. I can't believe you have kept it all these years without showing it to us."

"I didn't even know it existed until yesterday. Come upstairs with me and I will explain. It's a long story that involves Jake." She took Evie's arm and headed for the house. "Personally, I believe the watch is a tool of God that led Jake and me together."

Evie frowned. "This whole situation the last couple of

days has been so strange." She stopped and grasped Randy's hand. "Mother, are you *sure* about going on this trip?"

Randy glanced over at Dallas's cabin again. "Oh, I am *very* sure."

"You aren't going because ... I mean ... you aren't worried about that woman and Daddy being alone together, are you?"

Randy chuckled. "Oh, Lord no! At least not for the reason you are suggesting. The danger of them being alone is your father wanting to *kill* Dallas. Besides, he is leaving her in Denver and going to Wyoming without her. I just want to be there for him in case he gets sick or is wounded, and I should be there for that little girl. And I hope that bringing Dee Dee home will finally get rid of all the shadows from Jake's past." She put an arm around Evie. "Come on. I'll give you the watch and explain how I got it. It's all a part of those shadows I just mentioned."

PART 2

How many times had they done this? He never tired of her.
She was too special, too sweet, too beautiful and devoted.
He did not deserve her and never had. In spite of being sure
that bringing her along was wrong, he was glad she was
here.

CHAPTER EIGHTEEN

Sadie Mae and Tricia stood with their arms around each other as the whole family gathered around Jake and Randy and those going with them to Wyoming. Randy felt like part of a small army. A mixture of rifles and shotguns rested in scabbards attached to everyone's saddles, and every man carried at least two sidearms and extra ammunition.

Randy's little Remington pistol rested in a pocket on her riding skirt, but she doubted she would have need of it, not with Jake and Lloyd and three extra men along. For now, Jake carried only one of his .44's, but he had packed the other, along with a .45 and plenty of bullets. *Are we going to war?*

Thunder shuffled sideways and shook his mane, as though the big gray and black speckled gelding knew he was headed for something important. Man and horse were so used to each other that Thunder often reflected Jake's mood and purpose.

Randy took a deep breath as she mounted up. She wore a split, rust-colored riding skirt with a blue checkered blouse and a leather vest. She'd packed four extra shirts, three more riding skirts, and one heavy fur-lined jacket, just in case the higher mountains were cold at night in spite of this being mid-summer. She'd learned years ago that mountain weather could never be trusted. There was nothing fancy in her bags, no dresses or sparkling hair combs or fancy shoes. Such clothing would not be necessary where they were going. She'd even left behind the rose-petal diamond necklace Jake bought her in Chicago, and the beautiful diamond wedding ring he'd surprised her with in Denver. Instead, she wore the plain gold band he gave her when they first married. Jake had warned that fancy jewelry would just be a temptation for thieves in outlaw country.

And where we are going, you, my dear, will be even more valuable than that jewelry, so stay close to me at all times.

Jake's warning did not worry her. She never feared a thing when she was with Jake. She adjusted her wide-brimmed leather hat to keep the sun from her face and flexed her feet inside brown leather knee-high boots. This was going to be a long journey, and she already missed the family who all watched now, the little girls and Evie crying. Earlier, Brian had to practically pry the still upset Sadie Mae and Tricia off of Jake so he could mount up, and now Evie walked up and took her father's hand. "Good luck, Daddy. *Dios esté con ustedes."*

"Cuando pensé que me estaba muriendo hace tres años, mi madre vino a mí en una visión y me dijo que Dios aún no estaba listo para mí. Me imagino que ella también estará conmigo ahora, así que no te preocupes, niña".

Randy drew a deep breath. She'd learned enough Spanish from Jake to know what he'd just told Evie. *When I thought I was dying three years ago, my mother came to me in a vision and said that God wasn't ready for me yet. She will be with me now, too, so don't you worry, baby girl.*

Katie sat in front of Lloyd on his Palomino for a last goodbye. Randy watched them kiss. Yes, things were better. She said a quick prayer that Lloyd would make it back, her own tears wanting to come at remembering when Lloyd was shot at the cattlemen's ball in Denver and she thought he was dead. What a terrible time that was for Katie. And she had done so much of her own waiting and worrying when Lloyd rode with Jake as a deputy marshal.

She glanced at Dallas, who would ride sidesaddle on an easy-going small white mare called Sugar. Dallas met her gaze and nodded. "You're really going then," she said.

"I really am. I'm not letting Jake out of my sight this time. If something goes wrong, I want to be with him."

Dallas shook her head. "I didn't believe it when Gretta told me."

Randy shrugged. "I'm not the weak little woman you probably thought I was. If you're going to be married to Jake Harkner, you'd better be damn strong."

Dallas looked her over. "How well I know."

"Besides, Dee Dee will need her grandmother with her when we find her."

"*I'm* her grandmother, too," Dallas reminded her.

"That all changed when you came asking Jake to find her and bring her home with us," Randy reminded her. "And the fact remains she might need a woman's comfort, depending on how she's been treated. She wouldn't be in this situation if you had done the right thing in the first place."

"I suppose you know you will have to go into saloons and into those brothels if you're going to stick with Jake once you hit outlaw country," Dallas said, as though it would frighten or upset her.

"I am familiar with both," Randy answered. "And I can *handle* both."

Dallas sniffed and trotted her horse farther away. By then the others had said their goodbyes. One of the ranch hands helped Katie down from Lloyd's horse, but she stayed beside Lloyd as he gave some last-minute orders to young Jake, Stephen and Ben. All three boys sat their own horses, their backs straight, rifles attached to their gear, proud looks on their faces. They made promises to take good care of the ranch and make sure the women and children were always safe.

Randy glanced at the ranch hands staying behind. She could tell by their eyes that they were suppressing smiles at having to call the three young boys their bosses. But she knew who would really be running the place. Not a man left behind would let anything happen to those boys, and all of them knew what needed to be done while Lloyd and Jake were gone. She felt great relief at how dependable J&L men were.

She adjusted her hat, then took a brown leather cape from her lap and threw it around her shoulders against what would be a dusty trail. She pulled on leather gloves to protect her hands against hours of handling reins and against the western sun that so easily aged a woman's skin.

"Listen up!" Jake said in a loud voice, getting everyone's attention. He turned Thunder in a circle, facing each man as he spoke. "We will make the best time we can in our ride to Denver because time is important. Each of you is responsible for himself and his gear. You will each take turns cooking, and sometimes cooking will be every man for himself. I'm not bringing my wife along so she can cook for us every day just because she's a woman. She came along so she could be there for my granddaughter when we find her. This will be a hard trip for her, but Dallas managed it, so I'm sure Randy can, too. But any time I can't be with her, one of you will keep watch. Once we reach outlaw country, I don't want Randy left alone. *Ever.* Is that understood?"

Every man replied in the affirmative as Jake paused to light a cigarette.

"Hell, I'll watch her *all* the time for you if you want," Terrel joked.

Everyone present snickered. "I'm sure you would," Jake answered, tossing a match to the ground. He took a deep drag on the cigarette. "Just don't forget she will be carrying a shotgun and a pistol, and she's used both before. She even shot *me* once, so you had better turn your attention to *other* men's wives, Terrel."

The remark brought louder laughter and a couple of whistles.

"I want to time this trip so that we rest only one night in Denver," Jake continued. "Some of you will need one day to stock up on things you might still need, so I'm hoping to make Denver by midmorning the day after tomorrow, which means a hard ride. And I'm leaving Dallas in Denver. She will have to wait there because I don't want her with us when we reach Shelter. Her presence might give away things I don't want the men there to know, and that could end up causing more trouble than we need."

"Jake, I wish – " Dallas started to argue.

"We already talked about it!" Jake shot back. He turned Thunder in Dallas's direction. "If and when we get Dee Dee, we will stop to see you so that you know she's okay. Then we will head home, and you will go back to Shelter. Running your whorehouse and taking care of the women who work for you are apparently more important to you than my granddaughter. When this is over, I never want to see your face again. Understood?"

Dallas's eyes grew dark with hurt and hatred. "You can be such a bastard."

"Sometimes it's necessary." Jake backed Thunder and faced Charlie, Cole and Terrel again. "Each man is in charge of his own pack horse. I'll pay for whatever extra supplies you need when we reach Denver. We will take the Kansas Pacific from Denver to Cheyenne and then the Union Pacific to Wilcox. I'll pay your train fares. Once we get off in Wilcox, the journey starts getting rough. We will follow the Bozeman Trail for a ways, then the old Outlaw Trail to Hole-In-The-Wall. Shelter is about twenty miles north of there. If we get in a rough situation, we will need to work together, so don't any of you go off on your own and try to be a hero. I intend to get back home with all of you alive and well."

"You know you can depend on us," Charlie answered.

"Yeah, well, don't go getting carried away in the saloons or brothels," Jake warned. "From what I figure, this Ty Bolton has a lot of people on his payroll, including the sheriff and deputies, and likely some of the prostitutes. They will probably be afraid to go against him. The man who stole my granddaughter cut up the face of the woman who tried to help her, so don't trust *anyone,* and let Lloyd and me do the talking." Jake finished his cigarette and tossed it into the dirt. "Sun's up, so let's get going." He looked at Tricia and Sadie Mae. "You two get a room all ready for Dee Dee. Promise?"

"We will, Grampa," a sniffling Sadie Mae answered. "Don't get hurt."

"I'll be okay, Sunshine. You just say a little prayer for all of us every night before you go to bed."

"I will, Grampa."

"Me, too," Tricia told him. She wiped at tears with the palms of her hands.

"Then Grandma and I will be safe," Jake told both girls. He started off, but Young Jake trotted his horse closer to his grandfather and stopped him. Although only thirteen years old, the boy was almost as tall as his older cousin Stephen, who at 16 stood 6 feet. Both boys obviously took after the Harkner side of the family, dark and good looking, but Young Jake carried his grandfather's daring spirit more than the others. Poor Evie was losing her little boy to dreams of being the next Jake Harkner. Young Jake was the wildest, most daring of the grandsons, and he and his grandfather seemed to have the closest, though unspoken, bond.

"Grandpa, I wish you would let me go with you," he begged. "I'm already good with a gun, and – "

"You know you can't, Jake. This is not something for inexperienced younger men."

"But what if I never see you again?"

Thunder sidestepped anxiously, and Jake jerked on the horse's reins. "Jake, staying here and running the J&L is just as important as going with me. Remember that. And I'm leaving some good men behind, so you listen to them, too. Remember how experienced the older men are and respect their opinions. I feel good knowing you love this ranch and will take good care of it. And you will take good care of your mother, too. That means a lot to me."

Young Jake quickly wiped at an unwanted tear and sat a little straighter again.

So anxious to be a man, Randy thought.

"I love you, Grandpa," he told Jake.

"I damn well know it." Jake reached out and shook the boy's hand. Randy swallowed back her own tears, realizing

Jake understood that his grandson would not want a hug in front of the men. "Make me proud," he told the boy.

Young Jake nodded and rejoined his cousin and step-brother as the well-armed and well-supplied entourage resumed its exit. Randy rode a quarter horse named Jenny, gentle but fast when necessary. She favored the horse's golden color, set off by a blond mane and tail.

Most of the pack horses were mustangs, captured and broken by J&L men. They were a mixture of colors, and they were stocky, sturdy animals that did well on long journeys through rugged country. Randy pulled her own pack horse, their little train made up of five men, two women, and fourteen horses. After reaching Denver, Dallas and her horse would be left behind. The rest would continue north ... to outlaw country.

"Let's go get my granddaughter," Jake said loud enough for all of them to hear.

My granddaughter. Randy knew that's how he already saw Dee Dee. He would bring the girl home and love her like his own, and that would be that. Heaven forbid any granddaughter of Jake Harkner's should be left behind and in danger. Nor would Jake ever again question if the girl really belonged to him. It no longer mattered. She was a child in trouble.

In minutes they were over the high ridge on the north end of the homestead ... down the other side. The houses and outbuildings ... and the rest of the family ... were out of sight. Randy rode up beside Jake, who glanced sidelong at her. "You sure about this?"

Randy reached across the space between their horses, and grasped Jake's hand. "It's like Ruth said in the Bible. *Whither thou goest, I will go.* I have never been *more* sure of anything than this."

"Yeah? Well, I've never been more *un*sure." Jake squeezed her hand. "You just remember to do what I tell you if things get dicey."

"Yes, sir."

Jake snickered and shook his head. "Since when do you call me sir?"

"Since I decided to do this. Once we get home, *I* am in charge again. Got that?"

He squeezed her hand once more and let go. "Woman, you have *always* been in charge, even that first time we met in that supply store. I took one look at you and knew I'd been roped and tied." He urged Thunder into a slightly faster lope, and the others followed.

THE FIRST TWELVE miles left them still on J&L land. Randy felt a catch to her heart when she glanced toward Echo Ridge far to the right. A narrow road off the main path led to the ridge, and to the cabin that sat high and alone there. How many times had she and Jake gone there to heal? To talk? To make love? She trotted her horse a little closer to Jake, who stared straight ahead.

"I see it," he told her quietly.

"Let's go there as soon as we get back," she told him.

"Gladly. It's been too long."

"Looking forward to relaxing there is all the more reason for both of us to get back here as soon as possible," Randy reminded him.

"For more reasons than just relaxing," Jake added with a teasing hint.

Randy knew he was trying to keep her mind off the worst that could happen on this trip. Echo Ridge was one of the highest points on the ranch, with the big, beautiful Rockies to the west, and a view of the homestead to the south ... the houses and outbuildings just tiny dots a good twelve miles away. The cabin way up there was their private getaway ... the place where they went to heal after a major trauma ... the place where they could breathe the mountain air and feel the sun and be free of the troubles that had followed them all their married life. It was where Randy wanted both of them to be buried, side by side, in that sweet, peaceful spot that was just theirs. Such peace and beauty and grandeur belied the danger and lawlessness they had known when reality came calling.

"Can I ride with you for a while?" Randy asked Jake. "I want to feel your arms around me."

"Have I ever objected to that?" he answered. He sidled closer and reached out to pull her off of Jenny and help her settle into his saddle in front of him. "Charlie!" he called out. "Take up the reins to Randy's horse for a while."

Charlie obeyed, grinning as he took Jenny's reins. "Ain't always easy, you know, tuggin' three horses along."

"Randy brought extra loaves of her bread with us," Jake answered. "She will make sure you get an extra piece when we stop for the night."

"That's damn good payment," Charlie replied. "By the way, Jake, are we allowed to at least talk to that woman back there? I figure she's feelin' pretty lonesome."

"Dallas *deserves* to feel lonesome," Jake answered, "but go ahead. Just friendly talk. She can't be trusted, so watch yourself. If she can make trouble between you three, she'll do it. That's just one more reason I'm leaving her in Denver. The sooner we get rid of her, the better. The last thing we need is Dallas Blackburn along for this whole trip."

"I understand, Jake. I just don't feel right ignorin' her altogether."

"Yeah, well, you aren't the one she slept with so a bounty hunter could kill you just for money. I imagine what she really wanted was for that man to wound me but keep me alive. I was worth more that way. Three thousand dead. Five thousand alive. It wouldn't have mattered to her how much I might have suffered."

"Hell, Jake, I'm just tryin' to relieve the boredom. It will be a couple of nights before we reach Denver."

"Just don't get too close to her at night," Jake answered. "You know what I mean. And keep your eyes peeled. There might be more rustlers roaming around out here. Don't let Dallas distract you too much."

Charlie tipped his hat to Randy, then turned with the three horses and rode back to join Dallas.

"He means well, Jake," Randy told him. She leaned against his chest and relaxed at the feel of his left arm around her. "You know Charlie. He likes to visit."

"I know." Jake tightened his hold on her.

They rode on in silence for a few more miles. They would ride as late as daylight would allow, then get up and leave again before the stars disappeared to a rising sun.

"If we make good enough time, I promise to order a hot bath for you at the hotel in Denver," Jake told her. "I know a nice hotel room sounds great, but this is no pleasure trip, and the bad memory of Lloyd getting shot in Denver still makes me uncomfortable going there. So it will be for just one night."

"I understand." Randy closed her eyes for a moment, their bodies moving in rhythm to Thunder's gentle lope. "A hot bath and a real bed do sound nice."

Jake gave her a squeeze. "I'll bathe you myself."

Randy grinned. "I'm sure you will. Just remember how tired I will be."

"You will be even more tired after a few nights on the Outlaw Trail. The men and I can ride hard and skip hotel rooms and baths for two weeks or more if we have to, but I know that will be hard for you."

"I'll manage. You have forgotten how much traveling you and I have done together over the years."

He sighed. "I haven't forgotten any of it."

More silence, until Randy decided she should tell him about the watch. "Jake."

"Hmmmm?"

"I told Evie about the watch. I thought I should, just in case. I told her to keep it." She felt him tense up. "I hope you aren't angry that I told her."

More silence.

"Why would I be angry?" Jake finally asked.

"I don't know. It's just that we decided to wait until we got back. I did tell her not to tell anyone else just yet."

"How did she take it?"

"With mixed feelings, I guess, just like I did."

"Shit," he whispered. He slowed Thunder, waving the others on and asking Charlie to leave Randy's horse with him. Charlie handed over the reins, then kicked his thoroughbred into a gentle lope, asking no questions.

Jake just sat there with Randy still in front of him. He rubbed his hand back and forth over her stomach. "I'm so damn sorry, Randy."

"I know that. I just thought it best that Evie knows."

"She didn't say a thing to me before we left this morning," Jake commented.

"She wouldn't. Not Evie. She is too forgiving. She loves you beyond blame and beyond measure. If I, of all people, don't hate you for it, why would anyone else? I have made peace with what happened, and you should, too." Randy turned a little and looked up at him. He met her lips in a kiss filled with passion and regrets, then kissed her neck.

"Te amo, querida."

"And I love you."

Jake pulled Jenny closer and hung on to Randy as she moved onto Jenny's back. He checked to make sure the reins to the pack horse were still properly tied to a loop at the back of her saddle.

"Go on ahead," he told her. "I'll catch up."

Randy watched him light a cigarette, then gave him a loving look before kicking Jenny into a faster trot to rejoin the others. She knew Jake would stay behind a while. She had been through this too many times. He needed to be alone, to deal with feelings too deep to show in front of anyone else.

CHAPTER NINTEEN

Happy to finally make camp, Randy stretched muscles that she had not used in a long time. Riding dawn to dark for two long days was taking its toll. Everyone had unloaded saddles and bedrolls, hobbled their horses, and now sat around a campfire over which hung a pot of hot coffee that Charlie had made.

Dallas removed her hat and shook out her hair, which she had left down and brushed out for the journey. Plenty of gray showed in the roots as she pulled her red mane behind her shoulders. "After the long trip getting here from Wyoming, and now this, I feel like I've been dragged behind a horse these last two days instead of riding one," she commented. She sat down on her blanket near the fire, as did the others, who all rummaged through their supplies to take out various provisions they had packed to eat.

Randy also wore her hair long. She plopped her hat over the pommel of her saddle, realizing that once they got off the train in Wyoming, she would have to braid it and put it up under her hat to hide the fact that a woman was with their little posse. She untied a small cutting board from her supplies and dug two loaves of still-fresh bread from the burlap bag she had packed them in.

"I'm serving some of my bread to everyone," Randy told them. "I can also share a jar of honey. Take that into consideration when you decide what to eat."

"Well, now, that's bound to be a real treat," Terrel told her. "Nobody makes better bread than you do, Randy."

Randy handed the bread and cutting board to Dallas. "Slice these, please, and pass them around. I will find my knife for you."

"I have one," Jake told her. He pulled up a pant leg and took a six-inch hunting knife from its sheath at his right ankle.

"Has that thing been washed since the last time you used it to clean some animal?" Randy asked.

Everyone snickered as Jake sat down a couple of feet from Dallas. "Of course it has." He handed the knife to Dallas handle-first. "I'm trusting you not to stab me in the back with that thing."

Dallas grabbed the knife gingerly. "Don't tempt me."

"You're lucky it isn't the other way around," Jake grumbled.

"Jake, let's make the best of things," Randy told him. "Dallas, pass the bread around and I'll get out the honey and a spoon," she added.

"Randy, if we could go to the Fourth of July picnic at the Twisted Tree this year, your bread would win another prize," Charlie told her.

Randy recognized his attempt at keeping the peace between Jake and Dallas.

"I reckon we will miss the picnic this year," Charlie added.

"I hope the rest of the family will go," Randy answered.

She sat down next to Jake and handed him the honey and a spoon. "It will be good for the little ones."

The men traded jokes about dancing at the picnic as they poured honey on their bread. Soon the conversation turned to raving comments about how good the bread tasted. Even Dallas spoke her praise.

"Makes a whole meal all by itself," Terrel said about the bread. "We don't need anything more than this for supper. But it just ain't fair, Jake, you gettin' the best cook in all these parts, let alone the prettiest."

"And you need to stop eyeing the married women and start looking at the single ones," Jake answered. "And you had better start looking soon, before you lose your ability to make love to *any* of them."

The men all chuckled again while Terrel poured himself more coffee. "Speakin' of keepin' up with younger women, Jake, your own wife is ten years younger than you," he reminded him. "You got answers for how to keep up?"

Jake shrugged. "All you need is to love a woman so much that it hurts. The rest comes easy." He glanced at Dallas. "And it helps to be with a woman you know you can trust beyond all measure, not one who will lie to you that she loves you and then pay somebody to shoot you down for bounty money."

Dallas stared at the fire, and everyone quieted. The black sky sparkled with stars, and for a moment the only sounds were crickets chirping and firewood snapping and popping red and gold embers into the air. Randy pressed her hand on Jake's shoulder, sensing his sudden mood change. "What's done is done, Jake. Just stay calm and we will find Dee Dee and bring her home."

"Don't think too hard on it right now, Pa," Lloyd added. "Thinking too hard makes you do crazy things."

Jake lit a cigarette. "I just feel guilty sitting here joking around when my granddaughter might be going through hell."

No one knew quite what to say. Terrel took up a guitar he'd brought along and picked at the strings, then softly strummed a tune. Everyone knew that Jake's mood could turn on a dime when he was upset, sometimes leading to an explosion. Jeff Truebridge wrote in his book about Jake that he swore nitroglycerine ran in Jake's blood.

Terrel sang softly about nothing prettier than a starry sky and a good woman. He usually played guitar any time it was needed for a celebration or a dance, but sometimes he just sat and sang songs that he made up himself. Randy was sure he was trying to calm the moment, but when Jake took a long drag on his cigarette and then spoke Dallas's name sharply, they all jumped a little, and Terrel stopped singing.

Dallas sat up a little straighter. "What is it?" she asked Jake.

"I have a few questions I want answered in front of these men," Jake told her in more of a command than a request. "What is Ty Bolton like? What are his men like? And where is his home located in relation to Shelter?"

Dallas pushed some of her hair behind her ears. She tossed her remaining coffee out of its cup and turned to Charlie, who sat next to her. "I need a cigarette," she told him. "Got one?"

Charlie lit one and handed it to her. Dallas took a deep drag, same as any man would do, then put on a look of sassy confidence. Randy could see she was trying to pretend she was not the least bit intimidated by Jake's mood.

"Which the hell question do you want answered first?" she asked Jake.

"Doesn't matter. We need to be sure what we are heading into."

Dallas folded her legs in a very unladylike Indian style, covering them with the blue skirt she wore. She rested her elbows on her knees and took another drag on the cigarette before answering. "Ty Bolton is a sonofabitch who doesn't care about anything but money. A wild dog has more feelings than that man has. He's a cheat, a liar, and a brute who likes to bully people around, and he can bully people around because he has a lot of money. He is also very good looking, with the bluest eyes I've ever seen, and he dresses like a fancy businessman. He owns a gold mine in the mountains above Shelter called Red Rock Mining, and he even stole that. He forced the owner of the mine to sign it over, then threw the poor guy off a cliff and called it an accident. Nobody knows for sure that's what happened, but you can bet it's very likely true. They found the owner's body at the bottom of the cliff, after which Ty declared himself the new owner of the mine and that was that. There was no law around to do anything about it."

Dallas stopped to take a drag on her cigarette.

"Ty came to town a couple of years ago with a whole posse of men," she continued, "leftover renegades from an era when outlaws ruled, all ex-convicts, homeless men and the like. I think he formed the gang in Oklahoma and did pretty well until more settlers came in with lawmen and talk of making the territory a state. They have tamed what was once No Man's Land. I know you worked there as a Federal Marshal, Jake, so I figure you have experience with men like Ty and those who run with him. That's why I sent for you. I'm sure you had a lot of run-ins with such men."

Jake finished his cigarette and tossed the stub into the

fire. "More than I care to remember." He ran a hand through his hair. "How old is Bolton?"

"I'm not sure. Maybe fifty. He owns half the town and everybody in it," Dallas continued. "He is basically an outlaw with money, and places like Shelter have no law except the law of the strongest, richest and most powerful. Most of the common citizens want Ty and his men gone, but they don't know how to make it happen. I think the best way for you to start is to get rid of the town sheriff and his deputies, all paid by Ty Bolton." Dallas took another drag on her cigarette. "Ty's mansion of a home is made of stone and located about halfway between the town and the gold mine, along the same road into the mountains but around the back side of the high butte where the mine is. Getting onto his ranch, let alone into the house to find Dee Dee won't be easy. It's a fortress, much like how you protect your own homestead at the J&L."

Jake stared at the fire. "How does he ship the gold out?"

Dallas shrugged. "He doesn't have the means to extract and refine it at the mining site. There isn't enough water and no one with enough experience in amalgamation, so he ships it out as raw ore to places that can process it, usually by wagon down to Lander. From there it's shipped by train to various processing plants."

"Shipping heavy wagons of ore from up in the mountains all the way down to Shelter and on to Lander has to be a rough trip," Jake comment rather absently, as though planning the best way to do what needed doing. "It might be one of Bolton's more vulnerable situations."

"It is, but he pays his men well and keeps them well armed," Dallas answered. "They make the trip only once every couple of months. The mine doesn't produce a high amount of ore, but it's enough to keep Ty in good money. I think it will play out eventually. It's actually an old gold mine from around 1870. Ty just came along and did some new exploring – found a new vein."

Jake lit another cigarette, a sure sign he was upset. "Does Bolton go with his men on those trips?"

"Sometimes."

"Would any of your girls know when he's going along?"

"Possibly."

"Can they be trusted?"

"Once they find out who you are and that I sent you, they can be. They are afraid of Ty, but they will trust you to keep them safe. The woman most likely in charge right now is named Irene. She's about forty, and she's tough. She's one of the few who sometimes stands up to Ty, but she has been beat up once or twice for doing so. So have I."

"And what if I have to leave Randy at your place? Can the women there be trusted to keep her safe from the men who visit?"

"Jake, I'm going with *you*," Randy interrupted.

"Not always, especially if we attack one of those gold shipments."

"Believe me, if Jake Harkner tells my girls to protect his wife, they will do it," Dallas answered. "Once they meet you and Lloyd and the others here, they will be tripping over their own feet trying to please. They all hate Ty Bolton, and they have heard plenty about you and how good you are at what you do. Of course, they figure you're good at a lot of other things, but with the wife along – "

"That's enough!" Jake interrupted.

Dallas threw her cigarette butt into the fire. "Sorry. I am just explaining that my girls will help you."

Jake stood up, his growing anger palpable as he began to pace around the outside of the circle. "How many men does

Ty Bolton have riding for him, not including his store-bought sheriff and deputies?"

Dallas swallowed when Jake walked to stand behind her. She stared at the fire again. "I'm not even sure," she answered. "My guess would be twenty solid men who are paid well."

"Jesus," Cole muttered.

"Hell, that's only four men apiece," Charlie joked. "We can handle that."

Randy felt the nervousness in his remark.

"Add the sheriff and five deputies," Dallas reminded them. "And a few of the mine bosses are also loyal to Ty. Most of the general citizens who haven't left yet are afraid of him, so they aren't much help, but they won't betray you either."

No one said anything more as Jake continued pacing. "Do you think Dee Dee is at Ty's home?" he asked. "What about the man who took her? Where does he live?"

"He is Ty's number one foreman, so yeah, Dee Dee is most likely at Ty's house."

"He's the one called Dennis Gates?" Jake asked.

"Yes, and he's not a nice man. He's the one who cut up the girl who tried to pull Dee Dee away from him."

Jake let out a soft groan. "And Dee Dee saw all of that?"

"She couldn't help but see it. I wasn't there, but Irene said the girl screamed and cried all the way out of town."

Jake tossed his cigarette. "Jesus Christ, Dallas! Did you even go out there and try to get her back?"

"I couldn't! Dennis Gates would have beat the hell out of me or shot me!"

"You weren't willing to risk that to get your grand-daughter back? Do you know how bad I'd like to beat the hell out of you *myself* for that?"

"Then do it!" Dallas stood up and faced Jake. "I fucking *deserve* it. Right?"

Jake took a step toward her.

"Pa!" Lloyd rose and moved closer to Jake. "You live with enough regrets, and you know damn well you would regret going against the one thing you have never done in your life, in spite of all the other ugly things from your past!"

Randy remained quiet. She knew nothing she said would help. Even the men seemed to sense that this was something only Lloyd knew how to handle. They all sat quiet and didn't make a move.

Dallas stepped back a little. "I'm sorry, Jake, but getting myself beat up or killed would not have helped a thing, let alone it would likely happen in front of Dee Dee. Would you have preferred that? Dee Dee having to watch her grandmother beat in front of her eyes? You remember how it felt to watch your own *mother* beat to death when you were too little to help her."

Jake turned away. Randy quickly rose and hurried closer. She touched his arm. "Jake."

"Don't!" Jake told her, more of an order than a request.

Randy stepped back, but Lloyd walked closer to his father. "Pa, you asked Dallas to tell us what we are up against, and she told you. I think she's right in not going after Dee Dee. It could have turned out just like she said, and nobody understands what that would have done to Dee Dee better than you do, especially after that child saw a woman get cut up. Right now you need to calm down and think all this out. Remember how it was when we rode together in Oklahoma. You never let your emotions take over. You always told me that when emotions get involved, that's when mistakes get made and the wrong people die.

Remember? We have good men with us, as well as your own wife, and they are depending on you to think straight."

Jake drew a deep breath. "What a damn mess," he mumbled.

"And we will clean the mess up, Pa," Lloyd told him, "as long as you don't let anger and emotions get in the way. Right?"

Jake seemed to wilt a little. "Yeah." He reached out for Randy. "Come here."

Randy walked closer and he took her hand as he stood there with his back to Dallas. He kept a tight grasp as he asked Dallas another question. "What kind of man is this Dennis Gates when it comes to a girl Dee Dee's age?"

"What do you mean?" Dallas asked.

"You know goddamn well what I mean!" he yelled.

Dallas paused before answering, as though afraid of his reaction to her next words. She put a hand over her eyes. "I already told you that he likes his women young."

"That's the key word," Jake growled. "*Woman*. Dee Dee is a *child*."

Dead silence. Randy grimaced a little as Jake's hold on her hand tightened, as though he might explode in the wrong ways if he let go. "At what age does this Dennis Gates consider a girl a woman?"

"I'm not real sure." Dallas folded her arms. "Maybe twelve."

Jake grasped his stomach again and groaned, still holding Randy's hand. Lloyd stood close by.

"Pa, you can't think the worst or you will never handle this the right way. You can't go riding into Shelter like a crazy man with no plan."

"Jake." Dallas spoke his name almost pleadingly. "I honestly think Dennis will hold off. Dee Dee is only ten, and she looks even younger than that. I mean, she's just a tiny thing. She's flat-chested and still has a child's voice and she's ... well ... there just isn't one thing about her that hints that she is even close to being considered a woman. Dennis is more likely to try winning her confidence for now. He probably won't touch her because he'll figure some day she'll be worth a lot more if she's *not* been touched. I think he will just let her be a kid until she starts ... you know ... changing."

"Stop trying to make it sound better than it is!" Jake shouted. "You know damn well that's not true." He let go of Randy's hand and walked into the darkness beyond the fire. "Jesus Christ!" he swore.

Everyone remained quiet as they listened to his footsteps against the gravel. They could hear him turn and walk closer to Dallas again, until he could be seen in the firelight. Randy looked pleading at Lloyd, who moved closer and stood behind Jake.

"How many innocent young girls have *you* bought?" Jake asked Dallas. "Girls who were without family, or poor as a church mouse! Don't deny you've done things like that!"

"Not with ten-year-old kids!" Dallas answered. Her eyes were wide with fear. "My God, Jake, is *that* what you think?"

"I don't know *what* to think!"

"Pa, leave it be," Lloyd warned.

"Lloyd is right, Jake," Randy added. "Stop blaming Dallas and the son you never knew for all of this. Once this is over, we can help Dee Dee, and the last hidden remnants of your past will be banished. Don't let that past destroy all the good in your life."

Jake turned to face her. "You talk about the good, but

you are going to see plenty of the *bad* before this is over."
He looked over at the men. "So will you men."

"Jake, some of us have already seen it," Cole told him.
"I saw things I have never even talked about when we
went to Mexico and found where your mother was
buried."

Jake ran a hand over his eyes and grasped Randy's arm.
"Come with me." He paused and turned to Lloyd. "Bring
our supplies and bedrolls to us, will you? I need to talk to
your mother away from the fire." He walked with long
strides, causing Randy to nearly run in order to keep up. He
did not stop until they reached solid darkness. "Let's open
the bedding into one we can share. I want to hold you
tonight." He suddenly bent over with another fit of
coughing.

"Lloyd, bring us some water, too," Randy shouted.

Jake straightened and breathed deeply. "I'm sorry," he
told Randy, his voice rough from coughing.

"You can't help it." Randy rubbed a hand over his back.
"You need to calm down, Jake. I know how you can react
physically when a loved one is in trouble, but you can't
afford to neglect your health this time. You made yourself
sick from neglect when you went after Evie all those years
ago. You nearly died from lack of food and sleep. Don't do
that to yourself this time."

Lloyd sought them out in the darkness and set down
their bedrolls and a canteen of water. "I brought pillows
instead of saddles," he told his father. "The men and I will
take turns watching for any trouble. Get some sleep, Pa.
And don't make this any harder on Mom than it needs
to be."

Jake nodded. "We're really up against it, Lloyd," he said.
"This is going to be harder than anything we faced in Okla-

homa. If Dallas is right, we have a lot of men to bring down when we reach Shelter."

"True, but Dallas pulled me aside back there and said to take hope in the fact that half the town wants Ty Bolton gone." Lloyd bent down to help straighten out the blankets. "So once somebody like you comes along and shows them you mean business, she thinks you will end up with some help. You have a hell of a reputation, Pa. Don't forget that."

"Maybe so, but it isn't a reputation I wished for."

"In the meantime, I'm in this as deep as you are," Lloyd reminded him. "That could be Tricia or Sadie Mae in trouble. Dee Dee is no different. It's just too bad how evil some people can be."

"Apologize to the men for me, will you? It's hard for me to be around that slut over there."

"I know," Lloyd soothed. "And I have had plenty of experience over the years in stopping you from going too far. When that mean streak hits, you aren't a man who is easy to reason with." He walked back to the fire, and

Randy finished spreading out the blankets. She sat down. "Come lie down, Jake."

Jake did as she asked, pulling off her boots for her and then pulling off his own. He laid back and pulled blankets over him and Randy both. He stared at the stars for several long, quiet minutes. "I'm sorry," he told Randy. "Just know things like this will happen again before this is over. I try hard to control my anger, but when it involves a woman or a child ..."

Randy felt for his hand under the covers. "You are stronger than your demons, Jake. The fact that you have managed to be such a good husband and father and grandpa, and to keep your sanity after what you suffered as a boy is something I deeply admire."

"It is mostly due to you. You are my peace. *Te amo más allá de las palabras.*"

I love you beyond words. "I know, Jake. I know." Randy thought about his earlier words, when the men were joking about getting too old to make love. *All you need is to love a woman so much that it hurts. The rest comes easy.* There again was the poetic side of this man who could be as ruthless as he could be kind. "Get some sleep, Mr. Harkner."

"If we weren't dressed and lying out here with a bunch of men nearby who can hear an ant crawling across a rock, we wouldn't be sleeping at all."

Randy smiled. "You *need* to sleep. And so do I." She turned over. "Things will look better in the morning. I promise."

Jake rolled to his side and pulled her tight against him. "Things won't look better for me until that little girl is in my arms," he answered.

"And that, Jake Harkner, is what I love about you."

CHAPTER TWENTY

MARSHAL HAL KRAEMER looked up from his desk when the door to his office at Denver's City Hall opened. "Well, as I live and breathe." He studied the big man whose presence seemed to fill up the small room. "A dead man walking," he added as he rose. "To what do I owe this unexpected visit?" Tall, broad and graying himself, Kraemer reached across his desk to shake hands with Jake. "Last time I saw you, you had one foot in the grave and the other one was on wet clay."

Jake squeezed the man's hand. "If you go by age, I *still* have one foot in the grave."

"Same here. I retire in six months, and gladly," Kraemer answered. He looked Jake over. "Any health problems remaining after that shootout from hell three years ago?" He motioned for Jake to take a chair facing his desk.

Jake removed his hat and turned to hang it on a hat rack before sitting down. "I would list all my aches and pains, Hal, but it would take up too much of your valuable time. And they aren't just from that shooting. They come from all the others. I'm a scarred-up mess, but I guess the only lingering problem now is a pretty bad cough. It doesn't come often, but when it comes, it feels like my lungs are going to come right up through my throat."

Hal shook his head. "I never asked how you got that thin scar down the left side of your face there. That's not from a bullet."

Jake ran a hand through his hair, then rubbed at the scar. "I got this in a fist fight with my adopted son's father. I ended up getting tangled up with a shovel as well as the man. Long time ago."

"And you didn't kill him?"

"I wanted to. He was beating young Ben with a belt, so I grabbed the belt and gave him a taste of his own medicine. Lloyd managed to stop me before the man was nothing but a bloody pulp on the ground."

Hal chuckled. "My God, the stories you could tell."

Jake took a cigarette from his shirt pocket. "My stories would scare the hell out of anybody under fifteen, and a lot of people older than that." He held up the cigarette. "Okay if I smoke?"

"Of course it is. I think I'll have a cigar myself. Want one?"

"No thanks. I prefer a cigarette. I decided not to get used to cigars when my wife told me she hated the smell." Jake coughed a little before lighting the cigarette. "These things are all I have left that help keep me calm, other than my wife and grandkids. If I drank ... well ... you can imagine where that would lead."

Hal watched him warily as he lit his cigarette. "Out with it, Jake. What the hell are you doing in Denver? You hate this city because of what happened to Lloyd here and the trial that followed. There are also a few court officials who still don't care to see you around after barely missing getting your neck stretched. It's not often a man gets away with blowing another man's head off after he already has him pinned down. It was only the good graces and heartfelt testimony of others that saved your ass. As I recall, it was your daughter who really got to the judge. How is Evie, anyway?"

"My daughter continues to surprise others with the fact that she has my blood in her. It doesn't make sense that I should be the father of such a saint." He took a drag on the cigarette. "To answer your question, Evita Louise Harkner-Stewart is just fine and the mother of six now. Lloyd has five kids. His wife has had a time of it, though. She lost another one. Pregnancy seems to be dangerous for her, so Brian had to fix things so she couldn't have any more. She had trouble handling that, but she's a lot better now. Overall, the whole family is fine." Jake shifted in his chair. "Fact is, life in general was going along real good until a few days ago."

Hal lit his cigar. "Why did I already know that without you telling me?"

The warning bell of a trolley car clanged in the street below, and an automobile backfired. Jake looked toward the window. "Life sure has changed from the old days, hasn't it?" he commented. He turned his gaze back to Marshal Kraemer. "You and I remember when Denver was just a growing little gold town made up mostly of a bunch of shacks. No electricity. No telephones. None of those damn noisy automobiles. No factories and filthy smokestacks to ruin the skyline. I'll take the quiet remoteness of the J&L any day."

"I don't blame you, but you are avoiding the subject at hand, Jake. What are you doing here? You sometimes send some of your men here for supplies, but you almost never come with them."

Jake took another drag on his cigarette and leaned forward with his elbows on his knees. He stared at the cigarette between his fingers. "I want you to write up an order for me, Hal, and give me a couple of U. S. Marshal badges. One for me and one for Lloyd."

Hal groaned as he rubbed his eyes. "I knew it! Goddamn it, Jake, what the hell are you up to now? I have managed to avoid arresting you too many times over the years, and you expect me to let you pin on a *marshal's* badge? Who the fuck are you after now?"

Jake kept staring at his cigarette. "A man who illegally runs the whole town of Shelter, Wyoming. And I couldn't care less about that if it wasn't for the fact that he has my granddaughter. She's only ten. This man and those who work for him are the worst of the worst. They can't be trusted with a young girl, if you know what I mean."

"My God," Hal muttered. He shoved his chair back as he rose and walked to a window with the cigar between his lips. "Are you trying to cause me to lose my retirement pay? Maybe go to jail myself? I can't give you a marshal's badge without the approval of those over my head, which I would never get for a notorious former outlaw like yourself."

"Hell, a judge back in Illinois gave me one – part of a reduced prison sentence. That stint I did in No Man's Land as a U. S. Marshal was punishment for my former sins. And that job was, by God, punishment. There were times when I figured I'd rather be back in prison. My wife went through hell, too, always waiting to see if I would make it home alive."

"That's just the point." Hal faced him. "Serving as a marshal was a jail sentence. No judge in his right mind is going to pin a badge on you for any other reason."

Jake sighed with frustration. "Hal, I have plenty of

money. If you lose your retirement, I'll make up for it myself."

Hal rubbed the back of his neck. "Shit," he looked out the window again. "I don't want your damn money, Jake. And besides everything that is wrong with your idea, I might remind you that I have no authority clear up in Wyoming, certainly not in outlaw country. And putting on a badge in places like that is like pinning a target on your back. There are still men out there who probably wouldn't mind the reputation of being the man who killed Jake Harkner. You are lucky to be alive as it is." He walked back to his desk and sat down. "How in hell did men from clear up there in the Bighorns get hold of one of your grand-daughters in the first place? Getting that close to a Harkner family member on the J&L is like breaking into a government fortress."

Jake smoked again before explaining the whole situation, and the fact that this was a granddaughter he never knew about.

Hal remained quiet for a moment when Jake finished. "Holy Mother and all the Saints," he finally said quietly. "You just can't let go of your past, can you, Jake?"

Jake took a last drag on the cigarette that was now down to a stub, then smashed it out in an ashtray on Kraemer's desk. "I have been trying to let go most of my life, Hal, but my *past* won't let go of *me*."

Hal threw his head back and sighed. "I've never known a man I've both hated and loved, a man whom I totally respect but who I sometimes wish would just crawl into a hole at home and never come back out."

Jake met his gaze, and the rugged, experienced Marshal Kraemer frowned. "And there it is," he said, "right there in your eyes ... The old Jake Harkner, the snake-mean sonofabitch who kills without feeling and gets forgiven for it every time. If I didn't care about your beautiful wife and family and that good son of yours, I wouldn't ask this, but I'm asking. Why in hell do you want to go up there wearing a badge?"

"I need something besides my name to show I mean business, Hal. Illegal or not, I need something from you saying I have been deputized to go clean up Shelter, Wyoming. I'm going to end up needing the help of the townspeople. They might respect and maybe even fear my name, but they need proof I am truly there to help ... legally. Ty Bolton has a lot of men. I only have my son and three ranch hands who are all loyal and good with guns." He lit another cigarette. "Randy is with me, too."

"Your *wife?* Why in hell did you allow her to come along?"

Jake pulled on the fresh cigarette, realizing how Randy would hate it if she knew he was chain smoking. "You've met Randy, and you know how brave and stubborn she can be. She has stood up to you more than once, Hal, and she went with me into Outlaw Country years ago when we went looking for Lloyd after he ran off at eighteen. So she's not completely oblivious to that life. Hell, she *married* an outlaw. But those years when I was a marshal in Oklahoma kind of wore her out, waiting for me, living in constant worry I wouldn't make it back alive. That deal down in Mexico didn't make things any better, and then that shootout three years ago and watching me hang on to life. She was determined not to stay behind to wait and worry this time. She's been through hell in other ways and she only feels safe with me anyway, in spite of the danger we will be riding into."

Hal snickered and shook his head. "Once you get into

lawless country, you'd better have her wrap that beautiful hair into a bun and hide it under a hat, and wear something big and loose that hides the fact that she's a woman most men look at more than once."

Jake smiled appreciatively. "Believe me, I already thought of that." He shifted in his chair and couldn't stop another fit of coughing.

"Jesus, Jake, are you really well enough for this? I know your history with pneumonia. You're riding into higher country, you know."

"I am well aware, but I'll manage. Either way, when I get to Shelter, I want to be able to wear a badge and show what looks like an official order that more or less says that law has come to Shelter, Wyoming, and that I have a right to oust the current sheriff and his men."

Jake paused to clear his throat.

"Hang on," Hal told him. He walked to a small table in a corner of the room and poured water from a pitcher into a clean glass stacked there with others. He handed Jake the water.

"Thanks." Jake guzzled down the water and handed back the empty glass. "The men I mentioned are bought and paid for by Ty Bolton," he continued. "I want to announce that a special election will be held once the town is free of outlaws and thieves. Then the townspeople can elect an honest man for sheriff. But none of that will work without some kind of official authority, and without me killing Ty Bolton. I have to get rid of the source of all the evil in that town. Killing just a few of Bolton's men won't work. He'll just find somebody else to pay to keep people in line."

Hal shook his head. "You talk about killing the man as though it's no different from killing a bug."

"It *is* no different, at least not in Bolton's case. You can cut down a tree, Hal, but the damn thing will come right back up unless you get it out by the roots."

"And Ty Bolton is the root."

"You bet." Jake's eyes grew darker. "Bolton will be hard to get to, but I'll find a way. And I will go through the fires of hell to get my granddaughter out of there."

Hal shook his head. "Don't I know it?" He sighed, wishing he could hate Jake. If the man didn't have such a big heart under all that vicious persona, it would be a lot easier to say no to him. "You might have a beautiful wife and family, Jake, but way down deep inside, we both know who the *real* Jake is. In Oklahoma you were just an outlaw chasing outlaws. If it weren't for that wife of yours, you would have died a long time ago, or you'd be rotting in prison somewhere."

"You think I don't know that?"

Hal grinned. "She doesn't take one ounce of shit off of you, does she?"

"She orders me around like a damn army sergeant. She's the only person alive who can back me right down."

Hal chuckled at the remark. He opened a desk drawer, then pulled out two U. S. Marshal badges. He plunked them on his desk, then opened a different drawer and took out three deputy badges. "I'm not doing this for you, Jake, or even for Randy. I am doing it for that little girl. I just hope you can pull this off without getting me in trouble."

Jake rose. "You don't know how much I appreciate this, Hal."

"I think I *do* know. What time do you leave for Wyoming?"

"Nine tomorrow morning, by train, till the tracks north run out. Then we go the rest of the way on horseback."

"I will bring official orders to the train station in the morning and give them to you there. I don't want you to come back here today for them. Others will wonder why in hell you came to see me. Half the town knows who you are and you are probably already getting stares and gossip. Does Jeff Truebridge know about this? Or your lawyer, Peter Brown? God knows he's done plenty over the years to keep you out of jail."

"Jeff and Peter are in Chicago, so they won't know about any of this until it's all over. And so far, only the family and men back on the ranch know ... and now you. I want it kept that way for the time being."

"Well, I sure as hell won't say anything. I'd be digging my own hole full of trouble." Hal walked around and shook Jake's hand again. "Take care of the wife. I don't want to have to deal with Jake Harkner if he's lost her. I'd rather face down a raging bull."

Jake squeezed his hand, two big, powerful and sometimes ruthless men who understood the old life, and how lawless the West once was. But in some places in such big country, nothing had changed ... yet. Hal picked up the badges and handed them to Jake. "Please don't make me regret this."

Jake shoved the badges into his pants pockets. "You know me, Hal. Once I get in revenge mode, I'm pretty hard to stop."

"Which is why I am glad I never had to come after you myself. We've come close to being enemies, Jake, but I'll be damned if I haven't always had trouble seeing you that way. I've never known a man with such a bad reputation who was so easy to like."

Jake grinned. "The wife says it's my smile, so I smile at her a lot."

Hal broke into solid laughter. "Get the hell out of here," he told Jake.

Jake grabbed his hat and put it on. He opened the door.

"Jake," Hal spoke up.

Jake turned.

"I wish you good luck. My wife has me going to church now. We will pray for you. I mean that."

Jake smiled sadly. "If you are like me, you probably wonder if God listens to you at all, but I appreciate it, Hal. And I have my daughter praying for me. It doesn't get any better than that."

Hal nodded. "I agree."

Jake left, and Hal quietly closed the door. "God in heaven," he muttered.

CHAPTER TWENTY-ONE

Jake knocked on the door to the hotel room where he'd left Randy. "Randy? It's me."

No answer.

"Randy?" He took the room key from his pants pocket and opened the door to see clothes on the floor, the bed only partially turned down, and no Randy. He called her name again, then heard the sound of lightly splashed water. He closed and locked the door and set the key aside, then went into the wash room to find his wife asleep in a large, round, porcelain bathtub, her chin just above the water.

His heart went out to her ... so willing to put up with trail riding, probably more sore than she was willing to admit ... so loyal ... and so patient with his wild emotions. He threw his hat into the bedroom and quickly removed his boots and undressed. He climbed into the tub, glad to find out the water was still between warm and hot. His movement caused water to splash onto Randy's nose, and she woke up.

"Oh, my gosh! I fell asleep." She splashed water on her

face to wake up more. "Jake, I was going to wait for you, but I couldn't resist a hot bath."

"That's fine."

"How did everything go? Did you see Hal Kraemer? Did you get the supplies we need? Are the horses put up at the train station?"

"Yes to all three. I took a streetcar here from the train station. Made me feel like I'm a hundred years old and don't belong amid all this progress. Denver sure has grown from when we were stuck here waiting for Lloyd to heal from that shooting, and for the trial afterward."

"What did Hal say?"

Jake reached for her. "I don't want to talk about that. Turn around and come over here."

Randy smiled and turned, then let him pull her between his legs, her back to him. Jake grabbed a bar of soap and began running it over her arms, her shoulders, her back.

Randy bent forward. "Oh, keep massaging my back. That feels so good."

Jake gladly obliged. "You still have a pretty back." He ran strong hands over her shoulders, down her spine. "Woman, I can't think of anything nicer than coming back here to find my wife naked in the bathtub, all warm and slippery and relaxed."

Under the water Randy ran her hands over his thighs. "*Too* relaxed," she answered. "You might have to lift me out of this tub like a rag doll."

Jake ran the soap and his hands down and around to her breasts, pulling her closer again and embracing her. "There is a shower head over us. We will use that to rinse off."

Randy groaned when he massaged her breasts. "I love your arms around me like this."

Jake worked his way down over her belly and then soaped her privates.

"That's not part of a bath *or* a massage," Randy said sleepily.

"I beg to differ. It's the best part of both." Jake worked his fingers over familiar places, knowing every move this woman loved. "Remember when we took those showers in Peter's fancy bathroom in Chicago?"

"How could I forget?" Randy answered sleepily. She sucked in her breath when he ran his fingers inside of her. "We did some wicked things during those showers," she added. "And I've never had so much fun in my life."

Jake leaned around and kissed her cheek. "I'm all for doing some pretty wicked things right now," he told her. "This might be our last chance for quite a while, unless you are too tired."

·"For this? Never." Randy turned slightly and met his mouth in a deep kiss that turned into another groan as Jake laid claim to secret places with his hand, while leaning farther forward to lick the suds from her nipples. He loved how openly she allowed his every taste and touch. He kept his hand cupped over her privates while he reached over and turned on the hot faucet to warm up the water. He moved his free arm around her middle then and pulled her closer while he continued to massage places that had nothing to do with soothing her muscles.

"You have a wicked touch, Mr. Harkner. You keep saying you can't do this as often as you used to, but I haven't noticed any difference."

Jake kissed her hair. "I believe what I said is that the day is *coming* when I won't be able to do this. I didn't say that day was here."

Randy breathed deeply as she felt a climax building. "Don't stop."

"I wouldn't think of it."

A moment later Jake felt her shudder with a deep climax. She grasped his hand and pressed it harder against her privates. Jake continued massaging her breasts, working her nipples to taut, pink berries. "Turn around," he told her.

Randy obeyed. She straddled him and let him gently guide himself inside her in a rhythmic underwater union. Jake grasped her bottom to steady her while at the same time he invaded her mouth in the enticing sexual way he knew stirred her wild and bold nature, a side of her only he had the pleasure of experiencing in their private moments. She grasped his hair and offered her breasts again, bending her head and letting her hair fall around his face as he eagerly tasted each nipple. He ran his thumbs into the folds between her legs and her love nest, while she moved exotically over his hardness, her pelvic muscles pulling at him invitingly.

He never tired of her. She was too special, too sweet, too beautiful, too devoted. He didn't deserve her and never had. It always seemed he couldn't get enough of her, and in spite of being sure bringing her along was wrong, he was glad she was here.

Hal was damn right. Once on the trail, he would have to make her hide her beautiful blond tresses that shrouded his face now, and hide the beautiful curves these full breasts created. After all, they belonged only to Jake Harkner, and death to any man who thought he had a right touching her this way. Miranda Harkner belonged to him, body and soul.

"I love every inch of you, outside and deep inside," he told her, groaning the words as he left her breasts and hungrily invaded her mouth again. His penis literally ached in his desire to please her fully, even after all these years. He would never get over the fact that she had married him at all, or that she had put up with life on the run those first years, or waited four long years for him to be released from prison, and then put up with the hell of wild, lawless Oklahoma country. Eventually, even this beautiful woman had suffered at the hands of his enemies. So had Evie and Lloyd.

Yet here they were, all part of a big, loving family that never gave up on him. Here was this beautiful, gentle, loyal woman in his arms, naked against him, willing to ride into danger with him. Why? He would never understand it.

He climaxed inside her ... inside that warm, private nest reserved only for Jake Harkner. She leaned down and pressed her head against his chest. They sat there a few moments in the hot water, both knowing they might not get another chance to do this anytime soon. "Tell me again you are sure about this, Randy," he finally spoke up. "Be honest. There is still time for you to go back. I'll find someone trustworthy to take you home."

"No," she answered quickly. "I'm not leaving you."

He sighed in resignation, then bent his legs and rose, bringing her up with him. He pulled the plug of the bathtub. "Let's rinse off good and I'll wash your hair for you under the shower."

"I can do it."

"No. I like doing it."

Saying nothing more, they rinsed off thoroughly, washed and rinsed again before Jake soaped up her hair for her and massaged her head, rinsed her hair, then helped her out of the tub so she could dry off while he washed his own hair.

"Enjoy being clean because neither one of us will have

much chance to do something like this once we hit the trail," he reminded her.

"I know."

"Our best bet will be to find towns with a bath house, or a decent whorehouse where the women do a lot of bathing."

Randy vigorously toweled her hair. "I suppose you think I would let some prostitute help you take a bath and shave you and such," she joked. "I don't intend to leave you alone for one minute with such women." She stopped toweling off to look him over. "My God, Jake, you are a beautiful specimen of man."

Jake snickered. "Until you study my brain, and then all the outward scars. And by the way, I was often alone with the kind of women you mentioned when I rode far from home as a marshal," he answered. "Some of those places are the only ones where you can wash up and get a decent, home-cooked meal. You know damn well nothing ever happened. Whorehouses are like old home visits to me." He drank in the sight of her slender nakedness.

Randy wrapped her towel around herself. "Now I feel self-conscious. And don't tell me some of those women didn't do their best to entice you, and most women like that are much younger. I mean, look at you, handsome, infamous and dangerous. That's a tempting combination for a woman."

Jake rinsed his hair. "Is that why *you* were attracted to me?" He asked the question with a teasing smile.

Randy laughed. "No," she answered. "I was attracted to you because you were a challenge. I wanted to see if I could reform you."

Jake shut off the water and faced her. "Didn't work, did it?"

She walked closer and dropped her towel again, then

ran her hands over his hard-muscled stomach, over his chest and upper arms. "No," she answered, "because it didn't take me long to realize I loved you just as you were." She reached down and gently stroked his penis. "Like you said about me. I love every inch of you ... inside and out."

Jake groaned with the want of her all over again. He stepped out of the bathtub and picked her up in his arms to carry her to the bed. He heard the clang of another streetcar four stories below, thought about the world down there that had changed so drastically since he first met this woman back in Kansas ... that terrified, wide-eyed woman in that supply store who watched him shoot a man down.

Before this was over, he would shoot down a lot more men ... and hope they both lived through it. He moved onto the bed and settled on top of her. "Let's make the most of this bed," he told her.

Randy kissed his chest. "Do what you want with me," she answered.

He laid her back and took her again, realizing that the sun hadn't even set yet. They had time to do this for another couple of hours if they wanted to, and could still clean up again, get dressed, and go downstairs to the hotel's fancy restaurant for a decent meal.

Then again, room service might be even better. That would leave more time for making love to this woman he had no right touching in the first place all those years ago. But she by-God offered herself, and how was a man supposed to resist something like this?

He kept it slow and gentle, relishing every taste and touch, her unique scent, and every sweet groan from her lips, knowing that after tonight, such luxuries would fade into a grand landscape of tumbled rocks, vast horizons, hard riding ... and danger.

CHAPTER TWENTY-TWO

Randy watched from the train platform as the horses were loaded into a cattle car along with saddles and supplies. Dallas's horse and saddle would be left behind, already sold to the owner of the stable where everything else had been kept overnight. Charlie was assigned the dubious honor of riding with the horses to keep an eye on them on the way to Cheyenne. Cole would take over from Cheyenne to Wilcox. After that, each man would be responsible for his horse and gear as their little posse made the journey along the Outlaw Trail to Hole-In-The-Wall and on to Shelter.

"The train is leaving soon," Lloyd told Jake. "The marshal had better get here pretty quick."

Both men stood with Randy between them inside Denver's Union Station, all three of them waiting for Hal Kraemer to show up with what would be called official U. S. Government papers. The mixture of crowds talking, short blasts of train whistles, the rushed hissing of steam and a baby crying somewhere created a din of noise inside the station that seemed too loud to the ears of those used to nothing more than a few cows lowing and birds singing.

"I know the ride ahead will be hard," Lloyd commented, "but the quiet of big country sure will be easier on the ears."

"I was thinking the same thing," Jake answered. He scanned the crowd as he lit a cigarette. Several of those who passed by stared at him, glancing at the .44 he wore tucked into the front of his belt. Wearing a gun and holster in the city was no longer allowed.

"I think that's Jake Harkner," he heard someone say.

Randy felt like a shrinking violet between two sturdy trees, Jake on her right and Lloyd on her left. She straightened her shoulders, trying to stretch herself to a slightly taller stance, but she could only manage to reach their shoulders. Lloyd looked down at her and grinned, moving an arm around her. "It's not too late to change your mind, Mom."

"I have no desire to change my mind," Randy answered. "Not after coming this far."

"Here comes Hal," Jake said. He kept a cigarette between his lips as more people rushed past them and a cloud of steam poured from the side of another train engine.

Lloyd kept his arm around his mother's shoulders. "Stay close, Mom, or we might lose you in the crowd."

Hal reached them, a deputy by his side. The sandy-haired young deputy removed his hat and nodded to Randy, then looked at Jake as though he was eyeing the President of the United States.

"Randy," Hal said when he reached them. "You are as beautiful as ever." He also removed his hat, then bowed to her.

"Thank you, Marshal," Randy answered with a smile. She held her common, wide-brimmed cowboy hat in her hand. "I'm not exactly dressed like a proper lady. I am all riding skirts and leather, but where we are going, that's all that is necessary."

"I understand," Hal answered, "but I sure wish you would have stayed home on the ranch. I'm not real happy about what's going on here."

"Neither am I," Jake answered. "But she has her mind set."

Randy wore her hair in one thick braid down her back now, planning to keep wearing it that way, not just to hide her blond mane, but also to keep it from getting tangled on the long ride. Jake had braided it for her, deciding it would be easier to quickly twist the braid under a hat to hide it when necessary. He gave the braid a light tug now as he joked about "making a man out of her" on the trail.

Hal looked her over. "I don't think that's possible, Jake," he answered. He met Jake's gaze with a twinkle in his eyes. "I trust you won't do anything that means I would have to arrest either one of you," he added, hinting at the fact that more than once they'd had their differences over Jake breaking the law and getting away with it.

"I'll do my best to obey the law," Jake answered.

"But there *is* no law where you are going," Hal reminded him.

Jake grinned. "Well, then, there is your answer."

Hal laughed and turned his attention to his deputy. "Jake, Lloyd, this is Deputy Marshal Desmond Beaker. He wanted to meet the famous Harkner men and has vowed not to mention where you are going or why."

Desmond shook both men's hands. "It's an honor to meet you both," he told them. "I know you were marshals back in Oklahoma. There sure are lots of stories about those years. I've read everything Jeff Truebridge ever wrote about you."

Hating that kind of attention, Jake tolerated the hand-shake and what he felt was undeserved praise. "Jeff is a good man, and the only one who ever wrote the truth," he told the deputy. "Don't go believing the trash they write in those dime novels. It's all made up."

"Well, sir, a lot of people believe those crazy stories. And I suspect some of them are pretty close to the truth." He nodded to Randy again. "Ma'am, you are as lovely as Marshal Kraemer told me you were."

"Why thank you, Deputy," Randy answered.

"Give me that envelope," Hal told Desmond.

The deputy obeyed, and Hal handed an envelope to Jake. "There are your orders, supposedly issued by the U. S. Government, giving you permission to go to Shelter, Wyoming and bring law and order there."

Jake slipped the envelope into an inside pocket on his leather vest. "I will be forever grateful, Hal," he told the marshal.

"Just don't get me in trouble," Hal told him. "And I don't want to hear the sensational news that the famous Jake Harkner met his demise in an outlaw town up in Wyoming, and all the stories that would go with that. If I get asked how you got those badges and papers, I will have to say you must have somehow stolen them and forged the orders."

Their gazes held in mutual respect. Jake turned his attention to the deputy. "I take it you will have the same story if things go wrong."

"Oh, yes sir! But I'll still brag that I've met you."

Jake just shook his head. "That's nothing to brag about, Deputy Beaker, but I appreciate the fact that you think so."

The train they were boarding filled the inside of the

station with the noise of three short blasts of its whistle, followed by another blast of steam. Randy watched Cole and Terrell slide shut the door to the cattle car and climb aboard. Hal shook Jake's hand once more. "Watch your back," he said. "Remember that a badge in that country will paint a big red circle on you, front and back."

"I got used to that kind of danger back in Oklahoma," Jake told him.

Lloyd took an envelope from where it had been tucked into his belt and handed it to Marshal Kraemer. "Will you see this gets mailed out to the J&L for me?" he asked. "It's a letter for my wife."

Kraemer took the envelope. "Sure, I'll do that for you, Lloyd."

Lloyd shook his hand. "It's important. She's been through a tough time. We just managed to smooth things out a little when this happened. I hate leaving her right now."

"Of course you do." Hal squeezed his hand. "I'm sure things will work out, Lloyd. Nobody can handle a situation like this the way you and Jake can."

"I hope you're right."

"Stop and see me when you get back," Kraemer told Jake. "I want to hear how it went, and if possible, I'd like to know that you got your hands on that little girl."

Jake nodded. "I'll do that." He glanced past Hal to see Dallas hurriedly approaching the platform. She waited as Hal and the deputy said their goodbyes and left, then ran up the platform steps, holding on to her hat. She walked up to Jake and threw her arms around his middle. "Jake, I just had to see you once more and tell you how sorry I am about everything."

Jake grasped her arms and pushed her slightly away. "I don't give a damn how sorry you are, Dallas, but whatever happens, you keep quiet about it. Got that? I am using the law to *break* the law, and I don't need some judge knowing about it."

"I will never say anything about it, Jake. I just hope you get Dee Dee out of there without getting yourself killed." She wiped at real tears with gloved fingers. "Be careful, Jake. Don't trust anyone but my girls, and the men on that list of names I gave you." She turned to Randy. "I don't need to tell you to take good care of him. And you be careful, too. You can trust the girls at my emporium. They will hide you if you need hiding, and they will make sure you are comfortable if Jake has to leave you behind."

Randy noticed a flicker of genuine concern in Dallas's eyes. "Thank you," she told Dallas.

Dallas glanced at Jake once more. "Sometimes I look at you and it seems like the last forty years or so never happened. You're still the handsome, wild, reckless sonofabitch you always were, Jake Harkner. You wouldn't be doing this if you weren't."

Randy looked up to see Jake watching after her. "You loved her," she said, more as a statement than a question.

Jake met her gaze. "In another life, and when I had no idea what love is supposed to be. She sure taught me that I didn't know a damn thing about it."

Lloyd boarded the train, then took his mother's hand and helped her up the steps of the passenger car. Jake put his hands to her waist and lifted at the same time. They entered the passenger car, nodding to Terrel, Cole and Charlie before sitting down.

"I saw you hand that letter to Hal," Randy told Lloyd.

"Writing to Katie was a good idea. She will love getting that letter."

Lloyd rubbed at his eyes. "I feel so bad leaving her just when things are getting better between us. I miss her already."

"Lloyd, you can go back if you think you should," Jake told him. "I understand those kinds of decisions. God knows I've had to make the same choices myself."

"I'm not leaving you to this without my backup, Pa. Besides, time apart will help me and Katie see what's really important, and she has Evie and Brian, and her folks with her while I'm gone. It's just that ..." He shrugged. "I guess I have never loved her more than right now."

Jake glanced at Randy. "I know that feeling, too."

Their conversation was interrupted by the conductor, who walked down the aisle asking for tickets. He stopped when he saw Jake.

"Well, bless my buttons if it isn't Jake Harkner!" he said, loud enough for everyone in the passenger car to hear. "It was only a week or so ago that a woman who got off this train was asking me all kinds of questions about you, Jake. She was looking for somebody to take her out to your ranch. She ever make it out there?"

Jake scowled at him, hating that the conductor had brought everyone's attention to him, let alone the fact that he called him by his first name, as though they were great friends. "None of your business," he answered. "Mister, I don't even know you."

"Oh, but I know *you*. Last I saw of you, you were just home from a trip to Chicago with the missus. You going back? I believe you were visiting a lawyer friend, and that reporter who writes that column about you." The conductor faced the rest of the passengers. "Folks, this is the famous

Jake Harkner, flesh and blood! I was at the cattlemen's ball a few years ago when Jake put a gun to a man's head and –"

"Hey!" Jake yelled. "Do *you* want to live?"

The conductor turned, wide-eyed. "Sir?"

"I don't think it's your job to broadcast personal things about a passenger to all the others." Jake held out two tickets. "Take these, and tend to your job. Don't go bragging about something you really don't know anything about."

The conductor nodded. "Of course." He took the tickets. "But I *was* there that night, and I saw that shooting. I am going to save these tickets as souvenirs, Mr. Harkner, something touched by Jake Harkner himself."

"Well, mister, I could give you something to *really* remember me by, like the touch of my fist in your face."

The conductor stiffened. "I, uh, I'll settle for the tickets."

Charlie snickered loud enough for everyone to hear.

"You're messing with the wrong man," Cole spoke up from farther back in the car.

Charlie laughed even louder.

Some of the passengers snickered and spoke to each other in whispers. Some just stared, not sure what to think. A few actually looked afraid. The conductor slipped the tickets into his jacket pocket and stumbled a little when the passenger car jerked into motion.

"Is that one of your pearl-handled guns?"

Scowling, Jake looked across the aisle at a boy about Young Jake's age. He was staring at the .44 Jake had tucked into the front of his belt. "Don't be thinking that carrying a gun is something to brag about, son."

"Oh, I know. But can I see it?"

Jake pulled his hat down a little. "Absolutely not."

"Leave the man alone, Jack," the boy's father told him.

"Thank you," Jake told the man. He leaned his head back and pulled his hat over his face.

Farther up the aisle a little girl with a cascade of reddish-brown hair wiggled off her mother's lap and ran to where Jake sat. She poked his leg.

"Are you a bad man?" she asked.

Jake pushed his hat up and leaned forward. "I'm as bad as they come, sweetheart, but never toward little girls."

"Rebecca, get away from there!" her mother called to her.

Jake glanced at the woman. "Ma'am, I have eleven grandchildren, including two little girls about her age. She's no bother." He shifted and reached into his pants pocket, taking out a piece of peppermint candy. "You like candy?" he asked.

The girl nodded.

Jake handed her the peppermint. "Then you can have this. But you have to go on back to your mother and let me sleep."

The girl flashed a beautiful smile. "Okay! Thank you!" She leaned up and kissed Jake's cheek before running off.

Lloyd just chuckled and shook his head, leaning back to watch out the window as the train moved out of the terminal. Randy reached over and covered Jake's hand with her own. "It's a good thing that girl's mother doesn't know why you carry peppermint candy."

Jake squeezed her hand. "And I hope I'll find a chance to use it sometime on this trip."

Randy smiled as she gripped his hand tighter. The train sped up, not heading west to Chicago, but north ... to places nowhere near as civilized.

"I wonder how many of these passengers would ask the

conductor to stop the train and let them get off if they knew everything about me," Jake said quietly.

"They need to know all the *good* things you have done," Randy answered, keeping hold of his hand.

"Spoken by a very prejudiced woman," Jake answered with a sad smile. He leaned back again and pulled his hat over his face. "Enjoy the ride, Mrs. Harkner. This is as comfortable as you're going to be for quite some time."

CHAPTER TWENTY-THREE

Randy looked beyond the little town of Wilcox at the looming Big Horn mountains on the horizon. Their huge, purple outline reminded her that rugged country lay ahead. She checked the ropes and straps that held her supplies to her pack horse, making sure everything was secured. The rest of the men did the same after unloading the horses and gear from the cattle car.

Jake walked over to Jenny and adjusted the double rigged cinches he insisted Randy use. He gave Jenny's belly a little punch to make sure the horse wasn't puffing up to keep the cinch from being too tight. "Come on, girl," he told her. "I don't need my wife falling off because you didn't let her tighten this saddle properly."

"Jake, I checked. I told you I would take care of my own rigging."

"I can't help making sure." He yanked at the cinch. "I got another couple of inches out of this one." He checked the breast strap and britchin to make sure the saddle couldn't slip forward or backward. "We will be going up and down some damn steep inclines over the next several days. The last thing I need is for your saddle to slide forward and throw you over Jenny's head, or to get your neck broken."

"Stop thinking the worst. We have traveled this trail together before, remember?" Randy petted Jenny's forehead. "I take it you plan to get in a few miles yet today?"

"The weather is nice, and we have about five hours of daylight left. I figure to ride at least ten miles before we make camp."

Randy noticed a few men at a nearby general store watching them curiously. She figured Wilcox was not a common stop for travelers. Most passengers on this route were headed for Utah or California, not outlaw country. In fact, their little group of travelers were the only ones who got off here.

The train whistle gave out three short blasts that echoed against the surrounding mountains, blew off some steam, then chugged away. Four men sitting at the storefront were still there, staring. A woman wearing a purple feathered dress stood near them.

"We are being watched," Randy told Jake.

Jake finished checking the straps on her supply horse. "I am well aware. We have a lot of horses and supplies. Robbers watch for things like that." He walked back to where she stood and gave her a quick kiss. "And a woman getting off here only adds to their curiosity. You don't often see a bunch of men traveling with one woman." He looked toward the supply store. "Wilcox isn't much of a town. If I remember right, there are outhouses behind that store. If you need to use one before we leave, I'll walk you over."

"Sure."

Jake called out to Charlie. "Watch everything," he told him. "I'm taking Randy around behind the store."

"Sure thing," Charlie answered. "You figure on getting in a few miles before dark?"

"I do. Make sure your rigging is good and tight. There are a lot of steep escarpments in this part of the country, and the ground is mostly loose gravel and rock, so a horse can start to slide. It's rough country out there, hard on the horses' hooves and tendons." Jake took Randy's arm and led her toward the general store. A wagon clattered by, raising dust.

Randy noticed a sign that read "Main Street," which seemed silly, since it was the one and only street that comprised the little town. She glanced at one of the men watching. He chewed on a cigar as he nodded to her. "I have a feeling they think I might be a woman of ill repute," she quietly told Jake.

"Yeah, well you will get stares like that most of the time in this country. You stay close to me. Tomorrow I want you to pin the end of that braid to the back of your hair and keep it hidden as best you can. And I know it's too warm for a jacket, so I'm giving you one of my vests to wear. One that is too big for you will hide what gives your feminine attributes away." He walked her down an alley between the general store and a saloon.

"My feminine attributes?"

Jake grinned. "I love the fact that you are well endowed, Mrs. Harkner, but those curves can be dangerous out here."

"Then I will do my best to save them just for you."

Piano music poured from an open side window of a saloon as they walked past the buildings. Jake stopped in front of an outhouse that had "LADIES" painted on the front of it with pink paint. He knocked on the door, then opened it to check inside. He turned and looked down at Randy. "You're in luck. It's been freshly painted. Sorry about no indoor plumbing. Unless things have changed a lot up here, we won't find any real conveniences the rest of this trip."

"This is all we used when we first married, and for several years after that. I will be fine."

Jake pulled her close for a quick hug. "And you used to keep ours scrubbed and painted. I don't know how you did it, but ours were always halfway pleasant." He rubbed her back. "This sure isn't anything like the luxury of those beautiful bathrooms at Peter Brown's mansion in Chicago, is it?"

"I could never live in a city like Denver or Chicago, and you know it." Randy knew what Jake was thinking. He believed she should have married someone like Peter instead of a wanted man with no future. Peter was their lawyer and good friend who always managed to keep Jake out of trouble, including helping keep him from being hanged in Denver. Randy had worked for Peter back in Guthrie, and she knew the real reason Peter was always willing to help them. He did it for her. The man loved her, but he was wise enough to never cross Jake. The fact that Peter loved her was simply understood but never spoken. "Our own indoor bathroom back home is all the luxury I need," she reminded Jake aloud. "And I am fine with what we will have to put up with in the meantime."

"I already miss our bed at home," Jake told her. "Miss being able to make love to you whenever the need arises, and it arises every time I look at you." He opened the door to the ladies' outhouse. "Right now we had better get back to business."

They both took care of necessities and headed back down the alley to where Lloyd and the rest of the men waited. "Your turn," Jake told them.

"Hell, we was beginnin' to wonder what you two were doin' back there," Terrel teased.

"Just get the hell back there and hurry it up," Jake answered. He walked Randy to her horse and helped her mount up, giving her rear a quick squeeze as he did so.

"Hey, Mr. Harkner, keep your hands to yourself," Randy joked.

Jake grinned and walked over to Thunder, taking his gun belt from where he'd hung it around the pommel of his saddle. He strapped it on.

Randy watched him tie the holsters to his thighs, then drop his .44's into both holsters. He shoved his extra pistol into the belt behind his back. She had to look away, knowing it was very likely that before this was over, he would use those guns more times than she cared to hear them fired.

Lloyd trotted Cinnamon over to his parents, then sidled close to Jake. "Did you notice the men sitting in front of the store?"

"I noticed."

"There were four of them. While you and Mom were out behind, two of them rode off, Pa. You know what that means."

Jake sighed. "They are going after more men."

"I'd sure bet on it," Lloyd answered. "Lots of horses, supplies and a woman are quite a prize to men in these parts. That bunch probably waits at the train depot just to see who gets off and if they might have money and horses. We will have to be on the lookout. They know how many of us there are, so they will likely show up with more, figuring to outnumber us."

"That's nothing new to me, Son. You either." Jake paused to light a cigarette.

"We had better keep Mom between us," Lloyd suggested. "And if they don't show up before we make camp, she'd better sleep between us, too."

"I already thought of that." Jake took a drag on the cigarette and turned to Randy. "Do you still have that extra barrette in your hair for hooking that braid up under your hat?"

"I do."

"I was going to wait till tomorrow, but pin it up now." He reached into his left saddle bag and pulled out a leather vest, then hooked the open sleeve around her saddle horn. "Put that on when you're done hiding that hair."

Randy knew he was worried. "And how are you going to hide those good looks and that great smile from the whores when we reach the next town?" she asked, hoping to lighten his mood while they waited for the rest of the men to come back from using the outhouse.

Jake grinned. "I'll give them my meanest, most ornery look."

"That won't help, Mr. Harkner. You look good no matter what kind of face you show."

Jake snickered. "My God, woman, you sure have a one-sided opinion of me."

"I'm a woman."

"Really? I seldom notice."

Randy smiled as she finished pinning up her braid, then slipped the too-big vest over her own. She sat up straighter. "That better?"

Jake looked her over. "Let's just say you'd better ride between me and Lloyd, and slump down a little."

Randy shook her head. "Do you know how much I love you?"

"Not as much as I love you."

Charlie, Terrel and Cole returned and mounted up.

"Keep your eyes wide open," Jake told them. "Trouble is brewing."

"We saw them," Charlie answered.

They headed out, but as they passed the general store, one of the men who'd eyed them called out to Jake. "Hey! Where are you boys headed?"

Jake kept his cigarette between his lips. "None of your business," he answered.

The man grinned. "You shouldn't have brought a woman along," he yelled. "Do you men share her? There's other men around who would pay good money for her. If you're all gettin' tired of her, we've got a couple of women here we can trade for her."

Jake halted Thunder and dismounted, handing Thunder's reins to Lloyd.

"Pa?"

"It's okay. You just keep an eye on the second man still sitting in front of the store." Jake walked over to face the man who had suggested selling Randy. The man sported a long, full beard and a big belly.

"Oh, shit," Terrel muttered.

"No man gets away with insulting Jake's wife," Charlie quietly added.

"You want to run that by me again?" Jake asked the bearded man.

The hefty man smiled through brown teeth and stood up then slowly came down the porch steps. He pushed back his hat and rested his right hand on the butt of his sidearm. "Run what by you?"

"What you just said about trading women."

The man faced Jake squarely, but stepped back a little. "I said I know men who would pay plenty to fuck that woman you brought along, if you're wantin' to sell her. I'm one of them. You're gonna meet the rest somewhere on the trail out of here. And they won't offer money. They will just take her, so you'd be wise to leave her here and take the two I can offer you."

"That woman is my wife, and she's not for sale."

The man spit out a wad of tobacco. "That's too bad, on account of you just made a poor decision, mister. Maybe you need to learn our ways out here."

To everyone's shock, Jake's gun was drawn so fast that no one actually saw him draw it. He fired three shots, all into the bearded man's chest, and in a matter of only one or two seconds. The saloon woman standing nearby screamed as the bearded man stumbled backward, his eyes wide with shock.

"Jesus," Charlie commented.

"It so happens that I *do* know men's ways out here," Jake told the man. "And now I'll have one less man to worry about when your friends try stealing our horses and supplies ... and my *woman*."

"You bastard!" the saloon woman screamed. "A minute ago Carl was sitting here minding his own business."

"And I was minding *my* own business, while he tried to figure out how he could get his hands on my supplies and horses," Jake answered. "And my *wife!*" He holstered his gun as the man he'd shot fell back against the wooden steps, then slid to the ground, leaving blood stains on the steps. Trembling and dying, he looked up at Jake.

"Who ... are you?"

"The name is Jake Harkner. And you should have asked me before you insulted my wife. Once I told you who she was, you should have apologized. Maybe then you would not be lying there dying."

"Jake Harkner is dead!" the second man in front of the store yelled. Tall and lanky, he stood up, but he was unarmed.

"He is very much alive," Jake answered. "And if it's true other men will be coming after us, you will end up losing a lot of friends today." Jake turned and walked back to Thunder.

"You fucking murderer!" the second man yelled as he hurried down to check on the man Jake shot. "What are you doin' here, anyway? Where are you headed?"

"I'm headed for Shelter, and plenty of men there will lose their lives before this is over unless I get what I'm coming for. You can go ahead and spread the word. Anybody who tries to make trouble will die, and I won't bother asking questions first!" Jake glanced at Lloyd. "Let's go."

"Jake, that man – " Randy wasn't quite sure what to say.

"That man needed to be out of the way," Jake answered before she could finish. "The sonofabitch would have shot me in the back the minute I turned around. Trust me on that." He kicked Thunder into a gentle lope, and the others followed.

"Let him be, Mom," Lloyd told her. "He knows what he's doing. Out here you have to show them right away where you stand, or you get trampled real quick. Pa told you that you would see that other side of him out here."

"Whoo-wee!" Charlie shouted. "I ain't quite so worried now. Ain't no better man to ride with than Jake Harkner." He rode up beside Randy. "You okay, ma'am?"

Randy put a hand to her chest to soothe her pounding heart. "I am fine, Charlie. I'm just worried about how many more men Jake and you and the others will have to face down before this is over."

"Don't you worry about that. With Jake in charge, we'll get that little girl and get the hell back to the J&L, all in one piece."

They headed north, the saloon woman and the dead man's friend still shouting curses at all of them.

CHAPTER TWENTY-FOUR

RANDY PULLED LOOSE the cinch straps for her saddle, then the breast collar and britchin. Before she could unload the saddle, Jake reached around her from behind.

"I'll get it," he told her.

"Jake, I told you I can do these things myself. When are you going to let me?"

"When hell freezes over, and I'll freeze with it because I'll probably be there." He hoisted the saddle off of Jenny. "Just use the blanket to rub her down," he added.

Randy watched him carry the saddle over to a grassy area and set it down beside his own. He had not said a word for the last ten miles or so since they left Wilcox and the man he'd shot. As well as she knew her husband, it still surprised her how unaffected he seemed to be over the fact that he had just killed a man. He walked back to her pack horse and began unloading items most commonly used when they made camp.

The sun was fast sinking behind the Rockies to their west. Charlie took care of Terrel's horses while Terrel made a fire and was already heating a pot of coffee on a grate over the flames. "Just lighten the loads on your pack horses for tonight," Jake called out to the others. "You don't need to completely unload them. And rub down your riding horses. Check their hooves for stones while we still have a little light left." He untied a couple of potato sacks full of personal supplies and set them on the ground.

Randy watched him as she shook out her saddle blanket, then used it to rub down Jenny's back. "Jake, are you all right? You haven't spoken or looked at me since we left Wilcox."

"I'm fine."

"No, you aren't." Randy paused, draping the saddle blanket over Jenny's back. She faced Jake, who was checking over the hooves of her pack horse by the fast-fading light of dusk. "Knowing you, you aren't upset over shooting that man back in town – not like some men would be. You're more upset by what he said, aren't you?"

Jake dug a little too hard at a stone in the pack horse's foot. "He shouldn't have used such filthy words in front of you. And any man who talks about buying and selling women like a damn mule deserves to be shot."

"And you know darn well that kind of talk is to be expected out here, Jake. If I'm not upset, why are you?"

He let go of the pack horse's leg and patted its rump, then faced her. Randy couldn't read those dark eyes, if he was angry, regretful, or hurt. "I hated what he said. That's all. I'm sorry you had to hear it."

"And I will very likely hear that kind of talk again. I have developed a pretty hard crust when it comes to things like that, especially after –" Randy hesitated at bringing up her kidnapping by Brad Buckley. It was something that ate Jake right to the bone. "You have to stop treating me like some china doll who has lived in a castle tower all her life,

Jake. You know better. When I decided to come along on this trip, I knew what to expect. And I promised not to be a bother, so let me take care of my own horses and supplies." She grabbed the blanket from Jake so she could finish rubbing Jenny down, but Jake grasped her arm, turning her to face him.

"Randy, it bothered me more than it normally would because I told you not to come with us in the first place. Do you know how hard it is on me to watch you be disrespected? I hate what men are thinking when they look at you."

"And do *you* know how hard it is on *me* to stay behind and wait?" Randy couldn't help raising her voice a little as she pulled her arm away. "I can put up with just about anything to be with you, and *willingly,* so please don't treat me like a fainting flower. I have seen and heard and done things far beyond what most women could handle, but here I am, Jake. I'm not going anywhere. And don't you dare tell me I deserve better. You've tried to push me out of your life for 37 years. When are you going to give that up and just accept the fact that I don't faint at the sight of blood and I don't gasp in horror at insults and foul language. Stop babying me. Think of me as one of the men if you have to."

Her last remark finally brought a grin as Jake looked her over. "Are you serious?" He took her arm again and walked her farther into the grove of trees where they had chosen to make camp. "I can accept everything else you said, but treating you like one of the men is not something I could ever do." He lifted off her hat and tossed it aside. "Woman, you might be as *tough* as any man, but I sure as hell could never *treat* you like one."

Randy broke into a smile and moved her arms around his middle, resting her head against his chest. "At least let me do my share of the loading and unloading and helping make camp on this trip. I am perfectly capable of taking care of my own horses and gathering wood and peeing behind rocks and washing in creeks. I promise that when things get rough or dangerous, I will do what you tell me to do, but only because you are leading this bunch and you know what *you* are doing in places like this."

Jake kissed the top of her head. "Then you need to understand that I didn't kill that man just for what he said. Keep in mind that I can read a man's eyes damn good, and he was considering shooting me the minute I turned around. *That's* why I shot him."

Randy pulled away a little and looked up at him. "That's what Lloyd told me. Whatever you do in situations like that, I understand, Jake. God knows you have handled such things a thousand times."

Jake touched her cheek. "Just remember that if you feel you need to use your handgun or that shotgun, you do it," he told her. "Don't hesitate. It's when a man hesitates that he dies. That's why I did what I did back there, and we are in lawless country now, so don't worry about the right or wrong of it. For the most part, men out here will respect you as my wife, but there will always be ones like that man back in Wilcox. I'm sure his friend has already ridden out to the rest of their gang to tell them I killed one of their own, so I want you to sleep between me and Lloyd tonight. And it's not because I am treating you lke a fainting flower, as you put it. It's because you are one of the prizes they will be after."

"Pa, if you two are done playing footsie over here, we need to make plans for keeping watch tonight." Lloyd was walking toward them, carrying his rifle.

Jake put a hand to the side of Randy's face and leaned

down to give her a quick kiss. "I know," he told Lloyd. "Coffee ready?"

"Almost. I set up my saddle and bedroll beside Mom's saddle. Some of the men are still hobbling their horses." Lloyd turned to go back to camp.

"Wait," Jake called out.

Lloyd stopped, and Jake walked closer. "I don't think we should hobble the horses. Put up a picket line in case we need to mount up and ride fast. We could get into a situation where we won't have time to untie hobbles."

"Sure."

"I'll bring you some more bread and honey," Randy called out to both of them. She finished rubbing down her horse, after which she carried her bedroll and the supplies Jake had unloaded over to where Lloyd had set his saddle beside her own. She wrapped a loaf of her homemade bread and the jar of honey and a spoon into a towel and carried it to the campfire while Charlie picketed the horses per Lloyd's orders.

Lloyd, Jake, Terrel and Cole sat around the fire drinking coffee and talking about who would keep watch tonight.

"Those fuckers back in Wilcox will be after our asses," Cole was saying. "You can bet on it."

Randy walked into the firelight and set down the bread and honey.

"Oh, hell," Cole said. "Sorry about my language, Randy. I didn't know you were so close."

Randy straightened and put her hands on her hips. "You don't need to baby me on this trip, Cole, or worry about offending me. Jake and I have already had a discussion about that. Some of you probably heard our little argument. It was my choice to come along, so whatever you men need to do or say, feel free. Just don't leave me out of your plans."

Jake grinned and shook his head. "My very brave and stubborn wife is determined to be fully a part of this," he told the others, "so don't worry about your language or anything else you think might offend her. Just make sure she isn't left alone ... *anywhere.*"

Terrel pushed back his hat. "Well, Jake, it's like this. Just a few hours ago we saw what you did to a man when he insulted your wife, so you gotta admit, you givin' us permission to behave like bunkhouse boys around her is a little unnervin'. We don't do it around any of the women back on the ranch, so it ain't likely we will do it now."

"This is different," Jake reminded them. "If you don't behave like men who can handle themselves, we won't be able to get the better of the powers that be in Shelter. Sometimes that will mean foul language and fist fights and shooting first and asking questions later. It could also mean visiting the bawdy houses to get information, not that Charlie and you, Terrel, would object to that."

The men all snickered. "You including yourself in that?" Cole asked.

"Wouldn't be the first time."

"And Mom is a saint," Lloyd joked.

"God knows she must be," Cole commented.

"I'll never argue that one," Jake answered. "And as my wife just reminded me a few minutes ago, she's no fainting flower. And she's by-God right. No fainting flower would have lasted three days married to me. Randy has lasted 37 years married to a sonofabitch she has more reasons to hate than any of you even know about."

"Why, hell, it's your handsome charms and that great smile that keeps her so loyal to you, Jake," Cole told him.

The rest of them laughed while Jake poured himself a cup of coffee. "If that's so, what's *your* excuse for attracting Gretta?" he asked Cole.

"Oh, well, I'm not what you'd call handsome, and I don't have that great smile, but I have charms only Gretta knows about."

That brought even more laughter, along with hoots and whistles.

Jake put out his hand. "All right. All right. Maybe we need to talk about something else. Let's get back to what we do about keeping watch tonight."

Randy smiled to herself and cut some bread while Terrel chewed on jerky and Charlie joined them with a can of beans he'd opened. He began eating them cold out of the can.

"I don't think anybody will come tonight," Charlie told them. "That man back there in Wilcox needed time to ride wherever he had to go and let them know about the man you shot. Then they will need time to figure out what to do about it and then ride out to find us. I think they will wait till light, and with treeless country ahead, we will see them coming from miles away."

Jake smoked quietly while Randy passed around slices of bread and the jar of honey. "I have enough bread for a couple more nights," she told them, "so you men should be able to make some of your food supplies last a little longer."

"We sure will miss your bread once it's gone," Terrel told her.

"Thank you." Randy sat down between Jake and Lloyd.

"Make sure you eat, too," Jake told her. He handed her his cup of coffee and took another drag on his cigarette before addressing the rest of the men, who had quieted because their mouths were full of bread and honey.

"Charlie is probably right about nothing happening tonight," he told the others, "but you can't be too cautious out here. That means that as we ride tomorrow, we will need to keep an eye out for places where we can take cover in a hurry if necessary. I figure once we spot men coming toward us, we shouldn't try to get ahead of them. That's too dangerous for the horses. My plan is to take cover and wait for *them* to come to *us.* Word spreads fast among outlaws, especially about men you'd best not challenge if you want to live. That's what I want these men to learn when they come up against us. It is part of the reason I shot that man back in Wilcox."

"Hell, just your name is all they need to hear," Terrel spoke up.

"Maybe so. Maybe not." Jake poked at the fire with a stick that had fallen away. "I am hoping that by the time we reach the town of Shelter, the men there will think twice about giving us trouble. And maybe on the way we can pick up a couple more men. There are a few honest ranchers out here who live normal lives. Granted they sell horses and cattle to outlaws, but they are otherwise good men. We will probably have to stop a time or two at some ranch to rest and clean up. Maybe we can find a couple of men who are willing to volunteer to come with us to Shelter."

Charlie finished his beans. "Makes sense. But we still should take turns tonight keeping watch."

"That's a given," Cole added.

"I agree." Jake finished his cigarette and threw the butt into the fire. "And I think we should douse the fire before we turn in. There is a bright moon tonight. The firelight detracts from what we can see beyond that, so if the fire is out, it will be a lot easier to spot movement nearby, and harder for those who might be out there to spot us. We need two men at a time. One to watch the horses, and one farther away to watch the surrounding area. Any volunteers?"

"I'll watch the horses," Charlie told them.

"I'll find a higher place to watch farther off," Cole added.

Lloyd took a chain watch from his pocket. "It's 9:30. Cole, I'll relieve you in three hours. Pa wants my mom between him and me, so you take my bedroll when I relieve you. My mother is the first thing you should think about protecting before anything else, because, believe me, I don't want to have to deal with my father if something happens to her. I don't think any of you want to, either."

"Hell, no," Terrel put in. "I'll take Charlie's place watchin' the horses. Same time. 9:30. Lloyd, you wake me up when you get Cole up."

"I will."

"It's settled then," Jake told them. "And tomorrow, I want all of you armed and have plenty of ammunition ready. We could end up in an all-out gunfight."

"That don't worry me when you and Lloyd are along," Charlie told them. He poured himself another cup of coffee. "I'm taking my bedroll over by the horses. "

"If anybody needs to take care of personals in the middle of the night, call out your name so I know who is moving around out there," Cole told them.

They all finished eating, doused the fire and turned in, everyone keeping their guns close and using their saddles for pillows. Jake leaned over and kissed Randy lightly. "If Lloyd or I suddenly jump up, or one of the men calls out, you stay right here, got that? Unless Lloyd or I come for you, don't even raise up your head."

"I won't."

"He means it, Mom," Lloyd told her. "Listen to your husband."

"I always do," Randy answered.

Lloyd snickered and turned over.

"Yeah, right," Jake added.

"But I do!" Randy insisted.

"Listening isn't the same as *doing*," Jake told her. "In this case, you need to do both."

Randy pulled her blankets up to her chin. "I am perfectly ready for anything I have to do, which is why I am sleeping with my clothes on, even my boots."

Jake chuckled deep in his throat and turned away from her. "Baby, I can think of a lot more reasons for you to keep those clothes on."

Terrel and Lloyd both laughed.

"I heard that," Charlie called out from where he'd bedded down.

Randy scowled. "Men," she muttered. "Before this is over, all of you will find out just how mean and ornery I can be," she told them.

"I can attest to that," Jake added. "She bosses me around like a damn warden. Try living with her."

"I would if you would let me," Terrel joked.

"And I can't believe some woman's husband hasn't shot you by now," Jake answered.

"I can attest to the mean and ornery," Cole yelled from somewhere. "Randy beat the shit out of me when she found out I let you ride off alone three years ago, Jake. She lashed out at me like a cornered cougar. It was all Lloyd could do to pull her off of me."

Randy smiled and closed her eyes, saying a quick, silent prayer that friends of the man Jake had shot would not come after them. But she knew better. Men in places like this did not let such things go without an attempt at revenge.

Somewhere in the distance wolves yipped and howled. The moon rose huge and bright above the dark outline of mountains to the east. Other than the wolves, the air hung dead quiet, so quiet that it almost hurt a person's ears.

CHAPTER TWENTY-FIVE

"Man, oh, man, this is the most wide-open country I have ever seen." Charlie rode up beside Jake as they made their way north. "Colorado is just as big and beautiful, but not so many wide-open spaces between mountain ranges. I think Colorado is greener, too. Wyoming's mountains are pretty barren." He used his shirtsleeve to wipe at sweat on his face. "Colorado is also cooler."

"Not in winter," Jake told him. "Winters are more fierce here."

"Yeah? I guess you should know."

Jake nodded. "I spent two full years here after that gun battle in California when Lloyd was a baby." His horse shook his mane and neighed as the riders kept their steeds at a gentle walk.

"Cole says he's been here, but it was a long time ago," Charlie said. "He says nothing has changed."

"I agree. We might be in the year 1902, but you wouldn't know it out here. The landscape tells you why outlaws and deserters and men who escape prison come here to get away from the law. The first time I came here I was only about sixteen. I came up here from Texas. Those redrock cliffs in the distance and the wild, yellow, endless grassland ahead looks the same as it did then."

"Had to be hard on a sixteen-year-old kid."

Jake paused to light a cigarette. "Not for me. Living with my *father* was a hard life. I found relief here." He took a deep drag on the cigarette. "This is where I learned to shoot fast and straight, learned to rustle livestock and picked up tips on how to rob banks and trains. I made friends with a man from Missouri, followed him back there. We fell in with a gang of cutthroats, and we did a lot of rustling, robbed banks and trains, ran guns during the war. My face ended up on Wanted posters. That's when I met and hung out with Dallas. After I left her, I met Randy, and she knocked the bad out of me as best she could."

"She's a wonder."

Jake nodded. "That she is." They rode silently for a while. Jake scanned the massive valley of grass in shades of gold, red-rock cliffs and mesas surrounding them on both sides. "I've been back here twice since Randy and I married," he told Charlie.

Memories cut into Jake's heart. He glanced back at Randy, who was talking and laughing with Terrel. He smiled and looked ahead again. "God knows me leaving Randy back in California for two whole years is just one of a long list of reasons she should have left me. She was pregnant when I left, had Evie all alone and nearly died. I met up with a close friend from my past out here and together we found a good job with a wealthy rancher in southern Colorado, so I took a chance at changing my name and I sent for Randy. I didn't think she would come, but she did, and she welcomed me like I had never left."

"You're a lucky man, Jake. Only woman I ever loved left me for a richer man."

Jake shook his head. "It takes all kinds, Charlie. How I ended up with such a good woman, I will never understand."

"You had better watch out, Jake. Terrel is flirting something awful with her back there."

"Terrel knows how far he can go," Jake said with a quick laugh. "I can tell when a man respects a woman, and all of you respect Randy."

"We sure do. How can you *not* respect a woman like that?"

Jake nodded. "She's put up with a lot being married to me. We lived in peace on that ranch in southern Colorado quite a few years, until a soldier who came visiting recognized me from somewhere, maybe an old Wanted poster. I was arrested, and Randy went another four years alone while I was in prison. Evie met and married Brian, but Lloyd kind of went to pieces and fled to outlaw country. When I got out of prison, Randy and I both came up here looking for him. He'd been captured by a man he'd wronged, and he was in a bad way – nearly died. We brought him home, which by then was Guthrie, Oklahoma. I had been sentenced by a judge to serve as a U. S. Marshal in No Man's Land. Believe me, that truly was a punishment. It was three of the worst years of my life, but at least Lloyd and I ended up closer than ever. He served right along with me as a deputy."

A hawk flew overhead and filled the air with screeches, a sound that only accented the vast loneliness of outlaw country.

"Lloyd met Katie in Guthrie," Jake said. "He had already loved and lost a beautiful young woman when we lived in Colorado. Her father sent her away because he believed Lloyd came from bad blood. When we ended up in Guthrie, Lloyd found out he had a son by that girl. That's Stephen. He found the girl, Beth, and married her, but she died, so Katie has been a mother to Stephen ever since she married Lloyd."

Charlie nodded. "Katie is one beautiful woman, I'll say that."

"She's had a lot of problems over losing babies, but those two are very much in love. They will make it okay." Jake wrapped Thunder's reins around the pommel of his saddle and let the sure and dependable horse amble on its own while he lit a cigarette. "I don't know why I am telling you all of this ... your remark about Randy, I guess. She went through hell with worry while Lloyd and I went after some of the worst sons-of-bitches who ever lived, and you know the things that happened later ... to Evie ... to Randy ... all due to my past. I should be dead and burning in hell by now, but here I am."

Charlie shook his head. "You underestimate how important you are to your family, Jake. Your angel of a daughter thinks you're a god, and your granddaughters have no clue what you really can be like. And Lloyd, he's a good man. A lot like you, except he is a little wiser about when to draw a gun. He's a bit more of a diplomat."

"Thank God for that. You need to be in this day and age. I come from old stock, the days when law and order was pretty scarce in a big part of the country." Jake crushed out his cigarette against a piece of leather he kept tied to the pommel of his saddle so as not to damage the saddle itself. He made sure the cigarette was fully out before he tossed the butt into the grass they rode through. He'd seen grass fires out here, and sometimes men and animals got caught in them.

"Jake!"

Jake turned to see Cole charging toward him.

"Dust in the distance," Cole told him. He handed Jake a pair of binoculars. "Maybe four or five miles back, but they're coming fast. They must have got a start late yesterday and maybe kept riding after dusk trying to catch up." He waited while Jake raised the binoculars and studied the approaching riders. "I guess they could just be a bunch of men who don't know anything about that man you shot yesterday," he suggested. "But we had better make sure. You want to just hunker down and wait for them to catch up?"

Jake turned Thunder and watched a bit longer while the rest of their party caught up and halted their horses. "There must be ten or twelve of them, maybe even more than that." He lowered the binoculars and handed them back to Cole. "They are raising a lot of dust. No normal gang of men or cowboys would ride that hard in country like this unless they were after something and probably plenty mad. There is no doubt in my mind it's friends of the dead man."

"We don't know for sure what's ahead, Jake," Cole reminded him, "as far as a good place to hole up. About five minutes ago we passed that low spot full of boulders. It's the only place I can think of where we could hunker down and battle it out. There's not a lot of choice out here till we get into the mountains ahead. This is some of the most treeless country west of the plains. I say we head back to that little valley of rocks. Might be kind of dangerous gettin' down in there. Looked like a loose, rocky slope, but it would be a good place to have it out with whoever is coming."

"And they would have trouble getting to us," Jake said.

"We would have the advantage. They would have to expose themselves trying to get to us, which would make them easy targets."

"It's gonna be at least two men to every one of ours," Cole reminded him.

"I've been through worse odds." Jake trotted Thunder back to the others, pulling his pack horse with him. "Head back to that rock-strewn low spot we passed a few minutes ago," he ordered. "Men are coming, but we have a good half hour or so before they get here. We need a place to take cover and there is nothing but wide-open country ahead." He trotted Thunder over to Randy. "Stay by me till we get there. Hang on to your saddle pommel when we go down and let me lead Jenny. It's a dangerous escarpment." He glanced at Terrel. "When this starts, I might be all over the place. You stay with Randy, no matter what happens, understand?"

"No problem."

"And make sure she stays down."

"Jake – "

"No arguments!" Jake told Randy. "I don't mind you protecting yourself once we reach town and maybe having to use that shotgun, but this is a different kind of gun battle. Bullets will be flying, and a shotgun won't do you any good. Just find a good place to keep your head down and then *stay* there. Do whatever Terrel tells you to do." He turned to the others. "Let's go!" He kicked Thunder into an all-out gallop.

The others followed, their horses' manes and tails flying. By the time they reached the rocky dropoff, Jake could see the cloud of dust coming toward them without needing binoculars. He took Randy's reins from her hands.

"Hang on to the pommel!"

Shouts of "Whoa!" and "Easy!" along with whistles and

curses filled the air as men and horses eased their way down a hill made up of loose rock and gravel, the riders leaning far back as their horses were practically straight up and down as they pranced and maneuvered their way to the bottom. Jake was quickly off his horse and yanked his rifle from its boot as the others dismounted. "Go ahead and keep your shotgun handy," he told Randy. "But you shouldn't need it. I don't intend to let even one man get anywhere close to you, but I sure as hell can't make any guarantees. Otherwise, you stay down like I told you."

There was no time or reason to argue. Terrel took Randy's arm and led her and their horses farther down and around a huge boulder. He quickly tied both horses' reins around a couple of old logs and left the pack horses tied to the lead horses.

Randy knelt behind the large boulder while men continued shouting back and forth. A couple of the riding horses reared and whinnied, sensing alarm. Jake, Lloyd and the others looked for advantageous places to hunker down.

"Stay in that shadow this side of the boulder," Terrel told Randy. "You will be a lot harder to see if you stay out of the sun. And if you lay all the way down, they won't see you at all. Keep an eye on the horses." He cocked his rifle and leaned against the boulder, his head just above it.

"Do you think they saw us come down here?" Randy asked.

"Bet on it," Terrel answered.

"Where is Jake?" Randy asked.

"Up and over to our right, but I'm figurin' he'll be all over the place once the shootin' starts."

"Let's get this over with and teach this bunch a lesson," Jake yelled. "If we take these men, we will send a message to anybody else who tries to stop us!"

The horses calmed down as things quieted while the men stood ready behind the tumbled boulders. Randy looked around, realizing there were no high cliffs in this area, which made her wonder where in the world the boulders came from. There seemed to be no place higher from which they could have fallen. Even the ground above was bare, other than smaller rocks, scrubby plants and high grass. It was as though God had picked up a handfull of boulders from someplace else and then threw them like dice across the high plains. There also was no explanation for the logs Terrel had tied the horses to. There were no trees around. Where on earth had the logs come from?

"God be with us now," she said softly. She realized then she had not had a chance to touch Jake or talk to him, to say a quick *I love you,* or *be careful.* For some reason, the shootout back in California between Jake and former gang members from his outlaw days became vivid in her memory. How Jake had survived that, she would never understand, but he'd managed to keep Lloyd, then just a baby, from getting shot. After that he spent two years right here in outlaw country, a place that seemed to have a way of continually drawing him back to his old life.

She could hear them then, the thundering hooves of horses ridden by men bent on killing all of them ... stealing their horses and supplies ... and maybe her along with it all.

CHAPTER TWENTY-SIX

SENSING the approaching danger and the tension of the men who lay in wait, Jenny and other horses began to balk and tug at their reins. Randy grabbed Jenny's halter, as well as the halter to Terrel's horse and hung on, a tough job because both animals had pack horses tied to them. Randy was forced to step out away from the boulder as she tried to calm them. "Whoa! Whoa!" she soothed.

"Stay against the boulder," Terrel ordered. He stood with his feet braced on a flat rock, his elbows on top of the boulder, rifle aimed above.

"That's hard to do when these horses get jittery," Randy answered. "They are pulling at the log!"

"Sweetheart, your life is more important, and I don't aim to answer to Jake if somethin' goes wrong," Terrel answered sternly. "Let them go if you have to. If they run off, we will go find them later."

"But those men might steal them along with our supplies!"

"We will make do."

The horses finally calmed, and everyone waited while

things suddenly fell quiet. Randy wondered what was going on above the cliff, until someone shouted, "Don't shoot! I'm comin' to talk. I've got no weapons on me!"

"Speak your piece," Jake yelled back. "Just keep your hands away from your body."

A bearded, middle-aged man appeared at the rim, arms stretched out. He wore the garb of any average cowboy, but a black leather vest instead of the more common brown one. "Would one of you be Jake Harkner?"

"I'm here," Jake answered from behind another boulder. "And I saw a couple of men sneaking around that half circle to my right. If they intend to shoot at us from a different angle, I guarantee they will die, and so will *you* before this is over." Jake turned to Lloyd. "Keep an eye on that ridge to our right."

"I'm just makin' sure you're the man we are after," the man above yelled.

"I have no grievance with any of you," Jake replied. "What the hell do you want?"

"You know damn well what we want, Harkner!" came the reply. The bearded man at the top stepped back a little. "I'm Joe Betz. The man you shot back in Wilcox was my *brother*, Carl."

"Then this is between you and me," Jake shouted. "Why should a lot of innocent men die for your brother?"

"Bullshit!" Joe yelled. "You really think I'm gonna go up against the likes of Jake Harkner on my own?"

"That's what a loyal brother and a brave man would do," Jake shouted back. "But apparently your brother isn't worth your life, unless you can gather a lot of other men and attack like a pack of coyotes! Is that what you are, Joe? A scared coyote?"

There came nothing but silence for the next several seconds.

"Why did you kill my brother, Harkner?"

"Because he was fixing to shoot me in the back!"

"Carl ain't no back-shooter!"

"Mister, I can read a man's eyes better than I can read letters! I didn't even *learn* to read until middle-age, but by-God, I've been reading men's eyes since I was old enough to know when my drunken father was getting ready to lay into me!"

"They say all Carl did was insult your wife, but hell, he didn't know you were married to the woman. He even offered to trade you two good whores for her. Two for one."

"For that I would have just beat him. But I saw those eyes, Joe. He wanted me dead. When I got off my horse and walked up to him, I was ready to take off my gun belt and have it out, but I could see he had other plans. So I would advise you to leave now, or lose a lot of men!"

"There is one looking at us from the right, Pa," Lloyd told him. "Rifle in hand."

"*Shoot* him," Jake told him. "They have to know we mean business."

Lloyd aimed his rifle and shot the man, who cried out and fell backward, out of sight. Lloyd stayed in position watching the half wall to the right.

Joe jumped back out of sight himself when the shot was fired. A good deal of yelling and cussing could be heard above, but no one peered over the wall.

"You okay?" Jake asked Lloyd quietly.

"I didn't like doing that, but I remember our days as marshals, and the kind of men we went up against. If they don't realize we mean business, we're the dead ones, not them."

"I'm sorry, Son, but that's how it's going to be out here, especially when we get to Shelter. Keep watching that ledge." Jake shifted his position and kept his rifle aimed above. "You want me, you come down here and get me, Joe!" he yelled. "I'll do this one-on-one, or all your men up there can join the party. We will gladly take you on, two men to one! No problem!"

"Speak for yourself, Jake," Terrel said under his breath. "More like six men to one when it comes to you, but I ain't no Jake Harkner."

"Jake would not have had you come along if he wasn't sure of your abilities, Terrel," Randy told him quietly. She huddled against the boulder, filled with dread. How many men had Jake taken on when he went after those who had threatened his granddaughters three years ago? Eight? Ten? She couldn't remember. The only thing she knew was the condition her husband was in when Lloyd brought him home, such a bloody mess he didn't even look like himself.

She let go of the horses for a moment and dared to peek over the boulder. Just as she did so, another man appeared above, brandishing a rifle. Jake shot him befoe he could say a word.

"Stay down!" Terrel told Randy.

She ducked back down as the men above again exchanged shouts and curses. "Joe, let's get out of here!" someone yelled. "That's Jake Harkner down there, and he ain't gonna give up. He can kill a man and then sit down and drink a beer like it was nothin'!"

"But he shot my brother!" Joe screamed.

"Carl wasn't worth my life," someone answered. "Maybe yours, cuz you are his brother, but he didn't mean all that much to the rest of us."

A shot rang out from above.

"Anybody else want to tell me my brother's life was worth nothin'?" Joe screamed.

"Sounds like he shot the man who wanted to leave," Jake told Lloyd.

"He just did us a favor," Lloyd answered. "Those men aren't going to help him now."

They heard the hoofbeats of horses galloping off.

"We'll stay, Joe," someone yelled.

"Not me!" another yelled. "I don't aim to tangle with Jake Harkner. It ain't *my* brother he killed."

Pounding hoofbeats told Jake and the others that even more men were leaving.

"I wonder how many are left," Jake muttered. He looked around at the others. "Be vigilant," he yelled to them. "Some of them are still up there." He shouted toward the top of the wall. "Hey, Joe! Are our odds better now?"

"You sonofabitch!" Joe yelled back. "I just lost half my men!"

"Seems to me like that's *your* fault, not mine. You will lose the rest of them if you keep shooting them for cutting out on you!"

More silence, then all of a sudden all hell broke loose. Seemingly every man up top came to the rim at once, too many to count before a barrage of rifle fire filled the air. Jake and his men had the advantage of cover, while those above had to show their heads in order to shoot. Those below fired at will, and one after another, the men above fell back, most of them shot in the head. Lloyd and Cole concentrated on the half wall to the right, while Jake, Terrel and Charlie picked men off along the main ledge.

Randy's ears hurt from so much gunfire, and the horses below whinnied and reared in terror, some of them breaking loose. Randy tried to grab Jenny's reins, but when the horse and Terrel's both scrambled in confusion, they pulled up the log they were tied to and it swung around and hit Randy across the side of the face. Randy grunted but didn't scream, afraid of distracting Terrel. Jenny fell then, nearly catching Randy's right leg. Randy managed to scrambled out of the way in time, but Jenny lay there twitching and kicking. The pack horse yanked itself away and ran off.

Randy saw blood on Jenny's neck. "Jenny! Oh, no!" She lay over the horse and clung to its mane. Terrel grabbed her arm and yanked her back behind the boulder. "Stay in the rock's shadow!" he ordered.

Randy huddled there, weeping over the fact that Jenny had been shot. The shooting finally stopped, and by then, Joe Betz lay halfway down the draw, sprawled in the loose gravel and bleeding from the chest. Two other men from up top also lay dead below, having jumped over the ledge to come after Jake and the others. Three more men were draped facedown over the ledge, none of them moving. All went silent above.

"I count six, Jake," Cole yelled.

"I'm going to see who is left up top," Lloyd told his father.

"Be damn careful," Jake told him. "Charlie! Go up top with Lloyd and see what's there," he yelled louder.

"My pack horse is down!" Cole yelled. "She's shot dead!"

"Jake! Randy is hurt and Jenny is down!" Terrel yelled. He knelt beside Randy. "Honey, I'm sorry I jerked you away like that." He set his rifle aside. "Damn, your face! Your right cheek is bruised and bleeding. It's starting to swell, too."

"The log," Randy answered. "It swung around and hit me when the horses reared."

"Shit," Terrel muttered.

Jake clung to his rifle as he ran to the bigger boulder below where Terrel and Randy had taken cover. "Randy!" He sat her up straighter. "My God, there is blood all over her shirt!"

"She ain't shot," Terrel assured him. "The horses got out of hand is all. Jenny's been shot, and your wife laid over her. That's Jenny's blood."

"Jenny!" Randy wept again as she leaned forward to stroke the horse's mane. "Jake, do something!"

Jake pulled her away from the horse. "You know I can't," he told her. "We will have to shoot her." He moved her back into the shade of the boulder. Her hat had come off in the melee, and hair from the side of her head had come loose from the braid. Jake pushed some of it behind her right ear.

"It's like she said, Jake," Terrel explained. "The horses reared and the log they were tied to hit her in the face while she tried to hang on to them. I'm sorry. She kept trying to hang on to the horses and I had to pull her back more than once. I might have bruised her arm."

Jake sat down beside Randy and pulled her into his arms. "Thank God she didn't take a bullet." He glanced back at Jenny. "Get it over with, Terrel." He held Randy's face against his chest while Terrel took aim.

Randy jumped and let out a little cry when Terrel fired.

"It's all over," Jake told her.

"Lloyd ..."

"Lloyd is fine. He went up top to see what's left of those men." Jake noticed a bruise forming on her left arm, in the perfect shape of a thumb and fingers.

Terrel noticed Jake studying the bruise. "Jake, I did

what I could to keep her out of range," he said. "The woman is so damn stubborn."

"You think I don't know that? I tried to argue her out of coming at all, but that doesn't work once she makes up her mind." He kept smoothing back Randy's hair. "Word will spread fast now about what happened here today. I doubt men will give us any more trouble until after we reach Shelter."

"Yeah, and then things will get really bad," Terrel reminded Jake. "A lot more men against us, and bein' in town, a lot more places to hide. And we won't know who is a friend and who is the enemy."

"We'll fnd out soon enough." Jake raised his voice. "Is anybody hurt!" he yelled.

"I'm okay," Charlie shouted. His words were repeated by Cole.

"Pa!" Lloyd shouted from above. "There are eight more up here. It's a real bloodbath. Most of the horses took off."

Jake gently set Randy back against the boulder. "Hang on," he told her. He stood up to talk to the rest of the men. "Leave the bodies. Some of those men will come back and take care of them," he yelled. "And they will find their horses. Hey, Charlie!"

"Yes, Sir."

"Check Joe Betz," Jake ordered. "He's the one in the black vest lying halfway up the draw. I doubt he's alive, but go check. The rest of you gather the horses."

"Sure thing," Charlie yelled.

Terrel set his rifle aside and took Randy's hand. "I'm sorry, honey, but I couldn't help you and the horses both, plus keep an eye on those men shooting at us."

"It's not your fault."

Jake came back to kneel beside her again.

"I don't mind bein' in charge of that beautiful woman under normal circumstances, Jake, but when she could get hurt, it makes me nervous as hell," Terrel told him.

"You did all you could. We'll get organized here and keep going. If memory serves me right, there is a decent ranch on our way north. My guess is we can reach it tomorrow or the next day. I'm sure we can get some help there. Randy needs to rest in a real bed for a day or so. She can ride with me the rest of today and tomorrow until we get there. Try to find her pack horse and load her saddle and gear onto it. We will get her another horse to ride when we get to the ranch."

Lloyd scrambled down to where Jake sat with Randy. "Mom!" He knelt beside them.

"She got hurt when Jenny reared and pulled the log she was tied to up with her," Jake explained. "Jenny was shot, so Terrel finished her off."

Lloyd took hold of Randy's hand. "Mom?"

"I'm okay," Randy answered.

"She sounds groggy." Lloyd frowned, looking closer at her eyes. "You'd better keep hold of her when we leave, Pa. I think she's half knocked out."

"Damn it," Jake muttered.

"Betz is dead, all right," Charlie yelled to the others. "Jesus, Jake, you shot him all to hell."

Terrel took his canteen from his horse and pulled a clean handkerchief from his supplies. He wet the handkerchief and knelt down to apply it to Randy's cheek. "Hold that there, Jake, and we will gather things together. Stay here with your wife."

The next 45 minutes were spent rearranging supplies taken from Jenny and from Cole's pack horse. Getting men and horses back to the top of the draw was difficult because of all the loose stone on the steep incline. Because Jake feared Randy would pass out on the way up, he had the men throw a rope down so he could tie it around himself and hang on to Randy with one arm as they pulled him up from above."

"Jake, I'll be okay," Randy insisted. "I just ... need some water."

Jake took his canteen from his gear and held it to her lips, advising her not to drink too much. He replaced the canteen and mounted Thunder. Lloyd helped Randy climb up onto the horse in front of him, and Randy settled in sideways. She rested her head against Jake's chest.

"I can ride on my own," she told Jake. "We don't need to do this."

"No, you cannot ride on your own," Jake insisted. "Besides, we won't have a horse for you until we make it to that ranch. Wrap your arms around me and don't argue."

"But I said I wouldn't ... be a burden."

"You aren't. You can't help what happened." Jake kicked Thunder into a rhythmic canter. He used his right hand to control the reins and kept his left arm wrapped around Randy. "It scared the hell out of me when I saw that blood on your shirt. I'll help you change clothes when we make camp." He gave her a squeeze and kissed her hair. "I love you."

Randy breathed in his familiar scent. How many of those men had he shot? Now here he was, holding her and talking about love. The man was an incredible mixture of ruthless and gentle, vicious gunplay and loving care.

They all rode away, leaving chaos and bloodied bodies behind. Jake Harkner was coming to Shelter, and by the time he got there, Ty Bolton and his men would know he meant business.

CHAPTER TWENTY-SEVEN

Lloyd kicked Cinnamon into a faster lope and rode up beside his father. "How is she, Pa?"

Jake kept his left arm tight around Randy. "I'm not sure. She's half out of it, and I know she's in pain. I'm worried she might have a cracked cheekbone."

"You want me to take her for a while? Your arm has to be getting tired, and you can't change her position to the other side or she'll be resting on her own wound."

Jake didn't answer right away. He just stared ahead.

"Pa? You're blaming yourself, and you don't need to. And don't baby her. It will just make her mad."

More silence.

"Pa, Mom would want you to take a break, so hand her over."

Jake bent his head down and kissed her hair. "I can't let go of her."

"Yes, you can. She's tough. She'll be okay." Lloyd remembered that awful day when they found his mother in an abandoned cabin after she'd been kidnapped by Brad Buckley and his bunch. Sometimes the worst memories came visiting when a man was extra tired. Jake Harkner could handle blood and guts and beatings and the ugliest of ugly, including death. But not when it came to his wife. It gave Lloyd the chills to think what life would be like if his mother died before his father. The family would soon lose both of them, because Jake Harkner would not go on living without her.

"Pa, she won't care if she rides with me for a while. I've helped you with her in a lot worse times, so hand her over. We've been riding for four hours now. It's a little early, but why don't you ride on ahead with a couple of the other men and find a good place to camp for the night."

"I'm keeping her with me."

"She needs off that horse and needs that wound cleaned up. Go make camp somewhere and we will get something into her stomach and let her sleep. We can take care of things in Shelter a lot better if you don't have to worry about Mom."

Jake heaved a deep sigh. "I fucking betrayed her, Lloyd."

Lloyd frowned with worry. "Pa, what the hell are you talking about?" Was that a trace of tears in the man's eyes?

"If it wasn't for me, she would have led a whole different life. She would have lived many more years back in Kansas with her father, probably married a banker, or a lawyer like Peter Brown, lived a nice life, had five or six kids, all with her husband beside her instead of alone. It all would have been different if not for me."

"But you followed her west and saved her life. Remember? If not for you she would be dead from a snake bite."

Jake shook his head. "You don't understand because you don't know all of it. She never should have had to sell her farm and head west in the first place, not alone anyway. She would have had her father with her."

Lloyd inched his horse closer. "You aren't making any sense. Now hand her over for a while and rest your arm and find a good place to let Mom rest. Riding this way can't be helping anything. Let's take care of her for now and then you can explain yourself." He reached over and grasped Thunder's bridle, then yelled for Charlie to help get Randy onto Cinnamon.

Jake kept a tight hold when Charlie dismounted and came over to help Lloyd shift her to his horse.

"Damn it, Pa, if you are so concerned, then do what I told you to do," Lloyd said sternly. "Hand her over and let's find a good place to stop and tend to her. She needs food and water, and so do the horses. We're riding through great grassland, so let's get all the horses completely unloaded and rubbed down and let them graze. It's been a hard day, and I'm sure the men need a little time to get over that mess we left back there."

Jake dropped Thunder's reins and moved his other arm around Randy while Lloyd moved his horse around to Thunder's right side.

"Randy, you awake?" Jake asked softly.

Her only reply was a groan.

"*Te amo más que a nada en esta tierra,*" Jake told her. "*Los arreglaremos a todos. Pronto te sentirás mejor.*"

Spanish. Lloyd sighed. Jake usually spoke in his mother's language only when he was feeling extra emotional. Jake finally pulled her to the right and let Charlie help hang on to her as Lloyd took her onto his horse. He glanced at Jake and saw devastation in the man's eyes.

"Damn it!" Jake said. "Look at her face! People will think I beat on her or something."

"The people who matter know better. Now go find us a place to make camp. Tomorrow we will make it to that ranch you talked about and she can get all cleaned up and sleep in a real bed."

"Keep a good hold on her."

"Do you really think I'd let my wounded mother fall off a horse?" Lloyd asked. "Now, get going."

"If she comes around, you explain why I gave her over to you. Tell her I just needed to ride faster and find a place for her to sleep."

"Pa, she will understand. Get going!"

Reluctantly, Jake kicked Thunder into a much faster gait and whistled for Terrel to help him scout for a place to camp. Charlie looked up at Lloyd. "He's really upset, ain't he?"

Lloyd looked down at his mother, then shifted her a little to make sure she was properly settled. "We had better hope she makes it through this without any more injuries," he answered. "God help us if she gets hurt any worse, or takes a bullet. None of you will want to be around my father if that happens, especially if he loses her. And I hope we find that little girl in good condition. If she's been abused, you won't need to wonder what hell is like. You will see it through Jake." He urged Cinnamon into motion, wondering what the hell Jake was talking about when he said he'd betrayed his wife. He figured it was just his way of looking at the fact that he'd married her when he shouldn't have.

"Jake?" Randy muttered.

"It's me, Mom. Lloyd. You're okay. Pa went to find a good place for you to rest. The sun will be down soon and it will be nice and cool. We should all be able to rest easy tonight."

Randy moved her arms around him and rested her head against his chest. "Jake, tell me ... you didn't get hurt," she said brokenly.

Lloyd just grinned and shook his head. The only thing on her mind was Jake. "No, I'm not hurt," he answered. If it comforted her to think he was Jake, then fine.

An hour later found them camped against a high cliff that shielded them from a west wind that carried with it a chill from higher, snowy mountains farther west. In spite of the heat of the July days, nights in this country cooled down fast when there was no foliage of any significance to hold the heat. There were no trees here, but the men had gathered wood and tied it in bundles from the camp they had made the night before in a small patch of pines.

"Gonna miss Randy's bread and honey tonight," Charlie said as he sat down near a fire and poured himself some coffee. "Guess it's hardtack and another can of beans."

They all noticed that Jake had said little since making camp. While the others took care of removing saddles and supplies from the horses and turning them out to graze, Jake had carried a groggy Randy behind a boulder so she could relieve herself. She was still unable to walk straight. By the time Jake brought her back to camp, she was wearing a flannel nightgown.

"Go get her things back there and burn that damn bloody shirt," he told Lloyd. "It's Jenny's blood and it will never come out, so I'd rather she didn't see it at all. Find a clean shirt for her and fold her clothes. Put them back in that canvas bag she uses. She'll sleep better in this gown than with all her clothes on again."

"I made up some comfortable bedding for her with your pillow and mine plus hers so her head will be protected,"

Lloyd told him. "A saddle for a pillow might not be good for her right now."

"Thanks."

The others watched Jake quietly as he laid Randy on a pile of blankets. He vigorously massaged her feet and lower legs, then wrapped her into the blankets, saying gentle things to her in Spanish. He wet a clean rag and laid it against her badly-bruised and swollen right cheek. She jumped a little when he touched it.

"It's okay," he told her. "The cool water will help the swelling."

"Hurts," she mumbled.

"I know it does." He left the folded rag on her cheek. "Are you warm enough?" he asked her.

"Jake?"

"I'm right here."

She opened her eyes and looked him over in the dim light of early evening. "Are you really ... okay? What about Lloyd?"

"We are both fine, and it's good to hear you sound more lucid." Jake leaned closer and kissed her forehead. "I want you to eat some bread and take a couple of those aspirin I take for my leg. Eat something first so the pills don't upset your stomach." He managed to get her to sit up a little and eat a piece of bread that Lloyd cut for her. She drank down a couple of aspirin with water from a canteen, then lay back down. In moments her eyes were closed and she seemed to be sleeping.

"I hope it's just sleep," Jake told Lloyd.

"It probably is. It's been a long day for all of us, Pa. Every one of us will sleep good tonight, but we still have to take turns keeping an eye on the horses. There are always wolves to worry about, but I doubt we will be bothered by any men."

Terrel finished his coffee and walked over near them. "I'm sorry, Jake, but I told her to stop worryin' about the horses and let them go if they ran off. She kept tryin' to hang on to them. Is there still a bruise on her arm where I forced her to get back behind that boulder?"

"There is, but you did what you had to do," Jake answered. "Sit here with her for a bit. I need to talk to Lloyd about something."

Terrel sat down beside her, and Jake motioned for Lloyd to walk several yards away with him. He lit a cigarette before he spoke. "You need to know the reason I was so angry when Dallas showed up, Son. It wasn't just the fact that she nearly got me killed."

Lloyd frowned with confusion as Jake took a deep drag ont he cigarette. "I could tell something was amiss," he told Jake. "I've never seen you behave around a woman like you did around Dallas."

Jake exhaled. "Yeah, well, when she showed up after all these years, it brought back another memory, something more than her betraying me like she did, something I had been hiding from your mother." He ran a hand through his hair and took a deep breath before telling Lloyd about the pocket watch. "Your mother told Evie about it before we left, but there wasn't time to tell you, too."

So, that's the betrayal you were talking about earlier. Lloyd turned away and let the story settle in his mind. "Pa, Mom told you she considered the watch a gift from God. It made her happy to have something of her family after all these years, so you shouldn't feel bad about it. How could you have known the man who died would end up being her father? Mom understands that."

Jake studied the moon, still big and bright but oddly shaped because one little slice of it was now in the earth's shadow. "But I knew later on, before I married her. I had no right marrying her without telling her the truth. It might have changed her life."

"Maybe. But none of us has any control over where God leads us, Pa. And He led you right to Mom. Something tells me that even back then she would have understood about that attack on her farm. She fell hard for you, so I don't think she would have turned you away. And if she can accept what happened, then you have to accept it, too. You know damn well that's what Evie would tell you, so let it go, Pa."

"I'm trying, but after keeping it in all these years, it's pretty hard to change how I feel about it."

"The fact remains that you finally told her, and that's what is important," Lloyd told him. "You took the risk and she loves you anyway. And right now she needs to wake up with your arms around her. Doesn't she always say your arms are her safe place?"

Jake took a last drag on his cigarette, which had burned down as he told Lloyd about the raid and the watch. He dropped it and stepped it out with a hard twist of his boot to make sure no embers were left. "My arms can be a real dangerous place sometimes."

"You know what I mean. Go over there and eat something and sleep beside Mom. Hold on to her so she doesn't wake up all confused."

Jake glanced over at the fire, then turned to Lloyd. "You aren't upset by what I just told you? The man we killed in that raid would have been your grandfather."

Lloyd shook his head. "How well do I know you?" he asked. "I know how much you regret it. I also remember how you nursed me yourself after I got shot in Denver. I don't think you slept for days. Knowing you were there helped me get well. I know your heart, and it's not black like some people think. The man who took part in that raid wasn't the man I've known all my life. And he's not the man who tends to Mom like she's made of fine china. I know both sides of you, and so does Evie, so don't think anything we find out about you is going to make any difference."

Jake shook his head. "Both of you help me figure I must have a little good in me. Look how you turned out." He put a hand on Lloyd's shoulder and led him back to camp. "How are things with Katie?"

"Better than things have been in a long time. We had a good talk that day we got back with those rustlers, and I sent her a letter before we left Denver. We'll be okay."

"And I'll bet you are real anxious to get back home to her. You two have a lot of making up to do."

"You're damn right," Lloyd answered. "And in the best way there is to make up."

Jake gave him a teasing shove. "Then we had better get ourselves to Shelter and get this business over with."

"I just hope we don't run into any more trouble before we reach Shelter."

Jake headed straight for Randy when they reached camp.

"She's been sleepin' this whole time, Jake," Terrel told him.

"Thanks." Jake ate a little bread and jerked meat before turning in. He pulled two more blankets over both him and Randy, then wrapped her in his arms. The blankets covered her head so that her nose and ears would stay warm. Jake bent his head and whispered near her ear. "Who do you belong to?"

Randy let out a little moan. "Jake Harkner," she mumbled. "Now ... and forever."

Jake kissed her forehead and smiled. He'd feared a head injury, may be a concussion, but she still had her wits about her. "I love you," he told her softly.

Randy's only reply was a deep sigh.

CHAPTER TWENTY-EIGHT

Randy awoke to the smell of coffee and bacon. The sun was peeking over a string of low mountains to the east. *Must be part of the Big Horns.* She took a moment to clear her head, then winced at the pain in her right cheek. She sat up a little and noticed all the men were sitting around a fire. *What on earth are all the men doing over there eating breakfast without me to help?* She shed her blankets and stood up, then gasped at the realization that she wore her flannel nightgown instead of her regular clothes. "Jake Harkner!" she yelled.

She grabbed one of the blankets and wrapped it around herself as Jake set his tin plate aside and stood up. "Be careful," he told her. "You've been really dizzy and only half conscious."

Randy scowled and marched closer. "Well I am just fine now. Why on earth am I in a nightgown?"

"We don't mind," Terrel teased.

"I don't reckon Jake would either," Charlie added.

"Ooooh, this is ridiculous!"

"Randy, last night you were in a bad way," Jake tried to explain.

"And I told you I would not be a burden or a weakling on this trip!"

Jake walked closer and pushed her hair behind her right ear, studying the wound on her cheek. "Getting wounded is a different matter. Nobody here sees you as a burden. Sit down and I will get you something to eat."

"You will do no such thing! I will get dressed and fend for myself! Where are my clothes?" Randy could see Jake was trying not to laugh, which only frustrated her more, especially when a couple of the men quietly chuckled.

Jake nodded toward a rock farther away. "Your clothes are all laid out over there, including a clean shirt. I burned the one with Jenny's blood on it."

Randy took a quick deep breath and put a hand to her chest. "Oh, my. Poor Jenny. Such a sweet horse." She felt unwanted tears come to her eyes. "I should have done a better job of keeping her calm."

"Honey, you are always telling me to calm down. You need to do the same. In a mess like what happened yesterday, you aren't going to be able to control the horses. Look where it landed you." He squinted a little and looked more closely at the wound. "Looks slightly better, as far as the swelling, but the right side of your face is a lovely purple color. I hope people don't think I did that."

"I'll give *you* a purple bruise if you baby me like this again. We are only a few days into this trip, and here I am being treated like an invalid!"

Jake folded his arms and frowned. "You *were* an invalid last night."

"Oh, honestly!" Randy marched over to her clothes and grabbed them up.

"Don't you want some coffee first?" Jake asked.

"In my *nightgown*? Are you serious?"

"I'm *always* serious."

"Well, sometimes you are *too* serious!" Randy picked her way over to the boulder behind which she could dress, saying the word "ouch!" several times as small stones poked her feet.

"Want your boots?" Jake called to her.

The men laughed louder at their bickering.

"No! I mean, yes! Just wait till I tell you," Randy yelled back.

"Don't you need me to help you pull the ties on your camisole good and tight?"

"I can do it, and you are a brat, Jake Harkner. A great big brat!"

Jake just shook his head and rejoined the men at the fire.

"You'd better watch out, Jake," Charlie spoke up. "She's mighty mad."

"God knows it's not the first time she's been mad at me," Jake answered.

"Don't press her too far, Pa. She might use that little gun you gave her on *you*," Lloyd told him.

All the men chuckled.

"Yeah, well, it wouldn't be the first time she did *that* either."

They all laughed harder.

"If you men are laughing at me, you will all regret it!" Randy yelled from behind the boulder.

"Damn, Jake, what happened last night that she woke up all better and full of vinegar?" Terrel asked.

"Definitely not what you are thinking," Jake answered. "Say one more thing and you will be way at the back of the line eating dust when we leave."

"Yeah? Well, for a man most other men are scared to death of, that woman over there ain't afraid of you at all," Terrel joked. "Does she beat on you sometimes?"

Jake lit a cigarette. "She damn well should have, about a *thousand* times. And no, she's never been afraid of me and knows she doesn't need to be. The day I lay a hand on that woman is the day I'll shoot myself in the head."

"Jake, I need my boots," Randy yelled. "Just leave them. I'll put them on myself, thank you. I don't need your help!"

Jake kept a cigarette between his lips. "God help me. She's going to scowl at me all day and carry on about not being a burden."

"Jesus, I sure am enjoyin' this," Cole told him. "That woman beat on *me* once, and she can throw a pretty good punch. And she damn well knew I couldn't hit her back 'cuz I would have had to answer to *you* for it."

"All right, listen," Jake told all of them. "I don't care to hear you jabbing at me all day long. And don't be surprised if she passes out again. I don't think she's as well as she thinks she is. I'm glad we don't have an extra horse yet. She would insist on riding alone, and I don't want her to. I can just see her passing out and falling off her horse."

"Well, Jake, if you don't want to put up with her scolding you all day, she can always ride with me instead," Terrel suggested. "I wouldn't mind that at all."

"Nice try," Jake answered. "I'll take my chances."

They all laughed again when Jake left them to get Randy's boots. He carried them over to her and set them beside the rock. "Here you are. How are you doing?"

"Just fine." She walked around the rock to pick up the boots. "And I hate to ask, but I need my hair brushed and rebraided. I will let you do that much for me, if you don't mind."

Jake folded his arms. "Oh, I don't mind, as long as you don't rant and rave at me while I'm doing it."

Randy leaned against the rock and grinned. "I won't." She looked him over. "You really aren't hurt?"

"No, ma'am."

"None of the others?"

"No. But we left a real mess back there, enough of a message to make the next bunch who thinks about coming after us give it a second thought. I hope the news travels to Shelter before we get there."

Randy sobered. "So do I. And if we get in another bad situation, you put yourself first, Jake Harkner. You are the most important person on this mission, so try to stay alive and unhurt."

"For the men's sake? Or yours?"

Randy leaned against the rock and pulled on her boots. "You know I mean for me. And Lloyd, of course." She sighed and faced him. "Was I really that out of it last night?"

"Do you remember any of it?"

"No. The last thing I remember is that log hitting me and then Jenny falling."

"Then there is your answer, Mrs. Harkner. Yes, you were that out of it. You even thought that Lloyd was me. You scared the hell out of all of us."

She put her hands on her hips. "Then you got just a teeny, tiny taste of what it was like for me when Lloyd brought you back from that shooting three years ago as limp and pale as a dead man." She stepped closer and poked at his chest. "And that is why I came along this time. Whatever happens, I want to be with you."

Jake grasped her arms and gently pushed her back behind the boulder. "Then please do whatever I or any of the others tell you, Randy. Terrel told you to stay back and let the horses go, but you hung on to them anyway. I know you don't like being ordered around, but in situations like yesterday, the men and I know what we are doing. So don't distract us by not listening to what we tell you. There isn't a man over there who thinks you are weak or not capable of taking care of yourself, so don't think that doing what they tell you takes away from the brave and able woman you are. Okay? They all care about you."

"I understand." Randy winced with pain when she leaned back to look up at him. "How bad do I look?"

Jake kissed her forehead. "Pretty bad."

"So bad that you don't even want to kiss me?"

"Never bad enough for that." Jake leaned down and met her lips gently.

Randy moved her arms around his neck. "I don't want the men to see me in my nightgown again."

"They didn't think a thing about it. I was just trying to make you as comfortable as I could so you would get a good night's sleep." Jake grinned. "Besides, I'm the only one who gets to see and touch what's *under* that gown."

"Keep treating me like an invalid and I won't let you see and touch anything under there for a long time."

"You have posed such threats before, and you never stick to it."

Randy scowled. "You are always so sure of yourself." She pulled away and gave him a little shove. "I just hate that I slowed everything down, Jake. That's the kind of thing I did not want to be responsible for."

"And if any of the men had been shot, the same thing would have happened. A wound is a wound, man or woman, so it still would have slowed us down. And you didn't cry or ask us to stop and let you rest. The men respect you for that."

Randy picked up her nightgown and the pillows. "I feel so bad about Jenny. Maybe it's my fault she got shot."

"Randy, it's *nobody's* fault. We are lucky that two horses and a wound you will recover from are all that went wrong. It could have been a lot worse. And now we have a little leverage. I hope at that ranch ahead we can find a couple of extra men to help us. And when we get there, I want you to take a bath and sleep some more. Don't argue with me about it."

Randy sighed in resignation. "If you say so. Just make sure they know it's your order, not something I asked for."

"Whatever you want. Come over by the fire and eat something. I'll braid your hair while the men load and saddle the horses so we can be on our way." He kissed her once more and helped pick up the rest of the blankets. "You really did scare the hell out of me, Randy."

She packed her nightgown into the canvas bag with her other things and closed it. "Just don't treat me like a baby today. I know how you can be." She started to leave.

"Randy."

She turned and met his eyes, dark and serious. "I told Lloyd about the pocket watch."

Randy paused, aching at the regret in his eyes. "All of it?"

Jake nodded.

"Well, I know my son. I'm sure he understood, just like Evie did."

Jake shrugged. "He says he understands. He also told me things are good with Katie. I think he's real anxious to get back to her."

"Then we had better get moving."

Jake watched her march off. She greeted the men, who all said they were glad to see her feeling better before scattering like scared rabbits. Jake smiled to himself. For such a small woman, she sure could raise a ruckus.

"Lloyd, please help your father pack our things while I drink some coffee and eat," Randy asked.

"Yes, Mother," Lloyd answered sarcastically. He squeezed her shoulder and stood up. "Good to see you are better. And I *am* Lloyd, not Jake."

Randy waved him off. "Get out of here!"

Lloyd snickered as he walked away. He glanced at Jake and shook his head.

"Jake, come brush out my hair and braid it for me," Randy called to him. "My brush is in that bag with my clothes."

"Yes, Ma'am," Jake replied with the same sarcasm as Lloyd. "And later tonight, if we can get a bed to ourselves, I will straighten out the matter of who is the *real* boss," he muttered.

"What was that?" Randy asked.

"Never mind."

"You're being bad, aren't you?"

"Yes, Ma'am," Jake replied. "As bad as a man can get." Jake returned with her brush.

"In your case, as bad as a man can get is *really* bad," Randy joked.

"Mmm-hmm." Jake sat down behind her and began brushing her hair while she ate a piece of bacon.

"Jake?"

"Yes, ma'am."

"I have to admit that I'm feeling a little dizzy, and my head aches."

"I knew your sudden recovery was too good to be true. I just didn't want to get yelled at for saying it."

Randy reached behind her shoulder and touched his hand. "I hope you know I was mad at myself, not you."

"I know."

"Do you have more aspirin? I don't want to take away from what you might need for your leg."

"I have enough. You are more important. Besides, God knows I am used to pain. My father pretty much made me immune to it."

She squeezed his hand and turned, kissing him lightly. "Don't lie. Do you really have enough?"

"Yes. I wasn't sure how this would go or if maybe one of the others would need something for pain, so I brought plenty."

"Good." Randy kissed him again. "Please don't tell the other men I feel dizzy and have a headache. Don't even tell Lloyd. I hate looking weak."

"I won't tell them, unless you pass out on me again. Then I won't have any other choice. And since we don't have a riding horse for you yet, you have a good excuse to ride with me without them knowing you *need* to ride with me."

Randy studied those dark eyes, knowing full well he had likely been very worried and upset when she got hurt. "Jake, I'm sure that I will be okay after a couple more days."

"Just take it easy. You could still have a concussion. That log probably knocked your brain around some when it hit you. That is nothing to take lightly."

"I know." Randy turned back around. "Finish braiding my hair, but let me drink some coffee first." She sipped some of her coffee.

Jake ran the brush through her hair a few times while

she ate a biscuit. He suddenly stopped and sighed. *"Te amo."*

Randy sensed the strain in his voice as he began braiding her hair. "I love you, too," she answered, knowing she didn't really need to say it aloud. She knew he was deeply worried about what lay ahead. "It will work out, Jake. This is God's doing, not Dallas's. He made sure she got to us safely. We will find Dee Dee and go home to the peace we find there."

Jake didn't answer. He finished braiding her hair and Lloyd helped clean up what was left of making camp and doused the fire with leftover coffee. They all mounted up, Randy settling in front of Jake, and they headed north again. Randy wiped at silent tears over the thought of leaving Jenny behind with no time to bury her. Jake squeezed her a little tighter. He knew.

CHAPTER TWENTY-NINE

RANDY STOOD on a hill watching the spectacular green valley below. She enjoyed the breeze that swept down from the mountains to her left, so cool that she wore a lightweight leather jacket as she watched Cole, Charlie, Terrel and Lloyd chase wild mustangs. Even from the distance she could hear their shouts and whistles.

"Those men sound like a bunch of Indians, the way they whoop and holler," she told Jake.

Jake moved an arm around her shoulders. "All cowboys love going after wild mustangs."

"And you would be with them if you didn't feel you had to stay here with me."

Jake scoffed. "At my age, I don't mind just watching. There is no better sight than wild horses running in a herd. I just hope they *are* wild and not branded, or we could end up in a fix with whoever owns them. I didn't like the idea of stopping, but when we spotted those horses, I figured maybe the owner of the ranch ahead would trade the cost of paying a couple of his men for fresh-caught horses. Trouble is, the men would have to be willing to ride into hell with the rest of us."

Randy moved an arm around his waist. "I have a feeling you won't have much trouble finding men willing to ride with Jake Harkner." She grinned. "And I am going to have to keep an eye on you when we go to Dallas's Pleasure Emporium in Shelter. I am not fond of you being around a bunch of harlots."

Jake laughed softly. "Our bedroom back home is *my* pleasure emporium."

"I aim to please."

"And you do a hell of a good job, Mrs. Harkner."

"You make it easy, Mr. Harkner."

Jake squeezed her closer. "How is the headache?"

"I had one for only a little while this morning. I think riding with your arms around me and being able to nap a little next to your heart helps. Plus the aspirin you gave me."

Jake pulled her in front of him and wrapped his arms fully around her. "You look and sound better today. I'm sorry you had to sleep on the ground again last night. I thought we were closer to that ranch and would get there before dark. We should be close now. Don't let it alarm you if they greet us with guns. That's just how it is out here."

There came more whistles and shouts as the men circled the herd of about twelve horses and headed north through a canyon between two mountain peaks.

"They are already heading out," Jake said. He gave Randy a quick kiss on the head. "Those horses must not be branded, so Lloyd is taking them to that ranch. Let's go." He led Randy over to Thunder and helped her climb into the saddle. He mounted up behind her and headed down the long, grassy slope that led to the valley below and across the expanse of grass nearly a half-mile wide.

"How far are we from Shelter?" Randy asked.

"Maybe ten days. We will pass Hole-In-The-Wall but we don't need to go up there. It's a really a high and dangerous trip. You probably remember that from when we came up here looking for Lloyd. I don't even know if there is any kind of town there anymore, but we will take the lower trail and go past it."

"Jake, I hope everything is okay ahead. I can't see the horses or any of the men anymore. They all disappeared into that canyon."

"I'm watching." Jake kicked Thunder into a harder run. It took a good twenty minutes to reach the canyon entrance. It curved sharply along a dried-up creek bed so that they could not see the men ahead until it finally straightened.

Jake slowed his horse. The men had stopped several hundred yards ahead of them. The wild horses were even farther ahead and being herded toward a homestead not far beyond the mouth of the canyon. They could make out several outbuildings in sight, as well as corrals that held horses and cattle. Facing the men was a string of ranch hands on horseback, all holding rifles in ready positions.

"I told you this could happen," Jake told Randy quietly. "Don't say a word." He guided Thunder up close to Terrel, who hung back a little behind the others. "Take Randy," he told the man. "And I want her behind you, not in front."

"So I take the first bullet?" Terrel teased.

"That's the idea."

Randy reached over and grasped Terrel's shoulders as Jake helped her settle in behind him.

"They are waiting for you," Terrel told Jake. "We told them who we are and where we are from, but not the reason we are here. They checked out the horses for brands, then herded them down to the ranch ... said they have orders not to let a bunch of strangers in without knowing why they are here. Once we told them Jake Harkner was the head of this bunch, they said you're the only one they will talk to."

"I figured as much." Jake urged Thunder forward.

"Jake, be careful," Randy called to him.

He didn't answer as he rode past the rest of the men and up beside Lloyd, who was sitting in the lead, totally relaxed on his horse and smoking a cigarette.

"About time you got here," Lloyd told Jake.

Jake nodded to a heavyset, broad-chested man who faced them. He sported blond curls under his wide-brimmed hat and rested his rifle on his thigh. "Keep your hands away from your guns," the man told Jake. "If you are Jake Harkner, I know that order might sound foolish, but I'd appreciate you respectin' the fact that we check out strangers who come onto Pine Ranch. Don't mean no offense."

"None taken," Jake answered. "And yes, I am Jake Harkner. We are only riding through on our way to the town of Shelter. We don't mean any trouble. You the foreman here?"

"Nate Willis." Nate began pointing out the other men. "Boyd, Boomer, Tucker, Sparky and Tom. The rest of the men who rode out to meet this bunch took those horses you came with and herded them up to a corral near the house. What's left are all good with guns and all have orders to keep out thieves, killers and rustlers."

Jake grinned wryly. "Men like yourselves, you mean."

Nate laughed from deep inside, a laugh that made his big belly move. "Takes one to know one," he answered. "None of us has done nothin' you haven't done yourself,

Harkner. And word is, you left a man dead back in Wilcox and left a bunch more dead back down the trail a ways."

"The man I shot in Wilcox insulted my wife, and it was his brother and friends who came after us for it."

"Why hell, Jake, if you're going to shoot a man for insulting your wife, you will have to shoot a lot *more* men if you keep going in outlaw country." Nate shifted in his saddle and adjusted his hold on his rifle.

All the men grinned and chuckled at Nate's remark as Jake took a cigarette and a match from an inside pocket of his vest. He lit the cigarette and took a deep drag. "Well, I'll tell you, Nate. I intended to just beat the hell out of the man for his insult, but I saw a familiar look in his eyes, one I have personally seen too many times in my life. He was fixing to shoot me in the back once I turned to leave. You probably know the look I am talking about."

Nate nodded. "I know it."

"As far as the men we killed in that gun battle a couple of days ago, I was just leaving a message that I hope will spread fast out here. I want men in Shelter to know I mean business. There will likely be a lot of blood spilled, but things will be easier if people there know I intend to get what I came for, no matter how many men I have to shoot to do it. How did you know about that run-in we had farther back?"

"One of the men from that bunch rode hard to get here by a back way only a few men know about, so we were pretty sure you would show up."

Jake kept the cigarette between his lips. "We rounded up those mustangs that are now in one of your corrals in the hopes that whoever owns this place will buy them from us. Better yet, I'll trade them for a couple of your best men. We will need the help when we get to Shelter. It's going to be risky business, so they need to be good with guns and not hesitate to use them."

"That would describe most of us. I will let you explain to my boss. His name is Ruben Prescott." He shifted his gaze to Terrel, who had slowly urged his horse closer. "Is the woman behind that man there your wife?"

Jake turned to see Terrel sitting only a few feet behind him. "That's her." He faced Nate again. "She got hurt in that gunplay to the south. She needs another day to rest, in a real bed if that's possible." He nodded toward Lloyd. "The young man beside me is my son, Lloyd. We were hoping to camp here for the night."

"Good lookin' woman," one of the cowboys commented. "She really your wife?"

Terrel and the others stiffened at the comment. Jake glared at the cowboy. "The last man who suggested she was something else is dead," he reminded the man. He rested his right hand on his gun. "Yes, she's really my wife. Her name is Miranda, and I'd suggest you talk about her with respect because she's the kind of woman who deserves it."

The man backed his horse.

"You watch yourself, Boomer," Nate told the cowboy. "This is Jake Harkner you're dealin' with, and he can take down three or four of you before you can clear leather. You already know he's touchy about his wife."

The one called Boomer scratched the stubble on his chin as he eyed Jake. "Sorry."

"Jake, you know what it's like out here. Boomer didn't mean no threat," Nate said with a frown. "Why did you bring a right proper woman along with you into country like this anyway?"

"That's my business," Jake answered. "And after a man

has been with one woman for 37 years, he learns not to argue with her."

Nate laughed even harder. The other men joined him with snickers and chuckles.

"Well, Jake Harkner, we ain't real anxious to start trouble with a man of your reputation, so you can ride in," Nate said, "but we will all be behind you, guns ready."

"Fine. Just know that if something happens to my wife, you don't have enough guns to stop me from getting to you before I go down. Just a fact."

"I believe you," Nate answered. "Ain't nothin' gonna happen to her. We ain't that kind. Mister Prescott is married, too. She was a whore before he married her and brought her out here, but she's good to him, so we all treat her with respect like we would any man's wife." He glanced at Randy again.

"Don't ask it and don't even *think* it," Jake told him. "My wife is a good woman from Kansas, the daughter of a respected doctor. She's never been anything else, if that is what you are wondering. Let's get down to the house so I can talk to your boss and dicker over those horses. I also need to buy a good riding horse for my wife. Hers was killed in that gunfight back on the trail."

Nate turned his horse and backed off. "Go on down. We will be behind you."

Jake motioned for the men to go forward. The Pine Ranch cowboys waited for them to pass, then followed them down to the homestead. More men emerged from a barn and the bunkhouse, all watching closely. When Jake and the others reached the main house, Jake dismounted and reached up for Randy, helping her down from Terrel's horse.

"So many stares," Randy told him. "I feel like I am being auctioned off."

Jake grinned. "You are a respectable, beautiful woman - the kind men don't see much of out here. Hell, if I didn't know you, I would be staring, too."

"Oh, Jake, I'm getting too old to be stared at."

"Not out here, and not anyplace else. Your looks defy your age." Jake kept her at his side as he walked up to greet an average-sized, bearded man with steely blue eyes who stood in front of a frame house with curtains at the windows. A stout, big-breasted woman with dishwater blond hair stood on the steps to the veranda. She smiled and nodded at Jake and the rest of the men.

The bearded man put out his hand to Jake. "Ruben Prescott," he said. "I own this place. The men who rode in here a while ago with a bunch of good-looking wild horses told me Jake Harkner himself was coming to see me."

Jake shook his hand. "I'm Jake." He kept an arm around Randy. "This is my wife, Miranda. And no, I'm not a wife-beater. The bruise and cut on her face are from the gun battle my men and I were in a couple of days ago. Her horse reared up and Randy got hit in the face with the log her horse was tied to. I'm worried she has a concussion and am hoping she can sleep in a real bed tonight. We all need a little break before we ride on."

Ruben nodded. "Sure. Your men can share the bunkhouse and you and the Mrs. can use a spare bedroom."

"They sure can!" The heavyset woman came down from the steps and took Randy's arm. "Come on, honey. I'm Rebecca Prescott, Ruben's wife. Most call me Becca. Come on in and rest yourself." She scanned the rest of Jake's men. "All of you board your horses in the corral over there by the barn and make yourselves to home in the bunkhouse. The cook should have some food left over from lunch." She swept Randy into the house before Jake or Randy could say a word. "Sweetheart, you don't know how good it is to see another woman," Becca told her as she herded Randy through the door.

Ruben shook his head. "My wife gets all excited over company," he told Jake. "She will probably try to talk you into staying a few days."

Jake grinned and folded his arms. "We wouldn't mind, but I'm on a mission to rescue a granddaughter in Shelter, and I'm anxious to get there. Fact is, I'd like to talk to you about that, and about those horses we brought in."

Ruben nodded. "Come on in. We have coffee, and I also have some good whiskey. You are welcome to both."

"Just the coffee. Whiskey tends to change my personality, if you know what I mean. Turns me into the man I hated most growing up ... my own father."

"I know the story. I am honored to meet you, Jake. Most men have heard about you."

"And most have heard the worst, I'm sure," Jake answered. He turned to Lloyd. "Go ahead and take care of the horses and supplies and get the men settled. I'll talk to Mr. Prescott about what we need."

"Sure, Pa." Lloyd dismounted and nodded to Ruben. "Thanks for your hospitality, Mister Prescott."

"Sure thing," Ruben answered. He shook hands with Lloyd. "What's it like having Jake Harkner for a father?" he asked teasingly.

Lloyd grinned. "We don't have enough time right now to answer that."

All three men laughed as Lloyd took the reins to Thunder and Cinnamon and led both horses and the pack horses toward the barn. Ruben showed Jake inside the small but well-kept house and sat down to a kitchen table with him. Jake glanced at Randy, who sat in a rocker and was already drinking coffee. "You okay?" he asked.

"Yes. Becca is heating some water so I can take a bath." She smiled at Ruben. "Your wife is so generous and friendly, Mr. Prescott.

Ruben chuckled. "Becca once led a life of being friendly to everybody she met. I found her at Hole-In-The-Wall and we have been together ever since. She's a good woman."

"And you are a good man, Ruben Prescott," Becca called from a bedroom at the other end of the house. "I reckon Mr. and Mrs. Harkner know how we met." She came to the door. "Out here it takes all kinds, and even women like me can fall in love." She glanced at Randy. "Hope that doesn't offend you. You don't have to associate with me if you prefer not to. I understand."

"Oh, don't be silly," Randy answered. "I've been married to Jake Harkner for 37 years. Nothing surprises me or offends me, and one of my best friends is Gretta MacBain. Do you know of her?"

Becca let out a hefty laugh. "Who doesn't know that name?" She walked into the kitchen to grab another kettle of hot water. "I'll have the tub ready shortly, Mrs. Harkner. You're a right sweet lady. If you want more coffee, it's there on the stove. Ruben got me that big coal-fired cook stove last year. Weighs a ton, but we got it up here to the mountains. I love that thing." She went back into the spare bedroom and Randy just smiled and shook her head.

Jake drank some of the coffee Ruben had poured for him, then lit another cigarette. He inhaled deeply and held up the smoke. "These things take the place of whiskey for me," he told Ruben.

"I understand how tobacco can calm a man, Jake."

"I appreciate you putting us up," Jake told him.

"Well, sir, knowing your reputation, I figure it's safer to be friendly than to be your enemy."

"A man treats me fair, he gets treated fair in return." Jake went on to explain why he'd come to outlaw country and was headed for Shelter. He offered the wild horses in exchange for two or three men who might be willing to join him and the others. "We have a big ranch down in Colorado, so I know how important every man is to you. If you can spare two or three, I'll do my best to make sure they get back here safe and sound. I intend to make it known real quick as soon as we arrive in Shelter that I mean business."

Ruben nodded. "I'll see what I can do. This country is full of no-goods, but most of them respect a man like you. And they respect a good woman and appreciate when a man gives them a decent job, food and housing. You know what I mean. You've lived this life."

Jake nodded, smiling at Becca as she fussed over Randy. Before Randy could agree or disagree, she had her in the bedroom, offering to help her bathe and get into bed. "You need some decent bed rest. I can tell," the woman carried on. "We will get you all cleaned up and into bed and I'll bring you some food and then you can sleep." She closed the bedroom door. "Mr. Harkner, you tell that good-looking son of yours to bring in his mother's overnight needs."

Ruben chuckled. "Your wife is in good hands," he told Jake.

"I can see that. I've been a little worried about her, so I appreciate the chance for her to get some decent sleep. And Lloyd knows to bring her things to the house. He should be here soon."

Prescott nodded. "Anybody can tell right away that

your wife is one of those educated, sophisticated kind. How in hell did you end up with a woman like that for a wife?"

Jake grinned. "Right place, right time, I guess."

"Is the rumor true? That you scared her so bad at first that she shot you?"

Jake drank more coffee. "It's true. Thank God she didn't hit anything vital, although she probably would have been better off if she had put that bullet right into my heart."

Ruben shook his head. "I saw how you two look at each other. It's one of them things that's meant to be. Same with me and Rebecca. No doubt you know her background, but she has been loyal, and she keeps this place clean and is a damn good cook. At any rate, her past doesn't matter to me ... or to most men in these parts. And I don't hire any man who abuses women."

"My son and I require the same on the J&L. I have a beautiful daughter and daughter-in-law and now some growing granddaughters to think about, let alone my wife."

Ruben chuckled. "What the hell is Jake Harkner going to do when those granddaughters are old enough to take an interest in men, and the other way around? You going to lock the girls up? Or kill every man who takes a second look? Hell, you killed a man just for insulting your wife, and she's a grown woman."

Jake grinned. "Those girls becoming women has been in the back of my mind. I figure I will have to leave those things up to the girls' fathers, but if I'm still around when they are old enough to be interested in men, I will have a hard time keeping my nose out of it. My father killed my mother when I was too little to stop him, and that left me with a real strong need to protect. It gets me in trouble sometimes."

Ruben nodded. "Me, I had a good childhood, but during

the War Between the States, marauders attacked our farm and burned down our house with my mother in it. They shot my father and held me back so's I had to watch it all and hear my mother's screams. Later I found some of those men and killed them. So I reckon there are a lot of different reasons for a man ending up on Wanted posters and living up in places like this with a lot of other outlaws. I don't judge a man by his past, and most of the time I don't even ask."

"Same here. After I killed my father, I ran off and ended up running with a mean bunch of thieves and marauders, robbed a lot of banks and trains, ran guns for both sides in the war. That's how my face ended up nailed to trees and porch posts."

Ruben finished his coffee. "Let's go outside and look at those horses. Maybe I can convince a couple of my men to go with you to Shelter if you let them pick out a horse for free. Some might want to go along just to say they rode with Jake Harkner."

Jake waved him off as he rose. "Riding with me to Shelter will be no picnic."

Ruben grabbed his wide-brimmed hat from a hook on the wall. "Believe it or not, I read that book about you, Jake. That reporter who wrote it talked about when you took him along as a marshal back in Oklahoma. Pretty descriptive. So I understand what you mean about riding with you being risky. If I didn't have this place to watch over, I would consider going along myself, just for the experience."

Jake put on his hat. "You are better off here. Believe me."

"Your wife might be better off here, too," Ruben said. He headed for the front screen door.

"I already thought of that," Jake answered. "I am going

to suggest it to her, but she will not be happy about it." He glanced at the bedroom door. Randy and Becca were laughing. He shook his head as he followed Ruben out the door, thinking how their treatment here at Pine Ranch was likely a stark contrast to what waited for them in Shelter. At least Randy would get some decent rest first.

CHAPTER THIRTY

Jake climbed into bed and settled in beside his wife. She ran a hand over his arm as he pulled her close.

"What time is it?" Randy asked with a sleepy sigh.

"About ten." Jake leaned over and kissed her bruised cheek. "Becca says you've been sleeping about three hours. That's good." He nuzzled her hair and kissed her behind the ear. "You smell good."

"Becca has a soap that smells wonderful," Randy answered. She turned a little and kissed his chin. "Do you mind that I used the soap of a prostitute?"

Jake broke into solid laughter. "You are asking *me* that question?" He laughed again. "Oh, Lord, Randy, you can say the funniest things sometimes."

Randy smiled. "I just wondered." She turned farther around and kissed him. "You smell good, too. And you shaved."

"I cleaned up over at the bunkhouse." Jake sobered as he ran a finger over her lips. "I have been out there talking with the men about what to do when we get to Shelter."

"Did you find any extra men to come with us?"

"Two more. Ruben vouched for their honesty and their ability with guns, so we have a couple more soldiers in our little army. Lloyd joked that he makes up for two and I make up for about five, so we really have fourteen men along."

Randy's smile faded. "I guess that is one way of looking at it, but it doesn't erase the reality, and you know what that reality is, Jake. I'm so scared for you."

"Which is why I think you should stay here when we leave. These are good people, Randy. You would be safe here."

Randy scooted back a little. "No! Jake, don't you dare break another promise. You said I could go all the way with you. If the worst happens, I want to be with you."

"Randy –"

She sat up. "I mean it! You don't know how devastated I was when we all thought you'd been killed down in Mexico. All I could think of was you dying alone down there, probably slowly and in horrible pain, me never seeing you again or even having a body to bury at home where you belong. I am going, and I won't take no for an answer."

Jake grasped her hand. "Damn it, woman, you are ripping me apart. I can't lose you. Understand? At least not to something that is my fault in the first place."

"You won't lose me. I feel it. Evie and a lot of others are praying for us, and for Dee Dee. And we have Lloyd with us. You know darn well he is just as dependable as you when it comes to protecting me. I am ready to face whatever I have to face."

"And you are already hurt. That could have been a bullet that smashed into your face instead of a piece of wood. If it had been, I'd be burying you out here in outlaw country, a grave I could never visit again. I'd damn well shoot myself and let Lloyd bury us together, rather than go home without you. Outlaw country is probably a more fitting place for me to be buried anyway."

Randy squeezed his hand. "You won't lose me, Jake." She lay back down, facing him. "Please don't leave me behind."

Jake couldn't resist another kiss. "Then you need to promise me something."

"What's that?"

"If we end up having to ride up to that mine or to Ty Bolton's home, you will stay behind in town with whoever I ask to watch over you. Going up to that mine or the ranch would likely end up with a lot of bullets flying. I can't be distracted in any way, so if you want me to live through this, you have to stay someplace safe in town while the men and I go after Dee Dee. Promise me that much, or I'm leaving you here when we head out tomorrow."

Randy sighed with reluctant agreement. "All right. I won't go to the mine or to Bolton's ranch with you. At least I will be close by so I can be with you if you come back wounded, or ..."

Jake rolled her onto her back and moved on top of her. "Or dead? I might remind you that you are the one who insists that won't happen. You having second thoughts?"

Randy leaned up and kissed his bare chest. "No. It's just hard to be positive in the light of reality. But I am trusting in God and prayer."

"Two things that don't do a man like me much good."

"And you have always been so wrong about that." Randy studied his handsome dark eyes. "We will make it home, Jake. And we will have Dee Dee with us."

"I hope you can make good on that." Jake kissed her again, this time more deeply.

Randy moved her arms around his neck. "Make love to me."

"I shouldn't. You need your rest."

"I need my *husband.* We have close to ten days of traveling before we reach Shelter, and we will be out in the open with the rest of the men. This might be our only chance for quite a while to be intimate. And we always make love before you go riding off into danger." She moved her hand down to gently toy with all that was man about him.

"You don't play fair."

"I don't intend to."

Jake sobered and braced himself on his elbows as Randy felt for the buttons on his longjohns and began opening them. "You sure you're up to this?" he asked.

"If you're slow and gentle."

Jake snickered and kissed her eyes. "That isn't always easy for a man."

"You have no choice," Randy answered softly. "We are in someone else's house and we have to be quiet about this."

"You make it sound like we are committing a crime."

"It certainly wouldn't be the first crime you've committed."

"Definitely not." Jake met her mouth in a deep kiss as Randy freed his penis from the confines of his underwear and stroked its fullness.

"I have always wondered how something could be so hard and yet so soft to the touch," she teased.

"Slow down," he whispered in her ear, "or I won't last long once I'm inside you."

Randy welcomed him between her legs. "Then get to it," she answered. "I've made it easy for you. I left my underwear off."

Jake moved a little to the side and reached down between her legs, sliding his fingers into her depths. "Feels like you *are* ready."

"Oh, I'm ready, Mr. Harkner. I have been waiting for you."

"Then you were not sleeping this whole time." Jake kissed her hungrily as he moved both hands under her bottom and let her guide him inside her. She stroked his hips, his back, his arms, pressing her fingers into hard muscle and shivering with desire. Jake strived to give her deep pleasure, taking joy in the fact that he was here and alive and strong and able. He relished these moments when their lovemaking took them out of reality and into a world of sweet desire and nothing more. It seemed as though as long as he was inside her, nothing and no one could take her from him.

She seemed so small beneath him that he always had to be careful not to put his full weight on her. She met his rhythmic thrusts with her own erotic movements as she arched against him until he could no longer hold back his release. He relaxed and kissed her hair. "You still drive me crazy with want sometimes," he told her.

"You do the same to me."

"You sure you're okay? No headache?"

"I'm fine. Make love to me again, Jake." She leaned up to meet his mouth, groaning as she kissed him.

Jake unbuttoned her nightgown and leaned down to gently arouse her breasts with licks and kisses. She arched against him again, welcoming his renewed thrusts, sharing the precious act of lovemaking so familiar to them, yet always as pleasurable and fulfilling as a man and woman in the throes of young love ... precious to them because both had been through brushes with death and loss too many times to take this for granted.

He loved being her lover, her protector, her life partner. He'd spent the first half of his life so starved for love that he still could not get enough of her, even after all these years. She was the gentle dream that kept his nightmares away. When they shared bodies this way, it was as though they melted into one person, as though neither could breathe without the other.

His release came in hard, quick thrusts, each one, in his mind and heart, branding her as belonging only to Jake Harkner.

They lay there quietly, naked, covers thrown off because of heated bodies in a warm room. Somehow Randy's nightgown had come completely off, but he had no memory of when or how.

"Do you know how much I love you?" he asked. He moved to her side and smoothed her hair away from her face.

"You just showed me," Randy told him. "And you can show me this way as often as you want."

Jake kissed her lightly. "Well, you were right that I won't be able to show you this way for quite a while once we get back to the trail tomorrow. And by the way, I picked out a really nice mare for you from Ruben's riding horses. She's mostly gray with some black and white speckles, which is why she is called Pepper. She's a little bigger than Jenny was, but still a nice size for a woman."

"Are you saying women can't ride big horses?"

Jake snickered. "You just rode one."

Randy grinned and pushed at him. "You know what I mean."

"Yes, ma'am. And no, I am not saying women can't ride big horses. But common sense says you want a horse that is comfortable for you, and one that has a gentle nature and is easy to handle because we still have a long ride ahead of us."

Randy leaned over and kissed him. "Thank you. I fully trust your judgment when it comes to horses." She ran her hands over his arms and chest. "By the way, Becca asked me what you were like."

"As a man? Or a lover?"

"Both." Randy smiled and ran her fingers into his hair. "I told her you were as stubborn and frustrating and hard to deal with as any other man, but she got me to admit that when it comes to this, I forget about the things you do that make me want to clobber you. Not that it would do much good if I did."

Jake snickered. "Lady, you can lay into me any time you feel like it. I usually deserve it."

"I'm not strong enough to do a man like you much harm, but sometimes you drive the whole family crazy, especially poor Lloyd, who is always trying to keep you out of trouble. But for me, all I have to do is see the adoration in those dark eyes and I can put up with the rest."

"It *is* adoration. You are my life, Randy Harkner, the only thing that keeps me away from that ledge that leads to a pit of hellfire and wickedness."

"Not always an easy job."

"You think I don't know that?" He kissed her breasts again, her neck, her lips. "It's the reason I love you so much. The reason I always take great pleasure in *making* love to you."

"Keep that up and we *will* end up making love again. I wouldn't mind at all."

Jake grinned and pulled a sheet over them. "You need your sleep."

"And you don't?"

Jake pulled her close and settled against his pillow. "The proud man in me wants to say no, but the one who is forced to admit his age has to agree that he needs his sleep. At least we don't need to rush in the morning. Becca wants all of us to eat a big breakfast, so we won't leave as early as we should, but I figured that's best. The men would appreciate a relaxing morning and a good breakfast before heading out."

"That's a good idea."

Jake kissed her hair. "As far as putting up with the part of me that drives you crazy, I am afraid you will see plenty of that when we reach Shelter and I put on that badge. Remember that I warned you about the other Jake Harkner, the one with a temper and the one who might end up tearing that town apart. There will be times when you will hardly recognize me, Randy, so you might want to keep your distance."

"You don't scare me, Jake Harkner."

"I didn't say you would have to be afraid of me. But you might have trouble finding that good heart you always say I have. You will only see the bad man side, and it's not pretty."

Randy felt a quick little pain in her chest at the thought of returning to reality. They were not riding into Shelter, Wyoming. They were more likely riding into Hell itself. Satan, in the form of Ty Bolton, would be waiting for them, and he would meet his match in the form of Jake Harkner. Evie often called her father an avenging angel. Randy thought it was a fitting title, considering things he had done in the past to rescue those he loved, and at times, people he didn't even know.

Now he had a granddaughter to rescue. She knew he would think nothing of risking his life to find Dee Dee, and he might end up doing some ugly things to get to her.

CHAPTER THIRTY-ONE

"W<small>HO DID YOU SAY WAS COMING</small>?" Ty Bolton laid down his cards and took a thin, freshly-lit cigar from the corner of his mouth.

"Jake Harkner, that's who!" Sid Becker swallowed as he pushed back his stained wide-brimmed hat. He scratched at the stubble on his face and took a deep breath against the excitement he felt, mixed with nervous anticipation.

Ty frowned with confusion. "Some say Jake Harkner is dead," he answered. "Died about three years ago in a blood-bath of a gunfight down in Colorado."

Sid shook his head. "He is very much alive, sir. I seen him myself, down in Wilcox. He shot Carl Betz just for insultin' his wife. I was sittin' right there and saw the whole thing. All Betz did was offer a couple of real pretty whores in trade for a woman who traveled with Harkner and five or six men who all got off the train there. Every single man and the woman had their own pack horses, lots of valuable mounts and supplies. Looks like they mean to light and stay a while in one place, and word is, that place is right here in Shelter."

"Did he actually say his name?" Ty asked.

"Yes, sir, and he's big and mean lookin', but also good lookin' like all the stories about him. And the way he looked us over, I reckon Harkner figured out real quick why we was all sittin' in front of the general store watchin' them get ready to ride out. A man like Harkner, bein' an outlaw hisself, he'd know what men like us was up to. We was figurin' the value of those horses and supplies ... and the woman."

"You and that bunch from Snow Ridge Ranch are always up to no good."

"Ha!" One of the prostitutes who worked in the Cowpoke Saloon chuckled. "You're no better, Ty, the way you take advantage of everybody in this town."

Ty gave her a warning look. "Shut your mouth, Irene, before I shut it for you." He pushed his cards to the center of the poker table. "Fold," he told the men he'd been gambling with. He picked up a shot glass and quickly swallowed the whiskey it held, then poured himself another before scooting back his chair. He rose and drank down the second shot of whiskey, then walked closer to Sid, eyeing the man closely. "Are you real sure about all of this?"

Sid stepped back a little. Ty Bolton's steely blue eyes had a way of making a man feel like he'd just been punched. "Yes, sir. Like I said, I seen the whole thing. And after Harkner shot Carl, he said as how the woman with him was his wife, and that he was headed right here, to Shelter, but he didn't say why. He just said that men here would get more of the same as what happened in Wilcox if he didn't get what he came for."

Ty frowned and turned away. "What on earth could that be?"

"That ain't all of it," Mr. Bolton," Sid added. "After it

happened, I quick rode out to Snow Ridge and told the men about it. Joe Nitz got a whole gang of men together and went out after Harkner and his bunch on account of Carl was his brother. They caught Harkner and his little posse in that little canyonlike area north of Wilcox ... Red Valley, they call it. Joe probably had three men to one of Harkner's bunch, but Harkner, bein' who he is, scared off some of the Snow Ridge men. They didn't figure Carl was worth dyin' for. Besides that, Harkner and his men had the advantage. Better cover. Every time a Snow Ridge man leaned over the edge of the bank leadin' down to the valley, he got his head shot off."

Ty squiggled his nose and mouth against Sid's bad breath and body odor. "Jesus, Sid, you need a bath. And do something about your breath. At least take a drink of whiskey." He poured some into an empty glass someone else had left behind and handed it out to Sid, then poured himself another shot and drank it down.

"You sure you aren't exaggerating all this?" The question came from the town sheriff, Charles McDonald, who stood at the bar listening. "You *have* been known to do that, you know."

"No, sir," Sid answered. "I ain't makin' more of it than it is. I rode out with Joe and saw everything that happened. A lot of Snow Ridge men who were left alive took off, and those left behind needed buryin'. Harkner and his men are damn good. I didn't stick around to see if any of the bodies still had life in them. I headed straight here to let Mr. Bolton know about it on account of Harkner said back in Wilcox that he was comin' to Shelter. I managed to stay ahead of them because they probably had to stop and rest after that gunfight, maybe stop off somewhere and restock their supplies. I know a couple of their horses was killed, so they would have had to get more before comin' into Shelter."

McDonald smiled at Ty. "Don't worry, boss. We have plenty of men to take care of Jake Harkner. Besides, the man is getting old. He might be able to outdraw one man, but he'll be facing a lot more than that if he comes here and tries to make trouble."

"I'm not so sure you aren't underestimating the man," Ty answered. The setting sun hit McDonald's hair just right, accenting its unusually white color, if it could be called color at all. McDonald's nickname was "Cotton" because in spite of his young age of only 27, he had pure white hair that was thick and curly and "soft as cotton," according to the whores. *His pecker hair is just as white and soft,* Irene once told Ty.

Ty couldn't care less about such nonsense. All he wanted was someone who liked to kill men and would do so on orders. Cotton filled the bill and was damn good with a gun. He paid the man well for using that gun in ways that benefitted his gold mine and his holdings in Shelter.

He stepped away from Sid to avoid the man's stink. "None of this makes sense," he mused. He looked at himself in the big mirror behind the saloon's bar and slicked back his hair with a comb he took from his pants pocket.

"I know it don't make sense, Mr. Bolton," Sid told him, "but back in Wilcox after he shot Carl, the look in Harkner's eyes would scare a mountain lion back into its cave. If that man was near dead three years ago, he sure ain't no more. Back in Wilcox, when he pulled his gun on Carl, I never saw anybody draw so fast. We was all in shock, on account of we never even seen him make the move, like for him it was the same as takin' a quick breath. And he damn well didn't show any regrets when I yelled at him that Carl didn't mean no harm. He said he can read a man's eyes and that Carl meant to shoot him in the back the minute he turned away, so he shot him."

Ty rested his hands on his hips, pushing back a fancy frock coat and revealing his own sidearm as he did so. "What in hell is up here in Shelter that a man like Jake Harkner would want?" he again wondered aloud. "I've heard he and his son have a hell of a big ranch down in Colorado. Why would he leave that and his big family to come clear up here into outlaw country, and bring his wife along to boot?"

"I don't know, Mr. Bolton," Sid told him. "I'm just lettin' you know what I seen and what he said, that men were going to die, with no questions asked, before he was done here in Shelter."

Ty picked up his cigar and began pacing. Others in the tavern stopped their drinking and card playing and just watched and listened. The prostitutes who sat among them perked up at the mention of Jake Harkner coming to town.

"Hey, Susan, I'll make you a side bet on which one of us can get Jake Harkner into bed first," Irene told another woman at the bar.

Susan scoffed. "Sid said Harkner's wife is with him."

"Yeah? Since when does that matter to us?" Irene joked. "Besides, I've always heard Harkner has a soft spot for prostitutes," Irene added.

"I told you to shut up over there!" Bolton ordered. "Don't make me say it a third time, Irene!"

Both women sobered and stepped back a little. When someone stirred Ty Bolton's anger, they usually paid for it.

"Sorry, Ty," Irene told him. "You have to admit, this is interesting news."

"You two can talk about fucking Harkner on your own time. See if any of the customers here need another drink."

The two women hustled the drinks while Bolton kept pacing. "I wonder if this has anything to do with why Dallas left town." he mused.

"I don't know, Mr. Bolton," Sid answered.

"I think Dallas left because her son is dead," Cotton suggested. "That took the starch out of her. And one of her girls got cut up bad that night her granddaughter was taken. I think she just needed to get out of Shelter for a while." The man used a shirt sleeve to polish his badge. "I questioned the other girls at Dallas's whorehouse like you asked me to do, boss, but they swear they have no idea where Dallas went. I even tried to beat it out of a couple of them, but I got nothin'. I think they are all tellin' the truth."

"They are," Irene barked at the sheriff. "And Dallas won't be happy at the way you and your men treated us. My guess is that she will be back soon. She has friends at Hole-In-The-Wall. She probably went there just to get away from familiar places. She wouldn't go clear down to Colorado to find a man she hasn't seen for forty years."

Ty walked up and grabbed her arm. "You mean she once knew the man?"

Irene jerked her arm away. "Yes. I have this vague memory of Dallas telling me once that she knew Jake Harkner a long, long time ago, way back when she lived in Missouri and was real young. She told me about it when we read about that last gunfight he was in, because by then she thought he was dead. She said Harkner was the best fuck she ever had, but he was wanted back then and hard to pin down. He took off one day and never came back. That's all she ever told me. She said she never heard from him again, and was surprised to find out he was still alive when we got news of that gunfight in Denver. But that was three years ago. She's never mentioned the man since. He couldn't have anything to do with why Dallas left or where she went. I think she just needed time alone to mourn the loss of her son and Dee Dee."

Ty leaned in closer, a sneer on his lips. "Are you sure?"

Irene glared right back at him. "I know better than to keep secrets from you, Ty. And I hardly think the fact that Dallas knew Jake Harkner forty years ago and hasn't seen him since would make any difference. After all these years, why would she go to the man now? And like Cotton said, he's an old man now anyway. I'll bet he wouldn't even recognize Dallas after all this time, and he probably doesn't look much like himself either. Thinking that the man coming here has something to do with Dallas is too much of a long shot."

"The fact remains he *is* coming here, and apparently he's not so old that he can't kill a man in a split second, and over something as trivial as insulting his *wife*." Ty picked up a bottle of whiskey sitting on the bar and poured himself another shot, then quickly slugged it down. "None of this makes sense," he repeated. "And you are probably right. Why would Harkner give a shit about somebody like an aging whore he knew years ago? And it's a hell of a trip clear down to Colorado. I don't think Dallas could even make it that far." He walked closer to Irene again. "If I find out you have lied to me —"

"How the hell many times do I have to tell you that I don't know where Dallas went? She just packed her bags after Wade was killed and Dee Dee was taken and said she had to get out of Shelter for a while. She claimed she wasn't sure exactly *where* she would go. She just left town all by herself. She must have found some men in another town to help her get where she was going. She surely wouldn't travel around dangerous country like this alone. Even a whore can be raped and killed, you know. Maybe she made it to someplace farther south than Hole-In-The-Wall. She could have met some man who offered to take her up to Billings or Helena if she would be his woman for a few weeks. That sounds like something Dallas would do. All I know for sure is that she told me to watch the emporium and the girls while she was gone, but she didn't say anything about where, or when she would be back."

Frowning with irritation, Ty walked back to his table to down yet another shot of whiskey. "Dallas was angry about Wade's death and about Dennis taking off with Dee Dee. I understand that, but I don't need her out there telling others what goes on here in Shelter. I wish she would get her ass back here." He sighed and paced again. "Whatever Harkner's reason is for coming here, it doesn't likely have anything to do with Dallas or with her granddaughter. And we have plenty of men here to take care of the sonofabitch."

"I ain't so sure, Mr. Bolton," Sid told him. "The man looked damn healthy and able when I saw him shoot Carl. Then again, if you saw his wife, you'd be hopin' Harkner *does* come here and get hisself killed. That would leave the woman up for grabs. She might be older, but she's a looker. Ain't a man I can think of who wouldn't want to fuck her. That's why Carl offered to trade a couple whores for her. And Harkner had four other men with him. Maybe he lets them all take turns as pay for comin' with him to help with whatever it is he wants. I knew a man once who used his wife to ask men for money cuz he was broke. She didn't seem to mind."

Ty shook his head. "You *idiot!* He killed Carl Betz just because the man *insulted* his wife!" he answered. "From everything I have read about him, there is no way Jake Harkner would let any other man touch his wife. He treats her like *royalty!*"

"Why in hell would you read a book about Jake Harkner, boss?" Cotton asked.

Ty scoffed. "I wanted to see if I could figure out what makes him tick. When I came here and took over this town, I figured maybe I could make a name for myself like Harkner has done." He paused to look into the saloon's mirror again. "I'm decent with a gun, and I'm only 45 and not bad looking." He turned to Irene. "Don't you agree, sweetheart?"

Irene smiled. "With that soft brown hair and those striking blue eyes and nice smile? Sure, Ty." She walked closer and pressed a hand against his chest. "You're the best-looking and richest man in Shelter. What more could a woman ask for?"

Ty turned and grinned at the others in the saloon. "By God, I hope Harkner *does* come here. If we have a big shootout with him and he dies, it will make me and this town just as famous as he is. And you men can bring his wife to me. When I am done with her, the rest of you can have your turn. Cotton, you warn the other deputies to be ready for Jake Harkner's arrival."

"Whatever you say, boss. I ain't afraid of the man. Like you said, he's getting old."

Irene snickered. "Something tells me you will regret that statement, Cotton. Maybe you, too, Ty."

Without warning, Ty backhanded her. She fell against Susan, who moved away when Ty grabbed Irene and pushed against the bar so roughly that it hurt her back when he slammed her into it. He kissed her so hard that her teeth cut into her lips a little. He shoved her sideways then and sneered at her. "Go on back to Dallas's place, baby. Take Susan with you. I'll be over soon to take care of *both* of you."

Irene pressed her fingers to her bleeding lip and winced with pain at her jaw where Ty had slugged her. "I'm supposed to work here at the saloon till midnight," she told Ty.

"And I *own* this saloon," he answered sharply. "I told you to go over to Dallas's place and get ready for me."

Irene gave him a look of disgust "Sure, Ty. Anything you say," she told him with a mocking tone. She turned to Susan, a dark-haired beauty with a skinny build who was fairly new among Dallas's girls. "Let's go."

Bolton scanned the rest of the men in the saloon. "If Jake Harkner really is coming here, we will be ready for him. Sounds like a wild time lies ahead for us, boys. And when it is over, we will be famous as the place where Jake Harkner finally met his demise."

They all chuckled as the two women left.

"Let's hope the story will turn out a lot different," Irene said quietly to Susan once they were outside. "Maybe Ty Bolton will meet *his* demise. I hope Jake Harkner fills him full of so many holes that the blood spews out like broth through a strainer."

Susan frowned. "That sounds gruesome."

"From stories Dallas told me about Jake Harkner, he is *capable* of gruesome. If he is really coming, I want a front seat when he gives Ty what he deserves."

PART 3

Everyone is a moon and has a dark side,
Which he never shows to anybody.

Mark Twain

CHAPTER THIRTY-TWO

"It looks small from here," Randy commented. She stood with Jake and the others on the rim of a flat-topped mesa that overlooked the town of Shelter.

"It won't seem very small once we get there," Jake told her. "Most would think that town is just a couple of miles away, but I'm betting it's a good four or five miles yet."

Randy shaded her eyes. "I swear, I will never get used to how easy it is to misjudge distance in such wide open country."

"Maybe a couple to three hours of riding, if we stay at a good gait and stop to walk the horses in between," Terrel spoke up. "We can make it there easy yet today."

"Seems so remote," Charlie said. "Then again, men will settle anywhere when gold is involved."

"Yeah, and then other men come in and steal somebody else's claim," Terrel answered. "Apparently, that's what Ty Bolton did. He must have had to kill more than the original owner to do it. Claim jumpers are usually shot or hanged, but Bolton must have had a lot of firepower behind him."

"Not enough, now that we are here," Jake said, still gazing through binoculars. "I came here to avenge that woman Dennis Gates cut up and to get my granddaughter back. And the people in that town will never sleep well until Bolton and his men are gone from this earth." He handed the binoculars to Lloyd.

Randy's horse nickered and nudged her shoulder. She kept hold of the mare's harness and petted her nose. Pepper had been just as gentle and easy to handle as Jake promised. "Where would a town like that get their supplies?" she asked Jake. "There is no railroad down there."

"Shelter might seem remote, but it isn't all that far from Buffalo and Gillette," Jake answered. "There are mountains on all sides, but going north it's fairly wide-open country. At the same time, Shelter is far enough from those more civilized towns to make their own rules without worrying about the law."

"There is some kind of smoke stack far up on the side of that big butte to the right, Pa," Lloyd spoke up. "That must be where the gold mine is." He handed the binoculars back to Jake.

"That's what I figure," Jake answered. "Dallas said they don't get much out of it anymore. Most gold towns are vacated real fast once the gold runs out, so it's a good thing we came when we did. A year from now most folks down there could be gone. Dee Dee would have had to go with them and we would never find her."

"Unless somebody already took off with the girl," Charlie said.

Silence followed, all of them realizing that was a distinct possibility. Charlie took off his hat to run a hand through his thick, sandy hair. "Sorry, Jake. I'm just figuring all the possibilities."

"Could you tell where Ty Bolton's ranch and house might be?" Randy asked Jake, trying to change the subject.

Jake raised the binoculars again and studied the landscape as best he could. "It must be around the other side of that butte. I don't see anything besides the town and the mine." He paused. "And there is a big frame house painted white over west of town. I can't read any signs, but it is probably Dallas's place. She described it to me."

"Might be best to go there first and make plans, Pa." Lloyd mounted his horse. "We need more information on the layout of the town and the habits of Bolton and his men."

"Shelter is bigger than you think," Jake told the others. He handed the binoculars to Cole. "Have a look. There are a lot of scattered homes all around, and a couple of streets that look like all homes. Off to the right are a couple of fairly large spreads, corrals, horses and cattle, barns and such. I see plenty of businesses in town, and this side of town I see what looks like a small church. It probably also serves as a school house."

"A church means families," Lloyd reasoned. "There have to be a lot of people down there who want Ty Bolton gone, so they might help us. Who is that woman Dallas left in charge of her place?" he asked Jake. "We should be able to get all the information we need from her."

"Her name is Irene," Jake answered. "And yes, we need to talk to her before we go charging into the thick of things."

Cole handed Jake the binoculars and Jake shoved them into his saddle bags. "We will probably have to camp out behind Dallas's place tonight," he announced. "I know it's a whorehouse, but I need you men to keep your thoughts on the business at hand. There are a lot of dangerous men down there, so don't let your guard down because you would rather share some woman's bed. Tempting as that might be, it's not worth your life, so save your needs for when we finish what we came here to do. I'm sure some of those women will give you a big, free thank you when this is over."

"Nice to be appreciated," Terrel joked.

They all laughed nervously as they remounted their horses.

Jake walked over to Randy and gave her a quick kiss on the forehead. "You do what I say from here on," he told her. "We can't be sure what we are riding into."

"I know." She took the reins to her horse as Jake turned away. "Jake."

He glanced back at her.

"I love you," Randy told him. "I need you alive when this is over."

He looked her over lovingly. "I need the same from you, so like I said, do what I tell you, Mrs. Harkner. For once in your life, obey your husband."

Randy couldn't help grinning as she watched him mount up. Still, she already felt the change in him. The old defensive outlaw in him was taking over. He was moving into that dark world she had a lot more trouble understanding or entering. Dread filled her as she mounted Pepper.

"Let's go!" he shouted. "The sooner we get down there and make plans, the quicker we get this done." Thunder snorted and tossed his head, as though sensing a change in his rider.

Randy took a deep breath against her worry of what could happen over the next few days. She hoped they could depend on the two extra men from Pine Ranch. Whitey

Loomis was around 30 and had never been married. His nickname stemmed from the fact that in spite of his dark coloring, the irises of his eyes were nearly white, which made him look strangely devilish. But Ruben Prescott had vouched for the man's trustworthiness and his ability with a gun.

The other man who had volunteered to help was 36-year-old Duke Grayhorse, who was half Comanche and good with a knife. According to Ruben, Duke had been raised by whites but had a wild streak that led to him running away from home at 14. He had long, black hair and dark eyes that showed a sureness Jake liked.

Randy plopped her floppy cowboy hat on top of her head and buttoned her jacket up to her throat against the still-chilly wind. Jake trotted Thunder over to a pathway down to a steep escarpment that opened into to the miles-wide valley below. Once they managed the precarious trip to the bottom, each man remained lost in his own thoughts as they silently covered roughly five miles before spotting several men on horses far in the distance … all headed their way.

Jake reined Thunder to a halt, and the others followed suit. Randy's heart pounded at the sight of a line of men in the distance.

"I count about ten," Jake told Lloyd.

Lloyd pulled his hat down for better shade and made his own count. "Eleven."

"Lord, help us," Cole muttered.

"Well, Jake, I guess they got the news we were comin'," Terrel said. "They must have decided to send us a greetin' party."

"Let me do the talking," Jake answered. "We need to get

these pack horses out of the way." He handed the reins to his pack horse over to Cole. "Take mine with yours and tie them under that big, lone pine tree to our right." He backed Thunder a few feet. "Charlie, take Randy's pack horse. All the rest of you take your extra horses over to that pine tree and tie them. Do it quick and get right back here."

Charlie took Randy's horse and rode off with the others. Jake dismounted and walked over to Randy. "Get down," he told her.

The look in his dark eyes told Randy not to argue. She dismounted, and Jake pulled Pepper around sideways, giving the horse's rump a shove so she was horizontal to the oncoming riders. "Keep this horse turned sideways as best you can," he told Randy. "Use her like a shield and stay right here, understand? Have that shotgun ready, but don't use it unless you have no choice, and do not move any closer until I come for you. *Promise* me!"

"I promise." Randy gave him a quick hug. "Jake, be careful."

He gently pushed her away and remounted Thunder. "You do what I told you. I'll send Whitey Loomis back here to stay with you. If Pepper goes down, you go down *with* her and keep using her for cover. And keep your head down." He rode Thunder at a gallop to meet up with the others, stopping to talk to Whitey, then heading with the rest of the men toward the greeters from Shelter, if they could be called greeters.

"God protect them," Randy said quietly. Her chest hurt at the realization she and Jake had not shared a kiss or an *I love you*. It probably did not matter. Jake was not in the mood now for either one. She waited behind Pepper and watched over the top of her saddle.

"You hear one shot, ma'am, you keep your head completely down behind that horse."

Randy turned to see Whitey had ridden up beside her. "I will."

Whitey dismounted and turned his own horse, resting his rifle on top of the saddle. He took aim ... and waited.

CHAPTER THIRTY-THREE

"KEEP YOUR RIFLES READY," Jake warned the others. He laid his own rifle across his lap and rested his right hand on his .44. "They have been in range for a while now. Each of you pick the two or three men right in front of you so each man is covered. And, by God, don't hesitate when you see any one of them make a move. Hesitation will get you killed."

"They all look like cowboys," Lloyd told his father. He rode at Jake's right, and Cole stayed close on Jake's left.

"I don't think they are a citizens' committee coming to welcome us," Cole commented. "They also don't look like lawmen. I don't see any badges. I'm guessing they were probably sent from Bolton's ranch."

"Their first attempt at scaring us off," Charlie scoffed. He rode on the other side of Cole. "Any man who thinks he can scare off a J&L man is crazy."

"Most of them are wearing red scarves around their left arms," Jake observed. "Dallas told me that means they are Bolton men. Remember that any man down there wearing a badge or one of those scarves is a killer, and one of them could even be the man who cut up that whore and stole my granddaughter. They deserve no mercy, so don't show them any. And move fast. Hesitation means death, take it from me."

They rode within about ten yards of the the questionable welcoming committee when their opponents' apparent leader shouted. "Hold up!" The big-bellied, bearded man rode closer while the rest of his men held back. He halted his sturdy roan gelding about ten feet from Jake and propped the butt of his rifle on his thigh. The men behind him raised their weapons, all pointed at Jake and his men.

"Word is Jake Harkner is coming to Shelter," the bearded man announced. "Might that be you?"

Jake took note of the man's size, and the fact that he was breathing heavily, both reasons why he would be slow with a gun. Big bellies sometimes got in the way. "Might be," he answered. "Who the hell are you? And why are we being greeted with weapons?"

"I'm Sam Caldwell, foreman on the Gold Strike Ranch. And I think you know exactly why you are being greeted this way. You come with quite a reputation, Harkner, and rumors that you have already caused unnecessary trouble. The owner of the Gold Strike, Ty Bolton, told us to come out here and make sure you don't make it all the way into town. Shelter is his territory, and he suspects foul play on your part. I should also add that Mr. Bolton don't allow armed men in Shelter. You need to give up those guns or suffer the consequences."

Jake held up his hands, indicating he was not drawing a weapon. He reached into his shirt pocket and took out a Duke's Best cigarette along with a match. He flicked the match and lit the cigarette, then tossed the match and took a long first drag on the smoke. He kept it between his lips as he slowly rested his right hand on the butt of his ivory-handled .44. "I don't give up my guns to *anybody*. Never have. Never will." He carefully moved his vest aside with his left hand to reveal his marshal's badge. "I am here on official business, and these men with me are my deputies. I have orders to come here and clean up your crooked town and Ty Bolton along with it."

Sam's belly jiggled as he laughed. "Well, now, that's a pretty big task, Harkner, seein' as how Mr. Bolton owns most of Shelter. You can see you are already outnumbered, and that doesn't even include the town sheriff and his men. There are about ten of them, and there are more back at the ranch and a lot of miners up at Ty's gold mine who do what he tells them to do. So how do you think you are going to clean up Shelter? And who says it *needs* cleaning up?"

"Dallas Blackburn says so."

"*Dallas*? How in God's name do you know that filthy whore?"

"Long story."

The Gold Strike men inched a little closer, wrapping their fingers closer around the triggers of their rifles.

"I would not be all that concerned about cleaning up your town if it weren't for the fact that one of Bolton's men cut up the face of one of Dallas's whores," Jake told Caldwell, "just because the woman tried to help a little girl. I am told his name is Dennis Gates and that he lives out at the Gold Strike."

Sam's chubby lips moved into a threatening frown. "Why would you care about Gates? Or that whore he cut up? And especially that little girl?"

Jake eyed each man closely as he continued to keep the cigarette at the corner of his lips. "I have no tolerance for men who abuse women, no matter if they are nuns or prostitutes. And that little girl is my granddaughter."

Sam's jaw dropped a little. "What?"

"You heard me. And any of your men who want to ride off right now so they don't die are welcome to leave."

"Sam, I don't like the look on his face," a skinny man with long, dark, stringy hair told the foreman. "Ain't you heard about Jake Harkner?"

"Shut up!" Sam squinted at Jake. "I will remind you that your men are outnumbered."

"It's not numbers that count, Sam. It's skill and speed that counts, along with right and wrong. One of Bolton's men has my granddaughter, and I have reason to believe she is in danger. You and that fat belly of yours and that slow hand with a gun can ride back to Ty Bolton and tell him I'm coming. I don't care if he has a *hundred* men behind him."

"You're crazy!" another of Bolton's men yelled out.

"I've been called crazy more than once," Jake answered, keeping his eyes on Sam. "It's probably true. I'm just crazy enough to shoot five or six of you without leaving my saddle, and before you can fire that rifle or clear leather with your pistol. I'll give all of you about fifteen seconds to turn and leave, or suffer the consequences."

Sam shook his head. "We ain't goin' back and answerin' to Ty Bolton for letting you get past this point."

"Wait, Sam," the skinny man told him. "Look at that younger man next to Harkner. Who does he look like?"

Sam studied Lloyd. A look of surprise swept through his eyes then as he lowered his rifle. "Jesus, he looks just like Wade Blackburn."

"That's because the man next to me is my son," Jake told him, "and so was Wade Blackburn." He tossed his cigarette. "Now, get out of our way. We are headed for

Shelter to get rid of Ty Bolton's thugs and then I'm going after my granddaughter."

Sam shook his head.

"Jesus, Sam, that's Jake Harkner," the skinny man protested again. "I ain't gonna stand up against him."

"There are more of us than them, and we have to do what Mr. Bolton sent us here to do." Sam kept a steady eye on Jake. "Turn back, Harkner. You ain't got a chance." He lifted his rifle, but he never got a chance to shoot it. In that split second, chaos erupted. Jake drew his .44 and held the trigger back as he fanned the hammer. Horses reared and screamed as Sam Caldwell went down first, followed by the four men closest to him. In a matter of two seconds those five Gold Strike men were dead, and by Jake's second shot, Lloyd and the rest of the J&L men were firing a barrage of bullets from rifles and six-guns at what remained of Bolton's posse.

When the smoke cleared, ten of Bolton's men lay on the ground, eight of them dead. The last man was already fleeing. Charlie and Cole chased after him, shooting over his head to make sure he kept running. Terrel and Duke whistled and yelled and fired their guns to send the dead and wounded men's confused horses running.

Jake dismounted and held the barrel of his second .44 against the forehead of the skinny cowboy who had warned his boss not to go up against him. The man stared up at Jake in terror while blood spurted from his chest.

"I emptied one of these .44's on you and your men," Jake growled at him. "But this other one has another six bullets in it! Where is Dee Dee Blackburn?"

The man opened his mouth to speak, but he choked on his own blood.

Jake pressed harder. "Tell me where she is, or you can

find out what it's like to have your brains blown out! Is my granddaughter still being held at Ty Bolton's ranch?"

The skinny man managed a slight nod.

"By Dennis Gates?" Jake asked.

The terrorized, bleeding man nodded again.

"Has Gates abused her?"

The skinny man struggled to breathe. "Don't ... know," he managed to answer.

"And no Gold Strike man tried to help her, *did* they?" Jake pulled the trigger, and the top of the skinny man's head disappeared. Pieces of skull and brain and blood spattered Jake's shirt. He leaned down to wipe off the end and the barrel of his .44 on the skinny man's shirt, then shoved it back into its holster. He pulled out the first gun and dumped the empty cartridges, then began reloading it.

Lloyd removed his hat and wiped sweat from his brow, then walked over to Jake, grimacing at the sight. "Pa, wipe some of that shit off your shirt and vest before you go back to Mom." He saw Jake struggling with his darkest mood.

"I can't go to her right now. Please go check on her yourself. If she's hurt, fire a shot and I'll come."

Lloyd sighed, realizing that, at the moment, the look on his father's face would even scare Randy.

Jake turned away. "Go check on her," he repeated. "I need time to calm down." He whirled the chamber of the .44 after reloading it and slammed the gun back into its holster. "If those fuckers think they are going to keep me from my granddaughter, they know now that it's not going to work. Leave the dead and wounded ones here and have everybody go back for their pack horses. We will ride to Dallas's place next. What just happened here will have Ty Bolton confused as to what to do next, so I don't think we will have to face any more of his men today. I doubt he will even send any to Dallas's place to try to roust us out of there." He mounted Thunder. "I have to get away from here and cool off. I just shot five or six men."

"Pa, wait!" Lloyd grabbed Thunder's bridle. "The top of your shoulder is bleeding. I thought the blood was from a man you shot, but it looks like it's yours because the stain is growing. Somebody's bullet must have sliced across your shoulder. Let me tend to it."

Jake touched the wound. "I didn't even feel it. Your mother will be upset. Tell her it's just a scratch." He turned and rode Thunder right over a wounded man who was rolling on the ground and screaming with pain. He paused. "You are lucky I don't put you out of your pain," he told the man. "But I'll let you live because I want you to tell Ty Bolton and Dennis Gates that I am coming for them. And tell your stinking town sheriff that I'm coming for him and his men, too!" He kicked Thunder into a gentle lope and kept going.

Lloyd watched after him. Jake always rode off alone after killing a man ... or men. He ached for his father because he knew the war the man waged deep inside over good and evil. *Pa, I wish you would talk to me.* Lloyd mounted Cinnamon and rode back to his mother, who hurried up to him with an anxious look on her face.

"Are you hurt?" She looked him over as he dismounted. "What about your father?"

"I'm okay. Pa has a scratch across his left shoulder. Compared to his condition in that gunfight three years ago, it's absolutely nothing. He said he didn't even feel it when it happened."

Randy looked past him to see Jake riding away in the distance. "He's taking off again."

"He always does, Mom. You know that. I think he's

heading for Dallas's place. He said to gather the pack horses and follow him there. Let me help you up on Pepper. Pa will be okay."

Randy wiped at tears. "He's *not* okay. Not right now. I know how he gets. How many men did he shoot?"

"I'm not sure. Six or seven, I think."

Randy shuddered. "My God."

"The last one ..." Lloyd hesitated. "I think he led Pa to believe Dennis Gates might be abusing Dee Dee. You know what that does to him. He blew the man's head near off."

Randy put a hand to her stomach. The gentle man who'd made love to her back at Pine Ranch did not exist for now. These rare moments when he went over the edge in revenge were the only times even she could not reach him at all.

"Mom, he knows guns and shooting, so he knows nothing reached you or he would have ridden back here himself. He told me to give off a shot if you were hurt. Thank God you aren't. I don't even want to think about his reaction if you were."

Randy nodded. "Yes, I know." She put a hand to Lloyd's chest. "How many men did you kill, son?"

"I'm not even sure. Two, I think."

Randy studied his eyes. "Are you okay?"

Lloyd nodded. "I got used to it when I rode with Pa back in Oklahoma. But it's harder on me than on him. He's of a nature unlike any other man."

Randy managed a sad smile. "You don't need to tell me that."

Most of the men now had their pack horses, a couple of them pulling extras. They rode over to Lloyd and Randy. "We're headin' out after Jake," Cole told Lloyd. "Your ma okay?"

"She's fine. We're coming, too. Somebody's bullet took a slice off Pa's left shoulder. If you catch up, see if you can get him to settle down and let you or one of the women at Dallas's place tend to it, will you?"

"Hey, I was with Jake down in Mexico," Cole answered. "And that was over a young girl he didn't even know rather than kin. I know how he gets. I'll straighten him out. Let's get goin'."

Lloyd helped Randy mount up, then climbed onto Cinnamon and rode beside her as they headed to the Dallas's brothel far in the distance. Other men kept hold of their pack horses for them.

Randy shivered at the dead bodies they were leaving behind. "What about the wounded ones?" she asked Lloyd, turning her head away from the sight of the one man who was still rolling around in pain.

"One of them got away. He will undoubtedly send help. And when Ty Bolton finds out what happened, he will get a good, strong message that we are here and we mean business." Lloyd kicked Cinnamon into a faster gait to get his mother away from the scene. He headed for Dallas's Pleasure Emporium.

CHAPTER THIRTY-FOUR

By the late-day setting sun Randy could see a few sorry-looking rose bushes in front of the wide veranda at Dallas's Pleasure Emporium. The grass between there and the hitching posts in front looked equally sparse and thirsty. The two-story, whitewashed frame home, obviously used for notorious doings, had red curtains at all the windows and a sign across the front of the veranda that verified they were, indeed, at the right place. Not only did it say Dallas's Pleasure Emporium in red, but the words were followed by a painting of a naked woman lying on her side.

As soon as Lloyd rode up to the hitching post in front, the red front door opened and a woman with blond hair piled high in curls stormed down the steps of the veranda and marched toward them. Her well-exposed, generous bosom bounced so vigorously that Randy wondered if her breasts might fly right out of the strapless, pink taffeta dress she wore. Deeper pink ruffles decorated the bodice, but their full flare barely covered the woman's nipples.

"Where is Jake?" Randy asked Lloyd. "I don't see his horse."

"Just calm down till we talk to this woman."

"But he's hurt."

"I told you it's a really minor wound. You know Pa. You would have to hit him with a full load of buckshot and then twelve arrows to kill that man."

"He came close enough three years ago."

Lloyd dismounted. "Stay on your horse until I tell you to get down."

Several more women sauntered out of the front door, some wearing fancy dresses, some only bloomers and corsets or frilly camisoles, one in a robe so sheer it was obvious she wore nothing underneath. They looked upset until Lloyd dismounted and they got a closer look at him.

"Hey, handsome!" one of them yelled.

"Shut up, Mary!" the blond woman shouted back as she stepped close to Lloyd. Her mouth fell slightly open when she got a better look at him. She stepped back a little. "My God, I feel like Wade Blackburn just walked back into our lives from the dead."

"He was my brother."

"*What?*"

"Dallas Blackburn says so," Lloyd told her.

The woman frowned and folded her arms, looking frustrated. "Apparently there are a lot of things Dallas did *not* explain to me when she left, and I would like to know what is going on. Business was fine earlier, until Jake Harkner arrived and came charging inside, ranting and raving and waving a gun and telling our customers to get out. He scared the hell out of my girls and nearly shot one of the men who tried to argue. Now I have no business, and Jake, somebody I have never met in my life, is out back washing up, over and over, I might add, as though he can't get clean enough. And three or four more men are back there with him, unloading horses and making themselves right at home without asking my permission. I would like an explanation!"

"Jake is my father. Are you Irene?"

"I am. Your father came in here acting like a crazy man and ordered me and the girls not to accept even one more customer tonight. He said you would pay us for lost business. He was a mess. I thought at first that he was going to shoot all of us. He had blood and some kind of pieces of flesh on the front of his shirt and even on his face. I don't like this! I don't like it one bit! I am left here with a bunch of horses for my liveryman to feed and take care of, and a crazy man who looks like he would just as soon kill all of us as fuck us."

"I'll ask you to watch your language. The woman with me is my mother."

Irene glanced at Randy. "You are *married* to that maniac?"

"He is no maniac," Randy answered. "Lloyd will explain, but I assure you, Jake Harkner has never harmed a woman in his life and won't harm any of you. Tell the other ladies here not to be afraid of him. He is just ... very upset right now."

"No doubt!" Irene looked her over. "You called them ladies. You look like a decent, kind of high-class woman. Why would you call a bunch of prostitutes ladies?"

"Because that is what Jake would call them."

Irene turned her gaze to Lloyd. "Well, now, this is a fine fix. I heard your father tell one of the men he chased out of here to tell Ty Bolton and the lawmen in town that he is coming for them."

"And he will," Lloyd told her.

"And you and your father are going to get me in trouble with Ty. I don't *need* that kind of trouble!"

"Don't worry. We are here to get rid of Bolton and his bunch," Lloyd told her.

"Ha! Good luck with *that!*"

"It could take a week, or a day," Lloyd said matter-of-factly. "My father moves fast, and it also depends on how much you can help us with things we need to know. We have already killed nine or ten Gold Strike men. I'm not even sure of the count."

Irene's blue eyes widened. "Oh, my God! You are really here to get rid of Ty and his henchmen?"

"Yes, ma'am. Can we please go inside so I can explain? I want to get my mother out of the hot sun."

Irene turned to the women still standing on the veranda. "All of you get back inside and into your rooms! These men are not here for your kind of business!" She looked back at Lloyd. "Right?"

Lloyd grinned. "Right. Pa and I and some of the others are married."

"That doesn't always matter." Irene glanced at Randy. "Sorry."

"I am not easily offended," Randy told her.

"Ma'am, even if my pa and I and the others were looking to do business, this would not be the time," Lloyd told Irene. "The reason we are here is too serious to be romping around with you lovely ladies and letting our guard down. A little war is going to take place here soon, probably tomorrow, so we have plans to make. My pa and I need you to help us with names, the layout of the town, the habits of Bolton and his henchmen, things like that. I can tell you right now that my father is sorry for storming at all of you like he did. He just needs to calm down. My mother is best at handling him. Now, can we *please* go inside? Do you have any hot coffee? I could use some."

Irene seemed more relaxed. She gave Lloyd a sly grin. "You sure you don't want whiskey?"

"Oh, I would *love* a shot of whiskey, but I have kind of a weakness for it once I taste it, if you know what I mean. Coffee will do."

Irene smiled. "I do know what you mean." She shook her head. "My God, you sure are Wade's brother. Wade was so handsome that the girls sometimes fought over him, but when he drank, he got mean and liked to beat on them, so his mood would take away from those looks." She turned. "Come on inside."

Randy remained sitting on Pepper. She leaned over and took hold of the reins to Lloyd's horse. "Lloyd, go on inside and have that coffee and explain to Irene what is going on. I'm going around back to see what the men are up to and to find Jake. I will take your horse with me. I just hope Jake hasn't walked off somewhere."

"He is a real wild man right now, Mrs. Harkner," Irene told her.

"I know the mood. Believe me," Randy answered.

"You aren't worried he might hit you or something?"

Randy smiled and shook her head. "No. Jake would slit his own throat first. Just go on inside with Lloyd. And thank you for anything you can do, and for putting up with all of this. Dallas told us you were the one to talk to."

Irene sobered. "Yes, well, it would have helped if she had explained about Jake Harkner and where she was going. Right now I would like to sock her one. I just thought she left because she needed to get out of Shelter for a while because of Wade being shot and her granddaughter being kidnapped. The man who took the child also cut up one of my prettiest girls when she tried to help Dee Dee."

"That is all part of why we are here," Lloyd explained.

He looked at his mother. "You should come inside and cool off, Mom."

"I'm fine. It's more important that I find Jake."

Lloyd took hold of Irene's arm and turned her toward the house. "Let's go."

Randy urged Pepper around the house to the back, where men and horses were gathered, some unloading their supplies, some checking guns, reloading, all in various stages of settling in for the night. Someone had already made a fire, adhering to Jake's orders to stay out of the house. They were all strangely silent, most likely lost in thought over what had just happened. Randy found Charlie and asked him to take care of her and Lloyd's horses. Charlie reached up for her and helped her down from Pepper.

"Where is Jake?" she asked Charlie.

Charlie looked concerned. "He tore off his shirt and started washing up at that pump over there," he answered, nodding toward a pump that fed a water trough. "He washed his hands and face over and over and ran water through his hair like he couldn't get clean enough."

"I know the ritual," Randy told him, aching inside for Jake.

"Soon as we got a fire going, he walked over and threw his shirt into it," Charlie added. "He gave us a few orders, and he thanked us, but hell, ma'am, we didn't have a whole lotta chance to shoot anybody. Jake did most of it, and Lloyd some. I've never seen a man so fast with a gun as Jake. He fanned that hammer so's bullets flew right across that line of men before they had a chance to shoot back, but I guess one of them managed because Jake has a pretty deep gash across his left shoulder. He wouldn't let any of us do anything with it. He just put a towel over it and walked off."

"Which direction?"

Charlie nodded toward the stable. "I think he went around behind there. I heard him coughin' real bad on the way. Maybe you should leave him alone for now, Randy."

Randy shook her head. "I can handle him. Lloyd is inside the house explaining to the woman in charge what is going on. All of you had better clean your weapons and reload and rest. I fear that what happened today is minor compared to what could happen tomorrow. Thank you for all you did today. Is anyone else hurt?"

"Just Terrel, but not a bullet wound. Cole's horse reared up and caught him in the back with a hoof. He's sore, but he will be okay."

"Find me some gauze and alcohol, will you? I am going to find Jake. Did he have a shirt on when he left?"

"No, ma'am. Like I said, he burned the other one and asked somebody to clean off his vest, then walked away holdin' a towel on his shoulder. Them scars on his back sure tell a man why he is the way he is. Cole said he saw a lot of that down in Mexico when they went down there to rescue Annie. Jake went to find where he once lived down there and then he found where he knew his mother was buried. I guess he really lost it for a while ... took a sledge hammer and knocked down what was left of that stone house where he was raised."

"I know, Charlie. And now he's worried about Dee Dee. I think Terrel carries the medical supplies we brought. Please get me that gauze and alcohol. I'll find Jake's pack horse and take out a clean shirt for him."

"Yes, ma'am"

They parted ways, both finding what they were after. Charlie caught up to Randy and handed her the gauze and alcohol. She thanked him and headed around the livery stable. Away from the fire, her eyes adjusted to a hazy dusk, that time of evening when daylight began to fade into darkness. She rounded the back side of the stable, where she could see the glow of a cigarette.

Alone. Jake could be surrounded by a hundred people, but totally alone on the inside. She walked carefully closer to find him sitting on a wooden bench, smoking. Everything was much quieter on this side of the barn.

"Jake?" Randy could tell he was glancing her way.

"I told you how it would be," he said. His voice was gruff and strained. "I told you it would be ugly." He turned away. "Tomorrow will be worse."

"You're hurt."

"It's nothing."

Just another scar, he usually said.

Randy walked closer. "You know as well as I do that any wound, minor or not, can suddenly get infected and turn dangerous. Let me put some alcohol on it and wrap it so you can put on a shirt without staining it."

He dropped the cigarette and rubbed it into the dirt with his boot. "Do whatever."

Randy cautiously sat down beside him. She set the shirt aside and used one piece of gauze to douse with the alcohol, then dabbed it onto what she could see of the wound. Jake jerked at the sting but said nothing.

"Lloyd is explaining everything to Irene," Randy told him as she cleaned the wound. "He will soften her up. He is good at that, especially with women. All they need to do is see him up close and they are putty in his hands. You have the same affect on females, I might add."

Jake snickered. "Not when I am in this mood."

"Yes, well, I think you owe those women an apology for storming in there and scaring them half to death. They are not the enemy, Jake, and now they are terrified of the consequences if you can't get rid of Ty Bolton. He will take his wrath out on them."

"I'll get rid of him. No doubt about that."

Randy could feel his rage. She put a hand on his arm and it was hard as a rock. "You have to calm down so you can think straight tomorrow."

He stood up and paced before she was finished cleaning his wound. "I talked to one of those men before I blew him away. I could tell by the look on his face that he had a pretty good idea Dee Dee has been abused." He ran a hand through his hair. "My God."

"Jake, sit down."

"That's not all. After I barged through that house, when I headed for the back door I saw that girl who got cut up. She was in the kitchen. She looked at me all wide-eyed, and I ... I couldn't help walking up to her and touching her face. I told her the man who did it would pay."

"How bad was it?"

Jake balled his hands into fists. "Bad. Real bad. He cut her from left to right. Diagonally. Across her left eye, over her nose, and down over the right corner of her lips. Real deep. Somehow he didn't actually damage the eye itself, but she's a pitiful mess. You can tell she was real pretty, and she still has a beautiful body, but she is scarred for life. This whole mess, the thought of Dee Dee maybe being abused, it brings back so many ugly memories."

"Jake, come back and sit down. Let me finish."

He did as she asked, but Randy felt like she was sitting near a powder keg that might go off any minute. She cleaned the wound a little more, then began wrapping it as best she could for its location. He winced when she told him to hold up his arm. "What did that girl say?"

"Nothing. She just cried when I touched her face. I

leaned down and kissed her forehead and she put her arms around me and cried and told me what a nice man I was." He scoffed and turned his head aside as Randy finished wrapping his shoulder. "A nice man!" He repeated with a hint of scorn. "Jesus Christ, I might kill ten or more men tomorrow! Who knows? And if I get hold of Dennis Gates, he will pay mightily for what he did to that girl! But when I think about all that, how evil some people are, how evil my *father* was, I realize I'm no different."

He faced Randy, and she felt his doubt and anger.

"Maybe *I* am the evil one," he suggested. "This whole mess has reminded me of all the evil things I've done myself, so why am I going after people like Gates and Bolton? For God's sake, I was in on the raid that killed your *father*! I've killed so many men, Randy, including my *own* father. What gives me the right to go after men who are just like me?"

"Jake, they are *not* just like you! They weren't brought up like you were, little boys afraid for their lives every single day. Little boys who did not have the slightest comprehension of what love is supposed to be. You are not evil, Jake. You go *after* evil, because you had to *live* with evil the first 15 years of your life."

"The fact remains that the judge in Denver assigned me that job of marshal in Oklahoma because he said that as long as I lived like an outlaw and knew how men like that think, I should be good at hunting them down. What that boils down to is that he's *right*. I *do* know how they think. And I know how they think because I am just *like* them! The only thing that keeps me from going back to that life is you ... and my son and daughter and all those grandkids. Sometimes it's so hard to keep that darkness at bay. I feel my father telling me, *Come on, you worthless sonofabitch. Come over to my side.*"

"Jake, everything you are feeling is as natural as breathing because of who you are. You asked what gives you the right to go after those men. Your *granddaughter* gives you the right. That young girl who is forever marked gives you the right, and all the others you have gone after in order to protect innocent people. I know you hate to hear it, but I agree with Evie when she says God is using you to right some of the wrongs. It must be true, because here you are, going after men who deliberately hurt other people. You have a big, big heart, but memories of your father keep trying to pierce the good in you and to convince you that you are bad. But everyone who has ever known you intimately knows different. That girl with the scarred face met you for five minutes, and already *she* knows different."

Jake rested his elbows on his knees and stared at the ground. "I am so fucking tired of my past hurting people I love, especially you."

"Your past, and your *father* are at fault. Not you, Jake. Never once has anyone who loves you blamed you for any of the things that have happened."

He rubbed at his eyes. "I'm sorry for what you saw today."

"Don't be. I walked into this with my eyes wide open, and I expect tomorrow to be worse. I just hope you live through it." Randy rubbed his back. "I *love* you, Jake. We have survived so much, and here we still are ... still together ... still in love."

Jake glanced sidelong at her. "You have a strange taste in men."

"Oh, no. I have very *good* taste. I know a real man when I see one, and I saw that in you back in Kansas. I cried and cried when you rode away. I was so scared to face life alone. I wanted you with me because I knew I would be safe and loved. We just have to get through tomorrow and go get Dee Dee. And when we get home, we will go up to Echo Ridge and feel the mountain air on our faces, smell the wildflowers, eat and sleep when we want, and make love all we want. Just keep all that in mind and remember your purpose for coming here. Don't worry about the ugly, or even the right or wrong of it, because there *is* no wrong in what you are doing."

Jake grasped her hand and sighed. "I want you to stay here tomorrow, Randy. It's not the best place to ask you to stay, but you won't be safe in town. And once I go after those men the ugly in me will take over. I know you say you can handle it, but I'm the one who can't. If something does go wrong, you will still be close enough to come to me. I can't have you on my mind in a situation like we will face tomorrow." He squeezed her hand. "Promise me you will stay here. I don't like you seeing me at my worst. Back in Oklahoma I was always away when I had to get ruthless. You never saw it."

"Jake, I saw you put your gun in that man's mouth back in California and pull the trigger. And I saw you shoot Mike Holt in the head at the cattlemen's ball. I *have* seen the ugly."

"You didn't see what I left behind in that bloodbath three years ago."

"I didn't need to. I saw the aftermath by the condition you were in when Lloyd found you. I will stay here if it means you won't get distracted and make a wrong move and get hurt." Randy stroked his hair away from his face. "But I know your heart. When you get like this, I understand. I know things about you that no one else sees, so don't hold back on your feelings for my sake. You don't need to. You can't have that peace you crave if you hold things inside."

Jake moved his arm around her shoulders, even though it hurt his shoulder to do so. "*You* are my peace," he told her. "You always have been. When I am with you it's like riding out of hot, rocky, barren land into a meadow of lush green grass and rippling water and shade trees."

Randy smiled. "So, now it's the poetic Jake showing himself, the rarest side of you."

He snickered. "You are the only person on this earth who can bring out that side of me."

"Pa? You back here? Is Mom with you?"

They both glanced to their left to see Lloyd's tall shadow coming toward them. "We're here," Jake answered.

Lloyd came closer. "Everything all right?" he asked. "Did you let Mom wrap that wound?"

"I did." Jake stood up and pulled on the shirt Randy handed him. "You really okay?" he asked Lloyd. "I was a mess after that shooting and I hardly noticed. I guess I just took it for granted you and the others were unhurt."

"I made it okay," Lloyd told him. "Terrel took a kick in the back from Cole's mare. She was shot across her neck and she went kind of crazy. Otherwise, nobody was hurt except you." Lloyd sighed with frustration. "Come on in the house, Pa. It's cooler in there. And Irene is drawing out a map of the town for us. She figures the word has spread by now, which means it's likely a rider will come here with a message from the one and only Ty Bolton, or maybe from the sheriff, probably with a list of demands. So we had better get back inside. I told the others to camp out here tonight, but I think Mom deserves a room and a real bed. I hate to see her sleeping in a brothel, but she'll be more comfortable, and Irene said she could put you two up in one of the better rooms. It has clean bedding and hasn't been ... uh ... used for three or four days."

Jake buttoned his shirt and tucked it into his pants. "Let's go then. We will grab what we need on the way, including my weapons. I need to clean them and reload."

"If you two need more time, I'll leave and wait by the back kitchen door," Lloyd answered.

Jake touched his arm. "I know I killed a lot of men today, Lloyd, but the two you shot would have brought me down if you hadn't been there. When eight or ten men are shooting back at you, six bullets in a couple of seconds still aren't enough. I couldn't have got through that without your backup."

"We went through it plenty of times back in Oklahoma. I just picked up on an old habit."

"It's more than that. Don't think I don't know it. You are one hell of a son, more than I deserve. I hate you risking your life like this."

"I never worry about it when you are right there with me, Pa. I just want to get this over with and get home to Katie. That little girl isn't just your granddaughter. She is my niece, and I would do the same thing for my Tricia or for Sadie Mae."

"I know you would," Jake answered. "I just hope this is the last time something from my past affects the whole family."

Lloyd gave his father a quick hug. "You be goddamn careful tomorrow, understand?" He let go. "Don't let that temper make you do something too risky. I still need you." His voice broke on the last words. "I'll be over by the back door."

Lloyd left, and Randy moved an arm around Jake. "There. You see? He loves and needs you, Jake, and so does the rest of the family. There is your reason for helping Dee Dee and for just plain living." She wrapped her arms fully around him and rested her head against his chest. She breathed in his familiar scent, all wild, all sureness, all man.

"If you say so," Jake told her. "Right now we had better get into that house and see what we need to know about tomorrow. Are you okay being around a whole bevy of bawdy women?"

Randy looked up at him. "I have to be. I'm not about to turn you loose alone in there. I'll have to keep an eye on you."

Jake pressed her close. "And I always have eyes only for you."

"Yes, well, we will see about that when you are faced with a bunch of loose women."

Jake laughed softly and kept an arm around her as they headed for Dallas's "pleasure emporium." Randy wished she could turn off her worry about what might happen tomorrow, but she knew this would be a long, sleepless night. "I love you, Jake. You do like Lloyd said and keep your wits about you tomorrow."

His reply was to give her an extra tight hug.

CHAPTER THIRTY-FIVE

Jake, Lloyd and Randy were greeted by a kitchen full of the same skimpily clad women who'd stood on the veranda earlier. They stepped back a little when Jake walked in with the bandalero and his gun belt draped over one shoulder, his rifle in his other hand. Lloyd still wore his gun on his hip and carried both his rifle and the shotgun they would leave with Randy, who at the moment carried two carpetbags.

The women whispered among themselves and stared at both men, looking them over appreciatively.

"Mind your business, ladies," Irene told them. "Neither one of them is available, and Jake there has his wife with him." She turned to Jake with a grin. "You sure know how to fill up a room. I explained the situation to these women, but they wanted to see you as your normal self instead of ranting and raving and chasing out their customers with a gun."

Jake nodded to all of them and gave them a reassuring smile. "I apologize," he told them.

"It's okay," a skinny, dark-haired young woman answered. "Irene told us your son said Dee Dee is your granddaughter," she explained. "We understand why you would be so upset. We hope you can get her out of there and take her home with you."

"My gosh, *look* at him," another spoke up, nodding toward Lloyd. "It's like Wade himself was standing there."

"It's true then," said another. She kept her eyes on Jake. "Wade Blackburn was your son?"

Jake set his gunbelts and rifles on a counter behind him. "I never knew about Wade, but if he looks so much like Lloyd here, then it must be true that he was mine. Dallas and I were close once, until she betrayed me for bounty money."

"That's terrible," the skinny one told him. "Dallas can be kind of mean sometimes, but I never thought she would do something like that to a customer."

"It doesn't matter now," Jake answered. "What matters is that I know Dee Dee is my granddaughter, and we are here to take her home with us. If we can rid the town of Ty Bolton and his thugs at the same time, all the better."

"We all hate Ty Bolton," the same girl answered. She pointed to a bruise on the right side of her face. "See this?" She put her hands on her hips. "Ty Bolton did that. He takes pleasure in hurting a woman while he ..." She paused, glancing at Randy, then back to Jake. "You know what I mean. We will help you get rid of that man however we can, but this has to work, or he will come out here and beat on us and probably burn down Dallas's place."

They all nodded and offered their agreement to what could happen.

"I read about you." A redheaded, freckle-faced woman said, sauntering a little closer. "It said you were raised in places like this."

"Sweetheart, I am not here to talk about my past. I just

want my granddaughter and then I want to get home. I'm sorry all of you have to give up your business for a night or two, but you will be paid. This beautiful woman who just sat down beside me is my wife of 37 years. Her name is Miranda, and I want her to stay here tomorrow while my son and I and the men out back go take care of business in town, so it will be a hard day for her. I want all of you to be good to her and understand what she will be going through."

"What you want to do won't be easy," one of the others spoke up.

"He's Jake Harkner," Irene told them. "He has quite a reputation. And all of you saw him when he first got here. He about scared the pee out of me. I have a feeling some of Ty's men will take off running before he even comes after them. They know what this man can do."

"My father and I served as U. S. Marshals in the worst parts of Oklahoma for three years," Lloyd reminded them. "Some of the men we went after don't come any worse. We know what we are doing."

"In the meantime, I want all of you to dress proper tomorrow around Mrs. Harkner," Irene told them. "And I doubt she appreciates you flaunting your best qualities in front of her husband and son, so go on back to your rooms now. If you have to come down here for something, put on decent clothes And hands off the men outside. They will be risking their lives to free us from Bolton and his bunch tomorrow. I am going to have Martha cook them a fine, big breakfast in the morning, so some of you should offer to help her. And she will have hot coffee ready all night long. I want you to take turns helping serve those men out there, but don't be offering something more than food and drink, understand?"

"You sure are making this hard, Irene," one of the girls complained.

"Just do what I asked. Once this is over, if any of those men wants a free one, you give it to him, but some might come back from town tomorrow injured, so be ready for that, too."

A free one? Randy couldn't help a little sting of unnecessary jealousy. She glanced at Jake as he lit a cigarette. She could tell this environment was old hat to him. He glanced sidelong at her, then took her hand and gently squeezed it.

The women snickered and smiled and scurried off, and Irene told an older woman named Martha to serve their guests some fresh coffee. The woman gladly obliged, then put several tin cups on a tray along with the pot of hot coffee and headed outside with it. Lloyd jumped up and opened the door for her.

"Why thank you," Martha told him with an appreciative smile.

Irene sat down to the table and told Jake and Randy to sit also. "Martha is our cook and housekeeper," she explained. "That's all she does here. She lost her husband and needs the money." She turned her gaze to Randy. "I hope it doesn't offend you to be in here," she told Randy.

Randy shook her head. "Being in this place doesn't matter to me. It's what Jake is up against in going after Ty Bolton that matters. I'm sure you can appreciate that."

'I do." Irene rose to take a sheet of paper from the countertop behind her and placed it at the center of the table. She'd pulled a button-front shirt over the bodice of her dress so that her "attributes," as Jake would call them, did not hang out for all to see when she bent over to explain the drawing. "I did what you asked, Jake. I made a drawing of Shelter's main street so you don't go in there blind."

Jake turned to Lloyd. "Get Terrel, Cole and Charlie in here," he told him. "They should see this." He turned to Randy while they waited. "You okay?"

Randy felt a sudden need to cry, but she struggled not to show it. "I don't know."

Jake set his cigarette in an ashtray. "Randy, we don't have to stay here if you don't want to."

"No. No. It's not that." She looked at Irene. "I appreciate sleeping in a real bed. We have been on the trail and sleeping on the ground for several days. I just ..." She quickly wiped at tears. "Jake, I'm so afraid for you. I can't go through what I did three years ago. I just can't. And you had that doctor from Chicago then. I'm not sure you would have lived without him. It took him and Brian working together to save you." She looked at Irene. "Is there a decent doctor here in Shelter?"

Irene sighed. "When he isn't drunk. But honey, you are in outlaw country. High-class doctors don't come to places like this. But I know Doctor Baker can take out bullets and knows how to keep my girls ... well ... healthy, I guess you would say."

Randy broke into tears. "Jake, I'm so sorry. I said I would be strong about this."

"Don't be sorry. Don't you dare be sorry. Remember how I always used to say I will be back from whatever I was riding into?"

Randy nodded.

Jake moved an arm around her shoulders. "It's like that now. We won't be far apart this time, but I will get through this just like all the other times, and I will come back from town and the next day the men and I will go get Dee Dee. Simple as that."

"I wish it *was* that simple. The last time you came back, you were one breath away from death."

"And Evie is praying for us," he reminded her. "Plus, I am not alone this time. I have some very able men with me."

Lloyd returned with the three J&L men. Randy quickly wiped at her tears with a handkerchief from the pocket of her riding skirt and scooted back her chair so they could all lean over the table and look at Irene's drawing.

"It is only about a five-minute ride from here to town," Irene told them, "and the first building here is a place called Pat's Rooming House. Next to that is the hardware store, then a barber shop, a cafe, a store that sells livestock supplies and tack, then a restaurant, an ice house, and then the Cowpoke Saloon, where Bolton and his men usually hang out. After that is a farm supply store, and the jail is at the end of the street. It faces the whole street. Sheriff McDonald, who they call Cotton, is usually at the jail mornings with two or three of his deputies. You can't miss him. His hair is white as snow, even though he's not even thirty years old yet. Around the corner from jail and heading back up the street here is the doctor's office, then on up this way is a place that sells mining supplies, and a lawyer's office. By the way, he's crooked. And he is paid by Bolton. No surprise there. Then here is the White Mountain Saloon, a millinery, another restaurant, a place that sells fresh meat, a grocery store, a ladies' clothing store and up here, kitty-corner from the rooming house, is the Mountain View Hotel, which Pat also owns. Her husband died a couple of years ago and she runs everything herself."

Irene straightened and eyed all of them. "Bolton's men will be everywhere, and those sons of bitches will shoot you in the back if they get the chance. There might be a couple of men on rooftops, too." She pointed to the tack house and the restaurant down and across the street from the rooming house. "These are their favorite rooftop locations, and you can bet one of the deputies will be on the roof of the jailhouse. You can tell which ones are Bolton men because they wear red scarves around their left arms. That will help keep you from shooting somebody innocent. There will likely be at least three men on rooftops and at least three inside the jailhouse. But you can bet more will be lurking in the alleys."

"Sounds like we will be outnumbered probably two, maybe three to one," Lloyd told Jake.

"Familiar odds," Jake commented.

Cole snickered. "There you go again, Jake, actin' like this will be easy. You just remember that if somethin' happens to me, Gretta will light into you like a wildcat."

The men all laughed nervously.

"I'm used to women like Gretta," Jake joked in return. "And my own wife might not be from the same stock, but she can be just as ornery. I can handle anything after living with her for 37 years."

"Oh, thank you," Randy spoke up, trying to be as light-hearted about the situation as the men were. "In those 37 years, who has put up with the most chaos?"

"The whole damn family," Lloyd answered.

More nervous laughter followed.

"Pa, I think our main job will be looking for snipers," Lloyd said. "You know damn well their primary target will be you. They probably figure that if they can get rid of you, the rest of us will run. You have my promise that isn't going to happen. And if something does happen to you, we will still go get Dee Dee."

Jake looked around the circle of men. "I can't tell all of you how much I appreciate this. When we go into town tomorrow, don't watch me. Just watch the alleys and rooftops until we get close to the jailhouse. But I have a feeling Bolton and that sheriff and the others will be waiting here." He pointed to the Cowpoke Saloon. "It's their main hangout, so the saloon and jail are our primary targets. But they will try to gun us down before we even reach the jail."

Randy knew the others were thinking the same thing she was. How could he talk so calmly and matter-of-factly about going into so much danger, as though he was simply planning when to plant a crop or where to find stray cattle?

"Every Bolton man out there wants us dead," Jake reminded them, "so don't give any man the chance to shoot first. And remember to look for those red scarves on men's arms, or men with badges, and shoot without hesitation. Do just like I did when those men lined up against us earlier today. They didn't expect me to just start shooting. When you take a man by surprise, he gets all befuddled and scared and confused. That's your advantage."

"But you still need to be damn fast," Charlie said.

Jake glanced his way. "Fast is not as important as ruthless. Don't think about the right or wrong of it. Don't think at *all*. Just *act*." He scanned the circle of men. "All of you know Evie is praying for us. I truly believe my daughter's prayers give us an advantage. And we have to survive this so we can go get my granddaughter. Think about Dee Dee and *only* Dee Dee. With any luck, all this will be over in one day, but we might still need to head for Bolton's ranch to find my grandaughter. We will do all of this hard and fast so they don't have much time to make their own plans. We need to keep them confused and unsure. A quick strike will do that."

Various sighs and swallows and the sound of clearing

throats took the place of talking as the men straightened and nodded their thanks to Irene.

"God be with all of you," she told them. "Let part of your incentive be that there is a house full of women here who will be very grateful if you are successful. I think you know what I mean."

"You bet, pretty lady," Terrel answered.

They all shook hands with each other, and Irene reminded them about breakfast early the next morning. "Go get some sleep, if that's possible," she told them.

They all headed outside, but Lloyd paused to lean down and give his mother a kiss on the cheek. "It will be okay, Mom," he told her. "I figure God sent us here, so he's not going to let us fail. Okay? And you do like Pa told you. Stay here with the women tomorrow."

Randy nodded. "I will." She reached up and patted his cheek. "You remember Katie and all those children back home need you. And if something happens to your father ..." She hesitated and wiped at unwanted tears. "I will need you, too."

Lloyd squeezed her shoulder. "Hey, I abandoned you and Evie years ago when Pa went to prison. I came up here to outlaw country and tried not to care, but that didn't work. I'll never abandon you or anybody in the family again. And Pa will be coming home with us. Got that?"

Randy nodded. "You'd better go out there and keep the men's spirits up."

Lloyd turned to his father. "Take good care of her tonight, and don't be ornery." He left, and Irene showed Jake and Randy to their room. Randy studied the gawdy surroundings. White lace curtains and red velvet wallpaper. The bed was topped with a frilly pink quilt, and fuzzy pink rugs decorated the wood floor.

Irene left, and Randy could not help a light laugh as she removed her vest. "I feel like one of the girls," she told Jake.

Jake tossed his gunbelts and hat into a red velvet chair, then set his rifle against the wall. "Baby, if you were, you would be a rich woman. Men would steal from each other and shoot each other to be first in line to bed you."

Randy gave him a flirtatious smile. "And just think. *You* get me for free." She hoped the remark would keep things light and keep Jake's mind off of tomorrow.

Jake grinned. "You bet." He sobered again as he started undressing. "You don't belong in this place, Randy, but I can't help thinking how you are ten thousand times more beautiful and more desirable than any woman here." He walked up and hugged her from behind, kissing her hair. "Find your brush and I will undo your braid and brush your hair out for you."

Randy fished her brush out of her carpetbag and sat down in a small chair covered with pink satin. She relished the comfort of the scalp massage she gleaned from the brush's strokes. Jake was always gentle about it. They looked at each other in the mirror, and Randy couldn't keep the tears from her eyes.

"I hate seeing you cry," Jake told her, "mainly because I am usually the cause of your tears."

"I don't mind the difficulty of the trip, Jake, or staying in a brothel. But I ache for you and what you are going through."

Jake set the brush down and lifted her out of the chair. He carried her to the bed, then set her on her feet while he ripped down the quilt and sheets. He laid her on the bed, her hair spread out against the pillow. "You are so damn beautiful," he told her. He pulled off her boots, her stockings, her riding skirt, then unbuttoned her blouse and untied her camisole, pulling both open.

Neither of them spoke. It was not necessary. Randy drank in the sight of her husband's fine build when he finished undressing, studied his handsome face and great smile, loved seeing the desire in his dark eyes. He reminded her sometimes of a wild animal that only she could tame.

Here they were again, wanting each other because they knew this could be the last time. Jake joined her on the bed and moved his knees between her legs, forcing them apart as he leaned down and began kissing her, lightly, deeper, then hungrily, needing her, wanting her, just as she needed and wanted him. It was always like this when danger and death hung in the air.

Jake worked his way down, removing her panties, kissing private places, then trailing back up over her belly again, her breasts, her nipples, her neck, her eyes, her lips, all her body parts adored with deep, deep kisses that brought pleasant desire to her insides.

Randy pressed her hands to his face. "Jake."

He paused, meeting her gaze.

"Just be you," she told him. "I don't want the angry Jake, or the Jake who rode away to be alone, or the Jake who thinks he might lose me. You will never lose me. I just want the Jake who takes joy and satisfaction in making love to me, as I do in *letting* him. Let's just be us, like it is when we go to Echo Ridge."

"That's where I am right now. Alone with you up on that ridge, looking across the J&L and knowing my great big family is down there, and you *gave* me that family." He settled on top of her, meeting her mouth again, groaning with what she knew was a need to savor her body like fine wine … just in case … just in case.

Nothing more needed to be said. He was in command now ... in command of himself and of her body ... and her soul. For now he was in the present, the best place to be. His kisses deepened. This was her Jake now, the Jake who zeroed in only on her, who loved only her, needed only her. This was the Jake who wanted to please and own only her.

So many personalities. So tortured deep inside. He tried so hard to be what he knew she needed and wanted, and in spite of how he was raised, he could be incredibly gentle and loving. He moved over her with a velvet touch, velvet kisses, moves that brought out every womanly need imaginable.

"Eres todo lo que he necesitado para mantenerme vivo," he told her.

You are all I need to stay alive.

No matter how hard she tried to follow her own advice of not thinking about tomorrow, she could not help letting the reality of it sweep through her being like an evil demon. She grabbed on to him and gave all she could, and Jake gave all he could in return, hard love that penetrated deep and claimed every part of her. She was lost beneath broad shoulders and the power that was Jake. He was her safe place ... her wonderfully safe place. She had managed to pull him back from the abyss that held his past and constantly beckoned him.

They made love with intense passion, wanting to remember every curve and scent and every inch of each other's body. Their kisses were like another form of mating, an intrusion of souls, a sharing of spirits. He took her with wild abandon, commanding, a man in complete control of her, body and soul.

Just as passionately as he took, Randy gave back with the same intensity. She resolved that nothing was going to take him away from her. God would not allow him to die tomorrow. And all the women in this place meant nothing to him. Nor did all the women he'd known before her. She had never worried about losing him to another woman, because his *past* was the other woman. His past, and that dark abyss that often beckoned him, were her competition, and she would *never* let the shadows from his past win. She absolutely would not allow it.

CHAPTER THIRTY-SIX

A NIGHT of lovemaking left Randy sweetly exhausted. She awoke to the sound of a bird twittering just outside the still-open window ... and there stood Jake at the window, clean-shaven, dressed and fully armed. Reality hit her like a sledge hammer. She jumped out of bed. "Jake, what time is it?"

"Only about 7:30." He studied the grounds below. "The women are down there serving breakfast to the men." He smiled. "They are all dressed like school teachers."

"Jake, you should have woken me."

"We have time. I'm going downstairs to see about some coffee. I'm too worked up to eat, though. I think Lloyd is already down there, and it looks like Charlie and Cole are coming in. You stay here and get dressed."

"Jake, don't leave yet. Promise me. I'm sorry I overslept."

He walked over to the bed and leaned down to kiss her. "And I'm sorry I wore you out."

Randy gave him a shove. "And here I thought I wore *you* out."

He tousled her hair. "Get dressed. Bullets will be flying soon."

"And I meant what I said, Jake. Don't leave yet."

"Don't worry." He looked over as she got out of bed naked. "My God, you are beautiful when you are all sleepy and your hair is a mess. I love knowing I did that to you."

She rushed over to him and flung her arms around his middle, ignoring the bandelero around his chest. "I love you. I love you. I love you."

Jake moved his arms around her and kissed her hair. "Baby, it will be okay. Just be ready to meet the husband you haven't met yet. That God of Evie's didn't send me all the way up here to fail, so I will do what it takes to make sure of it."

She looked up at him and he kissed her deeply. "Get dressed and come downstairs. I promise I will be there."

Randy touched his shirt, pushing his vest aside to see he wore the U. S. Marshal badge. She moved her hand over his heart and felt something under his shirt. "You are wearing your mother's crucifix."

"What's left of it."

The memory made Randy's blood chill. She stepped back. "You look nice. A clean white shirt. A marshal's badge. So tall and handsome."

"This clean white shirt will have blood on it before the day is over. If it's not mine, it will be someone else's. You just make sure you stay out of all of it." Jake kissed her once more. "I had better leave before I decide to stay here in bed with you all day. I have to get you out of my blood and let that other Jake take over."

"I don't like that other Jake. I can't control him."

"Baby, you control him more than you realize." He kissed her once more, then turned and left.

Randy hurriedly washed herself and cleaned her teeth. She brushed the tangles from her hair, sexual desires pulling at her insides when she thought about last night. Once she got Jake completely away from his nightmarish past, she felt him come fully to her spiritually. That was when their lovemaking was its best, and knowing the danger that lay ahead made it all more forceful and deep ... soul deep. They became one, each trying to make sure every touch and taste and kiss and penetration was remembered ... just in case this time was the last time.

Don't think about that now, she told herself. She quickly dressed, white blouse, brown suede vest, matching suede riding skirt. She stood in front of a stained mirror and put a little color on her cheeks and lips. She wanted to look nice for Jake. She tied a yellow scarf around her neck. Jake liked yellow. His last memory should be ...

Stop it! She chided herself again. This was going to be a *good* day. Surely God would never take her Jake away from her. Today he and Lloyd and their men would rid the town of its crooked lawmen and then they would ride to Ty Bolton's ranch and get Jake's granddaughter.

And then ... home. *Home!* The word sounded wonderful. Jake would be with his grandchildren again. That always drew him out of the past better than anything. That passel of kids brought him so much badly-needed joy. She hated it when he talked like he did last night, about wanting to sleep forever. She feared he meant more than just normal sleep. There were so many dark corners lurking in the deep recesses of his mind, hidden crevasses she could not reach. She feared some day he would go there and never come back.

She heard men's voices downstairs as she pulled her hair back at the sides and secured it with plain combs. She pulled on her boots and took her pistol from her supply bag. She dropped it into a pocket on her skirt along with a few extra bullets. Jake had left the shotgun standing in a corner. She grabbed it and opened it to make sure it was loaded, then hurried out.

Jake, Lloyd, Cole, Terrel, Charlie, Whitey and Duke were standing in the kitchen talking about how and when to ride into town and what each man's job would be. All seven of them were heavily armed. Randy thought how, if she didn't know them, she would be scared to death of every one of them and the hard looks on their faces. Irene stood at the kitchen sink wearing a simple calico dress, her arms folded as she listened to the men talk.

Randy glanced across the hall at the dining room to see three of the prostitutes sitting at a table looking skeptically at Jake and the others. Their plates held food, but none of them were eating. Randy noticed a deep scar across the face of the woman who sat farthest away. The woman quickly turned away, as though she hoped Randy would not notice it, but Randy walked into the dining room and pulled up a chair beside her. "Are you Brenda?"

The young woman stared at her plate. "Why else would I try to hide my face?"

"Don't do that," Randy told her. "You are a brave woman, and I came in here because I want to thank you for trying to keep Dennis Gates from taking Dee Dee. I'm so sorry for what he did to you."

"You shouldn't be sorry," Brenda said quietly. "You had nothing to do with any of it. And you are too much of a lady to be sitting in here with a bunch of prostitutes."

"I beg to differ." Randy touched her arm. "Brenda, please look at me."

Brenda raised her head a little and met Randy's gaze.

Her eyes were a beautiful sparkling green, and her dark hair was brushed out long and lovely.

"You are still very pretty, and you should know that you are part of the reason my husband is going after Bolton and his men today," Randy told her. "It's not just for his grand-daughter. Nothing stirs revenge in his soul more than an abused woman. His mother was horribly abused when he was too little to help her. He has been making up for it any way he can ever since. I can promise you that if he succeeds today, you and these other women won't need to worry about Bolton and his men again, ever. Jake usually accomplishes what he sets out to do. And please believe me, neither Jake nor the other men out there in the kitchen care about that scar. Do you want to know what Jake told me when he said he'd seen and talked to you?"

Brenda looked back at her plate and toyed with her food, scraping it around with a fork. "God only knows. He's a handsome man with a beautiful wife."

"Well, thank you," Randy answered. "But I was just going to tell you that he said you are really pretty, and in his words, *she still has a beautiful body.*"

One of the other women burst into laughter. "They are all the same, aren't they, sweetheart?" she asked Brenda. "They always notice the body more than the face."

Brenda couldn't help grinning. "Thank you, Mrs. Harkner. But didn't that make you mad? I mean, weren't you upset that he noticed something like that and said it right to you?"

Randy smiled. "You don't know my Jake. He has a deep appreciation for beautiful women, including women who work in places like this. His father hung out in brothels, and the women there often protected Jake when he was too young to fight off his father's drunken rages. But believe me,

Jake knows who he belongs to now. I have ways of reminding him."

One of the other women snickered. "I'll bet you do."

Randy joined in their laughter as she stood up. "Jake also knows how sorry he would be if he ever strayed," she told all three of them. "I already shot that man once. And he knows I also have a big fist."

They all laughed harder at the remark.

"You're a real corker, Mrs. Harkner." The words came from a heavyset, dark-haired woman whose belly shook when she laughed. She wore a blue checkered dress in an attempt to look modest, but her hair was back-combed into a pile of dry frizz on top of her head and held there with sparkly combs. She wore heavy makeup and so much black on her eyelashes that Randy wondered if it made her eyelids heavy.

The woman reached out to shake Randy's hand. "My name is Tina, and this other gal at the table is Linda. You should know that we are all praying that your husband and all those other men out there make it through this. God knows we all sure wish your Jake wasn't a devoted married man, let me tell you. And that son of yours ..." She fanned her face. "God bless them both, and those men out there who are willing to help."

Randy squeezed her hand. "Thank you for your prayers."

"You might think women like us have no right praying, but God is supposed to love everybody, right?"

"You are exactly right," Randy answered with a smile. "I have always had trouble convincing Jake of that."

"He's a good man," Brenda told her.

Randy pressed Brenda's shoulder. "He is. And you remember how beautiful you still are. Don't let anyone tell you different." She headed for the kitchen, where every man looked her way when she entered. Jake hurried around the circle of men to put an arm around her shoulders.

"Jake, if you succeed, the whole town will be cheering for you and some will probably help you go after your granddaughter," Irene told him.

"I hope you are right," Jake answered.

"Like I said, you are already the talk of the town, Mr. Harkner." The words came from a medium-built, graying man who wore a dark suit.

Jake pulled Randy closer. "Randy, this is Hank Miller. He owns a hardware store in town and came to tell us that last night those men we shot were brought into town. That man you saw in pain yesterday lived. He has Bolton and his thugs stirred up and ready for action. They walked up and down the street last night and again this morning brandishing weapons and warning citizens that anyone who helped us, if we came into town today, would die." He gave her a squeeze. "Mr. Miller, this is my wife, Miranda," he told Hank.

Miller nodded to Randy. "Ma'am, I'm glad to meet you. From that book about your husband you are almost as famous as he is."

"Infamous is the better word," Jake said.

Miller sighed. "Infamous or not, we need you, Mr. Harkner."

"Call me Jake."

Miller scanned the circle of men. "Word spread fast after everybody in town found out what happened and who did it. We are all excited that we might see Ty Bolton get what he deserves today. Some of us citizens had a secret meeting last night and they sent me here to warn you what's going on, and to let you know they will do what they can to help. They don't want this drawn out because that gives Bolton's men more time to plan and to threaten and torture citizens into staying out of it. They are good at scaring us out of the street and behind closed doors, so if you act now, while everybody is worked up, a lot of us are ready to help." He zeroed in on Jake. "If you and your men intend to go up against Bolton and his bunch, you are definitely risking your lives. Getting it done fast is your best bet." He sipped some coffee Irene had given him.

"I've been up against men like Bolton most of my life," Jake answered. "And usually alone."

Miller set the coffee aside. "Be that as it may, Bolton is in town this morning, and he's lit up like a torch. I've never seen Shelter so alive at this hour. Bolton's excuse of a sheriff and his men are armed to the hilt and ready for you to come in. In fact, I'm supposed to deliver an invitation for you to come and face Cotton one-on-one. Cotton is what they call Sheriff McDonald because although he is only around 30, he has white hair that kind of looks like cotton, and he's damn fast. I'm talking *lightning* fast, Jake. I think he wants to face you down alone."

Charlie scoffed and others laughed. "He's an idiot," Charlie said. "Ain't nobody gonna win a gunfight with Jake."

Miller sighed and looked Jake over. "No offense, Jake, but he's probably thirty or forty years younger than you."

This time *all* the men laughed, including Lloyd.

"Mister, you ain't never seen Jake go up against it," Cole told Miller.

Miller smiled. "Well, I am sure his reputation is well-earned. But times change, and new people move in and take over. The way I see it is that they will let Cotton have his moment because Bolton and the others believe he can beat

Jake and put himself and Shelter in headlines all over the country. And once it is over, all hell will break loose, so be ready. You might be able to take care of Cotton, Jake, but as soon as he goes down, you will all be targets. If *you* go down, the rest of your men will be targets, along with the citizens who dared help you."

Randy put a hand to her stomach. Jake noticed her anxiety and squeezed her shoulders again. "Is Dennis Gates in town?" he asked.

Miller nodded. "He rode in last night. After Bolton sent those men out to confront you and your men yesterday, he stayed in town all night, too. He sent a man back to his ranch to get Gates, who is his right-hand man and body-guard. Bolton wants to bring you in so he can hang you in front of the townsfolk as a warning that nobody, not even Jake Harkner, can stop him and his men from taking over."

Lloyd scoffed. "If Bolton's men brought a hanging rope to town, they might end up seeing Bolton himself hang instead of my father."

Miller smiled slyly. "I hope you are right. We are all praying you and your father are the ones who can put an end to this. Up to now, we have had no one behind us who had your skill and daring," He paused nervously, looking intently at Jake. "Or – uh - your ruthlessness, according to rumors. A couple of territorial lawmen came here different times and tried to clean things up, but they are buried south of town now. I think it's because they tried to do things lawfully, arrest certain men, that sort of thing. I warn you, that won't work here. It's either kill or be killed. I hate to put it so bluntly, but that is what it will take, and from all I have heard about you …" Miller paused. "Well, again, no offense, but --"

"You don't need to say it, Miller."

"Let's hope one of us doesn't end up under a marker on that hill of gravestones I seen when we rode in," Cole spoke up.

They all smiled and snickered, but the tension was high.

"Jake, you are the talk of the town this morning," Miller told him. "The wounded man they brought in told us what you did to Skinny Martin. They say that more than one man threw up at the sight when they went out to get the bodies."

Jake took his arm from Randy's shoulders. "The only way to be successful with men like that is to move fast and surprise them with proof that you mean business. Some will give up and go home without drawing a gun. The rest will wish they had done the same." He smashed out the cigarette he'd been smoking and lit yet another one.

Randy knew what that meant. His mind was whirling fast with what he needed to do. She had already detected a change in Jake from the man who slept with her last night to a near stranger. He took a deep drag on the cigarette and kept his eyes on Hank Miller. "Do you have any idea where my granddaughter is? She is the sole reason I am here."

Miller glanced around at the other men, as though trying to warn that what he was about to say might set off an explosive violence in Jake and send shock waves throughout Dallas's Pleasure Emporium. He glanced at Randy and frowned. "Ma'am, maybe you shouldn't be in here."

"I can handle any news you have." Randy put a hand to Jake's back, already sensing Dee Dee's situation was not good.

Miller looked at Jake and swallowed. "Like I told you, Gates is Ty Bolton's right-hand man, so he gets away with just about anything he wants."

"And?" Even with speaking just one word, Jake's voice was husky with dread.

Miller ran a hand under his collar, as though he might die any minute. "Please don't think I go along with any of this, Jake. I am just the bearer of whatever you need to know."

"Get to the point, Miller."

Miller looked around at the rest of them, then pulled a chair backward up against himself as though he needed some kind of defense. "Well, sir, everybody knows that Dennis Gates likes young women."

"She's not a woman," Jake said. Randy felt the heat emanating from his body. "She's a fucking *kid!* No older than two of my granddaughters back home who are only nine and ten!"

"Jake," Randy said quietly, hoping to keep him calm. But she already knew that would be impossible.

"Out with it, Miller!" he demanded.

Miller looked around the room again, then back at Jake. "I have a ten-year-old granddaughter myself, Jake. I know that kind of love, and I always felt she was safe in Shelter until Ty Bolton and his bunch rode through and took over. We keep our family close now, keep younger girls off the street, especially at night."

"God dammit, Miller, stop beating around the bush!"

"Pa, Mr. Miller is not the enemy," Lloyd gently reminded him.

Miller cleared his throat. "Just remember I'm only here to help. And most in town are also ready. The look in your eyes is pretty intimidating, Mr. Harkner. Right now I feel like a small rabbit being eyed by a bobcat."

"Just tell me what's going on and be fucking glad you aren't the one in my sights. And remember that I have seen and heard every rotten thing a man can experience in his life. I killed my own drunken maniac of a father for raping a young girl, so just say it like it is!"

Miller ran a hand through his thinning hair. "Well, sir, your granddaughter is actually in town."

"*Where?*"

"In, uh, in a room over the Cowpoke Saloon. Dennis Gates brought her in last night after he heard what you did to those men who tried to stop you yesterday. He, uh, he had a couple of Cotton's deputies drag the town preacher and his family out of their home and into the main street. They held guns on the man's wife and two sons and said they would kill all of them and burn the preacher's house if he didn't, uh ..." He paused. "If he didn't marry him and Dee Dee right then and there. He said that you couldn't take Dee Dee away from him if she was his legal wife ... said you can't do anything about it, and that somebody should tell you that before you bother coming after her, think twice. He said you wouldn't be rescuing some innocent girl, so why risk your life for her? The preacher half cried through the whole thing, but he knew Gates meant business, so he married Gates and the girl. Gates put a ring on her finger and carted her off to the Cowpoke Saloon and forced her upstairs, or at least that's what people tell me happened after that."

"Jesus Christ," Cole muttered.

Various other grumbled cuss words filled the tiny kitchen.

"My God," Irene muttered, turning away. "Even I didn't think Gates was that bad. The women here and I would never allow something like that, and that includes Dallas. She will be devastated."

"*Will* she?" Jake rumbled. "She could have told me about Dee Dee *years* ago! She had to know what a sick environment this was for her. Maybe my son loved his daughter, but he let whiskey come first, and look how that affected an innocent little girl! Dallas *knew* something like that could happen, so don't stand there and tell me how devastated she will be to learn this."

Miller cleared his throat. "Jake, Dennis Gates buys and trades young women. He, uh, he usually doesn't mess with them himself, or so I'm told. I am not familiar with such sinful behavior. I just think ... hope, I should say ... that Gates was saving Dee Dee for prize money. She's awfully pretty. He probably never touched her wrongly, so maybe last night was the only time he ... you know."

Randy wondered if the sky actually darkened outside, or if it was just the room that darkened from Jake's fury.

"The *only* time?" Jake suddenly roared the words. "The *only* time? One time or many, what difference does it make to a ten-year-old *child*! I know goddamn well what terror and helplessness feels like at that age, whether it's a little girl getting raped or a little boy getting the *shit* beat out of him!"

No one spoke for a few tense seconds.

Miller wiped sweat from his brow. "I'm real sorry to bring such news," he said, looking around at all of them again. "Just know that the whole town is ready to back all of you when you go after Bolton and his bunch."

Lloyd moved to stand closer to Jake. "You had better leave," he told Miller.

"They should *all* leave," Jake added. "All except you and Randy." He grabbed the back of a chair and leaned on it, hanging his head.

Each man quietly made his way outside. Irene walked into the dining room, closing the kitchen door behind her.

Randy touched Jake's arm and realized he was trembling. He jerked his arm away again.

"We're too fucking late," he said, his tone that of someone attending a funeral.

"Pa, don't be blaming yourself."

Jake rocked back and forth, his breathing heavy. "That animal deliberately did the one thing he knew would bring me running! But no matter how this turns out, the damage to that little girl is *done.*"

"Jake, Dee Dee is a Harkner," Randy reminded him. "They don't come any stronger. And just like Evie got through what happened to her, Dee Dee will do the same. And if anyone can help her, it's Evie, so all she needs is to go home with us. No one will show her more love than her Grandpa Jake, let alone Katie and Evie and Brian and Lloyd and me, and that whole big bunch of Harkner cousins."

Jake shoved the chair aside and rushed over to the kitchen sink to vomit. Randy hurried over and touched his back. "Jake --"

"Don't touch me!"

"Pa, I remember how you reacted to the news that Evie had been taken. You would not sleep or eat, and your body started to shut down. Your own emotions nearly killed you physically, and I hate to remind you, but you're older now." Lloyd walked closer as Jake rinsed his mouth, then grabbed a flask of whiskey sitting near the sink and uncorked it. He took a mouthful and used it to rinse his mouth and spit it out, then took a swallow.

"Pa, stop it!" Lloyd grabbed his arm and knocked the bottle out of his hand into the sink. The glass broke, and the whiskey trickled down the drain. Jake whirled and shoved Lloyd away. Randy stepped back. This was a father-son moment, and one of those times when Lloyd had more control than she did.

The two men just glared at each other for a long, silent moment. "Is this what you want?" Lloyd asked. "To turn into a drunken wild man like your father? In front of Mom? In front of those men out there? They need you *sober,* Pa! And so do I. After all these years, the last thing you need is to give in to what you have always preached at me to avoid! And if you want to help Dee Dee, it's even *more* important that we go into town with you at full capacity."

Jake turned away and leaned over the sink again. He made a groaning sound as if in pain.

"Pa, right now I have a pretty good picture of what your angry, drunken father was like. Just by watching *you!* If you take one more swallow of whiskey, I'm not backing you up," Lloyd told him, "and neither will those men out there. I'm sure you would do one hell of a job trying to get to your granddaughter alone, but even Jake Harkner can't shoot his way through that many men without some help. And it works the other way around. The rest of us can't do it without Jake Harkner. And if we fail, we have lost Dee Dee forever to that filthy animal! *Think* about it! You will have failed Dee Dee, and might lose your son and even maybe your wife, because if something happens to you, Mom will be left here on her own. Is that what you want?"

Jake pumped more water into his hand and splashed his face, then wiped it dry with a towel. Randy knew he was wiping at tears along with it.

"Mom is right," Lloyd told him. "That little girl is a Harkner. She's strong. I bet you will be surprised at just *how* strong she is. And you did *not* fail her. Dallas Blackburn failed her. Her own *father* failed her, but none of it would have happened if you had known she existed. And now you have a chance to get her out of this situation. Nobody is better at defending his family than you are, Pa. But you can't do the job if you are so angry you can't see straight, and you *definitely* can't do the job if you down another slug of whiskey."

Jake braced himself against the counter and bent his head, taking several long, deep breaths. "Go make sure the men and horses are ready," he told Lloyd. "I'll be out in just a couple of minutes."

Lloyd glanced at Randy. "Should I leave?"

Randy wiped at her own tears. "Yes. Just give him a minute."

Lloyd scowled with concern and backed away. "One minute, Pa, or I'm coming back in here to make sure you aren't doing something crazy. Lord knows it wouldn't be the first time." He turned to leave.

"Lloyd," Jake called to him. "I'm sorry I shoved you."

"Hell, Pa, I'm sorry you didn't swing at me. I could have finally knocked you on your ass. I have wanted to do that for years, ever since you slugged me in prison for leaving Mom and Evie."

Jake wiped at his eyes with his shirtsleeve. "You wish," he answered.

"Yeah, I do." Lloyd grinned and walked outside. Randy heard him shouting orders to the men to mount up.

Jake splashed his face again and straightened, running wet hands through his dark hair. He didn't look at Randy as he grabbed a glass and pumped some water into it. He drank it down, then put on his hat before taking a cigarette from his shirt pocket and lighting it. He took a deep drag, exhaled, and turned, the look in his eyes all outlaw determination. "You stay here, understand? Don't you dare go into town."

"I understand."

"I mean it. It will be too dangerous. And if you think you have seen the worst of me, you haven't." He picked up his rifle. "Tell Irene I'm sorry for the mess I made." He headed for the door.

"Jake!"

He paused.

"I love you," she told him, her voice shaky. "I need you to come back."

"I'll come back, and I will have my granddaughter with me." He put the cigarette between his lips and walked out. Moments later came the sound of pounding hooves as Jake and the others headed for town.

Randy grasped her stomach and bent over, sinking into a kitchen chair.

Irene opened the door a crack and peeked inside. "Oh, my God," she said. "He left?"

Randy broke into heaving sobs. "He left. And I'm scared, Irene. I'm scared I'll never see him alive again."

CHAPTER THIRTY-SEVEN

THEY RODE HARD, HORSES' manes and tails swaying up and down with the rhythmic gallop, sod springing in all directions from under pounding hooves. Jake was in the lead, Lloyd and Cole just a nose behind on either side of him, all riders ready for whatever was to come. They leaned forward, as though in a race. Jake Harkner's granddaughter was being abused, and vengeance must be had.

Just before they reached town, they slowed their horses when a small posse of men rode out to meet them. Their apparent leader carried a white flag and waved it as both factions stopped roughly twenty yards from each other. Jake warily eyed them, counting.

Fifteen.

All wore red scarves on their arms.

The lead man again waved his white flag vigorously. Thunder snorted and pawed the ground.

"Get out of our way!" Jake ordered.

"Ty Bolton wants to talk," the lead man told him. "You Jake Harkner?"

Jake saw the quick glint of a raised rifle to his left. Lloyd saw it, too. Years of riding together left them nearly able to read each other's minds in such situations. For years the agreement was that Jake would always go for the lead man, even if it was one of the others who raised a gun. Lloyd would take care of that one. In half a second, Jake's .44 was drawn and fired. At the same time Lloyd shot the man to their left just as he took aim at Jake. By then Jake had shot three more men. Lloyd wasn't even sure which men fired after that because J&L men were also shooting. In seconds every man who had come out to "talk" was on the ground. Dead or alive, it didn't matter. The white flag meant nothing. There would be no talking.

Jake again urged Thunder into a hard run and headed for Shelter, Thunder's hooves pushing the white flag partially into the ground as the horse ran over it. The road from Dallas's house of prostitution led straight into town, and that was where he was headed. They thundered past barns, animals grazing in corrals, homes. People stood outside waving to them, but no man stopped to wave or to look back. They were on a mission.

Back at Dallas's place, Randy stood outside, shading her eyes and watching in the direction they had ridden. She'd brought her shotgun out with her, and her heart raced at the sound of the initial gunfire. "Jake," she muttered. Her son would be riding right beside him. She clung to the shotgun as she ran to the barn, then set it aside as she hurriedly put a bridle on Pepper.

"Ma'am, wait!" the livery man yelled. "Jake told me not to let you leave here!"

Irene had run out behind her. "Randy, don't!"

"I can't wait here! I can't!" Randy answered. "My husband and son might need me!" She picked up the shotgun and pulled Pepper from her stall and out of the barn. The liveryman grabbed the horse's bridle, but Randy turned and aimed the shotgun at him. "That's my husband and son riding into a hornet's nest of gunfire!" she screamed. "Get out of my way!"

The liveryman and Irene backed off. Randy led Pepper to a crate. She managed to hang on to the shotgun as she stepped up on the crate and slung her right leg over the unsaddled horse's back. She glanced at Irene. "I'm sorry." She kicked Pepper's sides and headed for town, holding the shotgun in her left hand and controlling the reins with her right. She'd forgotten her hat and thought what a silly thing that was to be concerned about.

In minutes she reached an area where several horses lingered, all riderless. Men lay scattered on the ground. Quickly she took in the sight, her brain working faster than normal as she made sure neither Thunder nor Cinnamon were among the grazing horses. A quick inventory of the dead and wounded men told her Jake and Lloyd and the J&L men were still alive and among those involved in a barrage of gunfire in town. Her blood chilled at the sound of constant shooting. "God protect them," she spoke into the wind. She charged ahead.

The hard ride caused some of the combs in her hair to come loose, and her blond locks were beginning to fall into a windblown tangle that didn't matter now. Only her husband and son mattered. Learning to use the shotgun she held was pointless if she couldn't use it to help them.

You stay here, understand? I mean it.

"I'm sorry, Jake. I can't stay behind this time. I can't!"

More gunshots! She kicked Pepper into a full gallop, pressing her legs tight against the horse's sides to keep from falling off. She rode past people standing in yards and on porches, noticed a couple of men running with rifles in their hands. They weren't wearing red scarves. They must be citizens ready to help.

Don't let them die! she prayed. The hotel came into sight, then a ladies' clothing store, a rooming house, a grocery store, a hardware store. More men were gathered in front of the stores and holding rifles, but most of the shooting occurred at the other end of town. She could see the word JAIL at the very end of the main street.

She slowed Pepper, eyeing the citizens with rifles. "Why are you standing there?" she screamed. "Get down to where the shooting is and help my husband and son!"

A couple of women grabbed their children and rushed them inside. Three men with rifles started walking closer to all the gunfire. Randy dismounted and ran up the street. Where was Jake? Where was Lloyd?

"Randy, get the hell out of here!"

Someone ran out and grabbed her arm.

"Charlie!"

"What the hell are you doing here!"

A gunshot. Charlie went down.

"Charlie! Oh, my God! Charlie!"

Someone with a red scarf on his arm headed her way. Randy raised the shotgun and fired both barrels, sending the man flying half way across the street. It was then someone grabbed her from behind and knocked the shotgun from her hand.

"I've got her!" a man yelled. "Let's get her down to the saloon. This will stop Harkner in his tracks!"

Randy kicked and screamed and scratched, but to no avail. Someone yanked her around, and a big fist landed into her left eye. The buildings began to float around her as someone picked her up then and threw her over his shoulder. She could see the dirt street. She thought she saw familiar horses trotting around aimlessly. One was Cinnamon. *Lloyd! God, not Lloyd!* The other horse was Charlie's. Then she saw him. Thunder! Then Terrel's horse. Bullets seemed to be flying everywhere. Bodies everywhere.

"The fucking barber shot that deputy named Matt!" someone yelled.

Good. Randy thought. *Some of the citizens are finally helping.*

"Where is Harkner?" another man yelled.

"They are making their way down to the Cowpoke Saloon!" another yelled. "The fucker is leaving a trail of bodies behind him!"

He's alive!

"Somebody shoot his ass!"

"He's too goddamn fast!" another shouted. "A man can already have his gun raised and Harkner still gets off the first shot!"

You are all finding out what Jake Harkner is like when he is angry and trying to save someone he loves. Randy felt strangely unafraid. The man who was carrying her walked past a horse that was on the ground and bleeding from the shoulder. The animal was snorting and whinnying, tossing its head and feet as it tried to get up. She thought how someone should put it out of its misery, but her abductor kept walking. Everyone seemed so absorbed in killing each other that none of them paid any attention to the wounded horse. As they walked past it, she noticed the horse was black with a star on his forehead. *Cole's horse!* Was Cole hurt? Or dead?

"Keep herding Harkner and the rest of them down toward the saloon!" someone yelled. "He's after the girl!"

"Ty and Dennis are down there!" another yelled.

"He won't get past Cotton!"

Randy came around enough to start kicking at her abductor again. He threw her to the ground.

"I ought to rape you right here in front of everybody!" he growled.

He started for her. Randy had presence of mind enough to reach into her pocket and pull out her little Remington, so small that the man who'd grabbed her didn't even realize she carried it. He came down close and ran a hand under her riding skirt. "My God, you're a pretty woman," he said, grinning. "And I aim to find out what Jake Harkner has been enjoyin' in his bed."

Randy shoved the little gun into his face and fired, wincing when blood and flesh sprayed onto her own face.

Her abductor screamed and rolled away, holding his hands to his face.

"My eye! My eye! Oh, my God, my eye!"

Randy scrambled to her feet and put the gun back into her pocket, then continued running up the street. She wasn't sure why the shot she'd fired did not go into her abductor's brain and kill him, but she vaguely remembered Jake telling her the little gun could slow a man but would not usually kill him because of its low calibre.

Maybe a bone stopped the bullet. It didn't matter. She had put the man's eye out. He deserved to suffer. Jake would tell her not to regret doing what she did, and he would probably praise her for her quick thinking. *Never hesitate.*

She kept running toward the heavier gunfire, but someone new grabbed her and yanked her into an alley. "Stay away from the saloon!"

It was Duke. He was bleeding.

Randy fought him. "No! I have to go to Jake!"

Suddenly Charlie showed up. The top right shoulder of his shirt was soaked with blood.

"Charlie! You're alive!" Randy embraced him. "Thank God!"

"You shouldn't have fought me, damn it!" Charlie told her. "How am I supposed to explain to Jake that you got away and you're hurt? Who the hell hit you?"

"It doesn't matter! I shot him! Charlie, my God, I shot him! I've shot *two* men! Please let me go! I have to go to Jake and Lloyd."

"No you *don't*! You will just be a distraction. If Jake sees you covered in blood and your face all beat up, he might get himself shot." He let go of her and started reloading his .45.

"You don't understand!" Randy pleaded.

Duke suddenly sank to his knees, growing weak from loss of blood.

"Yes, I *do* understand," Charlie told Randy. "But all you have to defend yourself with is that useless little two-shot Remington."

"Then give me your gun!"

"I *need* it, damn it! Now stay here and help Duke!" Charlie cocked his gun and took off toward the saloon. Bullets seemed to fly everywhere, men with red scarves on their arms shooting at Jake's men and also at citizens, both groups shooting back, men running everywhere, several lying dead in the street, most of them Bolton's men, but also several citizens.

Although he sat against a wall bleeding, Duke took aim at a man on a rooftop and fired. The man fell off and landed in the alley with a hard thump. Duke slumped farther to the side. Randy felt bad for him, but there was no time to stop and try to help. She took advantage of the distraction and grabbed his gun, then ran the rest of the way down the alley and around the back way, stepping over a dead man as she headed toward the Cowpoke Saloon. She stopped in the alley beside the saloon and checked Duke's gun for bullets. Three were missing. She ran back to the dead man and grabbed his gun instead, quickly loading it fully with bullets she yanked from the man's gunbelt. She realized then that the shooting had stopped.

"Come on, Harkner!" someone yelled. "You have our promise no one will shoot, because I'll kill you myself! I want a showdown."

Randy looked around to see if anyone was close. She saw no one. She snuck her way to the front of the alley, then peeked around the corner to see a young man with white hair standing in front of the jail with his arms raised, signalling for others not to shoot at him.

"Let's see how fast an old gunslinger is against a young one with a newer, faster gun!" the man shouted. "Come on, Harkner! Before this is finished, I want everybody in town to watch me kill the famous Jake Harkner! Then your men can try to save your fucking granddaughter, and when they fail, what's left of us Bolton men will have their own good time with her!"

Randy closed her eyes for a moment, feeling nauseous. She glanced at a window above the Cowpoke Saloon. Was Dee Dee up there? Was Dennis Gates with her? Or was he in the saloon, waiting to murder Jake?

"Harkner! This is Ty Bolton!" The shouted words came from near a window downstairs in the saloon ... and not far from where Randy was crouched. "You have my promise no one will shoot if you come out from wherever you are and go one-on-one with Sheriff McDonald!"

"Don't do it, Pa! They will kill you!"

Lloyd! Randy looked around desperately to see where Jake and Lloyd might be. Lloyd's voice came from somewhere near the mining supply store across from the saloon. She ducked behind a barrel at the side corner of the saloon when someone inside threw a gun out onto the steps, then walked out through the swinging doors with his hands in the air. He was a well-dressed man, wearing a dark blue suit, his hair slicked back, his shoes amazingly shiny for living in such a dusty town.

"There is my proof, Harkner!" he yelled. "I'm Ty Bolton, and I am standing here unarmed! I am trusting you not to shoot me, and you have my word no one will shoot at you if you face off now with Cotton!" He stepped out farther. "Everybody in town wants to see this, even my own men! They will hold off until you are lying dead in the street! Then we will finish off your son and the rest of your men!"

"Jake, don't," Randy whispered.

"Your sheriff is as good as dead, Bolton," Jake shouted in reply. Randy determined he was inside the mining supply store. "Once I kill him, you're next, armed or not."

"We have you covered, Jake!" Randy heard Terrel yell. She stayed low, worried that if Jake saw her, it would change everything. She only wanted to be close in case he was badly hurt, but already things had gone wrong. She felt sick over Charlie getting shot. Where was he? Her ears still rang from getting punched in the face, and waves of dizziness made her grab on to a post at the side of the saloon to keep from falling over. She shivered at realizing she was splattered with another man's blood. It hit her then that she'd blown one man nearly in half, and the other still lay farther down the street rolling around and screaming about his eye. She kept hold of the six-gun she'd stolen from the dead man lying farther back in the alley and stayed hidden.

"Come on out, Harkner," Cotton yelled. "I'll bring you down in front of the whole town, and then any citizen who helps your men will die for it!"

Randy peeked around far enough to see several business owners standing at their doorways with rifles and shotguns. Most of them shrank back a little as Cotton kept challenging Jake. It was obvious to Randy that if it looked like Jake would lose this battle, none of them would do any more to help.

She saw him then ... Jake ... coming out of the door of the mining supply store. His guns were in their holsters, and his arms were outstretched. He held no rifle.

"Pa, don't do it!" Lloyd yelled.

Jake slowly walked toward Cotton, and the whole town quieted. Randy moved farther behind the barrel and watched through a crack, not daring to let Jake know she was anywhere close.

"You asked for this, McDonald," Jake yelled for everyone to hear. "But if you want to brag about being the one to kill me, then do it right ... just you and me. If this is a trick, you can't take credit for a legal gunfight."

"Everybody back off!" Cotton yelled. "I asked for this! If you want to witness Jake Harkner legally go down, don't be doing anything to take away my glory!"

One man laughed. "We will enjoy watching the show, Cotton!" someone shouted.

Ty Bolton moved down the steps of the saloon, keeping his arms up. "I won't interfere," he yelled. "This will be a pleasure."

Cotton smiled and pushed back his hat. "There's gonna be a hot time in town tonight, Harkner," he said. "We will display your body in a coffin box with a sign that says *Outlaw Jake Harkner, killed by Sheriff Charles McDonald, July tenth, 19 and 02.* Men like you are outdated and outgunned today, Harkner."

Jake walked closer, moving his arms down to his sides. "The ones who die in a gunfight are the cocky sons of bitches who think they are fast but have never gone up against a real gunman before," he told Cotton. "I really hate to kill such a young man, but considering what you and your henchmen have done to this town, I will take pleasure in watching you die. I will even let you draw first, just so I can call this self-defense. Everybody here today is witness."

"What you did, charging into town shooting, that wasn't legal for a marshal either," Cotton answered.

"I'm pretty sure every citizen in this town will tell a different story," Jake told him. "And I have friends in all the right places when I get back home. And by the way, I intend to take my granddaughter with me when I go."

Cotton laughed. "Your granddaughter is no little girl anymore," he said, intentionally torturing Jake and goading him into drawing first. "Dennis Gates made sure of that last night. She's his wife now, and you can't touch her."

"I guarantee Dennis Gates will suffer like no man has ever suffered before," Jake answered. "You hear that, Gates?" he yelled louder. "Wherever you are, I will find you before noon, and you will be food for buzzards! I'll drag you out into an open field and let those hungry birds make a meal out of your eyes and your privates so that you are nothing but bones by nightfall! And I will make sure you are alive to feel it every time those birds yank at another piece of flesh!"

"Ty!" the sheriff shouted. "Count to three! Let's get this over with!"

"Gladly." Bolton stepped a little closer to both men. "Make peace with your maker, Harkner."

"Not necessary," Jake answered. "If I die, I won't likely meet my maker. It's more likely I will go to hell."

Ty chuckled. "You men out there," he yelled louder, "hold off! Let's keep this legal!" He folded his arms and waited a long, tense few seconds. "You ready, Cotton?" he asked.

"Oh, you bet," Cotton answered with a grin. "Harkner says he's going to hell, and I am ready to send him there."

Ty stepped back a little. "One," he shouted. "Two." ...

He'd barely finished saying the word "three" before Cotton made an early draw. Jake's gun was out and fired so fast that the boom made Randy jump. It happened in a millisecond. Randy was not even positive it was Jake who had drawn and fired. Sheriff Charles McDonald stood there wavering for a moment, still holding his gun. From her position, Randy could not determine where he had been hit. He turned his head and looked at Ty Bolton, then slowly wilted to the ground. It was then Randy could see a bloody hole in his forehead. It took a few seconds for onlookers, both the Bolton men and the citizens, to react. They all stood there in shock.

"Jesus Christ," someone said aloud.

"Pa, get out of there!" Lloyd yelled. He no more shouted the words than all hell broke loose again. Jake grabbed his thigh and went down.

"Oh, my God!" Randy whispered, still afraid for Jake to know where she was. He rolled behind a wagon, firing his gun at Bolton men who didn't have time to take cover after the gunfight. Several went down, and Lloyd came running out of the mining supply store, shooting like a madman. Two men with red scarves fell from rooftops. Randy couldn't see all the men doing the shooting, but Ty Bolton also cried out and went down. She knew J&L men were involved along with some of the citizens.

Things suddenly quieted.

"Ty is down!" someone yelled from the saloon.

That was when someone grabbed Randy from behind and squeezed her wrist until she dropped the gun she held. A strong arm came around her, pinning her arms to her sides. "You're Harkner's wife, aren't you? They say she's damn good looking and has blond hair." He felt her breasts. "And has nice tits. Yeah, you're her." He jerked her tight against himself. "Before the day is out, sweetheart, your man will be dead, and I'm gonna find out what kind of woman he's been sleeping with all these years. I'll fuck you *and* your granddaughter!"

Randy felt herself being dragged into the street and toward the saloon. She fought to wiggle away, but her abductor was too strong.

"Everybody stop shooting!" the man screamed at the top of his lungs. They were out in the middle of the street now, and terror moved through Randy's blood when she felt a knife pressed against her cheek. "Fire one more shot and I'll cut this woman's face open like I did to that whore who tried to keep DeeDee from me!"

His words told Randy who he was.

Dennis Gates!

CHAPTER THIRTY-EIGHT

"Randy!" Jake yelled. "Let her go, Gates!" He shimmied out from under the wagon and grabbed the side to pull himself to his feet in spite of his denim pants being blood-soaked at his right thigh.

"Pa, stay down!" Lloyd told him. He stood only about ten feet from the wagon and perhaps twenty feet from where Gates held Randy.

"It's okay, Jake!" Cole shouted from somewhere. "Some of the others are takin' off, and we have our sights on Gates!"

"Don't shoot!" Jake ordered. "You might hit Randy!"

Citizens emerged from doorways and started chasing men wearing red scarves on their arms. The barber raised his rifle and waved it back and forth. "We did it!" he shouted. "But Gates has Mrs. Harkner!"

"That's right!" Gates warned Jake. "I've got your woman, Harkner, and I swear I'll cut her till you don't recognize her if I don't get your promise you will let me go! I'm trading her and your granddaughter for my life. Let me ride out of here!"

Lloyd moved closer to Jake, both men holding guns on Dennis Gates. Randy's heart pounded at the feel of a steel blade against her cheek. *Jake, I'm sorry,* she wanted to tell him. This could still get him killed. She held his dark gaze and tried to ignore everything else. Wasn't that what he always told her? *Watch a man's eyes. They will tell you everything.* Right now Jake was telling her to stay calm and trust him.

"Randy, remember what Evie told you about what happened when she was taken," he said calmly. He held his gun straight out and steady. From her perspective, the gun seemed to be aimed directly at her.

"I –"

"Shut up!" Gates ordered, pressing the knife hard enough to cut into her cheek a little under her eye.

"Randy, don't talk and don't move," Jake told her. "Remember Evie," he repeated.

It seemed as though the whole town had gathered to watch. A couple of citizens shoved rifles into the backs of three of Bolton's men, warning them not to try to help Dennis Gates. With Jake and Lloyd both standing close, Randy was not afraid … except for the knife pressed against her cheek. She reminded herself that holding the knife left Gates only one arm to pin her tight with.

"Randy, look at just me," Jake ordered. "Only me! Don't worry about anybody else. Keep your eyes on me and remember what Evie told you. Think about it." He inched closer. "Remember what she said about that bullet?"

Daddy saved me when he shot that man who held me. I knew he could do it, even though that man held me right in front of him and daddy was way up on a hill with a rifle. I will never forget the feel of that bullet skimming right past my ear. I moved my head aside, and in the next second it was like a big bug had suddenly flown near my ear, and that man went down. I fell with him, and Daddy came charging down that hill. In seconds he was holding me in his arms.

Randy's problem was that Gates was short, and he kept his head right behind Randy's. Moving her own head would not expose much of his.

"Somebody shoots me," he shouted to Jake, "and no matter if it's from front or back, the bullet is bound to hit your woman, Harkner. I'm gonna take her into the saloon. I'll leave her there and go out the back if you promise not to come for me. Otherwise I'll cut her face open like that whore's face. I'll bet you have seen it. Ugly, ain't it? You have about five seconds before I do the same to your wife!"

Jake kept his six-gun aimed at Gates and Randy. "Don't shoot when this is over, Lloyd," he said quietly, his eyes on Randy. "I want him alive."

Gates started counting.

"Randy, remember what Evie told you!" Jake yelled the words a third time. Before Gates reached "five," Randy suddenly lifted her legs so that Gates had to support her fully with just his left arm. The surprise move and sudden full weight caused Gates's hold on her to slip just enough that he dropped his knife in order to try grabbing her with both arms.

Too late. Randy managed to twist away from him, and Jake fired. Twice. Randy heard a cracking sound, like a branch snapping. Gates screamed as he crumpled to the ground, taking Randy down with him. Immediately, Lloyd was there pulling his mother away from Gates. He held her close as Jake's .44 boomed two more times.

The bartender for the Cowpoke, who'd been watching it all, hurried down the steps and ripped off his apron, kneeling beside Lloyd and Randy and holding a clean part of the apron to the small cut on Randy's cheek

Gates rolled around in the street, screaming as though someone was skinning him alive. Randy looked his way to see Gates's legs were all twisted because his knees no longer held his thighs to his calves. He was grabbing at his legs with bloody hands as Jake limped closer to him.

"You bastard!" Gates screamed in a high pitch, almost like a woman. "You fucking bastard!" He began crying. "No man does this ... to another man!"

"Well, now, I'm not *like* any other man," Jake sneered, "especially when it comes to the people I care about. Where is my *granddaughter*?" he demanded.

"Don't shoot any more!" Gates begged. "She's ... upstairs. She ain't hurt!"

"The preacher told me you made her your *wife. Did* you? In the Biblical sense?"

"She's old enough. But she ain't hurt, Harkner. Let me go! You've done your damage!"

Jake cocked his .44. "I haven't done near *enough* damage, you filthy snake!" He fired twice more, both bullets hitting Gates in the privates. Onlookers gasped and looked away, as did Randy, sure Gates's screams could be heard clear down in Colorado.

"The knees were for you touching my wife!" Jake yelled. "Your privates were for what you did to my granddaughter! You'll never fuck another child again, or even a grown woman! Then again, you won't live long enough for either one, but you will damn well *suffer* as you slowly bleed to death!"

"You said if I didn't cut your wife, you would let me go!"

"I never said any such thing." Jake put his gun to the man's head. "And even if I did, sometimes I lie, Gates," he sneered. "I am what you might call a sinner, but then you know all about that, don't you? *Sinning*, I mean!"

"Pull the trigger!" Gates pleaded. "Get it over with!"

Jake put the gun's hammer back in place and holstered it. Gates bawled like a baby. "I can't live ten more seconds this way, Harkner! Kill me! Kill me!"

Jake limped over to where Gates's knife lay in the street. He picked it up. Randy glanced at Gates, who was covered in blood. She saw Jake approaching with the knife. "Oh, dear God!"

"Mom, don't look."

"No! No!" Gates wept.

Lloyd pressed the apron harder against his mother's cheek and moved a little, trying to keep her from seeing what Jake was doing.

"You need to know how it felt when you cut that young woman who tried to help Dee Dee!" Jake growled. He limped closer, leaning down and grabbing hold of Gates's hair. He yanked the man's head back and plunged the knife into his left eye, then ripped it diagonally across his face, deliberately cutting Gates in the same way he'd slashed Brenda's face.

"Oh, my God!" Randy said softly when she heard Gates's screams.

"Lord help us!" some man moaned.

More screams, both from Gates and from onlookers.

"Pa, just kill him!" Lloyd shouted.

"That's too good for him!" Jake roared. "Let him die slowly!"

"Jesus," Lloyd muttered. "I've seen Pa do a lot of vicious things, but it's never been this bad."

More people screamed, some running back inside buildings.

"This is far more satisfying than killing you, Gates," Jake growled. "If you do live, you will never walk again, and you will never *fuck* again! People won't be able to look at you without throwing up! You will have to go live in a cave because no one will want you around! Every man who might help you is *dead,* including those who called themselves lawmen, and a lot of Bolton's hired killers. Shelter is back in the hands of its citizens, and my granddaughter is coming home with me and my wife!"

Gates lay writhing in the dirt street, blood pouring from his left eye and the deep cut across the rest of his face. Combined with his other bleeding wounds, Lloyd doubted there was any chance the man would live, and that was what Jake wanted ... a slow death. Gates no longer screamed. He was too weak, and too wounded to function in any way, other than to lie there groaning like an animal. Lloyd thought how normally, Jake would shoot a wounded animal to put it out of its misery. But he was not going to do the same for Dennis Gates.

A couple of the town's citizens shoved two of Bolton's men toward Gates. "Get him out of our sight," one of the citizens ordered. "Haul him out of Shelter and let him die someplace else! Our women should not have to see this."

One man in the distance vomited. Children and women could be heard crying. Other citizens cursed at the mess left in the street. Another Bolton man grabbed someone's supply wagon and drove it wildly up to Gates. "Help me get him in the wagon!" he ordered the other two.

The man who had vomited was crying now. He shook as he helped pick up Gates, not an easy job because his legs were so badly separated. The two men laid Gates into the wagon bed, and all three of them drove off, heading down the street and then in the direction of Ty Bolton's ranch.

Jake threw the knife aside and stumbled into the center of the street. "All you people!" he shouted. "Clean up this town! Bury the bodies ... and get yourselves a decent sheriff! Stand up for yourselves and don't let this happen again! If it does, you will have no one to blame but yourselves!" His voice was breaking from all the yelling he had done to this point. He stood there a moment, as though gathering his thoughts, then turned and stumbled toward Randy.

Terrel jumped down from a porch roof next to the saloon and walked over to where Bolton lay. He knelt beside him. "Jake!" he yelled. "Bolton is still alive."

"Get me up!" Close bystanders heard Bolton growl the words. "I'll kill him! I'll kill the fucker!"

Terrel helped Bolton to his feet, and the man grasped a post that supported the roof over the Cowpoke Saloon's veranda. His fancy shirt and vest were covered with blood. He raised a .45 and aimed it at Jake, but his arm wavered. Terrel knocked the gun out of Bolton's hand and threw the man into the street. Citizens immediately swarmed to drag Bolton down the street with shouts of "Hang him!"

Bolton screamed resistance, but to no avail.

Jake collapsed beside Lloyd and pulled Randy into his arms. "Jesus! Jesus!" he lamented. "Lloyd, look at her face! Somebody hit her. Her eye is already purple and swollen. And she's cut! She's cut!" He held Randy against his chest and rocked her.

Lloyd could see his father was not thinking straight. All the man knew was that his precious Randy was bleeding. "Pa. It's not a big cut. You know how bad the face and head bleed from the smallest of wounds. Let's get her some help. And you're shot. You need help, too. Let's get out of the street."

"I have rooms upstairs in the saloon you can use," the

bartender told Lloyd. "You can take them there." He turned and yelled. "Somebody help these people upstairs, and send the doc over!"

"Where is my granddaughter?" Jake shouted to the bartender.

"In one of the rooms upstairs," the bartender answered, his eyes wide with fear of Jake. "They held me at gunpoint, Harkner. I swear! I wanted to go to her, but Bolton held a gun on me and told me if I tried to help her, he'd shoot me."

"Calm down, Pa," Lloyd told Jake. "You need to take care of yourself and Mom. I'll find Dee Dee for you."

"Be careful. She'll be scared. Don't let her run away Lloyd."

Lloyd detected tears in Jake's eyes. He'd just displayed incredible cruelty against Dennis Gates, and now he was weeping over an abused little girl. "I know what to do, Pa. I have daughters of my own, you know. Don't worry about Dee Dee. I will find her and she will be okay."

"Give her a hug ... or something," Jake told him as he still held Randy close. "Tell her I love her ... and I'm sorry for all that happened."

"Pa, I will take care of it."

Sudden cheers from the crowd of vengeful citizens filled the air as Bolton's body was hauled up with a pully at the front of the hardware store. A noose stretched his neck as he kicked his legs for several seconds before going limp.

"Come on now, Pa. Let somebody help you and Mom get to a room and let the doc tend to you. Dee Dee shouldn't see you like this. All the blood and the look in your eyes right now will scare her to death."

"Jake, I will be okay," Randy told him. "You have to let go of me."

Jake kept her close. "He cut you," he lamented. "He cut

you. I ... have to stay with you, but Dee Dee needs me, too. Lloyd, I can't leave Randy."

"Jake, it's just a nick," Randy told him. "Let the doctor do something about your leg."

"Why did you come here?" Jake asked. He kissed her hair. "*Why*? I told you it would be ugly and dangerous. Why didn't you listen to me?"

"I just wanted to be near you ... if you got hurt bad. I couldn't ... stay behind, Jake. I couldn't! Please calm down."

"I didn't want you to see the worst of it ... the worst of *me*."

"Pa, she needs a doctor's attention, and so do you," Lloyd again urged. "Your pants are soaked in blood. Remember three years ago? The doc back then said all that blood you lost probably damaged your organs, so let's get that wound taken care of before you end up with a heart attack. I will go find Dee Dee. I promise she will be all right. I know you want to go to her, but she shouldn't see you like this." He turned. "Somebody hurry up and help Jake get upstairs! He just saved your sorry asses from hell! Come and help!"

Somehow things suddenly became more organized. Men dragged bodies into piles and yelled for others to bring wagons to load them in. Citizens who finally believed all the shooting was over hurried to help get Jake and Randy upstairs. Terrel and Cole hurried behind them as others dragged the town doctor over to help. The man tugged back when he saw Jake.

"Is he done killing people?"

"Of course he is," Terrel answered. "Him and his wife both need your attention, and they come first, so you see to it."

The few patrons who'd hidden in the saloon through the entire gunfight joined in helping Jake and Randy.

"Tell the other wounded men to line up downstairs here and the doc will get to them soon as he can," Cole yelled to those who watched. The doctor ordered men to put Jake and Randy in separate rooms.

"No!" Jake insisted. "I need to be with my wife!" In spite of his own leg wound, he kept an arm around Randy while she held the bartender's towel to the cut on her cheek. "Take care of my wife first and let me stay beside her. I know how stitches feel! And you'd better do a good job of it so she's not left with an ugly scar!"

"Jake, it's just a little cut," Randy told him. "The doctor should take care of you first. I won't need stitches."

"It's *not* just a cut! That bastard was going to carve up your face!"

"Pa, you need to calm down for Mom's sake," Lloyd again urged. "And the sooner you get that leg taken care of, the sooner you can be in shape to meet Dee Dee."

Jake clung to the railing and looked at Lloyd with wild, bloodshot eyes. "Oh, my God. That poor girl! I need to go to her."

"Not like this! Right now the look on your face would scare a bobcat! Leave Dee Dee to me!"

Jake pulled Randy close and leaned against a wall. "*Find* her, Lloyd. You look like her father. That might comfort her. I just hope she is still here somewhere. She might be so scared that she ran off."

"I'll find her, Pa," Lloyd assured him yet again. "She's the *reason* for all of this." He helped his parents into an upstairs room. Gaudy dresses hung along the wall and the bed was a crumpled mess.

"Find a clean sheet to put over that damn bed!" the doctor insisted.

Cole scrambled through a trunk sitting nearby and found a sheet. Terrel had already ripped off the blankets and old sheets, and both men threw the clean sheet on the mattress and tucked it in as best they could. Jake helped Randy lie down and ordered the doctor to take care of her first.

"Remember that I don't want her left with an ugly scar! She doesn't deserve that!"

"I will do my best," the doctor told Jake. "For God's sake, Harkner, it doesn't help worrying you might shoot me if you aren't happy with my work."

"Pa, the man can't do his best if his hands are shaking because he's afraid of you," Lloyd reminded Jake.

Jake smoothed back Randy's hair. "This woman is my *life*," he told the doctor. He took Randy's hand and held it to his cheek. "Goddamn it, Randy, you should have stayed behind like I *told* you to do. When are you going to learn to do what I tell you?"

"I couldn't stay behind, Jake. I just couldn't." Randy could not stop the tears that came then. The horror of all that had just happened began to overwhelm her. " I heard all that gunfire. I just had to be here in case you were hurt bad."

"Speaking of that, let somebody tie something tight around your leg, Mr. Harkner," the doctor ordered. "If you insist I tend to your wife first, you'd better try to slow that bleeding."

Cole grabbed a long, feathered boa from the wall and hurriedly tied it around Jake's right thigh.

"I'm going to find Dee Dee," Lloyd told his father.

"Wait," Jake asked. He reached into an inside pocket of

his vest and pulled out two pieces of peppermint, one of the few things on his person that wasn't blood stained. "Give this to Dee Dee. Tell her it's her grandpa and grandma's favorite candy and that there is lots more of it back home."

Lloyd took the candy and noticed tears in Jake's eyes again. "I will find her and she will be fine," he assured his father. "Just get yourself fixed up and wash off all the blood." His father's stark contrast of personalities always amazed him, especially how easily the man could turn from ruthless torture to weeping over an abused child. And as dire as their situation was when they left this morning, Jake had thought to grab candy for his granddaughter.

He squeezed his father's uninjured shoulder, noticing the gauze his mother had wrapped Jake's wounded neck and shoulder with last night had some fresh blood on it. "Take care of Mom and take care of that leg, Pa, and don't forget about that wound by your neck. It looks like the bandage needs to be changed. When I find Dee Dee, I will get her out of here and head for Dallas's place. Okay? She shouldn't meet you or Mom until you are cleaned up and changed, and *calmer!* Understand? *Calmer.* I'll have somebody let you know I have Dee Dee and that she is okay. It's probably best this way instead of meeting all of us at once."

Jake nodded. "You're right. I shouldn't meet her yet, considering this mess. I'm just glad you aren't hurt, Lloyd. Go find Dee Dee, and find out what shape the rest of the men are in."

"I can answer that," Cole told Jake. "Everybody is alive except Duke. He was shot in the street fighting back there and didn't make it. They shot my horse from under me and nicked me through the ribs. I'll be sore for a while, but otherwise I'm fine."

"Charlie got hit from behind in the right shoulder," Terrel added.

"Oh, that's my fault!" Randy lamented. "He was trying to protect me." She burst into tears. "Jake, I shot a man with my shotgun! He flew half way across the street. And I shot another man in the eye with my Remington. It was awful! But he's the one who slugged me, and he tried to do more."

"Jesus," Jake muttered. He looked at Terrel and Cole. "Anybody else get hit?"

"Charlie is downstairs," Terrel told Randy. "Don't you worry about him. He'll be okay. The bullet went clean through, but he still needs the doc's attention."

"Your neck is bleeding," Jake told Terrel.

Terrel put a hand to the wound. "Well, sir, a bullet skimmed right across it. I'll be fine, too. Whitey is unhurt, far as I know. By all rights we should *all* be dead, but I guess that God of Evie's decided to spare us."

"Make sure Duke's body is properly tended to," Jake told him. "We should take him back to Pine Ranch to be buried there when we head back."

He sighed and closed his eyes, holding Randy's hand tightly when she winced as the doctor dabbed alcohol to the cut on her face. "Lloyd, go on now and find Dee Dee," he said.

"I'm going. And I will make damn sure she knows she's loved and doesn't need to be afraid. You just watch over Mom and let the doctor fix that leg wound."

Lloyd left, his chest hurting at the sound of his mother crying out with pain. *What a fucking mess.* He would find Dee Dee and they would all go home ... home to Colorado ... home to Katie. God, how he missed her.

He opened the doors to three of the other rooms, calling Dee Dee's name and looking under the beds and into closets. He opened the door to the last room and felt sick. The bed was a tumbled mess, and there was blood on the sheets. "Dee Dee?" he called out. "You in here?"

He heard whimpering from the direction of a curtain-covered doorway. He strained to listen closer. "Dee Dee? That you?"

The whimper turned to sobs.

CHAPTER THIRTY-NINE

LLOYD MOVED CLOSER to the curtained doorway. "Dee Dee? My name is Lloyd, and I came all the way from Colorado to find you so I can take you home with me."

"Go away! You will just hurt me like Dennis did."

"Dee Dee, if I meant to hurt you, I could reach right in there and pull you out, couldn't I?"

She did not answer right away. "Yes," she finally said.

"But I didn't , did I?"

"No."

"That's because you are very special and are part of my family. Did you know you have uncles and aunts? I am one of your uncles. In fact, I am your father's brother. My kids are your cousins. And my father, who was your daddy's father, too, is your grandpa."

There came a long pause. "I don't understand." The girl sniffed and made a little gasping sound. "My father ... had a brother?"

"Yes, ma'am. I know it's confusing to you now, but it's true. If you would come out of there and look at me, Dee

Dee, you would know I am telling the truth. Your Grandma Dallas says I look just like your daddy."

"You know my Grandma Dallas?"

"I do. She is the one who sent us here to take you to your big family in Colorado, where you will live in a nice house and have all kinds of toys and a pony. We didn't know about you till Grandma Dallas told us." *God help me with the right words.* Lloyd took a cigarette from his shirt pocket and lit it, taking a deep drag and struggling to think straight as he exhaled. "So now you have two grandmas, because my mother is married to your grandpa."

Another long pause. "I don't believe you," Dee Dee said when she broke her silence. "Men are mean. You are fibbing about all those things to trick me."

"I don't lie, Dee Dee. My father taught me not to lie. Like I said, he is your grandpa, and he has two other granddaughters your age who really, really love him because he is so good to them. He would never hurt you, and neither would I. Not in a hundred, million, gazillion years."

He heard another sniff. "You aren't very smart. There is no such thing as a gazillion years."

Lloyd smiled. "Sure there is, I bet. Even if there isn't, that means I'm not as smart as you, so I need you and all my other kids to help me learn to count. They all go to school on the ranch where we live, and your new grandma, Grandma Randy, teaches them. I have five kids, Dee Dee. If you come home with me and your grandma and grandpa, you could play with the ones your age and help babysit the littlest ones. Betsy Jane is only one year old. Jeffrey Peter is four. Donavan is five. Tricia is nine, almost the same age as you. And I have a sixteen-year-old son named Stephen. Their mommy is a beautiful woman named Katie. She's my wife, so she is also your aunt. All your cousins are real excited that I will be bringing you home with me. And I have a sister who has six kids, so that's even *more* cousins."

"I still don't believe you."

"But it's true.You have a whole great big family who loves you."

After another pause, the girl finally spoke up again. "You're trying to trick me."

"No, baby girl. May God strike me dead if I am trying to trick you."

"Where's ... Dennis?" came the tiny voice.

"Oh, we sent him away and he's never coming back. Your Grandma Dallas said he was a bad man, so we made sure he can never come back again to hurt you. And you know what else?"

"What?"

"Your new grandpa is the one who chased Dennis away. He risked his life for you, and now he is hurt, so the doctor is fixing him. That is why he did not come with me, but you will get to meet him soon. And your new grandma is named Randy. She's my mom and is married to your grandpa. She is beautiful and kind and she and your grandpa already love you even though they haven't met you. And all those kids I told you about are real excited to meet you."

More sniffles. "Dennis is a bad man. He killed my daddy and he hurt a nice lady named Brenda. He cut her real bad, and he made me ... do bad things."

"I know all about that, Dee Dee. But only Dennis did bad things, Sweetheart. Not you. Dennis *made* you do those things. That's why my father and I sent Dennis away forever. We will take you someplace where nobody will ever hurt you again. Your grandpa is anxious to see you and hug you and tell you he loves you. Please come out and let me help you."

There came no reply.

"Please talk to me, Dee Dee," Lloyd coached. "When you see how much I look like your Daddy, you will know I am telling the truth that I am your uncle."

Several more silent seconds passed before a small hand slowly pulled the curtain aside. A skinny young girl with big blue eyes, stringy blond hair, an angelic complexion, and a runny nose peeked around the corner at Lloyd. She blinked.

"You *do* look like my daddy, but he didn't have long hair. It makes you look kinda like an Indian."

"Other people have told me that. For some reason, my wife likes my hair long, so I leave it that way. "

Dee Dee kept studying him. "How can you be my daddy's brother?"

Lloyd stayed right where he was, worried the girl would be frightened if he suddenly reached for her. "Well, it's kind of complicated. Your Grandma Dallas was a friend of my father's before he met and married my mother. His name is Jake, and he and your grandma had kind of a disagreement. So my father left, but he didn't know your grandma was carrying a baby. That baby was your daddy. Now Jake knows about you, and he is real sorry he never knew your daddy. He's a really good daddy himself, and a good grandpa. He never would have abandoned your daddy if he knew about him."

Dee Dee knit her eyebrows. "Is he nice?"

Lloyd had a sudden urge to burst out laughing, considering what he'd just seen Jake do to Dennis Gates, not to mention all the men he had shot his way through to get to this child. "Yes. He is the nicest man you will ever meet, and he has always been good to me and all my kids. Every-body loves him. He's big and can be ornery, but only with people who try to hurt somebody he loves. He is the one who sent Dennis away so he can never hurt you again."

Dee Dee pushed the curtain all the way aside and stood up, folding her arms over the ragged little calico dress she wore. "Do I really have a lot of cousins?"

Lloyd got to his knees so he could face her more evenly. "You really do. I told you about my wife and kids, and I have a sister named Evie. She has six kids. One is just a three-month-old baby boy, and then there is baby Marybeth. She's about fourteen months old. Cole is four, Esther is six, Sadie Mae is your age. Ten. And my nephew, Little Jake, is thirteen."

She frowned. "How will I remember their names?"

Lloyd's smile broadened at the hope that Dee Dee was finally beginning to trust him. "Honey, once you start playing with all of them, you will remember. They all go to school and to church, and they all have their own ponies. The girls have dolls and pretty dresses, and they fixed up a special room, just for you. If you come with me and your grandpa, you can see it, and you can live there and have all the same things they have."

Dee Dee pursed her lips and took on the look of someone who knew what she was about. "Don't call me honey," she told Lloyd. "Dennis called me that, but he was mean to me."

Lloyd frowned. "I'm sorry. When I call a little girl honey, it means I love her and want to protect her. I would never lie about those feelings or try to trick you." He took the peppermint from his shirt pocket. "Grandpa told me to give this to you. It's his and your grandma's favorite candy."

Dee Dee looked at the candy, then at Lloyd. "Uncle Dennis gave me candy." Her eyes welled with tears. "And then he hurt me. He called me his wife, but I'm too little to be his wife."

Lloyd put the candy back in his pocket. "OK then. No candy." He folded his arms. "Dee Dee, if you cry, then *I* will start crying."

"Uh – uh. Men don't cry."

"Oh, yes they do. My wife lost a baby a few weeks ago, and I cried over that."

"You like babies?"

"I *love* babies. That's why I have so many back home."

Dee Dee wiped away her tears and watched him quietly.

"Dee Dee, listen to me," Lloyd told her. "I know Dennis was a bad man, but not all men are like him. And he was not your uncle. I am. And you are right. You are too little to be a wife. Wives should be grown-up ladies."

Dee Dee nodded.

"And I *love* you like your daddy did. I know he did not take the best care of you, but I believe he loved you. He never hurt you, did he?"

Dee Dee shook her head.

"Of course not. Did your daddy hug you sometimes?"

Dee Dee nodded again.

"And did you feel safe when he hugged you?"

Another nod.

"Then let *me* hug you. You will always, always be safe and loved when you are with me and your aunts and uncles and especially with your grandpa Jake. I am telling you the truth, Dee Dee. We want to take you home and give you your own room and your own pony and let you go to school and learn about Jesus and go to parties and wear pretty dresses and have anything you want. *Nobody* is ever going to hurt you again. Understand?"

Dee Dee swallowed and followed him with her eyes as Lloyd stood up. She stepped back a little. "You're kinda big and tall, like daddy was."

"That is because we have the same father. Your grandpa is big and tall, too. He can be mean to bad men, but when he is with little girls, they couldn't be safer. He has a great big heart to match his size."

Dee Dee finally smiled a little. "If he has a heart that big, how does he keep it inside his body?"

Lloyd grinned. "Sometimes he doesn't. Sometimes he wears it on his sleeve."

Dee Dee knit her eyebrows again. "Huh? How can he do that?"

Lloyd leaned against the wall. "Well, wearing it on his sleeve is just a way of saying a person sometimes loves so much and so big, everybody can tell how big his heart is. So they joke and say he is wearing his heart on his sleeve because they can see how much he loves."

Dee Dee frowned in thought, as though trying to picture something like that. She pushed some hair behind her ears and looked down at her plain dress. "I feel kinda dirty." She looked up again. "Can I go to Grandma Dallas's house? My Aunt Irene lives there. She isn't really my aunt, but I call her that. Can you take me there so she can give me a bath? I have some pretty dresses there. I want a lady to give me a bath, not a man."

"Then I will take you there right away."

Lloyd daringly reached out, and Dee Dee placed her small hand in his big one. Lloyd gently pressed her hand. "I love you like my own already, Dee Dee. In fact, when we get home to Colorado, you will live with me and my wife sometimes, and with my sister sometimes. All the kids do that. And sometimes they sleep at Grandpa's house."

"Really?"

"You bet. We are one big happy family. And those aunts I told you about will treat you like their own daughter."

Dee Dee blinked. "They will be like mommies?"

"Like mommies."

"My real mommy died when I was born. They say she was real pretty."

"She must have been, because *you* are real pretty."

Surprisingly, Dee Dee kept her hand in his. "I guess you can hug me now."

Lloyd smiled. "I thought you would never let me. I miss my kids, and I really need a hug myself right now." He got back down on his knees, and Dee Dee fell into his arms. She put her head on his shoulder and broke into sobs. Lloyd got to his feet again and carried her to a nearby wooden rocker, where he sat down and kept his arms tight around her. She curled onto his lap and continued to cry.

Lloyd thought how odd life could be. Moments ago he was shooting men down like bottles on a fence. Now he was holding a little girl and trying to convince her she was safe. "Cry all you want, baby girl," he told her. "Like I told you, sometimes it feels good to cry."

"I never had an uncle before ... or a grandpa," she said brokenly through sobs.

"Well, you do now. And a whole great big family to go with it." He rubbed her back. "Hey, do you want to know something funny?"

She sat up a little, then used the hem of her dress to rub at her eyes and nose. "What?"

"Well, it's Tricia and Sadie Mae's job back home to take care of the chickens, gather eggs and such. The mean old rooster who watched over the hens always let those girls go inside the chicken coop and never bothered them. That rooster died just before we left to come up here to Wyoming, and the girls had us bury him in the family grave-yard because they loved him so much. But guess what?"

"I don't know."

"Your Grandpa Jake hated that old rooster. Every time he walked past the chicken coop, that rooster chased him. He squawked and pecked at your grandpa and would never let him near the other chickens. I swear, that rooster is the only thing on earth that ever scared your grandpa. He wanted to shoot it, but he didn't because Tricia and Sadie Mae loved that grouchy old bird."

Dee Dee smiled through tears. "Grandpa was really afraid of a chicken?"

"As God is my witness."

That actually got a laugh out of the girl. "I wish I could see the rooster chase him. I never knew a man who was scared of chickens."

"Well, I'm sure that by the time we get home, my wife and my sister will have bought another rooster. When you come home with us, we will see if Grandpa Jake can get along with the new one."

Dee Dee giggled. "I hope the new one chases Grandpa, too. That would be funny."

Lloyd grinned at the thought of how annoyed Jake was going to be when he found out he'd told Dee Dee about the rooster. He took the candy from his pocket again and handed it to Dee Dee. "You want this now? I promise it's not a trick."

She took a piece and licked it. "I like it."

It was only then that Lloyd noticed a small bruise on her cheek and a cut on her bottom lip. He quietly studied her skinny arms. They were covered with bruises. He fought his anger, struggling to stay friendly and upbeat for Dee Dee's sake. "Your new grandma's name is Miranda. She is married to Grandpa Jake, and she is a true lady."

"She's your mommy?"

Lloyd nodded. "She is."

"I didn't think big men had mommies."

"*Everybody* has a mommy."

Dee Dee continued studying his eyes, as though to make sure he wasn't lying to her about anything. "Can I really have my own pony?"

"You can really have your own pony. We live on a big, big ranch and have lots of horses. You will get to know all the cowboys there, and you will be safe with all of them, too. In fact, some of them came with us and got hurt just so they could get you away from bad people and take you home with us."

Dee Dee bit off a piece of peppermint. "Can I be like a princess?"

Lloyd ran a hand through her blond tresses. "You *are* a princess. Your grandpa has nicknames for Tricia and Sadie Mae. He calls them Sunshine and Button. I will tell him our nickname for you should be Princess."

"And my grandpa is your daddy?" she asked again.

Lloyd realized she was still trying to get it all straight in her mind. "I know it's confusing, Dee Dee, but you will figure out who is who when you come home with us. Like I told you, Jake is my daddy, and he risked his life to come for you because you are his granddaughter. And he is the best daddy and the best grandpa a child could ask for."

Dee Dee studied him curiously. "But you are all grown up."

Lloyd chuckled. "Yes, I am, but Jake is still my father, and I need him and love him like if I was still a boy."

Dee Dee smiled. "That's funny." She put her head on his shoulder again. "Is he really a nice man like you said?"

Lloyd suddenly felt completely worn out from all the horror and tension of the day. "Yes he is, Dee Dee. It's just like I said earlier. He's the nicest man you will ever meet." *As long as nobody threatens somebody he loves.* "Come on. Let's go find my horse and I'll take you to Grandma Dallas's house so Irene can clean you up and you can meet Grandpa Jake. That okay with you?"

"I guess so. But keep holding me. Don't let Dennis get me."

"He won't. I told you Dennis is gone for good. That's a promise. Grandpa Jake made sure of that." Lloyd rose and carried her to the doorway. He waved Cole over. "Tell Pa I have Dee Dee and she's fine. I'm taking her to Dallas's place so Irene can give her a bath. She wants to put on a pretty dress to meet her grandpa and grandma."

Cole tilted his head to try to see Dee Dee's face, but it was buried against Lloyd's neck and her hair shrouded the rest of her. "I can tell by that hair she's pretty. She okay?"

"Well, you know how it is. She finally warmed up to me, but I'll feel better when I hear what Irene thinks. She is all bruised up." He nodded toward the bloody sheets on the bed.

Cole grimaced and looked away. "Bastard!" he grumbled.

"Just make sure Pa knows she seems to be all right. You know how he is." Lloyd swore he saw tears in Cole's eyes.

"I know damn well. I was with him when he went through all that hell findin' Annie. Go on. Get the girl out of here. Terrel went and found your horse. It's out back. Try to keep the girl from seein' all that mess on the main street."

"Sure." Lloyd walked away with Dee Dee, aching at how a little girl could bring a bunch of men to their knees and make them cry. Even the hardened ones like Cole, who didn't even have a family ... and like Jake. They didn't come any harder than Jake Harkner.

CHAPTER FORTY

"Why in hell am I nervous?"

Randy finished tucking combs into the sides of her hair, then watched Jake in a mirror as he pulled on his boots. "You are nervous because you are trying to change from a vicious outlaw to a gentle, loving grandfather. And because when you meet Dee Dee, it will be very hard for you to hide your anger over what happened to her." She saw him grimace when he tried to pull on the right boot. "Let me do that. You shouldn't even be walking, Jake."

He sighed and gave up trying to get the boot on. "The doctor said the bullet went clean through the flesh. Once we got the bleeding stopped there wasn't much for him to do. He said my thigh will just turn purple and hurt, but there is no major damage. I guess it won't matter if I stay off the leg or not."

Randy walked over to the bed and put the boot over his foot. "You push as best you can and I will pull. But it certainly should help if you stay off your leg as much as you can the next few days."

Jake grabbed the railing at the foot of the bed and

winced as he pushed. "I *can't* stay off of it. We need to head home."

Together they got the boot most of the way on. Jake put his foot on the floor and managed to finish the job. Randy pulled the bottom of his denim pants down over the boot.

"I would like to leave tomorrow," Jake continued.

Randy sat down beside him and rubbed his shoulders. "I think you should wait a few days."

Jake rested his elbows on his knees and hung his head. "Leg wound or not, we have to get Dee Dee out of this fucking town."

"Jake, watch your language around the girl. Right now your anger over what happened to her is consuming you. You can't let that show when we go down and meet Dee Dee."

"I am trying."

Randy leaned in and kissed his cheek. "I agree we need to get her out of this place and out of Shelter, but for now you have to show a whole different side of yourself to her. I just don't know if you can shed yourself of either attitude yet."

"I can do it, for Dee Dee. My God, here we are, staying in a house of prostitution. It obviously doesn't bother me any, but I want to get my granddaughter out of this atmosphere as fast as possible. I feel the same way about getting *you* out of here. I know Irene isn't allowing any male visitors tonight because of all of us being here, and because of what the girl has been through. But I want tonight to be the last of it."

"I know, but these women understand. They won't expose Dee Dee to anything that might scare her."

Jake put a hand on her knee and squeezed. "You should have stayed behind this morning. I still can't believe you rode into town like that. I could have lost you."

The tense strength of his hand told Randy he was still wound up. His hand was hot, his demeanor still emitting danger and power. She could hardly believe all that had happened in one day. People back in town were very likely still cleaning up the mess Jake and the men had left behind. "Jake, the cut is just a nick that luckily needed no stitches," she reminded him. "I will be just fine. And if you want to go downstairs and meet Dee Dee, you have to get your emotions under control. And don't forget that she doesn't like to be called honey."

He nodded. "I know." He rose and rubbed his hands over his face. "What if Dee Dee won't come to me? What if she is scared of me?"

Randy smiled at how the man could turn to mush over a little girl. "My darling husband, little girls love you, even ones who don't know you well. I've watched kids gather around you at the Fourth of July picnics. You have a certain charm and an exciting mystery about you that draws them to you. And I think they sense that you are someone who would always protect them. Dee Dee will sense that, too, but it will be easier for her if you let go of all this anger and all the regrets. You did what you came here to do, and Lloyd and the men survived, except for poor Duke. Be grateful that things turned out as well as they did."

"I am grateful, but none of it should have happened in the first place."

Randy stood and wrapped both her arms around his torso, resting her head against his chest. "The trouble is, *big* girls gather around you for the same reasons as the little ones," she teased. "When we got back here that whole bevy of prostitutes downstairs fussed over you like I didn't even exist. Don't think I didn't notice, but that is a matter for another discussion."

Jake pulled her closer. "You are the only woman who matters. My God, you could have been maimed for life today -- or killed."

Randy rested her head on his shoulder. "Jake, no more *what ifs*. Let's be glad we are here and alive. And once Dee Dee gets used to life on the J&L and meets her big, new family, all of that will take over and she will gradually put things behind her and just be a little girl again. Children can be amazingly resilient. Look how you survived your own awful childhood."

"I'm not so sure I *did* survive it. What I did to Dennis Gates today comes from that deep, dark anger at my father. I still have trouble controlling that anger."

Randy leaned up and kissed his chin. It was warm. The aura of his burning rage lingered. "Jake, we have Dee Dee. The men who abused her are dead, or *wishing* they were dead. We will go home, and you can finally put your past to rest."

"Can I?"

"Yes. The last remnant of that life is gone. You finally told me about that raid on my farm and gave me my father's watch. You have your granddaughter, and you know now that you had another son. You have made up for never being there for him by coming here and risking your life for his daughter." She pulled away and stepped back. "Let me look at you, all cleaned up and shaved."

Jake shifted his weight, grimacing again at the pain in his leg.

"You look very nice," Randy told him. "As handsome as ever. Those women downstairs will be all over you. I have always liked that blue shirt on you. And stop worrying about whether or not Dee Dee will like you. Your other granddaughters think you are a saint."

Jake put a hand to the side of her face and leaned down to gently kiss her eyes. "What about you? I'm sure you don't consider anything about what you saw today as saintly. I never wanted you to witness the worst of me, Randy. Back in Oklahoma, when I went after men like the Boltons and Gateses of this world, you weren't there to see how I dealt with them." He pulled her close again. "I never wanted that for you."

"Do you really think I didn't know how bad it could get? I saw the shape some of those men were in when you brought them back to Guthrie to be jailed ... or hanged ... or buried. I have never been fooled by how good you are to me and the children." She looked up at him. "I know what is down deep inside, but it's time you dealt with those demons and allowed yourself to be free of them."

Jake studied her lovingly. "You never give up, do you?"

"Never. I know the good side of Jake Harkner."

"And you are often a very disobediant wife."

"It's fun to disobey you. I like to watch your reaction." She smiled. "And I love when we make up."

"We always make up because you always win the argument. That's why I pretty much gave up arguing with you a long time ago."

Their mouths were still close, and Jake met hers fully in a deep kiss that said so much. *Thank God we are alive. ... Thank God we can go home. ...* For Randy, flashes of what he'd done to Dennis Gates, the brutality of it, seemed such a stark contrast to the man kissing her now.

She understood now why he'd warned her to stay away, but she refused to admit how it had shocked her. It would shatter his ability to come back to a life of love and joy if she told him. She had fought too hard to keep him from falling into the dark abyss of lawlessness to do or say anything that would make him feel undeserving of her love. He was so strong and able, brave and devoted. He had such a big heart, but down inside he was so needy of knowing he was loved, knowing she would never leave him.

Someone tapped at the door then. "Pa? Are you two decent?"

Jake kissed Randy once more, grinning. "Son, how many times have I told you being decent is no fun?" he called to Lloyd. He walked over and opened the door, then stepped back. "How do I look? Tell me I won't scare Dee Dee away."

Lloyd snickered. "Sometimes you scare *me* away. But you look fine. Just stop thinking about the worst. Irene had a little talk with Dee Dee when she helped her clean up. I'm not sure what she said, but Dee Dee seems happy just to be here and she's anxious to see you, so put on your grandpa face and remember she's just a sweet little girl who needs your love. I didn't ask Irene for any details. For your part, Pa, don't get that look in your eyes that might remind Dee Dee of Dennis Gates. Keep her mind on the future." Lloyd leaned against the door jam. "And you need to do the same thing for yourself." He turned his attention to his mother. "How do you feel? I wish I had been there when that sono-fabitch slugged you."

"Well, he is very sorry for it now, if he is still alive. But I don't want to talk about that. I am tired, and I just want to go to sleep in Jake's arms later and bask in the knowledge that both of you lived through that horror. Jake wants to leave for home in the morning."

"No," Lloyd objected. "Both of you and those men

downstairs should sleep in tomorrow. Give it another full day at least, Pa. You should rest that leg at least that long."

Jake shrugged. "We'll see."

"Right now the women are waiting in the dining room with Dee Dee and a big cake," Lloyd told them. "So come and meet your granddaughter. The men are here, too, all cleaned up and keeping Dee Dee busy. She already has them all under her spell. She's quite something, Pa. Pretty, strong, full of life, and real smart. And by the way, she wanted a nickname like Button and Sunshine, so I told her we would call her Princess."

Jake nodded. "Fine with me." He headed out.

Lloyd took his mother's arm and followed, watching his father limp down the stairs. They could hear singing coming from the dining room when they reached the bottom of the stairs. Someone, most likely Terrel, strummed a guitar to the song, "She'll Be Comin' Round the Mountain." Everyone clapped hands to the happy beat, and Cole emerged from the dining room to dance in circles in the hallway with one of the prostitutes. He stopped when he saw Jake.

"Jake! How are you doing?"

"I'll live."

"Come on in the dining room. We are having just cake and drinks. And Dee Dee seems real excited to meet her Grandpa." They all followed Lloyd into the dining room, where, in spite of jeweled earlobes, painted faces and fancy curls, the women of Dallas's Pleasure Emporium were dressed demurely in simple cotton dresses that showed no cleavage. There was no doubt what they were thinking when they greeted Jake and Lloyd, but Randy couldn't help being grateful for their honest caring and generous hospitality. Even Brenda was there, but she wore her long, dark hair partially draped over her face. She stood beside Terrel as he strummed his guitar, and Randy felt pleasure and surprise at the way Terrel looked at her as he played. *Something is going on between those two,* she surmised.

"Uncle Lloyd!" Dee Dee opened her arms when she saw Lloyd walk in. The singing and guitar playing ended. Lloyd walked over and hugged Dee Dee while all the women exclaimed various words of welcome to Jake and Randy. They parted away when Lloyd carried Dee Dee over to Jake, who stood leaning against the doorway. He set her on her feet, and the room quieted. Dee Dee tipped her head back to study Jake. "You sure are tall, and you look kinda like my daddy, but Uncle Lloyd looks more like him."

"That is because Lloyd and your father were both my sons," Jake told her. He glanced at Randy. "She's beautiful."

Randy smiled and nodded. "Of course she is. She's a Harkner."

"Uncle Lloyd said that for a long time you didn't know my Daddy was your son," Dee Dee told Jake.

"No, I sure didn't," Jake answered. "And I am real sorry about that, Dee Dee, because it means I didn't know about you. Once we get you home, you will become a cousin to a whole bunch more pretty granddaughters."

Irene pulled a chair out for Jake. "Your grandpa hurt his leg today, Dee Dee, so he can't kneel down for you, darling." She touched Jake's shoulder. "Here, Jake. Sit sown so the girl can look into your eyes."

Jake grimaced as he lowered himself into the chair. Randy stayed beside him and rested a hand on his shoulder.

"What happened to your leg?" Dee Dee asked him. "I heard a whole bunch of shooting today. Did you get shot?"

Jake studied her closely. "I did. But I'm okay."

"My daddy got shot and it killed him. Dennis did it. He

cut Brenda's face, too. Lloyd said you sent Dennis away and he can't ever come back and get me."

"That's right. A grandpa always protects his grandchildren, Dee Dee. If you come home with us, you will always be safe. That's a promise."

The girl folded her arms and kept watching his eyes. "I never had a grandpa before. I just had a daddy and Grandma Dallas. Where is she?"

"She is in Denver waiting for you. She asked me to come and get you, Dee Dee, but she was afraid of Mr. Bolton, so I told her to wait in Denver and I would let her see you before we take you home to our ranch. Is it okay if you come with us and Grandma Dallas comes back here to her place of business?"

Dee Dee looked up at Randy. "You would be my grandma?"

Randy smiled. "I would. And the grandkids and I do a lot of things together, especially the girls. We will sew clothes and make quilts and cook roasts and fry chicken and bake cookies and shop for pretty dresses. That's just *some* of the things we will do."

The girl frowned. "What happened to your eye? Did Grandpa do that?"

"Oh, my, no!" Randy assured her. "No, no! Grandpa would *never* hurt me or any children, boys *or* girls. Don't ever be afraid of Jake, Dee Dee. He came here and got in a gunfight just so we could take you to live with us. That's why I'm here, too. A bad man hit me when I was coming to you. That's what happened to my eye, but not one man on our big ranch would ever hurt a woman or a child."

Dee Dee quietly studied her. "You are pretty." She looked at Jake. "Do you think she's pretty?"

Jake grinned. "Your Grandma is the most beautiful woman I ever knew, because her heart is also beautiful."

Dee Dee pursed her lips and folded her arms again, taking on a very serious look. "I think you are a nice man because Uncle Lloyd is nice. He told me you are, too. He said you are a good daddy."

Jake cleared his throat, taking a moment to answer. "Well, Dee Dee, I try. My own father wasn't a nice man, so I decided that if I ever had kids of my own, I would try real hard to raise them right. I have never yelled at my kids or my grandkids, or ever laid a hand on them. I don't believe in spankings and such."

"Uncle Lloyd said you should call me Princess. Will you? I have a book about a princess."

"Princess sounds like a good nickname, because you are as beautiful as a princess."

Some of the women snickered when Dee Dee came within about two inches of Jake's face and studied his eyes closer. "Are you mean sometimes?"

The J&L men chuckled.

"Honest?" Jake asked.

"Honest," Dee Dee answered.

"Yes. I can be pretty mean sometimes, but only to bad people. And sometimes it takes me a while to get over it, but at my meanest, Dee Dee, I never turn it on little girls or grown women. So don't ever be afraid of me when I am sometimes kind of mean to somebody. You saw it in my eyes, didn't you?"

The girl nodded. "I like you though. I believe you when you say I can trust you." She kissed his cheek. "Do you have more candy?"

Jake smiled, but Randy did not miss the way he wiped at his eyes. "I have all the candy you could ever want," he told her. He reached into his shirt pocket and pulled out a piece for her. "But I would like some of that cake the ladies made for us. You want some, too?"

Dee Dee nodded. "I already had some, but I will eat more." She took the candy and put it into a pocket on her dress, then stepped back a little. "Do you like my dress? On the way here Uncle Lloyd asked me if I had a yellow dress because you like yellow and Grandma wears that color for you sometimes."

Jake glanced at Lloyd, then back to Dee Dee. "Apparently Uncle Lloyd told you an awful lot about me."

"He did. I think it's because he loves you a lot. I think if a big man like Uncle Lloyd can love you, you must be as nice as he told me you are."

Jake reached out and tugged at her blond curls. "I have my moments of being bad, Dee Dee, but you will almost never see me that way. Right now I just want to look at my beautiful granddaughter and be glad I found her and that she will come home with us. That makes me very happy."

Dee Dee touched his cheek. "Do you promise Dennis won't come after me?"

"Baby girl, he will never *ever* come after you."

"Did you beat him up?"

The men snickered a little and Jake cleared his throat. "I beat him up pretty bad."

"I wish I could see it."

Jake shook his head. "That would *not* be something for a little girl to see, but Lloyd and every man in here promises you will never see Dennis Gates or Ty Bolton again." Jake scanned the men around the table. "Isn't that right, boys?"

A round of "you bets" and "sure enoughs" and "yes, sirs" circled the room along with eager nods.

Dee Dee smiled at Jake. "Can I hug you?"

"There is nothing I like better than hugs from my grand-daughters," Jake answered. "I cannot wait for the grandkids at home to meet you."

Dee Dee reached out and Jake pulled her into his arms.

Randy struggled not to cry. She heard sniffles from a couple of the other women.

"Hey, what about us?" Terrel asked. "Do we get a hug?"

Dee Dee turned, but stayed close to Jake. "I might hug you tomorrow," she told the others. "You aren't my grampas. Grampas are special."

"They sure are," Charlie told her. "And you have one of the best. Jake loves his grandkids a whole lot."

Dee Dee knitted her eyebrows and turned to Jake. "Are you really scared of chickens?"

"*What?*" Jake glanced at Lloyd, who backed up a little with fake fear as the rest of the men laughed out loud, some hooting and howling in teasing remarks. "Did Lloyd tell you I was afraid of chickens?" Jake asked.

"Yeah. He said you had a rooster that chased you and pecked at you and made you say bad words."

Jake looked darkly at Lloyd. "Your uncle and I need to talk about how much he tells you about me."

Dee Dee grinned. "I think it's funny. Lloyd said you will probably have a new rooster when you get home. Maybe he will chase you, too." The girl giggled. "You're too big to be scared of chickens."

"Well, Dee Dee, I guess everybody has *something* they are afraid of. Mine is roosters."

Dee Dee covered her mouth and laughed.

"How about more cake, everybody?" Irene asked.

The party began. Terrel played the guitar and sang as slices of cake were passed around. Before long, Dee Dee was laughing and singing with the others. Jake stood up and walked out into the hallway to light a cigarette. Randy followed, knowing he was upset but also touched by Dee Dee's acceptance of her new grandfather. He took a deep drag on the cigarette and wiped at his eyes with his shirtsleeve as he exhaled.

"Damn, that was hard," he told Randy.

"Jake, she is a Harkner. The courage she just showed says that. And she is smart and strong and can read people well, just like you can."

Jake wiped at his eyes once more. "I had to get out of there for a minute and have a smoke to relax." He took another drag, then set the cigarette in an ashtray on a hall table. He pulled Randy into his arms. "She sure is pretty, isn't she? I wish I could have known her father. Things might have turned out so different for him and Dee Dee both."

"God hands us what He hands us, Jake. Just be glad we have her now and she seems to be handling what happened, as long as she knows Dennis can't come after her. That seems to be her main concern. You took care of that, so Evie and Katie and I will just have to watch her for a while and love her through whatever might be going on inside. We will urge her to talk to us whenever she needs. You just be Grandpa and keep making her feel safe." She leaned up and kissed his chin. "Like you make me and the whole family feel safe. You think you have made life hard for us, but it's quite the opposite, Jake. You are the rock this family is built on."

"No," he answered. "That would be you."

"You totally underestimate your worth, Jake."

"Grandpa!" Dee Dee came out into the hallway. "Come and eat your cake!"

Jake let go of Randy and gave her a quick kiss on the forehead. "I'm coming, Princess."

Dee Dee ran over and grabbed his hand, pulling at him. "I had Irene give you the biggest piece!"

Jake looked helplessly at Randy as Dee Dee dragged him back into the dining room.

"You are running out of fingers for all your granddaughters to tie themselves around, Grandpa," she joked. She thought about the events of this very long day, and wondered how Jake Harkner balanced that dark ruthless side against the soft side he showed now toward a little girl who carried his blood. *You are an incredible human being, Jake Harkner, and I have never loved you more.*

CHAPTER FORTY-ONE

To everyone's surprise and pleasure, Terrel stayed in Shelter to run for sheriff and to marry Brenda. He was totally smitten in spite of her scar and announced he wanted to stay in Shelter to help rebuild the town. All those going back to Colorado stayed to watch the marriage ceremony, and Randy was glad for the distraction that kept Jake from leaving too soon. She was as anxious as anyone to get home, but memories of his long recovery three years earlier still haunted her. She did not want him to risk another brush with death because of an infection.

Brenda wept with joy at finding a man who saw the woman behind the scar, and all the women there shed bountiful tears of joy over the union. Terrel, the man who loved married women, took a lot of teasing over now being a married man himself.

"Now when somebody looks to steal your wife, you will know how the husbands of them women you snuck around with felt," Cole told him.

Jake could not have been happier for both Terrel and Brenda. He and Randy stood up for them, and Dee Dee served as flower girl. Charlie was ring bearer, and he took great delight in staying at Dallas's place for the two extra nights they were all there.

He did not sleep alone.

Randy thought how strangely different things were in these unsettled places. She remembered, when she and Jake first came west, how strangers could meet and be married within days, or start a whole new life far different from what they had always known. She and Jake had been no different. Terrel and Brenda's marriage was considered perfectly normal in spite of knowing each other only a couple of days, and it was highly celebrated. The women of Dallas's Pleasure Emporium threw quite a party.

Leaving came with mixed emotions, their joy at Terrel and Brenda's marriage mixed with sadness when they passed the town graveyard on their way back south. After three days, graves were still being dug. Randy was glad when they made it to the top of the mesa that overlooked Shelter and down the other side. Shelter was no longer in view, and she and the others hoped to never see the town again.

They made the rough journey to Pine Ranch with Duke's body and stayed for his burial. Whitey Loomis stepped back into his old job, and after purchasing two more horses from Ruben Prescott to replace those lost in the gun battle, what was left of their small posse continued their journey toward Wilcox.

Randy ached to lie solely in Jake's arms again, but Dee Dee insisted on sleeping with her every night and riding with Jake or Lloyd by day, needing the reassurance that she was safe and would not be left alone. Their only dangerous encounter as they made their way closer to Wilcox was when seven road bandits rode down on them, waving rifles as they surrounded them.

Dee Dee shrank back against Jake, shivering. "I hope it's not Dennis," she whimpered when the men first approached.

"I promised that you would never see Dennis Gates again, baby girl," Jake reminded her. He halted Thunder beside Randy and quickly handed Dee Dee over to her as the bandits circled them and their leader rode closer to face Jake.

"Back out of the way," Jake told Randy quietly before turning to Lloyd and the others. "Let's try to settle this without a bloody shootout in front of Dee Dee. She has been through enough ugly, and I know men like these."

Considering that they were down to just Jake, Lloyd, Charlie and Cole, Randy could not help her pounding heart, especially since Jake had let the bandits ride so close without drawing on any of them. She clung to Dee Dee and moved Pepper farther back.

"How much for the women?" The apparent leader of the attacking outlaws asked the question.

"Only one woman and a child," Jake calmly answered. "And if you intend to try taking them, you will be the first to die, mister. We are not outlaws out to sell anything. We are family, headed home to Colorado. The woman is my wife, and the girl is my granddaughter."

"There are four of you and eight of us," the bearded man answered. "You have made quite a threat for a man up against two to one."

Charlie snickered.

"Telling you that you will be the first to die is not a threat," Jake answered. "It's a promise, so I suggest you be on your way."

"Who says?" the man asked.

"I'll ask your name first," Jake demanded.

"Abel Hayes," the man answered arrogantly. "Ever heard of me?"

"No," Jake told him. "Mine is Jake Harkner. Ever heard of *me*?

Abel's arrogance wilted a little.

"Sure you have," Cole spoke up. "Ain't many men who don't know that name. And Mister, Jake and the rest of us just cleaned out the whole town of Shelter, Wyoming to rescue that little girl who is riding with us, so I suggest you ride on away from here if you want to live more than another couple of minutes. Jake don't like threats to his family, and he can send you to hell quicker than you can clear leather or pull the trigger on that rifle."

Abel eyed Jake warily. "You're really Harkner?" He backed his horse a little.

"Why would I lie about my name?"

The bandits all looked at each other in obvious indecision. A couple of them raised their hands, rifles and all, to indicate they had no intention of using their weapons.

"I reckon I should warn you that news travels fast out here, Harkner," Abel told Jake. "We had some drinks at a saloon not far back where they were talkin' about Shelter and what happened there. Seems as though a couple of men from Shelter rode on ahead of you and are off spreadin' the news, askin' for men to come help finish the cleanup and tryin' to get more people to come in and help rebuild the town ... and help bury the dead, on account of there are so many."

"And we are responsible for most of those dead bodies," Jake told him. "Think about that."

Abel grinned slyly and nodded his head. "They say it's

such a big story that a reporter from Shelter took off for Lander so he could wire news about it to newspapers back east. I reckon you could be in a lot of trouble, Harkner."

"I could be," Jake answered, "but if I am, it was worth it to get my granddaughter out of harm's way. Just don't force me to add you to the long list of men who have regretted threatening me and my own. You're goddamn lucky I didn't shoot you onsight. I'm still in no mood for bullshit from men like you, but my granddaughter is with us and she's been through some bad times. I prefer she doesn't witness a lot of bloodshed here, and I am asking you to abide by that. There is a code out here involving women and kids. You damn well know that."

Abel chuckled and scratched at his beard. "I know it just like you do, Harkner."

"We don't want the kind of trouble you took to Shelter," one of the other men spoke up.

"Ain't nobody understands men like us more than you, Harkner," Abel said with a sly grin. "Takes an outlaw to know an outlaw, and to know the code. I should tell you that I wouldn't normally let some other party with all these valuables get off lightly. But you are highly respected by men like us, and I do believe I'll be dead if I use this rifle." He pushed his hat back a little with the end of his rifle barrel. "Glad to have met you." He turned his horse and rode off with the others.

"Whew!" Cole joked, after heaving a sigh of relief. "I sure feel a lot safer goin' home than I did comin' up here."

The others laughed nervously.

"I'll feel a *whole* lot better when we are back on the J&L," Charlie said.

"And I will be one happy man when I feel Katie's arms wrapped around me again," Lloyd added.

Cole gave out a whistle and Charlie grinned. "I ain't touchin' that one. All I can say is you are one lucky man, Lloyd Harkner."

Jake looked at Randy and grinned. "Did you hear that about a reporter headed for Lander?"

Randy nodded. "That means Jeff will hear about this. He and Peter will probably share a drink over it. Jeff has been waiting for some exciting news. What happened in Shelter will certainly give him something for a new article about you."

"I'm sure we will get a wire or a visit. He will want to meet Dee Dee."

"Jake, you certainly know how to keep making headlines," Charlie told him.

"This one is a corker," Cole added.

RANDY SMILED and shook her head now at the thought of the news reaching Jeff. The whole journey, from beginning to end, seemed surreal as she and Jake stood with Dee Dee in front of the door to Dallas Blackburn's hotel room in Denver. The encounter with the bandits had taken place nearly two weeks ago ... two long weeks of hard riding, camping out, living with the elements and through a bad rainstorm and the sound of wolves howling at night.

When they reached Wilcox, the memory of that first shooting that started their dangerous journey north seemed like months ago ... another life ... and someone else. It felt good to breathe easy and be free of so much danger. The comfort of the train ride from Wilcox to Denver was welcome, and exciting for Dee Dee, who had never been on a train.

Now here they were, at the brand new Oxford Hotel in Denver. The worst of the trip was over. Tomorrow they would head for home, but first, as promised, they would let Dallas see her granddaughter once more and know that she was safe.

She touched Jake's arm. "I can't believe we are really here, Jake. It's been such a long journey, in more ways than one. And right now a real bed will feel so good when we get to our room."

"Lying next to you will feel even better," Jake told her.

"I liked riding the train!" Dee Dee told them, completely oblivious to how anxious Jake and Randy were to just be alone. Jake's leg was better, and Randy's bruises were fading. The cut on her face was healing well. All the danger and horror and tension and trauma of going into unspeakable danger to find Dee Dee was behind them now. It had been difficult adjusting to real life again, and their anxiousness to just be home consumed their nights apart and kept their nights wakeful.

Dee Dee let go of Jake's hand and twirled around in the hallway. "Grandma Dallas will like my new dress, won't she?" She shook her blond curls and smiled, waking up beautiful dimples in her cheeks. "Do I look okay?"

"You look just like a princess," Jake told her. "Go ahead and see if Grandma Dallas is in her room."

Dee Dee giggled with excitement as she knocked at the door.

"Just a moment," a woman answered.

"It's her!" Dee Dee whispered, clapping her hands.

The door opened, and Dallas stood there in a soft green day dress, her hair brushed out long. She gasped and put a hand to her chest at seeing Dee Dee standing there, then broke into a huge smile. "Dee Dee!"

"Hi, Grandma!" Dee Dee said excitedly. "See my new dress?"

Dallas wrapped the child into her arms. "Oh, Dee Dee, you are really here!" She looked up at Jake while she held her granddaughter. "Jake, you did it! Oh, my God, you did it!" She kept Dee Dee in one arm and hugged Jake with the other. "Thank you! Thank you! Oh, Jake, I was so afraid for you!" She pulled back and looked him over. "Tell me you didn't get hurt."

Jake leaned against the door jam. "A couple of wounds, fairly superficial." He reached for Randy, pulling her close. "Randy took a couple of blows. One from a horse that kicked at her and one from one of Bolton's men who attacked her. Her bruises are fading, but you can see they are still there. And that cut that's healing on her cheek is from—" He paused. "I won't say his name in front of Dee Dee, but you can guess."

"Oh, I'm so sorry. Randy, that man didn't do worse than that, I hope."

"No. Jake was close by. It's a long story, Dallas, but I can tell you that the man who slugged me regretted it. I shot him."

Dallas put both arms around Dee Dee and hugged her again but kept her eyes on Randy. "You are one hell of a woman, Randy Harkner. Just the kind a man like Jake needs. And you certainly are stronger and more able than I had you figured for." She looked back at Jake. "What about the men who went with you?"

"One man we hired from a rancher was killed, and you will be happy to know that when you go back to Shelter, Terrel will be there. He stayed behind to run for sheriff ... and he married Brenda. How's that for more surprise news?"

Dallas broke into loud laughter and asked them inside.

"I was flower girl!" Dee Dee told her.

"You were? I bet you made a beautiful flower girl." She turned her attention to Jake again. "What about Ty? And, you know, that other man we won't mention?"

Jake glanced at Dee Dee before answering. "Let's just say neither one will be bothering you or Dee Dee again, and the sheriff and most of his men are either dead or have fled town. The women at your place will give you more details. I would rather not go into it in front of Dee Dee. She's been through enough."

"Of course she has."

"We are leaving Dee Dee here with you for the rest of the day and overnight for a good visit," Randy told Dallas. "You can take her to eat, keep her with you tonight, whatever you want."

"We are leaving for the J&L in the morning," Jake added. "Dee Dee understands she will go with us. She's excited to meet her new family." Jake reached out and tugged at one of Dee Dee's sausage curls. "Aren't you, Princess?"

Dee Dee nodded eagerly. She stepped back and twirled around in her pink ruffled dress again. She wore new shoes and a little gold necklace Jake had bought for her. "Do you like my dress?" she asked Dallas. "Grandma Randy bought it for me. And new shoes! And Grandpa Jake says I can have my own pony when we get to the ranch. And I have cousins there who have lots of toys, and I'll have my own room and everything!"

Dallas's eyes teared in a show of emotion the woman seldom mustered. "I am sure you will have all of that and more, Dee Dee. I have been to Jake's home and have met his family. What he told you about them is all true. I am so happy for you. You understand, don't you, that it's best you go with Jake and Randy and live with your new family, instead of going back to Shelter with me?"

Dee Dee nodded. "Grandpa Jake is so nice. And so is Uncle Lloyd. And the men who came with us are, too. They are a lot of fun." Her smile turned to a scowl. "I don't want to go back to Shelter. "

"And you don't have to, Dee Dee. That is the reason I sent Jake to get you. You will be safe and loved on the J&L." She glanced at Randy, sharing a look that said it all. Each understood the other, and both loved Dee Dee. "Thank you for all you have had to put up with," she told Randy, "and for taking my granddaughter. I thought about you two a lot through all of this. I know I come across as tough and ornery, but I mean it when I say now that I'm happy Jake has the family he always wanted, and I'm sorry he never knew Wade. I am even more sorry Wade never knew his father."

"Grandma, look! A butterfly!" A monarch flittered past and down the hallway. Dee Dee ran after it, and Jake took the moment to let Dallas know the worst. He kept his voice low as he told her about what Dennis Gates had done to Dee Dee under the excuse of marriage.

"Oh, my God," Dallas moaned, holding her stomach.

"You should know because I'm not sure what she will tell you," Jake advised. "Anything you can say to make sure she doesn't judge all men that way and that she did not do anything bad will help."

"But don't mention it unless Dee Dee brings it up," Randy warned. "She seems happy and more adjusted than we expected. We just worry she is hurting inside more than she says. She did warm up beautifully to Lloyd and Jake, and she sings and laughs with Charlie and Cole and is very relaxed around them."

Dee Dee ran back to them with news that the butterfly had flown out a screenless window at the end of the hall.

"It's been so hot," Dallas commented. "The hotel is opening hall windows to get an air flow." She touched Dee Dee's face. "How would you like to go for a walk with me?" she asked. "I know a place where we can get ice cream and lemonade. Let's let your grandparents have some time alone. I'm sure they want to go to their room and rest."

"We definitely need that," Jake answered. "Our room is 327, on the floor below you." He turned and picked up a small carpetbag he'd left in the hallway and handed it to Dallas. "Here are Dee Dee's things." He leaned down to talk to Dee Dee. "How about staying the night with Grandma Dallas," he asked the girl. "You might not see her again after this. Shelter is a long, long way from the ranch. I don't think your grandmother will want to make that trip again, and Randy and I have no desire to ever go back there."

Dee Dee sobered. "I know. I don't want to go back there either."

"You go with Dallas now," Randy told her before turning her attention to Dallas. "We just got into town and wanted you to know as soon as possible that Dee Dee was okay."

"Of course." Dallas petted Dee Dee's hair. "The news had already reached Denver. Jake has been the talk of the town the last couple of days. I knew you would show up, but it's still such a wonderful surprise. I guess I didn't believe things had worked out all that well until I opened the door to see the three of you standing there." She smiled wryly. "I am sure you are ready for some privacy." She put an arm around Dee Dee. "Let's take that walk. I will get an umbrella for each of us for shade from the sun, and I have to put on some shoes first." She looked up at Jake. "Thank you. I don't know what else to say. You have so many reasons to hate me, Jake, and –"

"I didn't do it for you," he reminded her. "I did it for our granddaughter. She was worth the hell."

Dallas's smile faded. "Of course she was." She touched Jake's arm. "I am truly sorry, Jake, for all of it. Is there any way you can forgive me?"

Jake pulled away. "Right now I'm not in a forgiving mood," he told her. "I need time to unwind from what happened in Shelter, and I can't help still blaming you for it." He looked her over. "Besides, it's been too many years for it to matter. And you haven't changed, Dallas. You never will. I guess all I can do is thank you for giving me another sweet and beautiful granddaughter."

Dallas nodded and stepped back. "You two do whatever you want for now. I will keep Dee Dee overnight." She blinked back tears. "Thank you again. Both of you. " She turned away and closed the door.

Randy looked up at Jake, sensing how torn he was on the inside. "That is kind of like closing the door on your past, Jake."

He sighed and put a hand to the side of her face. "It will take me some time to close that door, especially when it comes to what you and our family have been through."

Randy grasped his wrist and kissed his palm. "I have already walked through that door. I am waiting for you to meet me on the other side."

He leaned down and kissed her. "I can't quite make my feet step over that threshhold," he answered. "And right now I need you in a hundred ways." He pulled her close and kissed her. "It's been almost three weeks since that mess in Shelter, and we have been too far apart in spirit." More kisses. "Feelings of love have been pushed away in trade for hatred and revenge and brutality, and I don't like feeling that way around you. I am so damn sorry for what happened to you, Randy, and for the ugly things you witnessed."

"I know the real Jake. That's all that matters."

Jake touched her cheek with the back of his hand. "There is a part of me you have never known and never will, and that's good, because it involves demons and pain. I never want you to know that Jake."

Randy gave out a little yelp when he unexpectedly picked her up and carried her to the elevator, then down the hallway on the floor below. "Jake, people are staring."

"Let them."

One couple snickered when they walked by. Jake set Randy on her feet just long enough to unlock the door to their room, then picked her up again and turned to kick the door shut. Randy noticed through it all that he grimaced several times as he carried her. "Jake, your leg. I know you are still in pain."

"God knows I have suffered far worse." He turned the lock with her still in his arms and carried her to their bed.

CHAPTER FORTY-TWO

How strange it felt to lie on the bed and let this man of men undress her. It had been so long since they had freely enjoyed sharing their bodies without the haunting fear that he could die at any time.

Randy studied the hard curves of his arms and shoulders, the cut across the top of his left shoulder nearly healed now. So many scars, and yet here he was, still a handsome man with a fine build. He was her protector, her helpmate, the man who had saved her life more than once, her passionate lover, her husband of 37 years. A white scar in the shape of a cross was emblazoned right over his heart, where his mother's crucifix had stopped what would have been a deadly bullet. He was so sure God did not want him, but the scars he carried spoke of a man God had protected since he was a little boy.

She had seen deeply into those dark eyes, deep enough to see some of those demons he talked about, but they did not frighten her. She was stronger than they were. Their love was stronger. Their devotion was stronger. So she faced them boldly and refused to let them claim his soul and pull him into the hell that haunted the edges of his mind.

He stripped her to her panties and camisole, but then suddenly paused. Sobering, he sat down on the edge of the bed and ran his hands through his hair. "I'm sorry," he told her.

Randy sat up beside him, realizing he wanted to make love to her but couldn't. The weight of all he'd been through was pressing on his mind and heart.

The demons! Don't let them win!

"Jake, you need time to really get over what happened, and to get over the awful visions of Dennis abusing Dee Dee. I know that, and it's okay. You don't have one thing to be sorry for."

"I can't stop thinking about reaching Dee Dee too late to help her."

"You did everything you could. If you had already known about her and never went to see or help her, it would be different, but you *didn't* know, Jake. This will pass. Dee Dee will meld into the family as though she has been with us since birth. I see it in her strength and her ability to care. And she is so much like you ... strong and sure. She's a fighter, something you have been your whole life."

Jake met her gaze, then leaned close and kissed her lingering bruises, kissed her eyes. "You have the prettiest eyes in Colorado. I never have figured out if they are gray or green." More kisses. "I want my wife. I want to get back to normal and make love often and tell you I love you a thousand times a day, Randy Harkner."

"I can wait for however long that takes. You are alive and well and coming home, and that is all that matters to me. You *know* that. Now finish undressing and lie down and get some much-needed sleep. It's been a hard journey, and you faced your demons too many times. It has worn you out." Randy got up and pulled at him, making him stand up. She helped him undress to his longjohns and told him to lie down. She wet a rag with cool water and ran it over his face and neck. "It's hot," she said gently. "Get some sleep, Jake."

She stepped away and removed her camisole, wearing only her panties because of the heat. Through the open hotel window she heard street noises below. Denver's progress reminded her of how many things had changed in their years together ... since she married a wanted man. A gentle breeze ruffled the curtains, and Jake leaned up to kissed the crowns of her breasts as she bent over him to wash his face again.

"I love you so much that it hurts," he said wearily. "When Dennis stood there with a knife against your face and I saw the terror in your eyes, I thought I would lose my mind ... and you. I can't get over that sick feeling that he was going to sink that knife into your beautiful face, or cut your throat with it and I would lose you forever."

"I'm right here." Randy walked around the bed and lay down beside him. She snuggled against his side in spite of the heat. "When we get home, Jake, after you are attacked by all the grandkids, you and I can go to Echo Ridge and be alone for as long as it takes to get back to normal life and share a normal conversation." She ran a hand over his chest. "And we can make love any time, over and over, night or day."

Jake suddenly grasped her wrist and rolled on top of her. He buried his face at her neck and whispered in her ear. "I have to do this. I *need* to do this." He reached down under her panties and pulled them over her hips, her thighs. "Let me try."

Randy raised her hips and let him pull her panties all

the way off. He freed himself from his longjohns and rubbed against her privates as he kissed her taut nipples, her neck, her lips. In moments his hard shaft pressed her groin, and she opened herself to him, knowing this might help him come back to life, to normalcy, back to her as the gentle, loving man she knew he could be. She returned his kisses with great passion as he took her, hoping it would help erase the memories ... old memories ... current memories that haunted him and tortured his heart.

Flashes of his brutality back in Shelter made Randy grab at him and try to be inside his heart and soul, made her want to bring him out of the anger and vengefulness ... bring him home to her ... to the family ... to the J&L. "Come back to me, Jake," she whispered. "I want the Jake who loves hard and with all his being, the Jake who protects me and adores me and has so much love inside."

His groans told her she had found the man who loved her beyond measure. She arched her hips to take him as deeply as possible. He thought he couldn't do this, but here he was, all man, still so full of love in spite of how equally fiercely he could hate and take revenge.

"Lo siento mucho por todo el dolor, Randy. Te necesito como necesito comer ahd respirar."

"I need you just the same," Randy answered as tears filled her eyes. "I need the man I fell in love with. Don't worry about hurting me. Nothing you have ever done has hurt me except when you think you should leave me. Don't ever leave me, Jake. And don't ever think I would ever leave you, no matter what you have done or will ever do."

Their strenuous reunion led to two more rounds of hard lovemaking, until they were spent. They had barely finished the third time when there came a knock on the door. Randy frowned. "Jake, it must be at least midnight."

"Just a minute!" Jake called out. They both scrambled to straighten the bed. Randy turned on an extra electric lamp and pulled on her night gown while Jake yanked on his underwear and put on a light shirt. He grabbed one of his .44's, not sure what to expect. He opened the door to see Dallas standing there with Dee Dee, who was in her nightgown.

"Sorry if we interrupted something," Dallas said with a sly grin. She could see Randy's hair was a mess, and Jake looked worn out. "Your granddaughter feels safer with you," she explained. "I remember when I did, too." She leaned up and kissed his cheek, then chuckled. "My, you're warm."

"It's the hot night," Jake answered.

"I'm sure it is," Dallas answered. She stepped back to let Dee Dee inside. "I hate to intrude, but Dee Dee wants to spend the rest of the night with you two."

Dee Dee threw her arms around Jake. "Do you care, Grandpa?"

Jake glanced at Randy with that helpless look he got when a grandchild took over his heart. "No, I don't care. Go lie down over there on the bed with Grandma."

Randy grinned and put out her arm. "Come on, sweetheart."

"Jesus," Jake muttered.

Dallas chuckled and touched his chest. "Goodbye, Jake. You don't need to come by in the morning. It's probably better this way." She set Dee Dee's carpetbag inside the doorway. "Remind her often that I love her, will you? And that she will live in my heart forever." She leaned up and kissed his cheek again. "And so will you, whether you like it or not." She turned and walked away.

Jake closed the door and looked at Randy. "I guess I will be sleeping on the floor the rest of the night."

Randy grinned. "I guess you will, Grandpa." She totally understood how Dee Dee was feeling. The girl wanted to be near Grandpa Jake, where she felt safest. *Just like Grandma Randy feels.* Those strong arms had always been her safe place. "I love you," she told Jake.

Jake grunted and swore as he spread a quilt out on a braided rug and laid down on top of the quilt. He punched up his pillow and settled in for the night. "You have terrible taste in men, Mrs. Harkner. Have I ever told you that?"

"A few times. But I never listen to anything you tell me, Mr. Harkner."

"I am painfully aware of that." Things grew quiet as Dee Dee curled up on the bed. "Good night, Grandma and Grandpa," she said. "I love you."

"And we love you," Randy answered.

"More than you know, Princess," Jake added. He set his .44 on a chair nearby. "More than you know."

CHAPTER FORTY-THREE

WEARINESS DID NOT MATTER. Wounds did not matter. Horses needing a rest did not matter. They were on J&L land, and had been for the last two days. They had already seen outriders Lou Younger and Billy Dooley, who whooped with joy at the sight of Jake and Lloyd returning alive and well. This morning they came across Skeeter and Win Lee herding some strays. They yelled and waved their hats, and Skeeter rode part way with them.

"Damn, it's good to see you both!" he told Lloyd and Jake, riding closer and shaking their hands. "Things have been okay. We caught a few more rustlers and had them arrested, but overall, no big problems while you were gone. Stephen and Ben and Young Jake did a good job, too." He turned to Lloyd. "I gotta say, you're comin' back to men, Lloyd, not boys. Your son has a real level head on his shoulders."

"That's good to hear," Lloyd answered. "Makes me proud."

Skeeter turned his attention to Jake. "You okay? No wounds?"

"A couple of minor ones. I'll live."

Skeeter nodded to Randy. "Ma'am, you're lookin' beautiful as always." He frowned. "That the remains of a bruise by your eye?"

Randy smiled. "It's a long story, Skeeter, but thanks for the compliment. I will be fine."

Skeeter eyed the young girl riding with Lloyd. "Is she the granddaughter?"

"She most certainly is," Jake told him with a big smile. He reached over and ruffled Dee Dee's hair. "This is Diana Suzanne Blackburn. I intend to legally change the name Blackburn to Harkner as soon as I can."

Skeeter gave Dee Dee a bright smile. "Welcome to the J&L, Dee Dee. You will find out this is the best place in the world to live, and you have the best grandma and grandpa you could ask for."

"I can't wait to see my new room. And Grandpa said I could have my own pony!" Dee Dee told him.

"Girl, you are gonna be spoiled rotten," Skeeter told her. He glanced at Lloyd. "I bet you are anxious to get home to Katie."

Lloyd grinned. "You have no idea."

"She's been doin' good, Lloyd. She's gonna be over the moon to see you comin' back unhurt." He turned to Jake. "And that daughter of yours, she made us all gather every mornin' to say a prayer for your safe return. You know Evie."

Jake sobered. "My daughter is probably responsible for me still being alive at all."

Skeeter nodded and smiled. "That I would have to agree with. That woman has an angel livin' inside her." He waved his hat to all of them. "Get on home!"

Skeeter rode off to tend to the strays, and Jake turned to

Randy. "Come over here and ride in front of me. I need to hold you, Mrs. Harkner."

Randy smiled and nudged Pepper closer. She took off her hat and hooked it over the pommel of her saddle. Jake reached out and grasped her about the waist to help her climb onto Thunder. "It isn't just Evie's prayers that have saved this sorry soul of mine, you know," he told her. "It all started with you 37 years ago, and you are still my main reason for living."

Randy turned slightly and kissed his chin. "And you are mine, which is something you have never understood, but it's true."

Jake kept an arm around her and nudged Thunder into a gentle walk as Randy clung to Pepper's reins. "We will talk about who loves who the most when we go to Echo Ridge," Jake told Randy. He leaned down to kiss her cheek. "I want to leave within a couple days of getting home. Maybe we will spend the rest of the summer up there alone."

Randy leaned back, loving the feel of his solid chest and the strong arm that was holding her. "That sounds wonderful."

They rode up the last big hill that led down the other side to the homestead. Charlie and Cole let out wild whoops and kept hold of their pack horses as they decided to kick their horses into a run and head down the other side. They crested the hill, and Jake gave out the whistle he always gave when coming home. Randy fought tears at the memory of how many times she'd waited for that whistle when he was riding into Guthrie after another dangerous trip into outlaw country.

He and Lloyd both paused to watch the scene below. As soon as Cole and Charlie were halfway down the hill, men began coming out of the bunkhouse and corrals and riding in from farther away. Kids poured out of the houses, and even from the top of the hill it was easy to tell the women apart. Gretta was running toward Cole. Evie's long, black hair was easy to spot. She was waving wildly, as was Katie, unmistakable because of her very red hair.

"There they are, Dee Dee," he told the girl. "All your cousins and aunts."

"Go, Uncle Lloyd! Go!"

Lloyd kicked Cinnamon into a hard run, clinging to a screaming, laughing Dee Dee as he headed for the homestead.

Jake paused and just watched. "Looks good, doesn't it?"

"It's the most beautiful sight I have ever seen," Randy answered, wiping at tears. "And it's all because of you, Jake. You know that, right?"

Jake halted Thunder and watched. The women were waving frantically, and the children were jumping up and down and screaming, "Grampa! Grampa!"

"I see it," he answered Randy. "And I know it. But I feel like two men. One belongs to you and that great big family down there. The other one has never belonged to a life like this and doesn't deserve all that love."

Randy reached up and patted his cheek. "Well, Mr. Harkner, you are about to find out just how much you *are* loved. Get ready for the attack."

They watched Lloyd stop below and dismount. Dee Dee quickly melted into a herd of children, and Lloyd swept Katie into his arms. Moments later Dee Dee, Tricia and Sadie Mae broke away and ran toward the hill where Jake and Randy sat watching.

"Grampa, hurry up!" Sadie Mae screamed. All three girls jumped up and down as they waved.

"You had better follow their orders, Grandpa," Randy teased. "For the next few hours you will be in their hands." She turned farther around to meet his lips in a kiss. "And in a couple of days you will be in *my* hands. You had better rest up for Echo Ridge."

Jake chuckled. "*You* are the one who had better rest up."

"Oh, but I am ten years younger than you. Remember?"

"And when it comes to getting you alone up there, age means nothing. In the meantime ..." He untied the holster cords from his thighs and unbuckled his gunbelt. "I had better get these things off before I am surrounded by all those kids." He draped the gunbelt over Thunder's neck and urged the horse into a gentle lope. Moments later he dismounted and was bombarded with grandchildren. He picked up two of the littlest ones while Stephen and young Jake and Ben all talked at once about things that happened while they were gone. Jake kissed a crying Evie when she walked up to hug her father. Randy thought how little Evie knew about what Jake Harkner was capable of. She only knew that her avenging angel of a father was home.

Randy watched with tears in her eyes. She wiped at them as Evie left Jake and approached her. Randy glanced at Jake's gunbelt ... and the ivory-handled .44's it held.

"Please, God, let this be the end of it all," she spoke quietly. She dismounted and was immediately wrapped into Evie's arms.

"Welcome home, mom," her daughter told her amid tears.

Home. The word never sounded so good.

For there are two heavens, sweet,
Both made of love,
One, inconceivable even by the other,
So divine it is ...
The other,
Far on this side of the stars,
By men called ... home.

TWO HEAVENS
Leigh Hunt
Taken from *The New Joy of Words*
J. G. Ferguson Publishing Company, Chicago, 1961

MORE FROM AWARD-WINNING AUTHOR, ROSANNE BITTNER

Jake Harkner is one of my favorite characters, rivaled only by Zeke Monroe (Lone Eagle) from my 7-book SAVAGE DESTINY series. SHADOW TRAIL takes Jake Harkner back to the beginning of this series, when he met Miranda in the first book, OUTLAW HEARTS, published in 1993. This story brought him full circle to a time in his life when he can settle for good after facing his demons one last time. Family is Jake's whole world, and protecting that family from his past has been Jake's never-ending quest through all six books of this series, plus a short Christmas story involving Jake and his family called A CHICKADEE CHRISTMAS. That story is in an anthology titled CHRISTMAS IN A COWBOY'S ARMS (Sourcebooks).

Watch my web site for the announcement of a future Outlaw Hearts story that will involve Jake's son Lloyd and his wife, and another story about Young Jake as a grown man. Jake's legacy lives on through his descendants. Family sagas are my favorite form of writing, along the lines of James Michener's CENTENNIAL and the movie HOW THE WEST WAS WON. My favorite subject is American history, especially the history of America's Old West and Native Americans.

I have been writing 40 years as of 2023, and I plan more books. Watch my web site at www.rosannebittner.com for news of books to come and to learn about the 75 other books I have written over the years, most of which have been reissued and are still available. I have traveled the West extensively for research and I base my stories on real American history, locations and events.

Enjoy!

Rosanne Bittner

USA TODAY BEST-SELLER

(rosannebittner17@outlook.com)   (www.rosannebittner.com) Instagram, Facebook, Goodreads, Sourcebooks, Diversion Books, Amazon